CASS COUNTY PUBLIC LIBRARY
400 E. MECHANIC
HARRISONVILLE, MO 64701

# WHAT BOYS LEARN

ALSO BY THE AUTHOR

. . .

*The Spanish Bow*

*The Detour*

*Behave*

*Plum Rains*

*Annie and the Wolves*

*The Deepest Lake*

# WHAT BOYS LEARN

## ANDROMEDA ROMANO-LAX

Published by Soho Press, Inc.
227 W 17th Street
New York, NY 10011
www.sohopress.com

Copyright © 2026 Andromeda Romano-Lax
All rights reserved.

This is a work of fiction. Names, characters, places, and incidents either are the product of the author's imagination or are used fictitiously, and any resemblance to actual persons, living or dead, businesses, companies, events, or locales is entirely coincidental.

Library of Congress Cataloging-in-Publication Data

Names: Romano-Lax, Andromeda, 1970- author
Title: What boys learn / Andromeda Romano-Lax.
Description: New York, NY : Soho Crime, 2026.
Identifiers: LCCN 2025026930

ISBN 978-1-64129-691-5
eISBN 978-1-64129-692-2

Subjects: LCGFT: Fiction | Detective and mystery fiction | Novels
Classification: LCC PS3618.O59 W47 2025 | DDC 813/.6—dc23/
eng/20250613
LC record available at https://lccn.loc.gov/2025026930

Interior design by Janine Agro

Printed in the United States of America

10 9 8 7 6 5 4 3 2 1

EU Responsible Person (for authorities only)
eucomply OÜ
Pärnu mnt 139b-14
11317 Tallinn, Estonia
hello@eucompliancepartner.com
www.eucompliancepartner.com

*To my editor Alexa Wejko,*
*who fears neither cold water nor deep revisions*

# PROLOGUE

I never meant to see what was in his drawer.
I was never a mother who snooped.

Not even when I thought a little snooping would help me better understand my stoic son. No—I'd drawn the line. Trust was more important.

In our household of two, trust meant that drawers and doors stayed closed. And yet, there I was on an unseasonably warm spring day, sweating through my tank top and baggy gym shorts as I packed up the apartment, alone, venturing into Benjamin's room to take care of the chore he'd neglected while he was off at the pool attending a lifeguard-hiring information session. It was all he talked about—*when* he talked. Improving his swimming. Getting a pool job. Saving money, most likely for a car, though any expenditure that promised greater independence would do.

I pushed the toothed edge of the tape dispenser against the newly assembled box to bite off the final piece of tape, feeling irritated by how little he'd done but also guilty that we had to move at all. The new place was only two miles away from our old apartment, and it wasn't a step up by any measure. No backyard. Smaller bedrooms. One bathroom instead of one and a half. Dark.

I dragged the empty box next to Benjamin's bureau and pulled the drawer open. The T-shirts inside were folded more neatly than my own. He'd been selectively tidy since turning fourteen, insistent on doing his own laundry, obsessive about showers.

I pulled out a stack of shirts and flopped them into the big box, grabbed the next stack . . . and then I looked down, puzzled by a satiny feel. I held up the skimpy fabric with two fingers. Sexy. Small. Barely enough to cover any woman's private parts, front or back.

I winced, wishing I'd left this box untouched. But then the feeling shifted, from embarrassment to something even less comfortable. As far as I knew, Benjamin had never had a girlfriend.

On closer inspection, the underwear didn't look new. Possibly not clean, either. I didn't think—not that it would have alarmed me—that he was curious about cross-dressing. Maybe he'd ordered them online from some woman who wore them for five minutes and then sold them at ten times their value. But Benjamin always laughed at people who fell for online gambits like that. Plus, he was broke. Like his mom.

The more likely answer was one I didn't want to name. With the underwear still in my hand, I took three steps back, trying to block the picture that was forming. It was my fault for looking. My fault for thinking . . . and there was that ringing again, the edges of my vision beginning to darken.

A truck rattled past the open bedroom window and I startled, fist closing tighter around the satin souvenir, if that's what it was. I didn't like that word. *Souvenir.* Or *trophy.* Even so, I left Benjamin's room and hurried to my own, headed for the closet and that shoebox I'd kept for years, the place for things that couldn't be forgotten.

# PART I

# 1

"Think of it as a mental health break," our dean, Kimberly Duplass, told me ten minutes into our private emergency meeting, tugging at the lapels of her white bouclé cardigan as she boosted herself higher in her chair.

"I'm sorry. A mental health break for who?"

"For you, Abby."

I loosened my grip on the dented folder in my lap. Inside was the printout of a speech I expected to deliver to an all-school assembly the next morning, reminding students to be kind and observant, to watch out especially for anyone who needed to talk. Summit High was a community, albeit a new one. The death of a student was a shock, but we'd get through this.

"I'm confused," I said to Duplass. "You want me to go home early? We have a lot to do, the sooner the better."

Glancing at her cell phone, which was vibrating for the third time in several minutes, she said, "A well-executed plan is better than a hasty one."

I could hear the air quotes around that phrase, like she

was repeating a line from an entrepreneur's how-to book. Summit was like that—businessy, private, highly focused on the bottom line.

"Hold on, let me take this."

Behind the dean, tall windows framed a sun-dappled lawn backed by giant oak trees. Students on break from their exams gathered in loose circles. Girls laughed and brushed back long strands of gleaming hair. Boys roughhoused and fist-bumped. None of them looked devastated. But wait until they went home and lost themselves in their phones, where gossip and misinformation would distort their first suppressed pangs of grief. They hadn't assimilated the news yet. I hadn't, either. *Come back*, I wanted to say. Never mind an assembly tomorrow. We needed to round them up and answer their questions now.

Duplass gave short, reassuring replies during her phone call—*yes*, *of course*, *absolutely*. After hanging up, she explained, "Worried parent. A mother who was texted a few minutes ago by her daughter. She wants to know that we're doing enough."

"My concern exactly."

I started to open the folder, but Duplass held up a hand. "Don't forget, you're not the only one our students can turn to. You're part of a team. A *growing* team."

A good friend of the dean's, Dr. Shields—an *MD/PhD*, Duplass had already said twice, as if I didn't understand what *psychiatrist* meant—would be sharing my office beginning tomorrow. To prepare for his arrival, I'd been asked to empty one drawer and half of a small bookcase. I still didn't understand how we'd collaborate or why he needed shelf space for only four more days of school, unless it was to display honors or publications to impress visiting parents.

"Is he a grief expert?" I asked. "Does he work with teens?"

"He's a friend of the board."

That's what mattered. Not just his pedigree, which outshone my recent master's degree in counseling.

"Graduation is days away," I reminded her, as if she needed reminding. "There isn't enough time for him to establish trust. A lot of kids won't talk to him."

I paused, on the edge of an uncomfortable insight. *A lot of kids won't talk to him.* Is that what Duplass and the board actually wanted? To prevent a long line to the counseling office from forming, so she could assure parents that every needy student was being seen and there was nothing more to be done?

"You're being defensive," she said. "That's not helpful. Take the afternoon. Go home. I imagine you need some time to think about your role in this."

I folded my hands across my lap to stop them from trembling. "I didn't have any suspicions that Sidney Mayfield was considering harming herself."

"As you've made clear."

"No. I think you're misunderstanding me. I'm not saying I missed the signs. I'm saying there were *no signs*."

"Every kid has problems."

"Small ones. Nothing she couldn't handle."

"But she had weekly sessions with you."

"Which is why I can say it with confidence." I kept remembering the way Sidney looked when she dropped into the comfy blue chair in my office corner, looking relaxed and content, like she'd only come to show me her latest high-cadence Spotify playlist so that I'd have better music for my biweekly runs. "No apparent depression or anxiety. No agitation. No long-term preconditions. No self-injuring behaviors, not even . . . not even—"

"Abby."

"Not even promiscuity. No sign that she wanted attention."

"Wasn't meeting with you regularly exactly that—a sign of wanting attention?"

Grace, the dean's secretary, rapped on the door once, opening it a crack to whisper, "He's here."

I smoothed my skirt, expecting either Dr. Shields or the detective who'd already talked with us this morning, returning with another round of questions.

Duplass mouthed the word *fuck*. In my year at Summit, I'd never even heard her say *darn*.

She closed her eyes and briefly steepled her hands in front of her lips. "Another reason I wanted to let you slip out and go home. Jack Mayfield is here, an hour early."

"But that's fine."

She leveled her gaze at me. "It's not fine." To the secretary she said, "Tell him—"

There was a small commotion at the door, Mayfield's hand on Grace's shoulder, which made her turn in surprise, stammering apologetically. Which is what we women do. Apologize for the touch of large, pushy men. We aren't supposed to let them know they've done anything inappropriate. We're supposed to make *them* comfortable.

In seconds, Mayfield was through the door, leaving Grace standing behind him, eyes wide, mouthing the word *sorry*.

"No, no," Duplass said, rising and stepping to the side of her desk with a warm smile pasted on her face. "Please, Mr. Mayfield, we're so glad to see you. The timing is perfect." She gestured to the empty chair next to mine. "I brought in Abby, our counselor, so we could all talk about this together."

"Of course I know Abby."

I stood and extended a hand, but Mayfield didn't take it, only looked me up and down, making me suddenly aware of the damp circles beneath the arms of my secondhand blouse. He, in comparison, looked fresh and well-dressed. Tucked-in polo shirt, belted khaki pants. Dark brown hair, damp and gelled. He even smelled good. But we all deal differently with shock and grief. Some people wilt and withdraw. Others don armor.

Jack Mayfield pulled out his phone, pointing to the screen. "This is all you've got?"

"I'm sorry," Duplass said, patting her chest for missing reading glasses. "You're showing us what?"

"Some stupid checklists."

He shook the phone in her face, then mine, too fast for us to see, but I didn't need to.

"The digital counseling forms," I explained, waiting for Mayfield to sit, then lowering myself slowly to my own chair, positioned uncomfortably close to his. "Those are the ones we sent to Detective Hernández, after he talked with us this morning."

They were terrible forms—Duplass hadn't let me change them—with room for little more than a "presenting problem" and one or two "action(s) taken."

*Topic: Friends/family*
*Action: Explore feelings. Develop trust.*

"His partner sent me copies," Mayfield said. "You might have done me the courtesy."

"We planned to," Duplass said. "But it didn't seem right to send emails until we'd talked to you first. We're so deeply sorry. We can't even imagine how you're—"

"I want the rest of it," Mayfield said, turning to me, his face so close I could see one bright red shaving nick, the size of a staple, on his neck. "Don't you scribble things down, beyond the checklist stuff? I want to know what you and my daughter were talking about week after week."

Duplass threw me a cautioning glance. Did she think he'd sue? But Mayfield loved Summit. Maybe he could sue me alone, and not the school.

"Most of our conversations were about career interests and general well-being, not acute mental health concerns." I hesitated. "But I can get those notes to you."

Mayfield slumped for a moment in his chair, like he'd been itching for a fight and was disappointed I'd given in so quickly.

"Good. Email me everything. I should get to see it first, don't you think?" His ire was rising again. "Didn't that occur to the two of you? Show the family first?"

Another glance from Duplass. It's what I'd proposed to her this morning. Family first, and promptly. But she'd had her own ideas.

"Did Sidney talk about her mother?" Mayfield asked.

"She was sympathetic to her mother's history of neck pain, but she was a little concerned Geneva was overusing prescription drugs."

*What can I say? My mom's self-medicating. We all do, one way or another.*

Sidney had made that comment while pointing to my desk drawer. In one of our first sessions, Sidney had complained of cramps and cravings. I'd told her about my dark chocolate supply. She'd asked if we could open a bar to share. I relented, warning her that if she told every other girl in school, I'd never hear the end of it.

*Our secret*, she'd said. *As long as you keep the good stuff coming. Orange peel or almond, next time, please?*

In that moment, I'd caught a glimpse of the daughter I'd never have.

Mayfield was still staring at me. "You'll confirm Sidney was upset about Geneva's pill problem, if the detectives ask?"

The impression I got from Detective Hernández was that they already knew, but I nodded. As Mayfield himself said, there was no doubt where the pills came from. The question was *why*. I had no answer for that.

"Did Sidney say anything to you about me?" he asked.

*It's not his fault.* Apologies from Sidney—for her father's attitudes, behaviors, absence. But she seemed resigned, even relieved, that the charade of her parents' marriage would end when she left for college, in a year. *I personally think they should separate now, but hey, it's up to them.*

"She loved you, Mr. Mayfield. And Mrs. Mayfield, of course. She loved you both."

His eyes grew glassy. His lips parted. The aroma of whiskey, half masked by cologne, settled like a warm fug between us.

"Small consolation," he muttered. "My daughter still killed herself."

The assumption of suicide seemed premature, but I bit my tongue. I wasn't a criminologist. I certainly wasn't a cop. But even I knew that crime scene assumptions could go disastrously wrong, especially when it came to supposedly self-inflicted tragedies. It had happened in Waukegan, where Benjamin and I lived before moving to Pleasant Park—the hanging of a sixty-year-old man, later ruled a murder, a case I only followed because it happened in our building and the man had been an upbeat, easygoing neighbor. I hoped local detectives wouldn't make similar mistakes. But a beautiful seventeen-year-old girl, found in her beautiful bed, empty bottle of prosecco on the nightstand, several types of pills missing from her mother's bathroom—it could give anyone tunnel vision.

When Mayfield swiped at his eye, I thought we were reaching a truce. But then he leaned closer. "You're a real piece of work, you know that? Fucking diploma-mill counselor. Summit deserves better than you."

I nodded, as if he'd just given me some helpful professional feedback. Then I cleared my throat. "Will there be a full autopsy?"

Duplass raked her neck with eggshell-colored fingernails. "Forgive the question. I'm sure it's too early. You and Mrs. Mayfield must be—"

"It's goddamn clear what Sidney took. *And* in what frame of mind." He was referring to a final text message from Sidney to her mother—the only form of a note detectives had been able to find. *Don't come into my room. I don't want you to see.* The detective had explained to us that the housekeeper had found the body, just after arriving at the house for her Sunday afternoon shift. Geneva had been hailed from a private tennis lesson, where she hadn't seen the text.

Mayfield added, "The timing was purposeful. Sidney waited until she was alone. She knew her mom wouldn't be checking her phone until it was too late."

I nodded, eyebrows lifted, trying to restrain myself from saying what came to mind. That if I were the parent, I'd wonder why there was no note, aside from the brief text. The majority of people leave notes. Young women, especially.

"It's obvious she was getting back at Geneva," he said, waiting for me to confirm.

I couldn't. If anything, Sidney seemed to favor her mother over her father. No part of the scenario rang true.

He kept staring at me, disdain etched on his face. "You don't think my daughter meant to kill herself."

"It doesn't matter what I think, unless it helps you feel better about the situation. The detectives and the medical examiner would be the ones—"

"So why are you fucking looking at me that way?"

Why indeed. Maybe because he reminded me of someone I hadn't seen in a long time and hoped never to see again. The arrogance. The narcissism. The temper.

Mayfield pulled a piece of paper from the tight pocket of his khakis. A list of names. "Sidney wouldn't have done something so harebrained unless another kid gave her the idea. I've heard about contagious behaviors."

"Nothing like this has ever happened to any other Summit student," Duplass reassured him.

"Just show me her best friend's records, then." He jabbed a square finger at the top of the list. "Izzy."

"We can't do that," I said, not bothering to look to Duplass for confirmation. "You have a right to Sidney's records, but the others are confidential unless they're subpoenaed. I'm fairly certain of that." I wasn't certain. I just hoped the word *subpoena* would allow him to back down and save face.

"They belong to the school, too, don't forget. Which means the board. I'm on the board, and I'm sure my fellow board members would agree I should see them."

"It's irrelevant," I said. "Isabella Scarlatti hasn't come to my office."

Thankfully, it was true. Not *to my office*, though we had talked once, in late September—my third week on the job—on a bench outside the east wing's doors. It was one of my tricks, meeting students wherever they gathered. I'd stroll down the hall to the nearest women's bathroom and mix with the girls who were pausing at the mirror to reapply their makeup. More than once, that's when a student had started confiding to me for the first time, from the next sink over.

*Can I . . . talk to you for a minute?*

*Of course.*

In Izzy's case, it happened outside, where she was sneaking a cigarette. I ignored the infraction and listened to her over the course of one full smoke, then a second. When she stood to leave, I asked her to make a follow-up appointment, but she wouldn't, and I knew why. Because she'd caught me judging her, in light of the stories she'd told. I'd failed.

"I think we could all use a cup of tea," Duplass said. "Actually, Abby if you could just pop out and ask Grace."

Grace wasn't at her desk. When I came back to the dean's

office, Mayfield was already on his feet, readying to leave, the creased list of names planted in the center of Duplass's desk. Duplass and I listened as he marched down the echoing hallway. Nearing the exit doors, he barked at someone—a janitor, probably—before slamming the crash bar unnecessarily hard to let himself out.

Duplass opened her desk drawer, unwrapped a tiny mint, and popped it in her mouth. We waited a moment longer, two women ready to pretend our minds hadn't just called up memories of other angry, unpredictable men.

"Isabella didn't come to school today," Duplass said. "Several of Sidney's friends didn't show up."

"They must have heard the bad news before the teachers."

On the five-minute drive to school, Benjamin had been glued to his phone, but I hadn't thought to question why.

Duplass turned her back to me, hands on her hips, staring out the big windows. "Geneva told me a month ago that she was close to leaving Jack. She'll blame herself for what happened, and she'll roll over in divorce court. Jack has what he wants. Why does he need student records?"

"Because his theory about Sidney makes no sense." From the annoyance on Duplass's face, I could see she'd been asking rhetorically. I continued anyway. "But I'm less worried about Sidney's parents at this moment than her friends. They might be struggling. We need to talk to Izzy and anyone else who skipped today. All the more reason I should come in early tomorrow."

Duplass turned back to face me, kneading the side of her neck. "Do you really think Sidney Mayfield didn't mean to kill herself?"

"It wouldn't be my first guess."

"You'd stake your reputation on it."

"No," I said quickly. "Of course not. I don't have all the facts."

When Duplass frowned, I should have left it there, but I was feeling judged. And I was getting angry.

I said, "If there's a reason you don't want me to counsel Sidney's friends—if you're worried there's something going on you'd rather people not know about—just tell me."

She looked shocked. "Such as?"

"Drugs, bullying, sexting. I don't know. Something Summit parents would prefer to pretend doesn't happen here."

Duplass's eyes looked pink and pouchy. I instinctively looked around for a tissue box, because it's what I did in my office when a student was about to cry. But she didn't cry. She hardened.

"Do you know why the board got rid of your predecessor?"

Rita, my friend who taught Spanish, had informed me. "Because she told one of the top-ranked students he could afford to spend spring break relaxing instead of studying."

"Not just any top-ranked student. He was the son of one of our founding families, and they did not send their son to Summit in order to slack off. We are not a public school."

That I knew. They paid only 60 percent of what a public secondary school pays. That also meant they were willing to hire someone straight out of grad school. It furthermore meant they could fire employees for minor infractions or even smaller misunderstandings.

"Sending you home wasn't a punishment," Duplass said.

"It was a tactic. To remove you from the board's sight. Just for now. In the hope they'd forget about you until we're through the worst of this. But you don't understand that, because you're—"

"Worried about the students," I interrupted.

"No. Because you are *inexperienced*, I was going to say. And far, far out of your depth."

I waited a moment for her to go further, as Jack Mayfield had. To say that I was unqualified. The closest thing they had to a scapegoat.

I said, "A girl like Izzy won't make fast friends with an older male psychiatrist she's never met before."

"I'm sorry," Duplass said, eyes boring into mine. "Did she become 'fast friends' with you?"

# 2

It was one fifteen when I left the school—a half hour after Jack Mayfield had slammed through the exit doors. I crossed the parking lot, squeezing the banker's box filled with books and framed photos, careful to peek around one side to watch for careless student drivers backing out without looking. If I'd known what my day held in store, I wouldn't have worn a pencil skirt, too tight around the knees for quick walking. When my ankle turned, I nearly dropped everything.

"Shit," I said. "Shit! Shit! Shit!"

I stifled a sob, focusing on the twinge in my ankle. I couldn't break down here. Pain was better than tears. Indignation was even better. I should be screaming. No one was listening to my concerns for our students.

I hobbled in search of my parked car, scanning the parking lot to see how many people had witnessed my stumble. Then I saw him. Standing near the bumper of his black car, arms crossed over his tight polo shirt, eyes hidden behind expensive-looking aviator sunglasses.

"Hey," he said from fifty feet away. "You owe me the rest of that conversation."

It felt wrong to say nothing, but any reply would embolden him. *Keep walking.*

"Bitch," he called out. "You talked to my daughter for months. You *know* something."

I kept my eyes focused on my silver hatchback, only three cars away. Over my shoulder I started to say, "I'm sorry—"

But then I saw him take a step, shouting, "You think an apology brings my daughter back?"

I opened the driver's door, shoved my boxes of office stuff onto the passenger seat, and pulled my door shut, locking it before I reached into my purse for my antismoking tablets. I hadn't had a cigarette in sixteen months, but the pills did triple duty: anticraving, antianxiety, and antihypertension.

Just when I was about to step on the gas, something slammed against the car's thin metal roof. I shrieked. Jack Mayfield's face appeared in my window, mouth open in a ragged, wailing expression of unprocessed grief. He motioned for me to roll down the window.

"No," I shouted through the glass. "Step away. Please."

"You're not even trying to help!"

I went back to college at the age of twenty-seven. I neglected my own child for nine years. In grad school, I took on a ridiculous amount of debt. All because I wanted to help. But not at this moment. Not with that raging face so close.

He ordered, "Roll down your fucking window!"

Sidney's father drummed his fist twice more against the

car's roof, delivering a final pound on the hood even as I backed out. I kept going, turning the wheel fast, knowing I was doing a shitty job checking my blind spot.

I couldn't focus on the parking lot ahead. I didn't want him following me or knowing where I lived. He'd have easy access to my old address, but not the new one we'd just moved to, a week ago.

When a slow-moving police cruiser came toward me from the direction of the parking lot's main entrance, I jammed on the brake and waved my hand. The officer stopped and rolled down his window.

"There's a man," I said breathlessly once I had my window down, too focused on the rearview mirror to make eye contact. "He was threatening me."

"Abby?"

I turned. "Robert?"

"You don't sound thrilled to see me." He half grunted, half laughed, the way he used to when he was feeling shy. "Someone bothering you?"

I gestured back toward the parking lot. "Jack Mayfield. Sidney's father. Big guy next to a black—what do you call it?—maybe a BMW."

"Oh," Robert said. As usual, he sounded relaxed. "I know Jack. And that's a Bentley."

We both watched as Jack Mayfield brought a phone up to his ear. I wondered who he was calling. Board president. Chief of police. Maybe one of his famously well-connected siblings. The Mayfields co-owned a major baseball team and a trendy bar popular among Chicago aldermen.

"We'll let him finish," Robert said. As he'd told me more

than once, a lot of good policing was just giving people time to come to their senses.

That aura of strong calm was the first thing that attracted me to Robert. It was the opposite of what I'd grown up with after my mother died and my father remarried. A house filled with bickering and cruelty.

"Your day going all right?" I asked him, trying not to sound as jittery as I felt.

"Only started. I'm on until nine."

Without taking his eyes off Jack, he asked, "Where's Benjamin, anyway?"

"He only had two exams today. I signed a slip to let him leave early."

"I'm just asking because I wouldn't want him wandering the parking lot while this guy is having a temper tantrum. He might want to take it out on the counselor's kid."

"You're right," I said, taking a deep breath, reminding myself that Robert wasn't being nosy, just cautious. "Benjamin took his bike. He should be at the pool by now."

"Public pool's open already? I thought they opened Memorial Day weekend."

"No, private. The Dartmoor." Fancy names. There are no moors in our part of Illinois. No summits either. "It opened three weeks ago. He goes there as a guest. And yes, the Mayfields belong." *Everyone belongs*, I resisted adding, except people like Robert, Benjamin, and me. "But I'm not worried about Benj while he's there."

"And how's he taking all of this?"

"I don't know. I couldn't find him at lunch. But I don't think he knew Sidney very well."

"Summit's small. Two hundred students, tops?"

"Hundred sixty."

"Probably only twenty girls in Benjamin's grade, then."

"Sidney was a year above Benjamin. But thanks for the math lesson."

"You're welcome."

Both of us kept watching Jack Mayfield.

A pressure had been building in my head all day, and now I heard the first telltale ringing in my ears. My childhood had infected me with a dizzying distaste for crime scenes—the yellow tape and spinning lights, the endless questions. That volatile past felt closer at times like this. My finances were a mess. My employment was in jeopardy. And yet, who could think about money? We'd just lost a student. An incredible girl.

Smart, pretty, popular Sidney Mayfield, who thought she might become a psych major at her future college, either Vassar or Brown, hopefully. *Which would you pick?*

Sidney, who wanted to know more about helping people, the marginalized and misunderstood ones most of all—and of course, friends, too. Izzy Scarlatti, for starters. And some person Izzy was dating. The additional problem being: Izzy was dating more than one person.

How to help.

*Asking for a friend.*

Sidney was aware of the therapeutic cliché—that someone will ask, *pretending* it's for a friend. But in Sidney's case, she really was asking for other people. She had to be. Or I'd misunderstood her completely.

Despite that disturbing thought, I was starting to feel a

little calmer. Maybe it was the deep breaths I kept taking, waiting for Jack to finish his call. Maybe it was the clonidine tablet kicking in. Maybe it was Robert's composure, reminding me. I was safe. Benjamin was safe.

I reached into my purse for a mental health hotline card.

"You could give Jack Mayfield this."

Robert took one look and snorted without taking his hands off the wheel. "You kidding me? That guy isn't going to be interested in counseling. Not after what happened to his daughter."

My hand floated above the windowsill, card still clasped between finger and thumb.

"You're right."

"Owe me a drink at Ray's."

"No, I don't," I said, no patience for that long-expired game. "I can't owe you anything, Robert. We've talked about that."

And then I left them at it—one enraged father, one laconic ex-boyfriend, one school that couldn't wait to get rid of me, because what was the point of counseling when it couldn't prevent a teenager from ending her life?

# 3

## BEFORE

---

She'd never felt this happy—happy and warm, both inside and out, sitting in the back seat alone, while the guys joked and argued about music, sports teams, whether girls (women) minded having sex during their periods, which should have made her embarrassed but didn't, because they talked and joked as if they trusted her not to be disgusted. They didn't ask, "Have you . . . ?" or "Would you . . . ?"

The only question she got from up front was, "Too breezy back there?"

"No. It's great."

"Let me know if you want the window up a bit, or we can close them all."

"No, it's good!"

Nothing to worry about, hair whipping in front of her face, loving the humidity, the darkness, the view of cornfields lit up by a half-moon once they got past the suburbs, the smell of cigarette smoke, which she liked, sometimes more than cigarettes themselves.

"You don't smoke?" he asked when they stopped at a liquor store to pick up another case of beer.

"Occasionally."

"Smoking is bad for you. And it's worse for a girl. You'll have wrinkles before you're thirty."

"You hear that?" came the familiar voice from the front passenger seat. Less kind, but not enough to ruin her mood.

"Yeah, I heard it."

"When *I* tell you not to do something, you talk back."

"No, I don't," she said, wishing he'd stop, wishing he wasn't here at all. But that was part of the package. Sometimes he'd let her come along with him and his friends. Sometimes he wanted to show her off. Sometimes he wanted to pretend she didn't exist. Whatever. She planned to have her own fucking great time.

The car was noisy and the back seat vibrated as they drove farther west, toward a forest preserve along a shallow river that smelled like mud on hot nights. The state cops rarely bothered people for hanging out there, as long as parties stayed small and quiet.

When her eyelids grew heavy from the beer and the heat, she forced them open. She pulled the can from between her legs and took another sip, even though it was the drink itself that was making her tired. She must have pulled a face, not a fan of beer but only of beer's effect, because he started laughing. It was a good-natured laugh.

She looked up in time to see his eyes in the rearview mirror, staring. She wiped the grimace from her face and sipped again, trying to hide her distaste. He was still staring. She looked down again, bashful and tipsy, the tips of her ears blazing hot, but he wouldn't be able to see that while driving. The back seat was her place. The better place.

She rubbed her sweaty palms on the thighs of her jeans. No doubt her face was shiny, her hair a mess of tangles from the wind. She was grateful for the darkness. All the windows were still down, and she liked this, too—the rush of air, the noise that covered the guys' voices so that she only got snippets, curse words, howls of laughter.

Back home, she'd stepped out the front door just as a new argument was brewing. That's why they'd let her go, even though it was late, because they wanted time alone, without an audience. Things were bad. They didn't ask questions about where she was going or when she'd be back. No mention of curfew at all.

Normally, she drank wine coolers, and never too many at a time. Two firsts, then. The beer, the no curfew.

No, *three*. Riding in a car with a much older man who had bought her the beer, let her choose the music, even if it was mostly drowned out by the roar of the wind. A man who was still looking at her in the rearview mirror, which made her nervous and excited at the same time.

*You'll hit a deer if you keep doing that*, she thought.

# 4

I was glad that Benjamin was at the pool when I got home, not that I thought of this new apartment as "home" yet. I needed time alone to recover from feeling threatened and shamed, and also to think. *Was it my fault? What did I miss?*

Suicide is multicausal. There are "distal and proximal risk factors." Fancy words. I was proud when I'd first learned how to use them in grad school.

The blinds were down, and when I walked in, I was struck by a wave of damp, dark heat. Only May, but we'd already had a string of eighty-degree days. I could open the blinds to the blazing summer sun. I could leave them down, but even with several lamps turned on, the low popcorn-ceilinged room was abysmally dim.

I raised the blinds halfway, checking the street for any sign that Jack Mayfield had followed me home. The distance from our neighborhood near the railroad tracks and his stunning Sheridan Road faux-Tudor mansion was only a half mile. Everything was close here, which was nice if you were walking around, grabbing a bagel, or hitting the secondhand boutiques before seeing a movie at the quaint second-run theater. And not at all nice when a neighbor wanted to remind you that you tragically failed his family.

I pulled the cord hard, blinds catching on the corner where a few of them were dented. Did Jack Mayfield know that Robert would be keeping a close eye on me? Did he know that Robert and I had dated for nearly a year? By the end, Robert's overprotectiveness had left me feeling stifled, but if he insisted on adding my new address to his patrol route now, I'd try not to think of it as stalking.

When the coast seemed clear, I gave the cords a final yank, working them up another six inches. Then I opened the room's only sash window. Even with my face up against the screen, I felt no hint of a breeze.

Our biggest standing fan was in Benjamin's new bedroom, but I didn't want to enter uninvited. I'd learned my lesson a week ago, and anyway, it was too easy to set him off.

Correction. It was too easy to *think* I might set him off, but that might have been projection on my part, as someone who had grown up without the privacy I craved. I had a habit of reading too much into things that may have been random. The day before, it had been a school notebook. On the back cover, he'd written a quote in all caps, decorated with a border of spiky triangles: "A harmless man is not a good man. A good man is a very, very dangerous man who has that under voluntary control."

I'd googled it, thinking it might be a lyric by some chest-thumping singer. It was a quote by a bestselling author and psychologist. *A good man is a very, very dangerous man.* I wanted to send him an email, scolding him for trying to rack up more followers with that toxic masculinity garbage.

Part of me wished I had a male partner who could be there for Benjamin when he needed to talk about guy stuff, so he wouldn't turn to loudmouth authors and podcasters. And part of me was glad I didn't. Better to have no husband or boyfriend than the wrong one.

*You don't really like guys, do you?* Benjamin asked me once, when he was twelve.

*Men? Yes, of course I do.*

*Other single moms go on dates.*

*You think I should?*

I tried. To find someone for me, someone for him. But it was especially hard when you went on every date worrying if the man would be a good enough role model for your son. I already regretted things he'd seen. Bad behaviors, normalized—including my own, when I'd failed to draw clear lines for fear of bruising a man's ego.

I wished I could erase the times I'd let Robert talk his way into our house, even on nights I'd already said I wanted a quiet evening alone. Or the first time I let Robert stay the night, even though my heart told me it was too early in our relationship for a sleepover, simply because Robert was too tipsy to drive and wouldn't call an Uber. Or the times we argued, and I made peace and shut things down quickly, capitulating, because I was embarrassed our disagreement would be overheard by an impressionable teenager. I should have demonstrated that it was okay to take a stand. Okay, also, to disagree, even argue, respectfully and without shame.

I couldn't be the only parent with a scale in my head: on one side, good memories and smart choices. On the other, mistakes and moments I didn't want to think about, now or ever.

A thick strand of hair had fallen in front of my eyes. I blew it away, wrinkling my nose at my own hot breath. On the next exhalation, I blew out more slowly, trying to ground myself as I contemplated the clutter of boxes occupying half of our small living room. I chose the easy ones first: kitchen glassware and extra towels, no complicated sorting. By the fifth box, momentum was building. I was about to reassemble a computer table I'd taken apart when the phone rang.

It was Duplass.

"Isabella Scarlatti was found in Wadsworth, near the Wisconsin border. She died from some sort of drug, a day before Sidney."

Duplass paused, like she was waiting for my reply, but I couldn't form a reaction. *Izzy? Dead? Wisconsin border?*

I parroted her last phrase back to her. "*Before* Sidney?"

"Her parents were out of town on Saturday and her older sister didn't raise any alarms, so she wasn't officially reported missing until Sunday night. It's our second suicide, Abby."

"No," I said, insensibly.

"Izzy left a note that hinted at a suicide pact."

"But Izzy and Sidney weren't even close friends anymore. They had a falling-out."

"So, you *do* have information you haven't shared."

Duplass seemed to be suggesting I was hiding something, intentionally. Even a hint of an accusation sent my blood pressure rising.

"Did I miss a checkbox I should have ticked? Normal teen drama?"

"You didn't mention it to her father."

"Breaking off a friendship is common. They were kids."

"It might be important, a girl getting cut off from her friend. It might lead her to do something she wouldn't normally do. So much for your theory."

"It wasn't a theory."

"Your doubts, then. It looks like these girls had a plan."

In the mirrored closet door, I saw my reflection. Mussed hair in a ponytail. College T-shirt, damp with sweat. I still looked and felt like a student, not an experienced counselor by any means.

Duplass said, "Don't come to school tomorrow. Let's call it a soft suspension. You'll get your final paycheck. We'll call when we hear more."

"Yes, keep me in the loop, please," I said. "Dean Duplass—"

But she'd hung up.

# 5

I was grateful to have an hour to myself before Benjamin arrived home, face pink with sunburn, shaggy dark hair still slightly damp from his swim.

"I have to tell you something," I said as soon as he closed the door behind him.

He evaded my glance, slipped his sockless feet out of his big running shoes, and proceeded directly toward the refrigerator. "I know about Sidney. Everyone knows."

"There's something else."

My plan was to deliver the news calmly and then embrace him, but he scooted away too quickly. I sank down into the couch and called out, "When you're done grazing, please come in here."

The apartment was tiny. The living room and kitchen formed a nondescript rectangle bisected by a laminate-covered peninsula. No entry hall. No front closet. No dining room. It looked more like a motel room with a kitchenette than a family apartment.

Finally, the fridge door closed and Benjamin made his way to the living room where he stood in front of me. Generic soda in one hand, turkey lunch meat in the other, dark brown eyes still pink ringed with the impressions left by his swimming goggles. He'd been in the pool a long time, but I could never tell if those endless laps were a sign of discipline, frustration, or something else he wouldn't share with me.

"Isabella Scarlatti was found dead," I said.

He pushed the lunch meat into his mouth. His expression didn't change.

"I'm sorry," I said. "I didn't know how to break the news. It must be terrible for you."

His eyes went to the ceiling, like he was thinking. Or angry. Or maybe just trying not to cry.

"Were you close to them?" I asked. "Sid, or Izzy? Both?"

"Not really," he said, his jaw moving. He hadn't swallowed the turkey completely. He was in shock, I told myself.

"I need to explain, or you won't understand tomorrow, when I drop you off and don't come in—"

"I can bike to school."

"Maybe. Or I can drive, but let me finish." I tried to sound matter-of-fact. "The dean doesn't want me to come to work."

"Students kill themselves and you get vacation?"

I closed my eyes at the ugly sound of *kill*. I opened them again and tried to look . . . not happy, of course, but collected. Solid enough that he could afford—if he needed—to be *less* solid.

"I wouldn't call it vacation. Duplass called it a 'soft suspension.'"

"How is that different from a hard suspension?"

"Honestly, I don't know."

He pulled his phone out of his back pocket and started typing with one free hand, left hand still occupied with the soda.

"'Soft suspension' only leads to car websites."

"Benjamin," I said, waving a hand to get his attention. "Hey. It doesn't matter what they call it. Our community has lost two girls. Schoolmates of yours. Girls I knew, and cared for, as well." My voice faltered. "People are upset."

"At you?"

"I meant upset in general." I tried to catch his eye, but he was still staring at his phone. "But yes, upset at me, too."

"Did you do something wrong?"

I hesitated. Too much to say and too little. But also, my mind had stopped turning smoothly. It was like Benjamin's old bike and the chain that kept dropping when he tried to shift. He'd long ago stopped telling me, but I always knew it had happened whenever he came home with black, oily hands. I wanted a new bike for him. I wanted lots of things.

"You didn't ask me how Izzy died," I said. "You said 'students killed themselves.' You assumed it was suicide."

"What about next year?"

"Sorry?"

"What about next year, when I'm a junior. It's the most important year."

"I don't know about that yet."

"Even if you don't work at Summit anymore, I still want to go there."

"Okay," I said, trying to see the bright side. After all we'd gone through, making the big switch to this high-class suburb, he actually tolerated—maybe even *liked*—Summit. Even if we didn't fit in with other Summit families. Even if he didn't seem to have friends. "But there's no way we could afford it without a tuition waiver."

When he didn't respond, I asked, "But you still have one more exam to take, right? They have a new counselor who will be available for students. You could stop by his office tomorrow, if you want to talk to him."

"About the tuition waiver?"

"No, Benjamin," I said, my patience waning. "About the deaths of your classmates."

When I patted the couch, he looked past me, down the hallway.

"I need to take a shower."

"You didn't take one at the club?"

"Not with shampoo."

He headed down the hallway, out of sight. I couldn't make him stay in the room. Couldn't make him open up to me. It didn't help to think of all the Summit students who confessed their problems and worries to me freely—admittedly, three-quarters of them girls. The boys were trickier. Benjamin was trickier yet. But of course, he was my own son. I knew him better and didn't know him at all, in ever-shifting proportions.

I heard Benjamin's bedroom door open. A drawer slid open and shut. Then another. And another. I'd put it mostly out of my mind—what I'd found—but as I listened to him search, I felt my own anxiety sharpen. On a different day, one with less bad news, I might have asked. But today was today. I didn't feel ready. Sidney was dead. Her best friend, Izzy, was dead. My own son didn't need to talk about it. It wasn't a question of pushing something under the rug so much as a rug being irrelevant when an entire tornado had just touched down, smashing everything it touched. I could still picture Sidney and Izzy, the last times I'd seen them. I couldn't reconcile those pictures with the fact that Sidney and Izzy were no longer alive. If it was hard for me—an adult, a counselor—to believe it, how much harder would it be for a child?

When Benjamin came back to the living room, I said, "Okay, so you don't want to talk about your schoolmates. But when you change your mind, I'm here. For now, we need dinner. I'm thinking pizza. Sound good?"

When he didn't answer, I answered for us both. "Of course it's good. Pizza is always good. Especially when it's too hot to cook."

I moved toward the refrigerator, where there was a coupon stuck beneath a magnet—a photo in a chipped frame from the last time Benjamin had played soccer, at age seven. He'd stopped after getting a concussion from an overzealous goal shot by a young player who didn't belong in our non-comp league. A week of nausea, headaches. A hospital trip for MRIs. A follow-up when the headaches still weren't going away.

There was no long-term damage, but it took me weeks to get over the feeling of almost losing my son. Weeks of making promises. That I'd do anything for him. Benjamin was the only real family I had, the only thing that mattered.

"I'll be back from Giuliano's soon," I said. "Keep the doors locked, okay?"

I'd told him about the deaths. But I hadn't told him about Jack Mayfield.

Benjamin was still standing in the living room, waiting for me to leave. "Nobody locks their doors here."

"Nobody who goes to Summit locks their doors, maybe," I said, not even believing *that*. "But we live on the other side of the tracks. So listen to me, Benjamin. *Lock the doors.*"

# 6

Giuliano's was so busy I could barely get the guys behind the counter to take my order. They said it would take forty-five minutes. That usually meant an hour or more.

I texted Benj. *Long wait.*

I thought about the talk we still needed to have, how important it was that I stay calm and open, neither fretful nor impatient, neither skeptical nor insatiably curious. He needed to learn that silence and walking away were only temporary solutions. I needed to learn that even an incomplete conversation was worth having.

I added a smile emoji to my last text.

His reply was quick.

*I promise not to eat the couch cushions.*

I hearted the message.

I was just leaving the pizzeria with a paid receipt but no pizza when a young girl called out from behind me. "Ms. Rosso?"

Her glossy black hair was pulled back tight in a ponytail and she wasn't wearing the thick eyeliner she usually wore at school. "Chandra. I didn't know you worked here."

She wiped her hands on her dirty apron. "Dishwasher. It's not too bad."

"Good for you," I said, wondering if her wealthy doctor parents were using the job to build character or to work off the several hundred dollars of clothes she put on their Visa account without permission.

"I just wanted to say thank you for helping me talk to my mom after spring break. Things are getting better."

"Oh, I'm so glad." I wanted to say something more, or maybe I just wanted to hold on to this moment. "You're sure you're doing all right now?"

"I am." She smiled. "I'll ask my manager to upsize your pizza."

"It's already the biggest size you make. But thank you, Chandra. Really."

She started to turn back, then changed her mind. "It's really sad about Izzy. Some people didn't like her. She was—you know—a show-off."

I didn't know what "show-off" meant—whether it was something about clothes, money, or grades. But I could tell Chandra wanted to say more.

After a moment, she added, "People tried to hassle her, but they couldn't really, because she didn't care about what people thought."

I nodded, encouraging her.

"There was a photo going around. It didn't matter, though. I mean, she was still popular."

*Oh, lord. One of those sexting things, probably. Didn't kids ever learn?*

"Do you think Izzy was being bullied?"

"No. She wouldn't let people bully her."

That didn't answer the question.

Chandra added, "Izzy was too—you know. Confident." She dragged a dusty forearm across her forehead, leaving a spot of flour above one eyebrow. "I'm saying this all wrong—"

"It's okay."

"No, what I meant to say—well, I didn't really *mean* to say it, but . . ."

I nodded and smiled. *Take your time.*

"Izzy wasn't being bullied," she said. "She was the bully. I mean, sometimes. She could be mean. To some boys, especially."

Chandra looked at me expectantly, as if we were playing a game of charades and it was my turn to guess. But I had nothing to guess. Nothing to say.

The pizzeria door opened. A middle-aged woman in an apron called Chandra's name. Our conversation was over.

Back in the car, I replayed Chandra's cryptic comments, but I could make nothing of them. *Izzy.* And *some boys.* I could ask Benjamin, but he'd already been mute about Izzy. They weren't even in the same grade. He'd never mentioned her—or any other junior or senior girl, for that matter. Summit was small enough for every student to recognize every other student on sight, but individual cliques inhabited separate universes.

Parked with the windows down, I googled for any news about the girls. Nothing. Our local newspaper covered charity balls and missing pets. No hard news. If a big-city paper like the *Chicago Tribune* picked up the story then we'd all know much more. But our town fathers wouldn't want that, and I wasn't sure I wanted it either, not if the girls' deaths were sensationalized.

I was still staring at the phone when I realized it was Monday, 7 P.M., the time every week that I called Willa, my late mother's closest friend. We sometimes called her "Aunt Willa" because she was a surrogate aunt, for lack of a better term. I was her surrogate, too, because she had no one else. Her only daughter died at the age of thirty-eight from breast cancer. As Willa got older, she seemed more regretful about the past—not visiting me often enough during my foster care years, for example. But I didn't blame her for that. It was enough that she'd tell me spontaneously, especially if she'd already had a drink or two, how much my mother had loved me. As for Ewan, she never mentioned him. I tried asking once, *How old was he, when he started getting into real trouble?* She said she didn't remember. I didn't believe it, but I didn't push, either.

It was too hot to make the call while parked outside Giuliano's. I needed to run the car and get the air-conditioning going, even if it meant wasting gas. With another half hour or more to wait until the pizza would be ready, I headed north on Green Bay Road, counting on the dense green trees of yet posher neighborhoods to bring the temperature down by at least ten degrees.

When I could finally put my window up, with the AC fully kicking in, I speed-dialed Willa's number.

"Happy Monday," I said, when she picked up. "Go for a walk today?"

"Are you kidding? In this heat?"

"Good point. I hope you're drinking a lot of water."

The weekly call was always quick, just enough time to establish that Willa wasn't broiling to death in her Winthrop Harbor mobile home, or freezing if it was wintertime, or sinking into depression. I didn't mind. I was grateful she let me feel useful. It's what I would have done for my own parents, if I still had any, or even for my brother, if things had worked out differently.

"Work okay?" she asked.

"Oh, you know."

"Pays the bills, right?"

"Some of them," I said, not even managing a fake half laugh.

"But it's almost summer, so that's good. What do you have—a few more days? You deserve a break. Or were you doing a summer school thing for them?"

"Probably not."

I couldn't bring myself to mention the student deaths, never mind my abrupt dismissal. She'd find out soon enough, and by then, there would be less irresponsible conjecture. Instead we talked about a book she was reading and a TV series she was rewatching.

"It was boring then and it's boring now," she said.

"Then why do you keep watching it?"

"The actor. *Whatshisname.*" I waited as she cleared her throaty smoker's cough and complained about how her memory was going. The AC was working but I lowered my window again just to take in the air: green, fresh. It smelled like garden parties and expensive brunches with fancy alcoholic drinks that didn't count as unhealthy because they were light and fizzy and full of fruit. Like boutiques where women shopped for blood-red Italian leather boots and expensive sweaters that couldn't go in the dryer. It smelled like not worrying about anything. The cost of private counseling for your child, if he seemed unable to make friends or process grief. The cost of a good lawyer.

When I reached the northern limit of Lake Forest, I turned in to the train station and made a U-turn, wishing I didn't have to go back.

"That's the worst thing about this."

"About what, Willa?"

"Getting old. It's terrible how much you forget."

It's what everyone said. They never seemed to realize. Forgetting wasn't so bad. Remembering was worse.

I was halfway back to Pleasant Park when my phone started dinging with texts. I glanced over and saw it was Willa, sending me photos of the actor she'd been talking about. Then the phone rang. Willa again. It was her pattern, to send texts and then to call, to make sure you saw the texts. I laughed but I didn't take the call. I'd already taken longer than I'd meant to, and the pizza would be waiting. When the phone dinged again, I silenced it and pushed the phone into my purse.

I'd just focused back on the road when my eye caught sight of a girl stepping out of a car that was pulled off on the shoulder. My heart leapt into my throat. It was Izzy—same long black hair, same pale pretty face, and she was slamming the passenger door. I stared, incredulous, watching as a muscular, light-haired teenage boy stepped out from the driver's side, hurrying to intercept her in front of the car.

He'd just grabbed her by a shirtsleeve when I passed them.

I checked my rearview mirror. A car was right on my tail. I tapped the brake but it was all happening too fast, and in seconds the girl was out of my view

*Izzy.* The cops had made a mistake. That dead girl in Wadsworth must be someone else. The police incompetence was staggering. But that was less important than the elation Izzy's family would feel as soon as someone told them. *Izzy is alive!*

I looked for a place to turn around, cursing and counting the seconds. One. Two. Three. I took a hard right, into a side street. Up the first driveway and fast reverse, avoiding a mailbox by inches. I turned back the way I'd come, impatient at the stop sign. My shock turned to euphoria, a smile spreading on my face.

Since hearing the news from Duplass this morning, I hadn't been able to stomach thinking for long about Izzy's parents, Sofia and Dominic. I'd talked to Sofia Scarlatti only once at a school fundraiser. Sofia, with the jet-black hair, square jaw, and enormous, knowing eyes. *Like Sophia Loren,* Rita had whispered, coming to take my place at the silent auction table, and I had agreed, wondering if Izzy, too, would blossom into that kind of bold, one-in-a-million beauty.

In thirty seconds I made a left-hand turn and was on Green Bay again, eyes scanning the road shoulder. And there she was, walking toward me this time, on the southbound side of the road.

Izzy.

Except it wasn't.

This girl was skinnier. A few inches taller as well. The same hair, yes, but not the same hourglass figure. Not even the same face, I forced myself to admit once I'd passed her a second time.

I found yet another place to turn around. More slowly, now, I retraced my route, swallowing my disappointment, checking my rearview mirror to see that no cars were behind me when I passed the girl and pulled up just behind her, on the narrow shoulder.

Opening the door, I called, "Are you okay?"

She didn't turn at my voice. I stepped out and shouted again.

She was wearing rolled-up jeans and a white midriff-baring shirt, rising high enough that I could see a large, blurry tattoo on her lower back. She wasn't carrying anything. Not a backpack, not a purse.

I jogged forward to catch up with her. At the sound of my feet on the gravel-strewn shoulder she spun around, eyes wild. Her cheeks looked tearstained. One of her wrists was bright red, like someone had been grabbing her hard. Or maybe she'd just done it to herself, twisting the skin, an anxious tic.

"I didn't mean to startle you. I just saw you back there, with your boyfriend, or whoever that was. I wanted to see if you needed help."

"I don't need help," the girl said, eyes full of fire.

"A ride? Can I drop you somewhere?"

"I don't need a ride."

I felt a surge of helpless frustration. *If you'd just let me help you.*

"What about shoes? Do you need those?"

She looked down with surprise, as if she hadn't registered that she was barefoot. She didn't seem drunk or drugged, only stunned. I knew that feeling. The numbness that took hold in the face of a man's unpredictable rage. The jumpiness that followed, until it faded into shivery exhaustion.

"They're still in his car. Fuck."

We looked at each other.

I was wearing an old pair of worn-out running shoes that I'd slipped on quickly, just to drive to the pizzeria. Holes where my big toes rubbed the fabric. No socks.

"We look the same size," I said. "I'm on my way home. There's a lot of glass and stuff on the shoulder. If you don't want a ride, at least—"

"Yes."

I stepped out of the running shoes without bothering to untie them. As she was bending over to take them, I offered her a ride one last time and asked if she needed just enough cash to get home or if she wanted to tell me her name. No, no, and no. She studiously avoided looking at me again as she untied the laces with trembling fingers, then worked her feet into the shoes.

She *did* look like Izzy, if Izzy were older—and then again, maybe I was imagining it. It bothered me. My fading delusion, clearly the result of my own guilt and need. Wasn't it obvious?

*If you'd just let me help you.*

"Thank you," she said softly, busy double knotting the bright orange laces.

*You'll get past this*, I wanted to say. *Whatever this is. A man, a moment, a mistake. Keep going.*

While she was distracted with the laces, I pulled my phone from my back pocket and took a swift, silent photo.

When I finally got back to Giuliano's, the pizza was not only ready but cold.

# 7

Pulling up to our apartment ten minutes later, I spotted an empty police cruiser parked at the curb. Robert. *Good.*

I would tell him about the girl. He could keep an eye out if she was around town somewhere, looking dazed on some park bench or at the train station, without enough money to buy a ticket. He'd probably laugh at my story—and even more at my bare feet. He'd scold me for not noticing the boyfriend's license plate, but he'd also understand the gravity of the situation. More than half of his patrol calls were about domestic disputes.

All those thoughts vanished a moment later as I approached the door, damp-bottomed pizza box in my hands. Something was wrong.

Robert had said he was working until nine o'clock. Even aside from the fact that we'd broken up six months ago, there wasn't a reason for him to be inside the house.

To the right of the door, the living room window was open. An insipid sitcom with a laugh track was playing inside. Benjamin hated sitcoms.

I inserted the key before realizing it was the wrong one. I fumbled, dropped the keys once and had to pick them up again.

"*Finally,*" Benjamin said when I managed to push the sticky door open.

"You could have opened up when you heard me struggling."

He ignored me, stood up from the couch, and turned down the hall.

"Hold up," came Robert's voice. "Don't disappear into your bedroom yet."

"She's home," Benjamin said, returning to thrust his palm in Robert's face. "Give me my phone back."

"Not until I talk to your mom."

Benjamin shot daggers at Robert before stalking away again.

"Fine," Robert relented. "Go to your room. I'll talk to your mom, first."

"Benjamin?" I asked. But his bedroom door had closed. "Robert? What's going on?"

He was wearing his patrol uniform and duty belt, but he had a paper plate of Cheetos on the coffee table, like he'd been hanging out casually, waiting and snacking. I slid the pizza box onto the counter. "Is there a reason you let yourself into my apartment when I wasn't here?"

"I came in with Benjamin."

"Even if he invited you, that's not the same thing as me giving you permission. We're not dating anymore. You *do* realize that, right?"

"This was a special occasion," he deadpanned, standing

up from the couch. He aimed the remote at the television set, killing the canned laughter of *The Big Bang Theory.*

"Have a seat." It didn't seem like a casual suggestion.

I looked to the blind-covered windows, worry replacing irritation. "You couldn't have texted me?"

"We did."

I retrieved my phone from my purse, where I'd stowed it after silencing the multiple texts and the callback from Willa. One missed call, two texts from Robert, one from Benjamin.

Robert tucked his thumbs under his belt. "Benjamin said you went to get pizza. I didn't think you'd be gone long."

"You know how Giuliano's is."

He unhooked his thumbs and lowered himself to the couch, gesturing to the spot next to him. "Abby, I think you should sit down."

There was no other living room seating except the small couch. I yanked a kitchen chair over and dropped into it from an awkward six feet away.

"So." He did the shoulder roll I'd seen him do in public when he was in uniform but trying to convey that everyone should relax. "Benjamin and I both figured maybe you got caught up meeting someone while you were waiting for the pizza."

"You want to know if I went on a quick *date*?"

It was all coming back now, the other ways Robert had tried to assert his control, even aside from dropping by unannounced and creating excuses to stay over. It was the way he wanted me to delete all my dating apps after we'd only seen each other for two weeks. It was the way he brought Benjamin presents—an Apple gift card for good grades, a pair of wildly expensive basketball shoes—when we'd only been dating one month. He moved too fast and tried too hard, and when it was over, he kept trying, even when I asked him to stop.

"You don't get to ask me about my dating life," I said. "Please just tell me why you felt it necessary to ask Benjamin to let you into our home."

"I didn't ask Benjamin to let me in, Abby. I picked him up."

My indignation shriveled. "What do you mean?"

"After I saw you at the school, I followed Jack Mayfield back to his house, and I checked back again an hour later, just to let him see the car and realize he should stay chill."

"And . . ."

"Then he comes out and tells me I don't need to keep hassling him, he's going away overnight to his brother's vacation house in Racine, to get some family support. I tell him that's a good idea and to convey my best wishes to Geneva, but he says she's already flown the coop. I pretend not to know that their marriage is on the rocks. I circle back a while later, just curious to see if the lights are all off—just wanting to see if Jack was blowing smoke. Obviously, there's no law that says he has to leave town just because he said he would—"

"Robert," I pleaded, wanting him to go faster.

"And when I'm just about to pull away I see a figure, halfway down the block, sprinting across the street, coming from the direction of another yard I recognize."

I hated how he was telling it like a story, trying to keep me in suspense.

"The person is wearing a Cubs hoodie, which I recognize, because I was the one who bought it for him."

I felt sick. This wasn't about Jack Mayfield.

Robert said, "Benjamin broke into the Scarlattis'—technically, there was an unlocked sliding glass door he knew about, but that's still breaking and entering."

I put a hand over my mouth. *Breaking and entering.* Which made no sense. Benjamin wasn't impulsive, usually. He certainly wasn't stupid.

"When I picked him up, he had something. A diary. That belonged to Isabella Scarlatti."

I was nearly speechless now, thinking of the future. Benjamin, with a police record. College applications. Misdemeanor? Something worse?

"What was he doing with Izzy's diary?"

"Exactly." Robert's expression turned grim. "I'm assuming that he wanted to know what Izzy was up to, just before she died. I mean, why else try to read the words of a dead girl, unless you were close to her—unless you cared?"

But Benjamin hadn't professed any strong feelings about Izzy's death. He hadn't even seemed curious.

"And I should tell you," Robert continued. "Saturday night, a bunch of friends showed up at Izzy's house for a party. Her parents were out of town. She'd invited a bunch of kids, evidently, but then she must have been in Wadsworth, already."

"Who let them in?"

"Her sister, Talia, home from college."

A Scarlatti sister. The comment reminded me. I started telling Robert about the long-haired, shoeless girl on the road and the argument I'd witnessed. How she looked and didn't look like Izzy. Maybe it was Izzy's sister. Maybe what I'd seen was Talia reacting to the stress of her sister's death.

Robert looked annoyed by my interruption. "Talia Scarlatti is a redhead. On top of that, she's with her parents right now, down at the station, providing statements."

I nodded, fingers to my temple, massaging away a headache just building. I needed a second to absorb it all. The girl I'd seen had nothing to do with anything except to demonstrate there's always a girl somewhere, having a bad day or night, walking a knife-edge of safety.

Robert continued, "Saturday, Talia left the house with her own plans and didn't call their folks or think it sufficiently strange that her kid sister wasn't home yet for her own party. She regrets it, of course. In any case, she ID'd all the friends this afternoon."

"Don't tell me."

I tried to remember where Benjamin was on Saturday night. Whether I'd gone to sleep early. Whether he might have slipped out to join a party less than four or five blocks away. Whether I heard him return.

Robert shook his head. "No, I'm not saying Benjamin was there. I'm saying he wasn't."

"That's a good thing."

"No, Abby. It's not. The other kids have an alibi."

"My kid didn't go to some party that shouldn't have happened in the first place, and he's the one in trouble?" I paused, the word *alibi* slowly sinking in. "You're making it sound like Izzy's death was a crime. But suicide isn't a crime."

"It's looking more complicated than that."

"What do you mean?"

The radio at Robert's belt squawked. "I can't talk about it yet."

He stood up and pointed toward one ear while glancing past me, down the hallway, where Benjamin was in his bedroom, no doubt listening.

I whispered, "They think someone hurt Izzy?" I couldn't bring myself to say *killed*.

"It's a developing situation."

"But wait . . . what about Sidney?"

Robert had rarely been tight-lipped before, even in those months when he was trying his hardest to be a rule follower, preparing for a promotion to detective that never came. He would tell me when he could. I knew that. But this was important. So important, I'd actually forgotten for a second about my own son's harebrained act of petty theft.

"So, you didn't book Benjamin?"

Robert looked at me with puppy dog eyes. "Of course I didn't book him. Abby, that would have been a big deal."

"But you can't just . . . Someone could . . ."

"Yes. Someone *could*. But you aren't going to tell anyone, and Benjamin isn't either. Listen, I've got to get out to the car."

"Wait. Where's the diary?"

"I shoved it inside the Scarlattis' front door mail slot."

"With a note or something?"

"No note. Hopefully, they'll just think a girlfriend or someone had it and wanted to give it back."

"But what if someone saw you?"

"I was in uniform. I can say I found it in the bushes. Who cares where I found it?"

I stood up, calling, "*Benjamin, come out here.*"

"I've got to go," Robert said. "By the way, I left two Cubs tickets on your fridge."

A classic Robert ploy. We weren't an item anymore, but I'd known him off and on since second grade, and he'd never stop trying to manufacture reasons to hang out together.

"And before you ask," he said, moving toward the door, "I don't have a third ticket and I wasn't trying to trick you into spending the whole day with me. Those tickets are just for you and Benjamin. But I understand you may not want to reward tonight's behavior."

"So then why are you giving them to me *now*?"

He stopped with one hand on the doorknob, the other worrying the spot above his top lip where a ginger-colored mustache used to be, before I told him I hated mustaches. He whispered, "Because you looked pretty wrecked this afternoon. And you look even worse now. That whole story about the hitchhiking girl—"

"I didn't say hitchhiking. If she was hitchhiking, she would have accepted my ride. I said she was trying to get away from someone. Her face was red. Her wrist was red, like someone had been twisting it. I saw him grab her shirt."

"But she got away, right?"

"I think so."

"You didn't see the guy's car again?"

"No."

"All right then. Forget about it. You can't save a girl today, much as you'd like to. That ship has sailed."

His comment hit me like a slap.

Softer, he said, "Go talk to your son."

"I will. But you've got to tell me. Why did you let Benjamin get away with it?"

"*Abby*," Robert said, arms lifting for just a moment, like

he was beckoning me to approach. I knew that gesture. He wanted me to hug him before he left, the way I sometimes still hugged him—unwisely—when we met at a bar for the occasional drink, to watch a game.

"You shouldn't have put your own reputation at risk."

Robert rolled his eyes, like it was no big deal, but it was. He could be in trouble.

"Benjamin did something incredibly stupid, but I was less worried about punishing him than finding out why."

"Thank you," I said, but carefully. Things were bad enough without letting Robert think I'd start dating him again just because he'd covered for my son.

He opened the front door an inch.

"Plus, Abby . . . I knew it would be an extra big deal for you, having Benjamin picked up for something."

I wished I'd never talked about my brother. Robert knew us both as kids, and he was in a few of Ewan's classes in high school. That only made it worse. He *thought* he knew him. Ewan could seem charming, especially in small doses. But the charm always had a purpose and a plan behind it.

"Benjamin has nothing in common with Ewan," I said.

"Of course. I gotta run."

My mind was still racing. "Thank you. For what you did. I just wish I knew what was in that diary. You didn't get a look inside?"

"Not a peek."

"You're sure?"

"There was no time."

Robert was looking down at the radio on his hip as if he wanted it to squawk again, just so he'd have a reason to bolt.

"I'll try to call you when my shift ends," he said. "If not, then tomorrow."

"I'll wait up."

"Don't. You need sleep."

He was avoiding my gaze, still.

"I said, *I'll wait up*."

# 8

"Come out here," I called a few minutes later from the kitchen, confident Benjamin had been listening at his bedroom door. A small load of dishes from earlier in the day was sitting in the drainer. I put each clean plate and glass away slowly, trying to feel like a person who felt safe in her home, safe in her life, not standing on the edge of a cliff about to do something she could never take back.

He hadn't done the latest few dishes, still in the sink, or taken out the garbage, either. Tonight of all nights, it wasn't a battle worth fighting.

Izzy. Sidney. A stolen diary. And a week earlier—I could ignore it no longer—the underwear I'd come across. Maybe there were other things I'd missed. Maybe there were things I didn't understand—like Chandra's comment about Izzy being a bully to boys, and something about a photo.

Anyone who assumes you think your kid is either a perfect angel or a perfect devil has never had a kid. And yet.

*Please tell me why you'd steal a dead girl's diary.*

I walked to Benjamin's doorway. Whether or not he'd

been eavesdropping before, he was wearing earphones now, staring at his laptop. Loudly, I said, "We're going to talk after dinner. I'm taking out the garbage first."

He nodded. I nodded back. Small wins.

Just as I was backing out of his room, I spotted a thin, shiny hardcover book on the floor, next to where he'd dropped his school backpack. It was the newest Summit yearbook, released a few days ahead of graduation so kids could collect signatures. Benjamin hadn't wanted me to pay for it, but I'd insisted.

"Your yearbook. Can I see it?"

He tugged off his headphones. "I'll bring it to you in the living room."

I took a step forward. "It's just right there. I'll get it."

"Mom."

"Fine. Bring it to me in the living room."

A few minutes later, he did as promised. The binding was still fresh enough to crack when I opened it. I scanned the inside covers, looking for signs of friendly last-week-of-school notes from schoolmates, but there were none. No "enjoy your summer" or "see you next year." Not a single signature. I flipped to the student portraits. Summit was small enough that every student got a page—Benjamin, too, though his was sparer than most, because he hadn't bothered to submit extra photos or add anything special to his page design. There was only his formal school photo—the same unsmiling mug shot that appeared on his school ID.

"Done looking?" he asked.

I could tell there was something he didn't want me to see, but the only thing I noted was the fact that he'd dog-eared about a third of the student pages. He'd smoothed out the corners before letting me see the yearbook, but he couldn't erase the faint creases. Most of the marked pages were for girls, a few for boys. Maybe these were kids he liked. Or actively disliked.

When he put out his hand for me to return the book, I hastened my search, flipping through the juniors until I found Izzy's page.

He studied me, looking more uneasy the longer I stared at the yearbook.

I pulled out my phone and opened to the photo I'd taken just before picking up our pizza.

"Do you think this girl looks like Izzy?"

He squinted. "No way. That girl's hotter."

"What do you mean?"

"What do I mean? Look at her."

Where he saw "hot," I saw a girl who looked anxious and miserable, with messy hair and a red wrist.

"Never mind."

I looked back to Izzy's yearbook page. In one corner, she'd included a family photo: parents plus Izzy and an older girl who must have been Talia, all of them standing in front of the Chicago lakefront, with the Sears Tower—I'd never get used to calling it the Willis Tower—in the background.

I asked, "Does Izzy have two sisters?"

"No."

Benjamin stuck his hand out again. I relented, returning the yearbook.

"You're being weird," he said.

Maybe he was right. Once I had the photos side by side,

the barefoot girl didn't look like a Scarlatti. She just looked like a slim, scared girl. A girl who was back home now, hopefully.

"Forward it to me," he said.

"Why?"

"I'll show you. But first you'll have to give me back my phone."

"Okay."

A moment later, he opened the photo and moved it directly into the Google search bar. The image-based results showed a bunch of girls who looked nothing like the girl I'd seen.

"The search engine is focusing on her shirt, which you can evidently buy from some place called Zara. It can't get a read on her face. Anyway, Google basically wants to sell you shit."

"I didn't realize you could search for a person that way."

He shrugged. "We're basically living in a totalitarian state."

He slid his phone into his back pocket.

"Pizza," I said, remembering. "It'll taste better if you microwave it. I'll join you in a minute."

The garbage cans were located near the entrance to the basement, with its shared laundry room, next to our downstairs neighbor's door. He was just coming out as I deposited my bag. Skunky smoke trailed behind him.

"Hey. Abby, right? You guys settling in okay?"

I tried not to make any rash judgments about his stringy hair or the egg yolk–colored stain on his dark Led Zeppelin shirt.

"Sort of."

"Cool."

I couldn't tell how old he was, but if he was using a word like "cool" it meant he was probably closer to my age than Benjamin's.

"I'm David, by the way."

"You told me. The first time we met. When you apologized in advance for playing your music loud." I heard my own tone—the voice of a mom who wasn't going to be fun to live underneath.

"Well, come down and say hi anytime. And tell Benjamin I'll show him another chord if he comes over again."

"Benjamin's come by?"

"Yeah, couple of times since you moved in."

Couple of times? Another sign I couldn't keep perfect tabs on my son's location at every time, day or night.

I returned with a stack of shiny mail in my hand and set it on the counter. At this point, it should have been junk mail only, because our forwarding order would take a few more days, and yet I was cautious, and rightly so. A small white envelope slipped out from between two electronics store flyers.

My heart sped up, as it always did when I saw an envelope like this. Name and prisoner number in small, neat capitals in the upper left-hand corner. American flag in the right. I ripped it open and read the message, expecting some variation on what I'd received about every six months for years: *I could use some help, you know. Most guys get visitors.* Or: *So I've got some new ideas about an appeal.* Or: *Never thought it was fair you inherited money from Dad and I only got a fraction.* What Ewan didn't realize was that our father had left him zilch. I'd taken $5,000 from my $18,000 inheritance and moved it into an account for him back in 2014, because I hated to see him getting nothing.

It was Ewan's fault he was still locked up. Regardless of what he'd done as a violent and remorseless eighteen-year-old, only the minor charges had stuck. With good behavior, he might have been out within a few years. But Ewan had never been good. His first prison fights were with fellow convicts. Then he broke a guard's rib. A year later, he gave another guard a concussion. Most infuriating to me was the time he attacked the prison dentist, who'd made the mistake of turning his back halfway through a routine exam.

Ewan's requests for money were galling. But his new focus, over the last three years, was worse.

*Must be about thirteen now.*
*Must be getting taller.*
*Must be almost ready to drive.*
*You won't be able to keep an eye on him forever.*

Today's letter was a short one.

*You're not being fair, keeping me from getting to know my nephew. There's a punishment for that.*

I shoved the single small sheet into the envelope and started to rip them both when I stopped. That envelope, missing something. A forwarding sticker.

I looked again, heart sinking. Our current address was on the envelope. Impossible. Unless someone had told him we'd moved.

Benjamin was back on the living room couch, wearing cut-off sweatpants and an unbuttoned short-sleeve shirt, already working on his second pizza slice.

"It's really hot in here, Mom," he said between mouthfuls.

"You already told me. Long summer ahead. You didn't bother with a plate?"

"Would you get me one?"

Reluctantly, I did, to give my mind another moment to settle. The letter from Ewan—that was bad enough. Benjamin stealing a diary? That was worse. Robert was withholding information—and he had a right to, but it made me nervous. Izzy. Sidney. *Bad things come in threes*, Willa liked to say, but we were way past three.

From the kitchen, I heard the couch creak, like Benjamin was getting up to get his own pop or a glass of water, something he did a dozen times every evening, less because of thirst than because of an innate restlessness. Sometimes I told myself it was the reason he had no friends. Not because of the things he said or did or didn't do. Not because of the stony look on his face when he was annoyed with anyone he deemed inferior. Not because of incidents like the time when he was eight years old and went sledding behind the local elementary school with a neighbor kid named Jacob. Benjamin came back an hour later, took off his coat and boots, and started reading a book. Jacob's mom called two hours later to say Jacob had broken his arm on the sledding hill. He'd been crying and screaming, but Benjamin just walked away.

*His mom said the bone was practically sticking out of his coat sleeve. You didn't notice?*

*He wouldn't stop making noise. It was giving me a headache.*

I had Benjamin screened for autism at his next appointment with a pediatrician, who found nothing worth noting and didn't recommend extended testing. The story of the sledding day had already changed by then, anyway. Later, Benjamin insisted he'd gone home before Jacob got hurt.

I wasn't going to let a story get warped this time.

"So, Benjamin. Why did you steal Izzy's diary?"

He had his eyeglasses off. The planes of his changing face were clearer to me that way. Cheekbones where there used to be only round, soft flesh. A few stubbly, light-colored missed hairs along his jawline. I tried to ignore the resemblance. I hoped that by looking and telling myself, *This is Benjamin, this is my son*, I could overwrite other associations. At some point, in three or five or ten years, the thoughts would go away.

"You knew Izzy well, after all?" I asked, when he didn't answer me. "Obviously, you knew that she kept a diary." I laughed. "Who even *keeps* diaries anymore?"

"Girls."

"Okay. But what were *you* expecting to find in her diary? Why was it important enough to risk breaking into her house?"

"I didn't break in. The back door was open."

"But you *knew* in advance the house would be open, or you wouldn't have bothered to run to their house. How?"

"I told you tonight, when you left! No one here locks their doors!"

"Okay," I said, checking my own memory, confirming. "Noted. But it must have been hard to find her diary unless you've been in her house before." The improbabilities were multiplying. "Have you been in her house before? Were you friends? Did you hang out with her?"

"Not friends. She pretended to like me."

"Pretended?"

"When we weren't in school."

"Then, when? Where?"

"At the pool. Dartmoor. She wrote me notes. I wrote her notes."

"Like, texts?"

"Not usually. She didn't want me to text too often, because her boyfriend always looked at her phone. We wrote notes on paper. I know she showed them to Sidney. I'm sure they both laughed at them. But Sidney was okay. She knew what Izzy was doing."

"And what was she doing?"

"Using me."

A muscle flickered at his jaw, but he wasn't getting that faraway look he used to get when he was fourteen and we'd start arguing. He wasn't looking past me, over my shoulder. He was looking me straight in the eye.

I asked, "Did you have any big fights with Izzy?"

"I wouldn't call them big fights. Arguments, maybe."

Izzy was gorgeous, wealthy, and smart. Out of Benjamin's league. I shouldn't have thought that, but I did. "You didn't ever . . . spend any time with her, intimately?"

He scoffed so loudly it came out more like an angry huff.

"So she really was more of an acquaintance then," I said. "But she *did* pass notes to you."

"She was just doing what girls do."

"And what's that?"

"Like I said. They use guys."

His cold certainty troubled me.

"Would you say that she bullied you?"

"No," he said flatly. "Bullying? Really, Mom?"

I waited.

"She never threatened me. She didn't intimidate me. She used me. If you don't know the difference between using and bullying, then I guess you don't know anything."

"Oh come on, Benjamin," I said, trying to sound casual. "Do we have to draw Venn diagrams? Using? Bullying? Teasing? Humiliating? Isn't there *some* overlap?"

He didn't laugh. Slowly and pedantically, he said, "Women . . . use . . . men. Even when they're trying to act sweet and soft and virtuous. They want *things*. They get *things*."

"What things, Benjamin? What things?"

The air had grown charged between us. My scalp was tingling. I knew if I looked in a mirror I'd soon see a psoriasis stress flare-up of scaly red streaks along my hairline.

"In any case," I said when it was clear he didn't plan to answer, "Izzy was mean. You implied it. Chandra *said* it—"

"Who?"

"Chandra," I repeated. "She works at Giuliano's. You know, Chandra Kapoor?"

His eyes narrowed. "Chandra is the Queen Bitch. She's way meaner than Izzy could ever be. Why was she talking to you? Why were you talking to *her*?"

"Relax." I didn't want to get stuck analyzing girl cliques, especially ones with no direct connection to Izzy or Sidney. "We barely talked. Chandra just said to say hello to you."

"She did not."

"She did." His cold glare flustered me. "Just in passing. We weren't talking about you mainly, we were talking about Izzy."

"Chandra Kapoor didn't tell you to say hello to me."

There was that certainty again, fortified by righteous anger.

He said, "You're a liar. You're a liar and I caught you, red-handed."

"Fine. I may have misremembered. Chandra gave me the impression that Izzy was mean to boys, and I found myself wondering if you knew anything about that, and she didn't specifically say hello—"

"She didn't say hello *at all*. Chandra would never say hello. I don't exist to Chandra. I don't exist to half the kids at Summit and I don't give a shit. They leave me alone. I leave them alone. Peaceful coexistence. That's good enough."

I interlaced my fingers in my lap and looked down, forcing myself to breathe deeply.

He said, "I don't want to go to school tomorrow."

"You have one exam left?"

"Chemistry."

"Then go to school. Take the exam. Come home."

"And then what."

"Then you'll be done with exams." He blinked. Except for the anger and the superiority—yes, those were easy to spot—I couldn't read him. And I still didn't understand about Izzy.

"Benjamin, did you read the diary?"

"I didn't have time."

He closed his eyes and rubbed his face hard, which felt like a reset for both of us. When he dropped his hands, Benjamin looked like himself again. Not quite so hard or embittered. Making an effort. I always wanted him to make an effort. Those years in grade school, when he didn't seem interested in anything; that freshman year in Waukegan, when he got called into the principal's office so often I knew he'd be expelled if we didn't move away soon; all the times he got in trouble and I was there to back him up, to believe him, to protect him.

"And Robert didn't have time to read the diary, either," I said.

Something changed in Benjamin's face, then—a shift so subtle I couldn't trace it to a furrowed brow or tensing jaw. Then his expression cleared again, like he was playing some internal meditation on a loop in his head, trying to bring himself back to some practiced state of mind.

"Robert ran back to the house," I said, testing him. "He put the diary in the front door mail slot. You were in his patrol car. You would have seen him do it."

"Yeah, Robert didn't have time to read it," he said, shrugging. It was an exaggerated shrug, like he was an actor reading from a script, but other than that, his expression and voice were convincing. "So, can I go to bed now?"

"Soon. I want to ask you about something else you took."

"The women's underwear," he said, saving me the trouble.

"Okay." I exhaled. We were getting through this. "Were they Izzy's, too?"

He paused—only a few seconds, but it was a pause I'd be reviewing in my mind for days.

"Yeah. She gave them to me."

"*Gave* them to you. But you laughed a few minutes ago when I asked if you were intimate with her."

"We were in a public place. She was wearing a skirt. She stepped out of them and gave them to me."

"Why on earth would a girl do that?"

"Because she wanted to. That was the only reason Izzy ever did anything."

He gave me a flat, dark look, like he'd put up with my questions far longer than any teenager should. And maybe he was telling me the truth. I'd talked with Izzy enough to form my own impression. Chandra mentioned some photo that was going around—a photo that Izzy supposedly didn't mind others seeing. Maybe Izzy was flirting, or provoking, or accepting a dare. It didn't mean Benjamin had done anything wrong that day. And as for later—stealing the diary, breaking and entering—they were all bad, and yet still not the worst things I worried about, where teenage boys were concerned.

My phone rang. It was late, and the caller was unidentified. I let it go to voicemail.

"Can we go to the pool tomorrow, after my last exam?" Benjamin asked.

"I don't know . . ."

"I answered your questions."

"Yes, you did."

I went to the kitchen to get my own plate of pizza and when I came back, Benjamin was watching a video on his phone. A male voice droned uninterrupted in a way that told me it wasn't TikTok. I didn't assume it was a coincidence he'd pulled up that video and was playing it now, when he knew I could hear it.

I peered toward his phone. "Isn't that the guy who believes climate change, white privilege, and the oppression of women are all lies?"

Benjamin shrugged. "He's a psychologist, like you are." He paused meaningfully. "Or *almost* are."

I made an effort to sound less critical. "He seems bitter, but maybe there's a reason. I wonder if some woman broke his heart."

Benjamin started to smile. "Damaged goods. You think?"

He entered the man's name followed by *childhood photos* into the search box. "Five-dollar bet he was an ugly kid. You up for it?" He held up a pointer finger, ready to search.

"No! That's not the point. You shouldn't be looking for reasons to shame him."

"Who said I wanted to shame him? I wanted to see if he was weird looking. To see if other people shamed him."

I turned away from the screen. "What an assumption."

"And your assumption, that he was a failure with girls, is nicer?"

"Just stop watching his videos."

He laughed. Of course he wasn't going to stop watching any video just because I said so. He'd probably watch them more. For now, he slid the phone between his thigh and the couch cushion.

"You don't want me to learn anything."

"Of course I want you to learn things."

I sighed, remembering the time I made him look up why a "Blue Lives Matter" T-shirt might be offensive, and explain it back to me, before I let him wear it to school on a casual Friday. He ended up writing an English paper about it, pretending to defend the slogan. When he got an A, he showed me the paper. Then he told me it was all a joke, a put-on, and the teacher had bought it. *Teachers are dumb. Cops are dumb, too.*

I knew he felt that way about social media and just about everything else. He was too smart to be influenced. On top of that, he deplored trends. If I asked him about something specific—sigmas, "looksmaxxing"—he'd wince.

*That's cringe, Mom.*

And I got that. If I saw some specific bit of teen slang decoded in *People* magazine, it was already three years out of date. Google searches could only take a parent so far.

When Benjamin left for the bathroom, I checked my voicemail.

"Mrs. Rosso? It's Detective Hernández. I'd like to talk to you again. Call me?"

He sounded friendly, the way he'd been when I talked with him for fifteen minutes, at school. Young, twenty-five or so, which is young for a detective, I guess. Round cheeks and a dimple that flashed when he smiled. No wonder Robert was jealous of him.

I called back and got his voicemail. "Ms. Rosso here, the counselor from Summit." I tried to sound helpful. No, I *wanted* to be helpful. "Given the terrible news, I imagine you'll need anything I've got on Isabella Scarlatti. I'll go through my notes and let you know what I find."

I'd sounded confident enough on the voicemail, but the moment I disconnected, I felt different. Unsettled. Like every next choice was bound to be the wrong one.

# 9

## BEFORE

She'd lost all sense of time by the third beer. At first the drive seemed to take forever and then, a moment later, they were pulled up at a brightly lit gas station that she recognized as being near the forest preserve and she was being told to buy chips and Red Bull. When she took too long to unbuckle, she heard the front passenger door open, but then: *No, you're too drunk and there's a cop in there. Let her run in.*

She steeled herself to walk into the gas station mini-mart. Blinding lights. Air-conditioning up high. Too many people in line and standing in the aisles, guy laughing at her as she tried to pull a refrigerator door open and let her hand slip, stumbling back.

Potato chips. Doritos. Red Bull. Hand trying to fish the folded twenty out of her pocket while she looked around for the cop. Maybe he'd gone into the bathroom.

"Anything else?"

She reached for a roll of LifeSavers and accidentally bumped several candy bars to the floor.

Man behind her. "You're a little young to be out drinking, aren't you?"

She ignored him.

The cashier took her money. She bent down to pick up the fallen candy and felt a hand on her ass. She spun around, ready to slap or swear, but it was him—not a stranger.

"You were taking a long time," he said. "Thought I'd check on you."

She let him guide her by the elbow. Open the door. "After you."

He wasn't as drunk as she was. Hopefully. Since he was the one driving.

Back in the car, a drawl from the front passenger seat. "About time."

She tossed a bag of chips forward. "Hey, I paid with my own money. Say thank you, maybe?"

"Thank you," came two voices, followed by laughter as they pulled away from the pumps.

And now she was happy again. They were the three musketeers. Now she could think back to the moment in the gas station, when she felt a hand touching the lower corner of her jeans pocket, a playful pinch, and instead of being angry she could watch the scene like a movie in her head and imagine what he was thinking when he did that, how he'd come into the store so they could have a moment away, just him and her, two instead of the three. Would they find a way to be alone? Would he take her hand and lead her into the trees? She had to get her head straight or she'd spoil it.

"Nice car, isn't it?" came the voice from the front passenger seat.

"I guess."

Truth was, she could smell gasoline from the back seat and the ride was bouncy, like there was something wrong with the shocks.

Didn't matter. In minutes, they'd be at the forest preserve, seeing the flick of lighters and flash of eyes in the parking lot hidden by woods, out in the warm summer air where she could breathe away the nausea stirring in her gut.

A yellow light turning to red. The last one, before they would turn down a smaller county road.

The half-moon, visible from the side window. Green light and they accelerated fast into the darkness.

"Your reward."

Another beer, not as cold as the first ones, being handed back, already opened. She didn't want it. If it hadn't been opened, she would have just set it down at her feet.

When they got to the forest preserve, she had to pee, that was the first thing. Not vomit. Just pee. Though everything was starting to spin as soon as she stepped out of the back seat, stumbling several feet across the parking lot until she felt his firm grip on her elbow.

"Whoa, hold on," he said. "Careful."

The sharp pinch hurt, but she needed it, too, like a slap that would shake all these bees out of her head.

"That's right," he said. No slur in his voice, no boyish nervousness. He sounded nothing like the guys at school and nothing like her father. She didn't know how to judge ages. "Come over here. That's right, honey. Just stand here. Get your bearings."

She leaned against the closed car door, listening to the

engine tick. It was hot. So hot. The door, the air, everything: a humid Illinois night that felt like a stifling blanket, covering her face.

"Try this."

She took a swig. It burned her throat.

"You like it?"

"No." She coughed.

That mud smell, rising off the river, which was really more of a creek, brown water running between big oak trees. Laughter at the far end of the parking lot, where maybe a dozen people were already gathered by their parked cars. She could hear the pop of cans. Smell smoke—pot, regular cigarettes. Music coming from somewhere, but not loud. Glints of light that may have been lighters, may have been fireflies. A light haze over their heads, obscuring most of the stars.

"I don't know," came a voice from the other side of the car. "Seems like a lot of money."

They'd been talking about the car for the last hour.

"Well, you gotta make up your mind."

She whispered, "*I've got to pee.*"

There was no outhouse in this parking lot but she didn't need one. Just darkness.

"Tell you what."

She heard the dull thunk of the released hood, the squeak and rusty scrape of the rod propped to keep it open.

"Too dark to get a good look."

"Should have thought of that before, when we were at the gas station. Anyway, you already looked, last weekend. You already drove it. What's holding you back?"

"Cost, like I told you."

She winced, hand on her lower belly, bladder full. *Blue book, battery, hoses.*

"I'm already giving you a discount, long as . . ."

Long as what? She didn't ask.

"You know I'm good for it."

Laughter. "I don't care if you're good for it. I care if *she's* good for it."

Louder, she said, "I really can't hold it. Be back in a sec."

# 10

My deepest wish had been to return to Summit, but the next morning, I was glad for the first time that I didn't have to. My mind felt shattered. I'd find myself standing in the middle of the living room, forgetting why I'd headed there in the first place. I put two eggs into a pot of water and set the pot to boil, and only remembered an hour later, when I smelled something burning. The water had evaporated.

Benjamin would be home from school by noon. I should have been wondering how his exam went, and whether this would be the first semester in his life when he got all As and Bs instead of mostly Cs. Instead, I was only wondering about his relationship with Izzy, if it was a relationship at all, and not some insignificant exchanges of flirting and teasing.

Around ten o'clock, needing to clear my head before I tackled my most important mental chore of the day, I tried going for a jog around our new neighborhood, but the heat and humidity were stifling. I felt like every person peeking out a window or pulling out of their driveway was looking at me as if to say, *Do you belong here?* Even a working woman in overalls, sliding open the side door of her panel van—GREEN THUMB PLANT THERAPY—turned to stare.

Other neighborhood women ran or speed-walked in the same kind of tank top and shorts I was wearing, but something about me must have given it away—I didn't have perfect caramel highlights adding pizzazz to my dull brown hair, or my eyebrows lacked definition, or a crease was forming in my brow even though I was only thirty-seven years old. Unless I was just being paranoid, the way my own mother was when she claimed some of the local roads were confusing on purpose, to keep newcomers out. Mom wouldn't have guessed I'd end up on this part of the North Shore, within a few blocks of Sheridan Road, the lakeside drive on which she frequently got turned around, attempting to drive the prettier route from Waukegan to Chicago.

In places, Sheridan Road just disappears. You have to look for signs, and where there are none, you have to trust that if you keep going in a generally north-south direction, with Lake Michigan nearby, you'll stumble onto Sheridan again. I needed to feel the same modest confidence that we'd all understand soon what had happened to Sidney and Izzy. There were no dead ends except the ones of my own making.

None of my fellow teachers had texted with questions about my suspension or intel about any investigations, though I kept checking my phone. When it came to Izzy, Dean Duplass had provided a rough location, and she'd mentioned a note, and some sort of drug. I tried to think what something "more complicated" than suicide would be, and the only thing that came to mind were those cases of kids being pressured into injuring themselves by sadistic online groups. Maybe it wasn't a group, only a person. But what kind of person would have so much influence on a girl as confident as Izzy? And how was it connected with whatever happened to Sidney, who'd simply overdosed? No, not *simply*, I reminded myself. None of this was simple.

When I got home, I traded out my sweat-soaked tank top for a looser T-shirt and dug through the box I'd brought home from Summit. At the bottom I found a legal pad where I'd recorded what I'd remembered from the only conversation I ever had with Izzy, on the bench outside school. These weren't privileged client notes, per se; she wasn't yet a client. In my mind's eye, I'd jotted only a few words. Once I had the legal pad on my knees, I saw there were more than a few words. I'd filled up a whole page. It was proof that she'd gotten under my skin. Proof that I thought she might be in trouble. Proof that I hoped she'd come to my office for a formal session, even if I feared that she wouldn't.

The first word I saw, now, at the top of Izzy's page was *Manny*.

That was Izzy's jock boyfriend. I'd forgotten his name. Izzy said he was jealous. She admitted she did things at times to *make* him jealous, and when I'd asked her why, she didn't avoid the question.

"Because I'm pretty sure we're breaking up soon? Because I've . . . I don't know . . . I've outgrown him? And when we fight then we make up, and that part is the only time I really feel close to him?"

The cops definitely needed to know about Manny.

But there, in the middle of my page of notes, was the more interesting confession. Izzy had also mentioned an "older man."

I remembered asking, "Is your boyfriend jealous of this other relationship?"

"He doesn't know."

But she'd just said she made Manny jealous on purpose. But not jealous about this person?

On the legal pad, I'd written: *Concurrent relationship. Age? Not student?*

"Older man" could mean anything. It could mean eighteen. It could mean thirty.

An older man.

I'd written no full sentences, only single words or phrases to nudge my memory. Below the questions about the older man's identity, I'd skipped several lines and written *Shrimp*. A third person. She hadn't told me his age, only that he went to Summit.

"So," I recalled saying to Izzy, "you like to make your boyfriend jealous, it's a game you both play. But he doesn't know about this older man. You say that he 'can't know.' Then . . . ?"

"He knows about the Shrimp. That's what Manny calls him."

"But you like 'the Shrimp'?"

"Not *that way*. He's disgusting! That's the whole point or it wouldn't work."

"By 'work,' you mean make Manny jealous. Because this other boy is beneath you?"

"It can't be someone Manny is threatened by. That would be serious. This isn't like that."

Izzy didn't want her boyfriend to know she was fooling around with the older man, or planning to. But Manny could know she was fooling around with the Shrimp. In fact, it was because of the Shrimp that Manny didn't think to suspect the real threat to her affection.

When I worded the situation back to her, she objected.

"I wouldn't call it affection," she corrected me. "Didn't you 'play the field' when you were my age?"

I could tell by the way she said it that no one called it "playing the field" anymore.

"My mom likes to pretend that people her age were so careful about sex, but you guys didn't even talk about consent. I did a paper on it. How there was a college in the nineties that drafted a consent policy and they were ridiculed for it, even on *Saturday Night Live*. Was it weird back then, everyone thinking a guy could fuck a girl even if she didn't say yes?"

I was trying to decide the best way to answer when she added, "Oh my god. Wait a minute. *Were* you dating in the nineties?"

"No," I said, smiling. "I was in grade school. But for you, I'm sure my dating years would still seem a long time ago. Brad Pitt and Jennifer Aniston were still together. Beyoncé was still part of Destiny's Child . . ."

None of that computed. Then she tilted her head, interest returning as she examined me.

"You were pretty, I bet. It doesn't last long, does it? That's what I hear." She made a sweeping gesture down the length of her body, like a television game show hostess drawing attention to a prize. "Evidently, I'm in my *prime*. I'm supposed to enjoy it while I can."

She'd said it wearily. Maybe ironically. But I think she believed some part of it, too. Izzy was involved in a three-ring circus of suitors. Or something more complicated. A secret infidelity, an unhealthy game. The Shrimp was a decoy.

I could remember, even now, the way Izzy had leaned back and looked up at the oak trees over our heads, their gnarled branches forming a thick yellowing canopy, and how she had blown a long, slow blue-gray stream of smoke that we both watched rise and dissipate, while I tried to find the words to say, *You think you've got this all under control, but trust me, you don't.*

"My life is fucking boring," she said. "And Manny is the worst of all."

"So maybe you should break up with him."

"My new friend isn't boring."

"The Shrimp?"

She laughed, which I took to mean no, the other one. The older man.

"Well, this was a mistake," she said.

"Can we talk again?" I asked. "Make an appointment. Please? I want to hear how you're doing."

But most of that wasn't written on the legal pad. It was all in my head, a mix of half-remembered dialogue and conflicted feelings, because much as I worried for Izzy, I also disliked her, which made me question myself yet again. It wasn't in my job description to like or dislike. My job was to care.

I thought back to what Benjamin had said. *Girls use guys.* Maybe they did, sometimes, but maybe that was their way of asserting power in a world of angry, frustrated, "dangerous" men.

I heard the sound of familiar steps, coming up the walk. The front door swung open. I flipped over the legal pad and jumped up like I'd just remembered I needed to defrost something for dinner.

# 11

When I was fourteen, my first year in the foster care system following my stepmother Martha's death and my father's institutionalization for dementia, I got in trouble for playing mini-golf.

Janessa, a girl in my home, had invited me and we had just enough scavenged quarters to play, especially after the pimply cashier was convinced to let us pay half rate. The place was empty. It was a beautiful fall afternoon, blue sky, crisp air. I'd never played mini-golf before, and the little windmills and bright green turf made me feel like a kid again. I *was* a kid, of course, but that didn't stop me from feeling like a jaded adult.

Janessa had played before. She rolled up her flannel sleeves to the elbows, and I spent lots of time standing beside her, looking down at her hands and thin wrists, gripping the club, thumbs pointed down.

"They're from my dad," she said at the fourth hole.

"I wasn't trying to stare. I was just watching how you swing."

She made a dubious sound, shook her arms so the flannel

sleeves settled farther down her scarred forearms, then smacked the little ball.

"You got anything like that?" she said after she'd finished the hole.

Cigarette burns?

"No."

No burns, no scars, no poorly healed broken ribs.

"Then what do you got?"

"She sent my brother away."

"Your mom?"

"Stepmom."

"But before that?"

"She hated both of us. But him, most of all."

"So, she never touched you."

I wasn't in the mood to visit any specific memory or to play the "my family was worse" game, so I said, "Not really."

"Then after your brother was gone, she kicked you out?"

"Something like that."

I didn't tell people my full story. Benjamin didn't know it; Robert thought he did, but I'd given him only partial details. My mom's death by stroke when I was eight. Martha's accident in the kitchen—one wrong step on a slippery floor, head cracked on the counter's sharp corner edge—shortly before I turned fourteen. Foster care for four years. It was only a couple of years ago that Benjamin did the math and said, *You were twenty when you got pregnant with me? That's not so young.*

*Oh, it was, honey. It was.* I skipped over the next seven years. *But things were better once I inherited a little money and could afford to start college.*

But neither Benjamin nor the dream of college existed yet, during that mini-golf outing, long ago. Janessa and I played a round, went home, and received a full reaming out: no dinner, lost weekend privileges, extra chores. My foster father—Dan Baxter was his name, a church pastor—lectured us with his hand over his heart, incredulous that we could have chosen to do something frivolous on that day of all days.

But what else was there to do? Sit at home watching the news endlessly replay smoke and terror? September 11. No wonder the mini-golf place was empty.

I thought about that time and again, whenever a tragic public event happened and I found myself deciding whether to go to a movie, or the beach, or in today's case, a private pool. It wasn't like sitting at home, reorganizing the pantry or cleaning a toilet, would be more respectful.

So I said yes when Benjamin asked if we could go to the pool together, my first full day home with my Summit career uncertain, his last day of exams, one day after I'd made him talk about the underwear. He'd admitted to having some kind of involvement with Izzy, and if I'd been his age, talking to my father or stepmother about some boy I liked but wasn't steadily dating, I couldn't imagine providing more details than he had. Even if the picture was blurry, he'd given me something. There had to be a reward for that, or at the very least, no punishment. And anyway, for Benjamin, the pool wasn't frivolous. He was preparing for a lifeguard test, hoping for a first job, trying to improve himself.

Once I was in the pool parking lot, sliding my Mazda between a blue Audi and a silver Lexus, I started doubting myself again. Maybe my judgment in this situation wasn't the best. Maybe anyone who knew us—including Rita, the Summit Spanish teacher who let us visit Dartmoor as guests, under her membership—would judge me for showing up, today of all days, at the pool.

So far, I'd signed in as a "guest of Rita" only once. But Benjamin had used her name a half dozen times. He blended in easily, arriving by bike, whereas I arrived in a car manufactured before Benjamin's birth. As my son liked to remind me, there were only two crappy cars that showed up on this lot. The *other one* belonged to a janitor.

I texted Rita. Instead of texting back, she called.

"Are you *okay*?" her voice boomed once I picked up. "I heard they gave you a 'soft suspension.' What does that even mean?"

"It means a day and a half off, so far, and no renewal of my contract, I'm guessing."

"Shit, woman, you need to come over for a glass of wine. It isn't fair! What are they thinking?"

"They were thinking about parents' donations and the school's reputation. They were thinking about the Mayfields and the Scarlattis."

"I can't believe they already found someone to replace you."

"Better than leaving students stranded for the last few days of school." There were only two exam makeup days, now. Benjamin was done; the kids who had skipped after hearing about Sidney still had exams to complete. "Hey, listen. I was texting to ask if it's really okay for Benjamin to keep signing in under your name. I don't know if there's a maximum number of visits."

"Don't worry about that. If there's a problem, they'll tell me. Dartmoor isn't shy about slapping members' wrists. But how about you?"

"Swim, you mean? I'd like to. I'm just not sure if it's a good look, coming here today."

"A good look?" She sounded confused. "Oh, *that*. I don't really see how one thing has to do with another. I mean, every Summit teacher is distraught about what happened. We're all still allowed to get some fresh air, aren't we?"

I lowered my voice, not that anyone could hear me. "You're allowed, maybe. I'm not sure *I* am."

"Oh, honey. Whatever the police and parents find out, I know you did your best. I don't know which is worse—that those girls took their lives, or that someone did something *to* them."

"Both girls," I said, testing her knowledge, trying to fill in the blanks left by Robert. "I heard something about Izzy's death being 'complicated,' or maybe both? If the detectives are saying 'homicide,' that covers a lot, even something unintentional, like an accident—"

"Abby," she stopped me. "They're not talking accident. They're talking *murders*, plural. And screw those detectives. Duplass is getting it straight from Geneva Mayfield and Sofia Scarlatti. Those moms are ready to rip this town apart if the police department doesn't get its shit together. Didn't you read what Duplass put in the chat?"

She was referring to a teachers' and support staff chat group from which I had been promptly removed.

"No. I don't have access."

Rita started talking about how she hoped I'd get back into

the group, and in the interim she could screenshot everything and email me later. But I didn't want to wait, and I didn't need screenshots. I just wanted her to tell me.

"They know someone was in Sidney's house when she took the pills," she said. "The family's security systems were turned off—"

"Why were they turned off?"

"Because Geneva and Jack had had endless fights about all the deliveries being made to their door, due to Geneva's shopping habits. She didn't like him getting the notifications. Anyway, the neighbors' doorbell cameras on either side showed a figure heading toward the house and then running away, maybe forty minutes later."

"A figure."

"Person. Man, probably. They couldn't see him clearly. And the police have gone back to dust for prints—especially in Geneva's bathroom, if that's where the pills came from—which they probably should have done the first time, right?"

"Right," I said. Even though the car was warming quickly with the engine and AC off, I felt a chill.

"And Izzy's parents took one look at her so-called suicide note and said it wasn't her handwriting. The whole thing could be a setup, like someone gave her the pills that killed her. It didn't take much, because she had an allergy that made her tongue swell up."

"That's terrible."

"Her parents told the police that Izzy's sister has an allergy to an ADHD drug, so they're wondering if it was something chemically similar."

"So, the person . . . knew that would happen?"

"Maybe not. Maybe he just wanted her—you know, drugged—and then she died. Inconveniently."

I thought about my attitude yesterday, talking to Jack Mayfield, feeling stubbornly sure that Sidney's death didn't look like a suicide. But now that the details were coming to light, there was no pleasure in being right, only an anxious distaste for the specifics. Every new fact conjured up a new image. Izzy accepting a pill, maybe thinking it was no big deal, a recreational drug to try in the presence of this person—friend—whoever he was, not realizing she had an allergy. Sidney drinking tampered wine, not realizing someone had put a cocktail of ground-up drugs into it. Different girls, different situations, but drugs in each case, and an unidentified person. Maybe the *same* person.

"Anyway," Rita said, "I think you should put it out of your mind for the day. Go for a swim. Say hi to Benjamin."

The car was sweltering now, the black steering wheel soft and greasy feeling. I'd mishandled things, at work, at home, in life—now and before. I felt lightheaded and anxious every moment I tried to imagine why someone would have wanted to hurt Izzy or Sidney. It didn't feel right to go into Dartmoor, just as it hadn't felt right to be at home. Nothing felt right.

I stared numbly at my phone for a minute before texting Robert. *You promised to call.*

I waited, but there was no reply.

I texted Benjamin back. *Sorry for taking so long.*

I saw Benjamin was typing. Before his next message rolled in, I added: *If you're ready to go I could just give you a ride home. I don't need to swim.*

*Come in*, his reply read. *Water's warm.*

# 12

When I entered Dartmoor, the young desk clerk was on the phone—an actual corded black phone so heavy and old it looked like it was from a 1950s movie. She waved away my driver's license, grabbing for a clipboard and a pen that she pushed toward me as she continued to talk to someone else.

Two spots above the blank line, Benjamin had signed in as a guest of Rita. I scrawled my name, thinking of other pools and fitness centers I've visited, with their membership card scanners and their fancy entryways, complete with couches, electronic message boards, and flat-panel television sets. This reception vestibule looked like it hadn't been freshened up since the Kennedy era.

Benjamin had no reference point for categories like upper-middle class and new rich versus old money. I'd told him that lots of people try to look wealthy. But the people who have had money forever try to look poor. Rich kids *and* their parents in our town wore scuffed-up shoes, weird golf pants, and polo shirts with worn collars. It was a preppy cliché, but

I hadn't grown up preppy, and Benj probably didn't even know the word.

"Am I good to go?" I asked the desk clerk, who was still talking on the phone, head in a cabinet, rustling through some stacks of paper.

While her face was hidden behind the cupboard door, I scanned the sign-in sheet. No sign today of any Mayfields. I flipped the page to check out entries from previous days. Until Memorial Day, the pool had limited hours. There weren't too many names. I spotted Benjamin's name yesterday, and around the same time on Sunday and Saturday. Two lines above his Saturday sign-in was Isabella Scarlatti. In at 11:10 and out at 12:50. I was looking at the way she spent her last afternoon. I was also seeing, with my heart in my throat, that Benjamin had signed out directly after her, with the same time: 12:50, almost as if they were leaving together.

"Okay!" said the desk clerk, hanging up the phone. "Do you need anything?"

I absentmindedly massaged my cheek with my fingers. "A lock," I said when it came to me. "Do you sell them?"

"No, sorry."

"Do you have any extras to loan out?"

She smiled. "We used to. Let me see. I'll check the back office."

She was gone less than a minute. When she came back, I swallowed down a trace of bile and shifted my tote bag, wincing when I heard it crinkle. I was just buying time, *until*. Until what? Until I understood.

"Here you go," she said, placing the lock in my hand. "Just drop it back when you're done. Enjoy!"

I mirrored her expression, keeping the smile pasted on as I made my way into the women's locker room, smelling that old familiar brew of chlorine, coconut-scented sunscreen, and fancy hair conditioner.

Then I saw the row of old lockers. Two of them, side by side, were decorated with black bows. Each one had a combination lock affixed, a swimming team Speedo hanging outside. The deaths were so recent. I supposed no one wanted to be the person to cut the locks off or remind family members they needed to retrieve the girls' suits. It was too heartbreaking.

Looking around to confirm no one else had followed me into the changing room, I reached for the nearest neon-green swimsuit, and then for the one next to it. On first touch, the second one still felt damp. My stomach did a sickening drop again. As if a recent death was more horrible to imagine than one farther back in time. But it felt that way, as if the past was close enough to reach back and grab, before anything bad happened or before the next thing did.

My fingers lingered, touching the fabric, which wasn't actually wet, just shiny. I thought of that moment at home—the wisp of satin, clenched in my fist. I got that old feeling, like it was my job to contain this, even ahead of understanding it.

*She gave them to me.* But also: *She was using me.*

When I shook my head clear, I automatically reached for the clonidine tablets I usually carried, but then I stopped, remembering I'd taken the last one from the small pill case I kept in my purse. The regular prescription bottle was back home, somewhere. The last time I'd seen it was during the move, and I hadn't spotted it since, because I hadn't had time to properly organize the recently unpacked toiletries, medicines, and first aid stuff. Some of it was in bathroom drawers, some in lidded plastic tubs in the hallway closet.

In place of a clonidine tablet, I tried some box breathing. In for four counts. Hold for four. Out for four. My only problem with box breathing is that I always wanted to stop in the middle. To hold for not just four, but longer than four. To make everything stop.

I allowed myself to picture the girls for a minute, the way I'd last seen each of them. Sidney, with her long blond hair and effortless, retro '80s supermodel tan; she'd probably been born with highlights. Izzy with her black hair, sleepy eyes, and devilish smirk; more Aubrey Plaza than Sophia Loren, come to think of it.

Even when they weren't in school uniform, they dressed the same, in a fashionably disheveled style: a men's button-down shirt slipped off one shoulder and tied at the waist, over a crop top. High-waisted jeans with shredded cuffs. An enormous set of neon hoop earrings that seemed to bounce from one girl to the other. The girls traded entire outfits. Lord knows they didn't have to, given their wealth. What else did they share?

I hurried to the pool deck in my old bathing suit with a beach towel wrapped around my waist, spotting Benjamin just as he finished a lap. His hand went up, waving.

"Mom," he shouted across all six roped-off lanes. "Over here!"

In the shallow end, two young women who were probably nannies played with two toddlers. In a lane next to

Benjamin's, an ancient, liver-spotted bald man performed the slowest and steadiest crawl stroke I'd ever seen.

"This is awesome," Benj said when I reached the far side of the pool. Pointing to the big swimmer's clock hanging over five lounge chairs, only one of them occupied, he said, "Here, time me."

So that's why he was glad to see me. No contacts. No way to see the clock.

"How many laps are you doing?"

"Three hundred meters."

"That means nothing to me."

"There and back, six times."

I waited for the second hand of the big swim clock to sweep up to the "60" position, a new minute about to start. "Ready, set, go!"

Swimming had built up his back, bulked out his shoulders, and tapered his waist. He gobbled protein bars between classes, then skipped lunch period in the cafeteria, going instead to the school's weight room—an alternative Summit allowed. I knew why he and other kids like him did it: to avoid the terror of the cafeteria—the stares, the cliques, that moment of wondering where you should sit or if you should just turn around, dump your tray, and flee. I was a kid, too, of course. The difference was I wanted friends, enough for me to overcome my shyness. When I told Benjamin that story, he corrected me. He wasn't shy, he said. He just didn't like most people.

In any case, the weight training had paid off. I couldn't believe that more girls hadn't noticed his good looks or the way he was shooting up. Already, there was too much ankle showing below the cuffs of his latest thrift-store jeans. He wouldn't be the shortest boy in his class forever.

Benjamin was coming in for the first of six completed laps when I noticed a man occupying a lounge chair in the shade. He caught me looking and shifted his gaze downward, to a yellow pad not unlike the ones I'd just packed up from my office. Lawyer, I thought, or architect. The latter guess only because he had an *Architectural Digest* at the top of a pile of reading materials next to his chair.

He was older than me by a decade. Slim, tan, and fit. Eyes hidden behind nothing-special sunglasses. Good-looking. Intellectual, if all that reading material was an indication. But not someone I knew from Summit, which was the important thing.

After his last lap, Benjamin hit the wall and yanked off his goggles. "Time?"

"Five minutes, forty seconds."

He slapped the water with his palm, face unreadable.

"Is that a victory slap?"

He ran a wet hand over his face then stared up at me, eyes bloodshot, brow furrowed. So, not a victory lap.

I asked, "Is it good enough for the lifeguard test?"

He dipped under the water again, then emerged, smoothing back his otter-dark hair. "There's no maximum time for the three hundred meters. You just have to swim it with a confident stroke and even breathing."

"Well, no problem there!"

But his expression had flattened.

"You probably need a snack by now," I said.

"No. What I *need* is to learn how to flip turn. Which will make me ten percent faster."

"But you don't need to go any faster."

"All real swimmers do flip turns."

"Are you sure?"

"*Mom.*"

Since he'd started visiting the pool this month, he'd had to swim laps alongside the real swimmers—*private swim team* swimmers. I got it. I lowered myself into the water and started doing the breaststroke, allowing him time to swim off his frustration, although I still didn't fully understand it.

For the next twenty minutes, we remained in our own worlds, our parallel lanes. When complicated questions or images began to form in my mind, encouraged by the mindlessness of my slow and steady breaststroke, I pushed them away. But I could not push away the silent words, surfacing like bubbles.

*He barely knew Izzy. He's got nothing to do with any of this.*

Another length, a tap on the wall, a slow turn, and back again.

*He's not like Ewan.*

But that wasn't a name I wanted to think about.

I mentally sidestepped, trying to think instead of my late mother. I could see her wistful, patient smile. I could remember tagging along with her to grown-up places—art galleries where she browsed but never bought; bookstores where she took her time in the fiction section.

Once, from a phone booth near a movie theater, she placed a call to let my father know that we wouldn't be home until late, and he mentioned a visit from a neighbor alleging something, graffiti or a suspiciously injured cat—and she should come quickly. Still, we went to the movie. It was *La Cage aux Folles*, in French, playing at the Fine Arts in Chicago—a little over my head, but I enjoyed it in the end because she did. The last movie we ever saw together.

My mother had done an admirable job of seeming even-keeled no matter what was going on around her. She didn't let her kids' moods or misbehaviors drag her down. Until the day she died of a stroke, one never would have known she was stressed or suffering.

If I were sentimental, I'd wish that she could have lived just a few years more. But I wasn't, and I didn't. It would have broken her already-weak heart to see how Ewan turned out. Unless I was misunderstanding everything and she always knew. Perhaps she was only waiting, full of dread, for the rest of the world to find out.

# 13

When I finished my laps, I lingered, watching as Benjamin swam toward me and then stopped, eyes impossible to read behind his tinted goggles.

"I'm not done."

"Okay then," I said, tone artificially bright, determined not to be affected by his bad mood.

I proceeded to the empty chair two seats away from the man with the piles of reading material. There was something about his profile—the straight nose and the full, thoughtfully pursed lips—that vaguely reminded me of a favorite college professor I hadn't seen in years.

"Gymnast?" the man asked me.

I followed his glance to the nearest lane, where Benjamin was progressing slowly, turning one somersault after another, kicking wildly enough that the nannies in the shallow end were staring at him, too.

"Oh." I laughed. "No. It's something he saw on YouTube. A way to practice your flip turn, away from the wall."

"Is *that* right," the man said, looking impressed. "My

daughter could flip turn from a young age, but only as long as she was wearing a noseclip. I don't remember how she learned. Not from me, that's for sure."

He turned in my direction, so attentive I didn't feel right digging into my bag for something to read.

"My daughter used to swim competitively," he continued. "She was on the Dartmoor team before she and my ex-wife moved hundreds of miles away."

Divorce, plainly stated. Was he trying to flirt?

"You really don't recognize me?" he asked, grinning.

"Sorry. I don't."

"Curtis Campbell. You were a student of mine."

He pulled off his sunglasses. That's when everything slotted into place: not just the nose and the mouth, but the thick eyebrows that had always reminded me of the actor Colin Farrell. Kind, dark eyes with long, thick eyelashes. Eyes that had made me feel safe. Like I belonged.

"Statistics for psych majors," he said. "Followed by Abnormal."

"*Dr. Campbell?*"

"In the flesh. But less of it."

Dr. Campbell was an extremely heavyset man in baggy brown Dockers and unfitted dress shirts. Dr. Campbell used to hide his face behind a scruffy beard and mustache. Dr. Campbell, nice as he was, didn't look like an Irish movie star.

"You applied to be my assistant," he said.

"Yes, but I didn't get the position."

Dr. Campbell had dyslexia. That's why he needed the help of an undergrad assistant. He was my only college professor who not only accommodated learning disabilities at a time when fewer teachers did, but honestly seemed to believe that one's differences could become one's strengths.

"I didn't fill it once I knew I was taking time off, to work on the marriage problem. Listen to me, going on about my personal life."

"No, please do. It's been so long. I want to hear all of it."

He smiled again—grateful, maybe a little shy.

"We tried to work things out. It was her idea to move closer to her parents, in Wisconsin. When we finally pulled the plug, I decided to come back to the North Shore."

"But you didn't want to return to teaching?"

"I decided to focus on my private practice and my writing. I'd had some unexpected success with a book about parenting."

"I had no idea. But everything's . . . good since? Aside from the divorce?"

"It was overdue."

All along, I thought I'd been passed over for the position because I wasn't good enough. I was about to ask more about his new book when my phone started vibrating.

The text read: *Handed in the diary. B has nothing to worry about.*

I was confused. Robert had said he'd returned the diary, without reading it, via the Scarlattis' mail slot last night.

"Sorry," I said to Dr. Campbell. "I need to take this."

I grabbed my phone and walked behind the lounge chairs, to a high fence that separated the pool area from several outdoor tennis courts, dialing as I went. On the closest court, a couple—lean, gray-haired man and a girl in a short tennis dress, probably his daughter—were finishing up a game and collecting loose balls from the court.

Robert had just picked up when I saw the gray-haired man lay a hand on the girl's behind.

"Oh," I said with disgust. Not his daughter, then.

"Yeah, hello to you, too," Robert said. "I just wanted to let you know Benjamin's name wasn't in the diary."

"You read it, then. You told me you hadn't."

"I had to, Abby." He sounded harried. I could hear multiple voices in the background, like he was calling from a hallway or break room. "They ordered an autopsy on Izzy."

"When will they have the results?"

I waited as Robert moved away from the hubbub to someplace that sounded echoey but quieter. He kept his voice low. "Preliminary physical exam, they already have, but analysis of fiber, DNA can take months. All depends on the backlog and the type of test. There didn't appear to be sex involved. Which is a different story than her friend. Sidney Mayfield had intercourse the day she died."

My head was spinning, all of my assumptions turned around. Izzy, the sexually precocious one juggling three men, died somewhere twenty miles from here in a small town. No intercourse was involved. Sidney claimed not to be interested in local boys and thought only about college. She died at home, in a short span of time when no one else was around. She may have had sex just prior to dying. Someone was with her—a man, face hidden, spotted hurrying away from her house.

"It may have been consensual," Robert said. "Or not. Hard to tell when there isn't clear evidence of trauma. And of course, she could have been unconscious by that point, on account of the overdose."

I groaned, caught off guard by the image of someone violating her that way. But Rita had said both girls were drugged. Why else would a man drug a young woman? Maybe Izzy's anaphylactic shock scared him off, but only long enough to set his sights on Sidney.

"There's a whole lot we don't know yet," Robert continued. "The department is keeping some details to itself, until we know more about who was with her. If we pick him up, we don't want to feed him information he can use to construct an alibi. You didn't hear all this from me."

The tennis players were chatting with their backs to me. I wanted to shout. To tell that old man to take his hand off that girl's nearly bare ass.

"So, you can see why I've been busy today," he said. "I didn't have time to update you on the diary. But once I saw what was in it, I had to hand it over to Hernández and his partner, Wood. They'll need everything they can get."

"You held on to the diary. You lied to me. And Benjamin knew you were lying. To me. His mother." The next part hit me hard. "Which means he was watching you get away with it."

"Whatever."

"Not *whatever*. Benjamin's hypersensitive to this stuff right now, and he seems to be getting more slippery with the truth. He's watching me. I'm sure as hell he's watching you. If a cop plays that fast and loose . . ."

Robert sighed. "I needed to make sure. I was worried Benjamin's name would be in there. But it wasn't. Lots of other guys, lots of innuendo. Nicknames and stuff."

"Nicknames."

"But Benjamin's name isn't in there. I swear."

"What kind of nicknames?"

"I don't remember." Someone in the background was calling for Robert.

I dreaded asking. "Was one of them 'Shrimp'?"

"Maybe. Actually, yeah. Shrimp. That was one of them."

The diary. The decoy. My son himself, as living evidence. The shortest kid in the class.

"That's Benjamin," I said. I couldn't believe it hadn't hit me before.

"Oh, shit." Robert lowered his voice. "Well, at least Hernández and Wood don't know that."

"But they will. Robert, they will. As soon as they ask other kids."

When I got back to the lounge chairs, Dr. Campbell asked, "Everything all right? You look upset."

"No. It's fine." I pushed my phone into my bag with shaky hands, the crinkle reminding me of what I'd already stashed at the bottom.

Benjamin continued flip turning down the lap lane. I wanted him to be finished, so we could leave, but it wasn't like leaving would make things any better.

"I heard you went on to a master's program," Dr. Campbell said, pleasantly, as if he hadn't noticed my distressed expression. "Are you teaching? Counseling?"

"Counseling. At a local private high school." I couldn't keep the dismay from my voice.

"Not Summit, I hope. The suicides?"

"They're investigating them as homicides now."

He took the statement in stride.

"You must be in shock. Of course you are. I'm sorry. It's hard for any therapist, losing a patient for any reason."

He glanced down, giving me time to recover before looking up again. Those eyes. I hadn't thought of Dr. Curtis Campbell in years.

"I've lost my job, too," I said. "They blamed me, at first, when they thought the deaths were suicides. They probably still do."

"No reasonable person could blame you."

"I knew those girls. I talked to them. Clearly, even if they didn't take their own lives, they were involved in something, and I had no idea. Everything I thought about them was wrong."

He nodded patiently. "You have malpractice insurance, of course, but do you have the support you need?"

"Not really . . ."

A shadow passed over my whole body. Cold water speckled my legs.

"*Mom*," Benjamin said, shaking his head like a dog.

"Hey!" I shouted, then wished I hadn't.

"Young man," Dr. Campbell said, swinging around to face my son, "you are one hell of a swimmer."

"Not really," Benjamin mumbled.

"No, you are. Take it from a parent of a former competitive swimmer who wouldn't do her laps without a coach."

I spotted the changing angle of Benjamin's chin as he looked up, taking in the praise. "Yeah, well. Motivation isn't everything."

"I'd gamble on you as the next Michael Phelps."

The compliment was too much, and we both knew it.

Benjamin frowned. "Phelps is six-four with an eighty-inch

wingspan. Genetically, he's made for competitive swimming. I'm pretty much the opposite of Michael Phelps." He looked at me and gestured toward the locker rooms with his chin, the message clear.

"Hold on a second," Dr. Campbell said. "You and I have met before."

Benjamin squinted. "I don't remember."

"You were seven or eight years old and sitting in the back of the lecture hall with a coloring book because your mom had to take you out of school that day."

I winced, remembering the reason: another exasperated call from his school principal.

Dr. Campbell said, "Your mother said you were having a hard day, but you were very well-behaved in my classroom. I remember our conversation because you were my daughter's age, with the very same birth month. December. Do you remember how we talked about how it's no fun having a birthday close to Christmas?"

"Not really." But Benjamin looked more interested now.

"I said you could choose another month to celebrate, and you said, 'That's cheating.'"

"Because it is."

"Exactly. It's interesting to see morality develop. Fairness and rules are so important between the ages of seven and ten."

I smiled. "And then a kid becomes a teen and all those concerns about the rules fade away." I made an exploding gesture with my hands.

Dr. Campbell laughed. "Oh, I wouldn't say that. Even older kids care about rules, especially the ones they decide for themselves."

Benjamin wrapped his towel tighter around his chest. "Mom," he said, more politely than before.

"Yes?"

"Home?"

"Okay."

Benjamin headed to the men's locker room while I packed my bag, looking around my chair to make sure I hadn't forgotten anything.

Dr. Campbell stopped me. "Abigail."

"Abby," I corrected him.

"Abby, I'm sorry about your job situation, and the work you have ahead, sorting out your own grief, never mind helping others. You'll find a way to do that, I promise. On top of that, lawsuits against school counselors are rarely successful."

He was trying to be reassuring but that word—*lawsuit*—made me want to crawl into a hole.

"By the way," he added. "I just gave notice at my own school—Grove Academy, in Lake Forest. I'm shutting everything down, my private practice included, in order to finish the new book. 'The book!' It's my albatross. Is that pretentious, too? To have an albatross?"

"I think it's great you're writing another book."

"Thank you." He picked up a water bottle I'd set next to my chair and stepped closer, to hand it to me. "I should get your email. Grove might need some help with their summer international students' program, and who knows what they'll need in the fall. Right?"

"Right," I said, not truly feeling right about anything. Jobs. Finances. My reputation. "Phone numbers, too?"

When we were finished exchanging contact info, I said, "Thank you, Dr. Campbell."

"Curtis, please. You're not my student anymore. We're colleagues. I don't suppose you'd like to . . ."

My phone buzzed. Benjamin couldn't be showered already. *Want to go home.*

"Sorry—it's part of being a parent, I guess. Pavlovian response to a text. You were asking . . . ?"

"I was going to ask if you'd like to go somewhere for a glass of wine."

"Things are a little shaky at home, so I'd better say no."

"Well, I hope we can stay in touch."

"I'd like that."

On the way home, I asked Benjamin to dig into my purse and pass me a piece of chewing gum, to stop me from thinking about the cigarette I wished I could smoke or the clonidine I wished I could take, in order to settle my nerves.

He held up the first thing he pulled out. It was the sign-in sheet I'd swiped from the Dartmoor. "What's this?"

I didn't answer.

"*Mom?*" He studied the sheet. "Why do you have this?"

"Because it looks bad."

He held up the paper, rattling it. "It looks like I left the pool. And Izzy left the pool. Because we'd both finished our laps."

"It's too close. You look like you left together."

"Oh, that makes fucking sense. I gave her a ride to her mansion on my handlebars."

"I didn't say *that*—"

"And then when she was still feeling sad, I gave her a ride

on my bike to a motel that's miles and miles away. A rich girl like Izzy would have loved that."

He kicked the speaker in the door's side panel, hard and loud enough to make me startle and yank the steering wheel. An oncoming car laid on its horn.

"Hey!" My heart pounded. "Careful! We could have had an accident."

For several more blocks, I massaged my chest with shaking fingertips. "Jesus," I said under my breath.

When we reached a red light, I looked over again. His expression had changed. A door closing. Flesh into stone.

When we reached the curb in front of our apartment, I said, "I didn't mean to sound like I was assuming the worst. I'm not assuming anything."

In a low voice I barely recognized, he said, "What you're thinking didn't happen."

He grabbed at the door handle.

"I'm sorry, Benjamin."

But he was already out of the car, heading for our front door and likely to his room, where he'd hide as long as he could.

Inside, while I hung our wet towels to dry, I kept thinking about my apology, wishing I'd phrased it differently. And then I replayed his sarcastic words: *I gave her a ride on my bike to a motel that's miles and miles away. A rich girl like Izzy would have loved that.*

To a motel.

*I gave her a ride to a motel.*

Dean Duplass had told me Izzy had died in Wadsworth.

No one had said Izzy died in a motel.

# 14

## BEFORE

She was squatting with her underwear down around her knees, fist grabbing the crotch to pull it away from the pee stream, when she saw the strobing lights. A megaphone-amplified voice startled her so badly she almost toppled headfirst into the tall grass, still peeing.

"Dogface, come on! Cops!" came a husky whisper from the shadows.

She grabbed at her wet underwear, hobbled by the jeans bunched around her ankles. When he reached for her, she thought he was trying to help and she reached back, but he slapped her hand away.

"You're a fucking mess," he said. "Pissed yourself."

She took a second to catch her breath. "Only a little."

"Get up. We gotta get back to the car."

Through the latticework of black tree branches they saw flickering lights and silhouettes, people standing, a few running.

"They'll arrest us."

"Not me they won't."

He knew he could talk his way out of getting arrested even after they checked his fake ID. Even if the cops smelled beer on his breath. He'd be charming. Tell a story. He'd done it before. He actually seemed to enjoy it.

She took a few steps and got the spins.

"You dork," he said, laughing as she vomited onto her shoes. One quick spurt, and then another, burning her throat. Back spasming. "Spread your feet. Jesus!"

Looking down, she saw orange flecks on her shoes, even in the dark. But worse was the spittle on her shirtfront. It smelled already. Just thinking of it made her want to gag again.

"Well there goes that," he said. "Grant's not going to want to fuck you now."

She wiped her chin. "What?"

Part of her—the tiniest part—was flattered. Grant was interested. But the slight spark of good feeling was doused by what he said next.

He came at her with a small stick and crouched down, flicking the vomity chunks off her shoes. "Good job, Dog-face. You've made yourself unfuckable. I'm not going to get the car now. Not at a discount. Not unless I find some other little bitch for him."

She stood still, fighting the urge to be sick again, glad he was cleaning her shoes, at least. Trying to see it as proof that he was willing to be nice. He couldn't mean the thing he'd said about a discount.

"Remind me not to let you eat Doritos again," he said. "Not with beer, anyway."

He pointed to her shirt. Not so easy to clean.

"Then again, Grant's pretty drunk," he said. "He may not notice that you smell. You *are* a virgin, right?"

"You're gross. Stop it."

She still felt lightheaded. She didn't know what to make of his words. He *was* helping her, after all. With Ewan, you never knew. Her entire childhood had been a series of jokes and tricks, some of them mean, alternating with occasional favors, like the time he stole money from Martha's purse to order them pizza. There was no point trusting, and no point *not* trusting, either—not if you ever wanted to go anywhere, do anything, get out of a house full of anger and shouting.

"C'mon." He grabbed her by her skinny upper arm and pulled.

"No."

She was worried about Grant, but she was terrified about the cops, and getting in trouble, and facing their dad and Martha.

"Stop—"

But this time, instead of humoring her, Ewan whipped around, hands clutching her throat. For a second, her feet were off the ground. She couldn't breathe.

"Stop?" he shouted. "Stop what? Stop talking back to me, skank."

Her feet were back on the ground, but his thumbs were still drilling into the front of her throat. She couldn't breathe. Couldn't speak. The only sound that came out was a series of clicks.

"You *cost* me, Dogface. I'm not fucking around."

When he let her go, she stumbled forward, landing on her knees. She stayed on all fours, coughing and fighting tears.

But she wasn't shocked. They'd been here before. She knew how far he'd go. *This* far, and she was still okay.

In the distance, a cop called over a megaphone, telling someone to stop running, but the cop sounded more annoyed than hostile.

"They'll catch you if you go back to the car," she managed to say over her shoulder.

"They won't." Her brother was never afraid. "Especially when I tell them my baby sister went missing and I need to hurry up and find her before she falls into the creek and drowns."

This last part he found hilarious.

She was clinging to the word *sister*. The entire phrase: *baby sister*. Even if he grabbed her and choked her and teased her, he would protect her in the end.

"Head that way, we'll pick you up at the next trailhead. Then we'll drive across the state line to make sure the cops don't follow."

When she got to her feet, he was gone. She walked the trail through a moon-silvered darkness, wanting her brother, the very same one who'd just hurt her and left her on hands and knees, breathing in the smell of dirt, mud, leaves. Would he be there, at the next trailhead, in thirty minutes? Would he rescue her?

The trail was wide and it paralleled the road so close she could hear cars speed by. She didn't want to walk the shoulder. It was safer staying hidden in the trees. The alcohol in her system kept doing funny things. For a few minutes after throwing up, she'd felt better. Ewan's choking had adrenalized her, sending fizzing Pop Rocks through her veins. But now that she was walking in the dark, her senses started to dull again. She was drunk, and it was only getting worse as the last few beers hit her. Twice, she fell down for no reason, ankles suddenly twisting.

When she made it to the trailhead, no one was there. Maybe Ewan and Grant had gotten there already and left. Maybe the cops did stop them after all. Or maybe they went joyriding elsewhere, to pick up more vodka or beer. She positioned herself near the entrance road, sitting on the grass, arms around her knees, head bowed. When she tried to look up at the stars, they were moving in circles, like in one of those time-lapse videos. She brought her face to her knees again and only woke once a car pulled up. Her brother called out the window: *Dogface. Wake the fuck up.*

The memories until then had been blurry, but from this point forward they were more than blurry, they were fragmented, tiny slivers of light and sound with great big black curtains separating them. Even when I tried, I couldn't bring more of them back.

The girl I was then and the woman I'd become were equally stymied trying to force more memories to the surface. But of course, the darkness protects as much as it obscures. The memories don't deserve revisiting.

The only part that can't be denied is the very end, when I woke to the sounds of Grant and my brother arguing—Ewan most of all, taunting Grant for something he'd done earlier that night or hadn't been able to do, calling him *whiskey dick, whiskey dick*. I didn't know what that meant. I only knew that men called each other dicks all the time. I woke up twice or maybe three times, when Ewan leaned on me too hard, pushing his way over the armrest and into the back seat to reach for a bottle of vodka. He came back with a pair of unfamiliar tennis shoes that he chucked out the window, and a girl's wadded-up underwear that he shook in front of Grant's face before pushing them into his own front jeans pocket.

The girl's abandoned clothing and the smell of something foul alerted me to the fact that something had happened back there—and yet I didn't ask. Maybe they gave a girl a ride during that hour I was on the trail and falling asleep in the trailhead parking lot. Maybe something else happened, too, but it had nothing to do with me. It had been a bad enough night, already, and I was embarrassed about all of it: the hope I'd had, the flirtation I'd imagined, the hurt I'd allowed, the way I'd acted like a little kid, getting drunk and vomiting and making a mess of myself.

As we sped east, staying on country roads just north of the Illinois border to avoid the state cops they'd already talked to at the forest preserve, I kept my eyes closed. I didn't ask questions. I surrendered to blackness again until I felt sudden physical pressure as Grant took a curve too fast and we left the road—the two of them still arguing, shouting—and barreled down a slope. My eyes flashed open as the car flipped.

Grant never walked away from that accident. Maybe he didn't deserve to.

Ewan and I did.

# 15

From Wednesday through Friday, nothing happened. No calls or emails from Summit, asking me to come speak to the board or informing me about my fall contract, or even answering my question about when I should come and finish emptying my office. No major news about the investigation of Sidney's and Izzy's deaths, although there'd been one press conference, clarifying that they were being investigated as homicide cases, possibly linked. No visits to the pool. Benjamin had stopped asking.

I was surprised that Curtis hadn't emailed, as promised. He'd seemed so friendly. Flirtatious, even. But in my self-critical state I could find plenty of reasons he'd change his mind.

Still, I succumbed to the temptation to google him. I found dozens of articles about his first bestselling book, *How Children Grow*. It had come out when I was in grad school, drowning in academic reading, with zero interest in a parenting guide about preschool children, especially since my own child was a preteen by then. My work and study schedule left no time for podcasts or magazine browsing during those years. But this next time, he'd be harder to miss. His publisher's website said a sixteen-city book tour was already planned. The cover and title were already uploaded to online bookstores: *What Boys Learn*.

That's exactly what I needed to know—what boys pick up from the world around them, and what they carry within, and what any of us—mothers especially—can do to make sure our boys become decent, undamaged, and undamaging men.

I thought of calling Curtis directly and asking him to accept Benjamin as a client, but Curtis had already told me. He was shutting down his practice. End of story.

For nine years, I had juggled college and grad school with single parenting, and for the last year, I'd stayed busy learning the ropes of a new job. Now, for the first time, I was unmoored, with too much time on my hands. Aside from a few boxes of books and some unrecycled empties in the living room, everything was put away. I'd even had time to organize better: spice bottles and spice refill packets coordinated, small toothpaste and dental floss samples from the dentist rounded up in one place, dry pens thrown away and good ones in a countertop jar where we could find them. I still hadn't located several missing things, but that was normal in a move. *Everything floats to the top eventually*, my mother had always said.

One of the final things I emptied was the banker's box from Summit. Several thick books were in the bottom, including a *DSM-5*. I lifted the psychological diagnostic manual in my hands, feeling its weight, and remembering how proud I'd been, buying it as a graduation gift to myself, to replace the previous, outdated edition I'd bought cheap as a first-year counseling student. The field of psychology changes, after all. Labels, treatments, assumptions.

I stood in the living room, fully aware that our limited bookshelves were already packed so tight even a slim book wouldn't fit, never mind this doorstop. But then my gaze went to the low black bookcase next to the couch. There *was* space, actually. A two-inch-wide spot on the bottom, in the middle of a shelf of college psych textbooks.

I wandered over and squatted, trying to understand what was missing, but all the old familiars were there—*Abnormal Psych*, *Intro to Clinical*, *Child and Adolescent Development*. It bothered me. Stress had a way of doing that—of making everything seem equally significant, from an argument to a letter to shit gone missing in a new and disorganized apartment.

Then I heard the sound of a whistling mailman, heading around the side of the house to drop our mail. The mail came earlier to this apartment than our last one. I'd have to be vigilant. I put the question of the missing book out of my mind and hurried to intercept the mail.

On Saturday, the next letter from Ewan arrived.

*Someone's been asking me about you. I could give you hints. I owe you that, don't I? You owe me a lot more, baby sister. A visit with my nephew would be a good place to start.*

Someone was talking to him about me, or he wanted me to think so. And he wasn't forgetting about Benjamin. I needed help.

I dialed before I could lose my nerve.

"Abby!" came Curtis Campbell's voice after two rings.

"I'm in my car. Can I call you from the house in fifteen minutes?"

"Perfect," I said, trying to match his optimistic tone.

"Before I let you go. I sent that job posting to you but it bounced back. I must have entered your email wrong. First name Abigail, last name Rosso, at gmail dot com, right?"

Relief flooded me. "You forgot the middle initial." I spelled out the full address again.

"Great! I'll be home in a few minutes. I'll send the email and call you then."

When he phoned ten minutes later, I heard keys clattering, as if into a bowl. I pictured him in the cool hallway of an impeccable house: gallery-style lights positioned to show off framed artwork, fresh flowers, underlit kitchen cabinets.

"Really sorry about that mix-up," he said, voice loud one moment and muffled the next. "Just a minute."

He greeted someone or something, his pitch rising.

"You have a dog?"

"An old one with a weak bladder. But now that Sammy's in the yard, I can pay better attention. There. Better." He exhaled. "*Abby.*"

He said my name as if he was charmed to have a reason to talk. No hurry. No agenda. Just a caring voice.

He asked, "Have things gotten any better at your school? Is there a professional question you'd like to discuss?"

"Yes. But it's also personal. I'm calling about Benjamin. He was closer than I thought to the girl who just died—actually, both girls. I think their deaths are upsetting him in ways he's not mature enough to confront."

"That would be natural."

"I'm afraid he'll go looking for support or consolation in the wrong places. He needs to talk to someone, and the new counselor at school . . . never mind about him. School's over now anyway."

This time Curtis said nothing. I didn't even hear an empathetic sigh.

"Dr. Campbell? My son needs help. You'd be the ideal—"

He cut me off. "Abigail, I'm very sorry. My book deadline is closing in."

"You're writing a book about boys. You'd be more likely to understand than anyone. And you know Benjamin, already. You've seen what he's like. Intelligent, disciplined, but oppositional as well."

In the pause that followed, I could feel him considering. "It's not just my upcoming deadlines, unfortunately. I'm also spending more time every week near Fond du Lac, checking on my father. He's determined to 'age in place,' but he isn't doing well."

"I'm so sorry."

Of course. Benj and I weren't the only ones with problems.

"Listen. We can find the right person for you, I promise. Someone with the right specialty." In the background, a screen door opened and banged shut. I could imagine all the things Curtis Campbell had to deal with. A dog, a father, clients, research, a book. Somewhere far away: a daughter, an ex.

"That's okay, I can google—"

"No, the wrong person is worse than no person at all. How about Raveena Adelman? Didn't you take classes from her?"

She was another one of my college professors, a specialist

in child development, her office only three doors down from Curtis's own. I'd taken Benjamin to see her once and it didn't go well.

"I tried her about five years ago. One session only. It wasn't a good fit."

"Not a good fit. That happens." He seemed to be ruminating. "Eighty percent of psychologists are women now. Men are disappearing from the field—as practitioners and as subjects. Boys' issues don't get much attention these days."

I'd managed to hit a nerve. "No, they don't."

"I sometimes think the world is afraid of teenage boys. What kind of message are we sending them?"

I let him mull that one as I stood at the counter, running a finger along the cheap laminate edge, staring at the letter from Ewan, with its strange, cajoling tone. I'd worried a few times about the day Benjamin turned eighteen, if he would ever decide to visit Ewan's prison. I hadn't worried about *this*: that they'd find a way to communicate even earlier, behind my back.

"Let me think about it," Curtis finally said. "I'll call you tomorrow?"

Around two in the afternoon, I was thinking about Summit's graduation ceremony and all the students I wouldn't be able to congratulate when I spotted one of Benjamin's journals on the side table, next to the couch. On the front cover, he'd written only his name. On the inside cover in angry capital letters, he'd written: "I go out and fuck and I come back to her and I don't care about her and I only love my girl. That's not cheating, that's exercise."

I recognized the name of the person written on the next line. I couldn't tell if Benjamin really thought the quote was clever or if he knew I'd riffle through his notebook and wanted to punish me for it.

After a late shower, I took a cup of coffee into the bathroom to sip while I detangled my ropy, wet hair. I kept thinking about that asinine quote. I knew what Benjamin was telling me. *You didn't like an actual author? I can move down the evolutionary ladder. Bring back some real Neanderthal shit.* Which, frankly, wasn't fair to the Neanderthals.

Maybe every family has its own tensions as each member jockeys for position, especially if money, love, or respect seem scarce. Maybe our identities are forged by teasing, provoking, resisting—saying, *You can't change me*, in the case of a teenager. *I refuse to play second fiddle*, in the case of a stepmother. Maybe it's natural, in other words. I worried too much, and I knew why I did—because I'd had a front-row seat to the development of a troubled boy into a troubled man. And at the same time, that perspective warped me. Confirmation bias, it's called—the tendency to search for what you already believe, or fear. Ewan deserved the blame for that. But he didn't deserve the blame for everything.

Every time I hit a snag in my hair, I remembered Martha just after she'd gotten engaged to my dad, when she was still pretending to care about me, yanking a comb through my hair without patience, then catching herself in time, remembering that this was a performance. I disliked the gentler combing as much as the rough kind.

After the wedding, photos of my mother were cleared from the living room. Then Martha started talking about how

Ewan had to go, on account of his volatility. If he was sent somewhere—military school, or any place that would take him—I'd be the only target in the house. A growing target, painted in even brighter colors by the unstoppable forces of adolescence.

When I needed my first bra, I was too afraid to ask Martha to buy me one, so I kept wearing my inadequate undershirts until the school nurse sent home an embarrassing note to my father. Martha intercepted it. Then she called me into the bathroom. She told me to take off my button-down shirt. Then my cotton undershirt, which I folded nervously and set on the carpet-covered toilet lid.

"Those too," she said, pointing to my underwear, which I stepped out of, slowly.

She pointed to my nearly hairless crotch. "You let anything or anyone down there?"

I was horrified. Speechless. Anyone? *Anything*?

I already dreaded getting a first period; I hoped she wasn't going to try to show me how a tampon fit or worse, where a penis went. When her hand hovered inches from my body, I pushed my knees together, confused.

When her glance moved upward, I felt a moment of relief until she leaned in close to my torso, so that I was looking down onto her head of tight brown curls. Her face was an inch away from the small, barely developed mounds on my chest.

"That's all you've got?" she said, leaning close. "Those are worth sending a letter home? *Those*?"

I thrust out an arm to grab for my undershirt. She countered with her forearm, blocking me. Then she seized one nipple and twisted hard. I yelped in pain. She clapped a hand over my mouth.

"You don't even know enough to realize I'm not the one you should be afraid of." She leaned back and laughed her husky smoker's laugh. "Oh, yeah. Trouble's coming."

I squirmed away and ran from the room. Hours later, I could still feel the painful tingle in that right nipple. I felt it again, a few years later, the first time a boy snuck his hand up my shirt, even though I wanted him to. I felt it even now, standing in front of the nearly cleared mirror, amazed to think that two degrading minutes could still take up so much space in my brain, no matter how much I'd tried to cram in there since. Pavlov's dogs, Skinner's box, Piaget's stages, Bandura's observational learning of violent behavior, it was all there, efficiently tucked into the gray folds, but beneath it all, a physical pain still pulsed, and below that, an even deeper humiliation.

I set down the wide-toothed comb and studied my expression in the steamy mirror. Frowning. Tired. Nearly overwhelmed—but that *nearly* was the key word, and underlying it was a self-pity I couldn't afford.

Martha was long behind me. I didn't have to feel this way anymore. I was the parent, now; I'd survived the sleep deprivation of Benjamin's babyhood, problems at day care and grade school, the sullen tween years. I refused to infect my son in the same way Martha and Ewan had both infected me—making me believe that adolescence was, by its very nature, a time when everything went to hell.

"Coming out soon?" Benjamin called from the other side of the door.

"In a minute."

"Your phone is ringing."

He handed it through the door to me. "It's probably your ex-boyfriend. Mister patrol-cop-who-can't-make-detective."

"That was six months ago."

"And he still talks about it."

It was the most consecutive words Benjamin had said to me in three days. I didn't care that he was being snide. I was just glad to hear his voice again.

But it wasn't Robert on the phone. It wasn't Curtis, either. I closed the bathroom door and took the call.

When I came out to the kitchen, Benjamin was pulling out the coffee carafe, about to fill a ceramic mug on the counter. I reached into the cupboard for a travel mug and held it out to him.

"Are we going somewhere?"

"You don't have to be mean to Robert," I said.

"Everyone's mean, Mom. Some people are mean, live in shit apartments, and lose their jobs because they can't stand up for themselves. Some people are mean and rich and popular and get people to do what they want."

*Use your words*, I'd always told him. And he was. He was using them to tell me that he was better prepared than I was for the world he'd soon face as an adult—a world in which presidents got away with rape and cops got away with murder, where older men dated young girls and used them up and threw them away.

"Get dressed. We need to go downtown."

"I need to shower first."

"No time. Detective Hernández is waiting for us."

# 16

I told myself I wasn't feeling anxious on the way to the police station, but once I saw all the cop cars lined up in the lot, something changed. I steered carefully into a guest parking spot, set the brake, and turned to Benjamin.

I said, "This shouldn't take long."

He shrugged, hand on the door handle, like he was eager to get it over with.

"Don't be nervous," I said.

"I'm not."

I thought of all the texts between us, Saturday and Sunday, an indicator of our schedules, proof we'd been in close contact on the days the cops might want to know about.

"Got your phone?"

"Of course." He patted his jeans pocket. "Shit. I left it on the counter. It was when you handed me the travel mug."

"Okay," I said, thinking, *He never forgets his phone.*

Under my breath, I said, "I wish you'd been at that Scarlatti party, Saturday night."

He let go of the door handle and turned to me, his focus so undivided I thought we were going to have a tender moment. Mother and son, together in adversity.

"Thanks a lot," he spat.

"No, I just meant—"

"I know what you meant."

"Benjamin," I tried.

"You think I don't wish I'd been invited to that party?" His voice cracked.

"You're still new here. There are cliques—"

"And another thing: You don't have to hide shit," he said, opening his door and stepping out. I hadn't even cut the engine yet.

I didn't know if he meant the underwear or the pool sign-in sheet. Maybe both. I followed thirty feet behind, heart hammering, trying to catch up before he reached the station's front door.

Over his shoulder he said, "I saw how you handle things. Maybe you can let me handle it from here."

"We'll handle it together."

But he wasn't listening, and now we were arguing within feet of the police station's front door.

"Fucking sucks my own mother doesn't trust me."

"It's the world I don't trust, Benjamin. Wait up!"

My own voice sounded wrong to me, like I was shouting into a tunnel. I pushed ahead, replaying Hernández's relaxed tone during our call, half an hour ago. *Stop by.* It sounded so casual. *Bring your son.* Completely casual.

My father and stepmother drove Ewan to the police station. They left me at home. Told me to stay near the phone in case it rang, but it didn't. Everything was casual, then, too. At first.

"Benjamin, wait."

No one even asked me to fill out a statement. Everyone knew I'd been blacked out for most of the night in question, as well as young and traumatized. Ewan was arrested and brought before a judge. Then he was out on bail. A week later, after Martha's death, he was brought in for questioning again, and I was alone with my father, preparing for Martha's funeral.

"Hold the door," I called louder. "We should walk in together."

But the smoky-glassed door had already closed behind him.

When I pulled on the handle, the door was surprisingly heavy. I had to lean back to get some leverage before the door opened with a suctiony pop and whoosh, the air-conditioning hitting like an arctic blast.

Benjamin was at the reception desk, trying to get the attention of a woman handling the phones. I caught up, turning as I heard Hernández coming toward us from a long hallway, raising a hand in greeting. The row of recessed lighting in the hallway ceiling caught my eye. Glowing spikes of light radiated from each hockey-puck-sized fixture, and then the spikes began to change color, from white to shimmery pink. The corners of my vision darkened.

When I opened my eyes, Hernández's face was directly over mine. An unfamiliar female officer crouched next to him. Cool, gentle fingers encircled my wrist.

"Mrs. Rosso?" the woman cop asked. "Can you hear me now?"

The back of my head hurt. I tried to straighten one kinked leg but it weighed too much to move.

"How about now?"

Hernández said loudly, "Did you take anything?"

In the background, I heard another male voice softly questioning Benjamin, who kept saying, "I don't know. I don't know."

Hernández repeated, "*What did you take?*"

"Nothing," I said.

A dull pain radiated down my legs. I couldn't tell which parts hurt from falling and which parts hurt from whatever was happening to change the proper pace of blood flowing through my arteries and veins.

I levered my way into a sitting position, head straining to catch sight of Benjamin. "Where's my son?"

The woman placed her hand on my forehead, then moved it to the back of my skull, cradling it as I leaned back again. Too dizzy to sit up yet. "The ambulance will be here soon."

"It wasn't something I took. It's something I *didn't* take. It was a stress reaction, or, or . . . my mother. She had . . ."

High blood pressure, and later, a lethal stroke. My blood pressure was high, too. I was careful about it, usually.

Someone said, "Get her a juice, maybe?"

My eyelids got heavy again. Doors opened and the entryway filled with too many bodies in high-vis vests. Strangers kept asking me the same questions. What's my name. Did I know where I was. What did I take. Did I have any health problems they should know about it. Was I on any prescriptions.

"Hypertension. I take clonidine."

"How many hours ago was your last dose?" a paramedic asked.

"I'm not sure."

"Why did you go off it?"

"I ran out of pills in my purse, and I have my regular bottle somewhere, but I couldn't find it. We just moved to a new apartment."

"What you're experiencing is withdrawal. Your heart rate and blood pressure got elevated, that's all. Next time, talk with your physician before you decide to go off your prescription."

"I wasn't trying to go off it. Life just happened."

The paramedic smiled. He looked so young. I bet his mother was proud of him. "Let's transport you just to be sure."

"No, I need to be with my son. They can't question him without me, can they? He's a minor. Where's the detective?"

The hallway lights no longer shimmered. I enunciated more clearly, "We came in voluntarily. Where did the detective take my son?"

# 17

When they let me into the interview room, I saw an open can of Coke and a flattened SunChips bag, Benjamin's hand scraping for the last crumbs as he mumbled in a low monotone.

"Hey," I said, even before the door closed behind me, waving my hands. "Stop talking. Benj. Hey!"

"Whoa there," Hernández said, brow furrowed. "You can't be here if you're agitated."

"I'm his mother. I have a right to be here, agitated or not."

"Not necessarily. You have a right to be advised we are questioning your son—"

"You didn't say anything about 'questioning.' This was not the impression I got from your call, Detective."

The sweet chubby-cheeked detective who had interviewed me briefly the day after Sidney's death looked like someone else, now. Thick eyebrowed, scowling. No dimple. Good cop and bad cop in one person.

"I asked you to bring Benjamin in," he said. "And you did. Which was smart. It always looks better that way."

I shifted my attention to Benjamin. "Did they explain what they're doing? Did they offer you a lawyer?"

"*Mom.*"

"This is *not* the time for 'Mom.'"

The detective pointed to a stackable plastic-molded chair several feet away from the interview table. When I tried to pull it closer to Benjamin, Hernández held his palm out. "Give us a little space, just until you're settled. Please. I'm warning you a second time. Any erratic behavior, and you're out of here. We can't proceed this way if you're under the influence of anything."

"I'm not under any influence and you know that, Detective. God damn it."

Benjamin's shoulders were shrugged up, his chin tucked into his chest. Even in profile, I could see the shame overwhelming him. He knew I took a prescription legally, but it was still embarrassing to see your mother pass out and make a scene.

"Your son has given us permission to do a cheek swab."

"But I don't give permission. We came here voluntarily. That means we can leave anytime."

"Not . . . quite," Hernández said. "That was true ten minutes ago. It's not the case now."

"What did he say?" I started to rise out of my chair, then forced myself to sit down again. "Benjamin, *what did you say?*"

I didn't know the lingo. Witness, suspect, person of interest. Everything was going too fast. "We need a lawyer."

"Your son was willing to talk without one."

I leaned forward, elbows planted on my knees, face as

close as I could get to Benjamin's. "Hey. Hey. You shouldn't say anything without a lawyer present."

His eyes were fixed on the can of pop. He was mad at me. Mad, hurt, and embarrassed. A dangerous combination.

"It's not your fault if you've said too much already," I told him. "This is what the police do. They're trying to manipulate you."

Detective Hernández leaned back in his chair. "Your mom is a little worked up. Don't let that be a distraction. You said you want to help, and I appreciate that. When someone's innocent, it's best just to get all the info out on the table—"

"He's not old enough to understand, and you know that. If he asks for a lawyer, you have to give him a lawyer."

"If he asks, yes."

I looked to Benjamin. "*Ask, Benjamin.*"

He turned his head toward me, slowly. "They already know I took the diary. They already know what it says. They already know Izzy and I saw each other at the pool. We hung out sometimes."

"At the pool," I said, hoping he'd confirm. School and the pool, only. Nowhere else.

"Mom, they need to know the situation so they can go and talk to the people who did it."

"People?" Hernández asked. "You think it was more than one?"

"Person," Benjamin corrected himself. "An older guy, like I said. The one she met up with in Wisconsin, or close. Wadsworth. Whatever. The motel."

"So you know about the motel?" Hernández asked. "That's not public knowledge."

"Everyone knows."

"Who's everyone?"

"Kids in our class. When it came out that she died, everyone was talking about it, that morning. Even before we got to school."

"We've talked to nearly everyone in your class, Benjamin. No one has mentioned a motel."

Benjamin stared straight ahead. Hernández glanced toward me, as if he wanted to make sure I had registered the point he'd just scored, then back at Benjamin again. "Now, let's go back to this car you saw. If you can describe it, that will help."

"I didn't see it."

"You didn't see it? But you were there, waiting for her ride to pull up on Saturday, the day she died."

I hadn't heard anything about a ride, or a car.

"No," he said. "It wasn't Saturday. I mean, I did see her Saturday, too. At the pool. But I was talking about a different Saturday, two weeks earlier, which was when the car thing happened. That's when she gave me her underwear, and I got on my bike, and I took off."

This part of the story was new to me, too.

Hernández said, "We'll be checking all those dates, just so you know."

I thought of the pool sign-in sheet. The page I had taken and pushed down into my bag.

Benjamin said, "Two weeks ago is when I knew she was being picked up by some guy who wasn't her boyfriend. I knew that for a fact because Manny was out of town visiting some college. You can check that, I bet."

"Okay, clarified. The underwear story was great, by the way. It establishes that you weren't just . . . for example . . . stalking a girl who didn't like you. I mean, if she *gave* you her underwear."

The skepticism in Hernández's voice was plain.

"We'll want the underwear," he added. "Just in case."

Benjamin didn't look at me or the detective. His gaze was fixed on the far wall, over Hernández's shoulder. "Ask my mom. She took them."

My face felt odd, my skin too tight. Like I'd applied one of those face masks and it had dried all shiny and flaky, and like my eyebrows were sitting too high on my face.

"Ms. Rosso?"

"Yes?"

"The underwear?"

"Yes?"

"That belonged to Isabella Scarlatti?"

"Yes?"

"We'll need to get that, as evidence."

"Yes. I threw them away."

I kept my eyes on Benjamin. His expression didn't change.

"You threw them away?" Hernández asked.

"Yes. I didn't tell my son I found them. We didn't talk about it. I threw them into the trash. Almost two weeks ago, just after he got them, I guess. We were moving apartments that day, so yes. A Sunday."

Hernández chuckled to himself. Silly people. Hiding underwear. Throwing away underwear. Making up stories about underwear.

"Funny thing—a kid willing to do a cheek swab. A mom

who won't let him. A kid who's willing to hand over underwear. A mom who already got rid of it. You got a reason to be more paranoid than your own son?"

*I'm an adult*, I thought. But that wasn't the only reason. I knew how much cops overlooked—the most obvious questions they neglected to ask, the tunnel vision that made them mistake innocence for guilt and vice versa. And I also knew a person could be sent away even when cops only knew a fraction of the truth.

Hernández shook his head. "The underwear would have been nice to have. But let's be clear. We don't need it to get Benjamin's DNA. We can get that with a warrant."

Benjamin made a disgusted face. I did, too, but then I realized. Hernández was only thinking what I'd thought, when I first found the underwear. That it was a souvenir from a sexual encounter. That it might contain traces.

Or then again, maybe Hernández didn't believe in the underwear. Maybe he didn't believe in the car. But if there was an older man she was spending time with, who finally met her at a motel, it made sense. A car.

The door opened and another detective popped his head into the room.

Hernández said, "Joe, can you bring in the binder? The one with all of Isabella Scarlatti's text messages and social media posts?"

Hernández said to Benjamin: "Did you know we can get even the deleted messages off a phone? Amazing."

I said nothing. I was looking at Benjamin, trying to see if he was surprised. Teens could be equally brilliant and naïve about technology.

"Wait, Joe. Can you bring a bottle of water for Ms. Rosso? Unless—you want a coffee instead? It's pretty good stuff—one of those machines with the pods."

"Keurig," Joe said.

"No, in the break room. That new machine. The one with the little pods."

"Keurig."

"No, the *little* pods, the shiny kind. The ones that look like chocolates."

"Nespresso."

Hernández gave me a look—*Can you believe this place?*

He'd already told me, the very first time we talked, that he'd worked in Waukegan around the time we lived there. When he mentioned pining for the tacos from a particular Washington Street restaurant, I'd sighed and closed my eyes. Even then, I'd gotten the sense that the detective was trying to bond with me over our shared outsider status here in Pleasant Park. But now it all felt like a ruse.

"Never mind," Hernández said. "Coffee will keep you up. Water's better. Two waters, Joe, cold if possible. Not from the case under Tina's desk. From the break room fridge. Please."

After the door closed, Hernández said, "We've got texts, we've got posts, we've got pictures, we've got cell phone data. Full toxicology will take a while but we may not even need it. Benjamin is just helping us tie up loose ends."

If I was rich and if I had a private lawyer, he would have been here already. I would have texted him even before I entered the room and now he'd be pulling up a chair next to Benjamin and no one would stop him. But a public defender? I didn't know what kind of hours they kept or how fast they came running.

"We can get a lawyer, Benjamin," I told him. "It doesn't mean you're not innocent—"

"But it does take longer," Hernández said, leaning back in his chair, eyes flicking toward the institutionally bland clock on the wall. "A lot longer. And like I said, every one of your classmates has already talked to us."

"But my son's the only one sitting at the police station."

"You offered to come in."

"And if we hadn't?"

Hernández stretched his arms and started what looked like a fake yawn, all show. It turned into a real one, followed by a second. He didn't bother to cover his mouth with his hand. I tried my hardest to stifle my own yawn, but it was catchy. Hernández chuckled as he saw the sleepy contagion he'd triggered.

I was mid-yawn, eyes watering, when I glanced to Benjamin. He wasn't yawning. He'd never caught a yawn from me.

My eyes darted to Hernández, wondering if he'd noticed. He had.

"Some people are just like that," the detective said. "Interesting, isn't it? What does that say about a person? Must be nice in some ways, like there's a barrier between you and the world. Do you feel that way sometimes, Benjamin? Like you can't read people? Or you can, but you don't want to? Stuff just rolls off your back? Other people's needs don't concern you? Yawns don't make you yawn? Your mom freaking out doesn't make you freak out? And even a girl asking you to stop—"

"Don't answer that," I said to my son.

Robert had said that no sex seemed involved in Izzy's death. And no one had pressed Benjamin on whether he'd had a relationship with Sidney. Yet the cases seemed to be linked. Izzy, Saturday. Sidney, Sunday. Someone had left a dying or dead girl in a motel and decided, the next day, to pay a visit to her closest friend and have sex with her, then somehow convince her to overdose. Or pills first, sex after. I was starting to see how that would make more sense, especially if the girl was unwilling.

"Here's a bit of trivia that knocks me out," Hernández said. "Do you know that psychopaths, when they go to prison, don't even mind it very much? It's 'cause they live in the present. They don't ruminate. That means, 'thinking stuff over, regretting the past.'"

In a low voice, Benjamin said, "I know what ruminate means."

"You take the SATs yet?"

"Yeah."

"How'd you do?"

Benjamin shrugged.

Above average: 640 math and 680 verbal, but he could do better. He'd retake it next year, if he got that chance.

I looked at Hernández, smirking. He was figuring it out—how to reach my son. Don't tell him he seems guilty. Question his intelligence. Benjamin thought too highly of himself to let people think he's stupid. *Arrogance. Grandiosity.*

The detective said, "Psychopaths are like genius monks in a way, right? Maybe we're the ones who are f . . . sorry, who are *messed up*. Right? What do you think about that, Benjamin?"

"Don't answer," I said.

Benjamin answered without delay. "I think that's really interesting, actually."

Hernández grinned. "There you go. Nut doesn't fall far from the tree."

I felt rage bubbling at the base of my throat. "What do you mean by that?"

Hernández screwed up his face, like he couldn't imagine why I was taking offense. How much did he know about my brother? How much did he know about my entire family?

He said, "I just meant that Benjamin might end up becoming a psychologist. Like his mom."

# 18

When I thought about a younger Benjamin I didn't remember one boy, I remembered flickering images, silly and happy and sad moments. I remembered being curled up next to him on a couch when he was two and a half, with an earache, and how his bright red feverish cheek felt against the back of my hand. I remembered listening to his breathing slow and feeling the deepest possible sense of peace looking at his relaxed, sleeping face, once the pain and fever had passed.

This was another fever. We'd get through it.

Joe came back with two bottles of water and a five-inch binder. It didn't have a label on the cover and there was nothing on the spine, either, plus the sheets inside didn't seem to take up much space. Hernández left it sitting closed on the table, his glance flicking toward the dark one-way mirror at the back of the room. I wondered how many people were watching and listening.

"I bet there's nothing in it," I said.

"Is that what your boyfriend told you, that we bring in

empty binders to manipulate people we're interviewing?" He chuckled once. "Go ahead, Mom. Open it."

With invisible eyes possibly watching, I flipped open the binder.

"Oh, that's a good page." Hernández nodded. "Read that top text aloud for both of us."

I squinted at the small font, reading BITCH and CUNT. So, the binder wasn't empty.

"That's one to Isabella Scarlatti from your very own son."

I kept reading silently. Hateful words, the kind you'd never want your son to say or text to anyone. Threatening, violence-filled words that appalled me.

"We've also heard from a few classmates that people call your son 'scary.' I guess he gives girls the creeps. Which isn't illegal. I'm just saying."

I tried to speak but my mouth was dry. It was cold in the room, even colder than the hallway and reception area. Hernández was wearing a suit. Benjamin was wearing a T-shirt. I was wearing a tank and in the last minute I'd started to shiver.

I said, "He'll need to eat some dinner, and it's friggin' cold in here."

"We can get him a second bag of chips, if that's what he needs." Hernández flapped the bottom of his tie, straightening it. "Benjamin, if you're anything like me, you can't sleep in a hard chair. Believe me, this is not a pleasant place to spend the night. You've done a fantastic job so far. Let's get this all finished before bedtime."

The wall clock read a quarter to six. Hernández was already talking about bedtime, like there were hours and hours of questions left. Benjamin gave me a pleading look, which I took at first to mean he wanted me to find a way to extract him and end the interview. I was wrong.

"Okay," Benjamin said. "Just ask me whatever you want to ask me. I'm tired of this taking so long. I want to go home."

Hernández smiled big enough that his dimple flashed.

"Smart kid. Let's start over with the person who was picking up Isabella—a couple of weeks ago, you said. You said you never saw the car. When I asked you for a color, the plate, anything, you said—"

"I didn't see it. I *heard* it, making a bunch of noises before it died. Then it started up again and I could hear it coming around the side of the building. Super noisy."

"Like, screeching when it turned?"

"I wouldn't know if it was turning because I couldn't see it. But no, it wasn't a screech, or a scrape. Not like a muffler hanging down or something. I don't think."

"I'll note the description in your interview," Hernández said without bothering to pick up his pen. "Squeaky car. Well, my car makes noises, too, but more so in the winter, when it's not warmed up. And this wasn't a cold day, was it, Benjamin?"

"Not squeaky," Benjamin said. "Ticking, more like."

"Like a bomb."

"No, like an old typewriter maybe."

I tried to imagine the sound he was describing. It came to me, the thing Benjamin had often said about why he preferred to bike to the pool rather than being dropped off. My janky car embarrassed him. *The only other person with a crap car who visits the pool . . .*

A jolt of adrenaline cut through my mental fog. "The janitor. There aren't many older cars in that part of town—especially not at the Dartmoor. Our car is a 2002 Mazda. It's in bad shape. There's another car, maybe one owned by the pool janitor. That's what you're saying, right Benjamin?"

"I'm not *saying* it was the janitor's car. I'm just saying it had trouble starting and even after it got going, it was still noisy, and Izzy went off with that person. So maybe that's a place to start. Figure out who she's been spending time with and see what kinds of cars they have. But it's not Manny. He drives a Tesla and that thing is silent, and anyway, he was out of town. But if she was dating another guy—"

Hernández interrupted. "We already know the other guy Izzy was dating, Benjamin. That person was you. Or was you at some point, based on the underwear story. From the diary, it's muddier. She called you the Shrimp. She made fun of you. You're aware of that?"

He nodded with the barest movement of his chin.

"Let the record show that Benjamin knows he was called 'the Shrimp,' the same one Izzy talked about in her diary. An object of scorn."

Benjamin muttered something.

"Sorry?" Hernández asked.

Benjamin cleared his throat. "Sometimes, she was nicer."

"Girls are like that, right? Fickle. Secretive. Manipulative." Hernández smiled. "Let the record show that Benjamin has been nodding his head. Okay. Let's finish up with the car business. If we had a color, or any other detail—"

"I told you I didn't see it."

"Even though you were just starting to bicycle away just as it was coming up to that half-circle drive under the—what did you call it?—the portico. Do you think, with time, you might remember?"

When Benjamin shrugged, Hernández looked to me. "Hypnosis works for things like that, doesn't it?"

It was the first time he'd asked me something without using a snide or sarcastic tone.

"Maybe," I said. "I've never hypnotized clients. That's not something you do in a high school counseling office, obviously. But yes, it's done in private therapeutic settings."

He nodded, interested. Maybe flattering me. Maybe honestly asking. The longer I talked, the less Benjamin would have to say.

"I'm assuming," I added, "that something said in a hypnotized state can't be used as evidence in court. You'd have to independently verify anything that comes up, because people under hypnosis still get things wrong. But as a way to generate leads? I don't see why not."

I didn't mention learning in a grad school forensic psychology unit that there can be problems introducing a witness if that person has already been hypnotized in pursuit of information. I didn't care if Benjamin was discounted as a future witness. My focus was on eliminating him as a suspect. Let Hernández continue to screw up his case. He'd been doing it from the start.

The detective said to Benjamin, "If you were willing to try hypnosis, it would demonstrate cooperation. And who knows, maybe you'd remember some other interesting things about the last time you saw Izzy."

Benjamin pulled a face. "I don't want to let someone mess with my head."

Hernández smiled. "No, I wouldn't want that, either. Because you never know what you'll find in there, right Ms. Rosso?"

I looked away, working hard to contain my rage.

"Let's move on to Sidney," the detective said. "You ever have sex with her, Benjamin, or touch her, even just a little?"

"No."

"You ever go to her house or anywhere near her house?"

"No."

"But you did call her on Sunday morning. Maybe four or five hours before cameras caught someone in a hoodie entering and leaving the Mayfields' house."

Benjamin blurted, "I called her because Izzy wasn't answering my texts. She was having a party, Saturday night. The whole school knew it. Her parents were out of town. But I saw posts from other kids saying she wasn't at her own house even at nine, ten o'clock. I called Sidney on Sunday morning to ask her."

"And what'd Sidney say?"

"That she and Izzy had been fighting, but she was still worried that Izzy wasn't answering texts."

"So you went over to Sidney's house to make her feel better."

"No," Benjamin said, more calmly than I felt.

"But you did go to Izzy's house."

"Yes."

*He did?* I tried my best not to look alarmed.

"Saturday, the day she died," Hernández confirmed.

"Yes."

"The house of the girl who called you 'Shrimp' and made fun of your appearance in her diary. The one you called the *b* word and the *c* word."

"Yes."

"And why did you do that?"

"I was hoping to have sex with her."

My mouth fell open. Hernández reached for his pen.

Benjamin gestured to the binder. "I called her names because I was mad at her. It didn't mean anything."

"You were mad before you went to her house? After?"

"After. We had a disagreement."

Hernández turned several slick binder pages until he came to the right one. "*I hope you suffer. I hope you pick up a nasty disease. Serves you right for being a whore.*" He closed the binder. "For two schoolmates who supposedly were friends—at times—you didn't text her very often. But that afternoon and evening, you texted her nonstop."

"Because I was trying to stop her from doing something stupid. Usually her boyfriend Manny was looking over her shoulder. He'd even ask to see her phone and open up her apps."

"The controlling type."

"Yeah. So me—and the older guy, she never told me his name—we didn't text her, or not often. I don't think you're going to find him that way."

"When was the last time you saw Isabella Scarlatti, Benjamin?"

"That was the first thing you asked me."

"I'm asking again."

"Saturday, around two. At her house."

"Last time you said it was at the pool."

"I did see her at the pool. But then we went to her house, after swim practice. I went hoping we'd hook up, like I said."

"Wait a minute," I interrupted. "I saw my son directly after his pool practice. He came home."

Hernández looked disappointed, like he was quietly fishing and I'd just roared past him on a jet ski, scaring away all the fish.

"True?" he asked Benjamin.

"Yeah, I stopped home first. But then I went to Izzy's. Like, five minutes later."

"Why'd you stop at home?"

"I wanted to drop my bike. I didn't want to leave it outside Izzy's house."

"You were worried about theft outside Izzy's house? She lives on a pretty posh block. And I'm sure they would have had room in their four-car—six-car?—garage."

"I didn't say I was worried about theft. I just didn't want to be the asshole pulling up on a bike."

"Fair," Hernández said.

I was still doubting, though. Why would *I* have stopped home at his age if someone cute had just asked me over? Probably to change into better clothes, fix my hair. Take a shower. But he was just at the pool. He already took a shower. Body spray? A fresh shave?

"So you go to Izzy's house," Hernández reminded him, "hoping to hook up."

Benjamin nodded. "We started making out, but she kept stopping to check her texts—a bunch from friends who already knew about her party and were coming that night, but she had somewhere to go first. She was going to meet the older guy at the motel."

"In the middle of the afternoon."

"Yeah. So?"

"Then what?" Hernández said.

"Then we started talking some more about the guy, and I made a crack about sexual diseases, and how if she and I were ever going to have sex, better now than later, because I didn't want to sleep with someone after she slept with lots of guys, but especially some older pervert."

"Go on."

"She said, 'He hasn't had sex in years, I know it for a fact. I'd be his first since he got out.' And I really thought she was pulling my leg. *Got out?* As in, prison? The whole thing was a joke. I said, 'First, I don't think you're going. Second, if you did, even your friends would think you were a skank. Sidney will never talk to you again.' And she said, 'Sid's the one who introduced us.' But I could tell I hit a nerve, that Sid didn't like him. Not that way."

"You're saying the person who met with Isabella Scarlatti also knew Sidney Mayfield."

"Yes!" Benjamin said, and now he was angry, his face flushed.

"And you think Izzy was willing to have sex with him but Sid wasn't."

"Yes."

"But you've got it backward, my friend," Hernández said. "If the 'older' guy even exists. Because someone did have sex with Sidney just before she died."

Benjamin twitched in surprise. He didn't know what I knew about Sidney—what Robert had already told me.

"No," he said.

"No?"

"No," Benjamin said again. "That's not what Sidney's like. She wouldn't just have sex with some random guy."

"Medical examiner differs on that point."

"Then he must have talked her into it, or made her do it." For the first time, he looked shaken.

Hernández said, "So, back to you and Izzy in her house. She says she's not interested in you at this point in your conversation. Or she never was. And then what?"

"I went home."

"Did you ever wonder why she invited you to her house if she didn't really want to have sex with you?"

"I don't know. Maybe."

"Did you ever wonder why she'd want to talk so openly about her sex life with multiple other . . . men?"

"She seemed nervous about the guy, now that it was getting real. Like she was having second thoughts. If she knew what she really wanted, she wouldn't have been talking at all, she would have just gone and done it."

"So she was treating you like a girlfriend," Hernández said. "Talking at you. Making you listen before she rewarded you with something better than 'making out.' Was she painting your toenails this whole time, too?"

I exhaled noisily. "Are you telling my son that spending time listening to a girl is *not* an acceptable thing for a boy to do?"

Hernández smirked. "All right, Benjamin, so what did you finally say?"

"I told her what I thought. Which she didn't like. Obviously."

"Are you popular with the girls?"

"Not really."

"Why not?"

"I just said. Because I tell them what I think."

"Have you ever wanted to hurt a girl?"

Benjamin glowered. "I've wanted a girl to shut up. Does that count?" He brought both hands to his head and pushed hard, on the tops and the sides. It was getting to him, finally. "No, I've never hurt a girl. I've told you everything I know."

Hernández said, "I'm going to ask you again, Benjamin. Why did you stop at home?"

"No reason."

"I think you stopped home to get something specific," Hernández said. "Condoms?"

I'd already mentioned birth control to Izzy, as soon as she mentioned multiple partners. She smirked when I asked her if she needed any condoms, perfectly happy to tell me she had a drawerful at home.

"Did you show her something? Threaten her with something?"

Benjamin stared straight ahead. "If you're talking blackmail, trust me. Izzy couldn't be blackmailed. Ask anyone. She did what she wanted to do."

"That's what you liked about her."

"Yeah. And no. Not when she was about to do something fucked-up."

I released my fists, which I'd been squeezing on my lap. It felt like we were almost done.

Hernández silently reread the statement he'd filled out, rustling the pages. Three of them. He seemed to have accepted the nonanswer about stopping at home. I hadn't.

Ewan was impulsive. Ewan bragged, because he thought the world was his oyster and if he could take something then it was always meant to be his.

Benjamin wasn't like that. He made good choices, usually. He kept quiet. Usually. The quiet worried me, but it proved something, too. He wasn't a raging narcissist.

But I was thinking too much. My job wasn't to think at this moment. It was to avoid thinking—to pray, even if I wasn't someone who prayed.

"Anything else?" Hernández asked when he was finished.

"Nothing else."

"You're sure? Take your time."

There was a knock at the door. Detective Wood entered. Hernández stood up, giving him his chair, as if it was an elegant exchange they'd prearranged.

"Hi, Benjamin. One other question," Wood said. "So, after Isabella Scarlatti turned you down, what happened when you saw her next, at the motel?"

Benjamin laughed. Not scoffed. *Laughed.*

"*That's* the way you get people to make a confession?"

He looked at Wood. He looked at Hernández. He looked at the one-way mirror at the back of the room.

"Fucking amazing. No, I didn't go to any motel. Not that afternoon, not any night, not ever. I don't know which motel she went to, but you do, because you found the body. So, you know that the guy you should be looking for recently 'got out' and you know he drove a noisy car and you should probably be able to figure out who checked them in to the motel or even if she used a fake ID, someone probably saw them together, right?"

Benjamin nodded. Finished. Confident. Triumphant. *Not quiet this time. Not quiet at all.*

"Okay!" Wood said a moment later, dotting a period at the end of the sentence he was writing. "Well. That was all very helpful."

Hernández, standing with his back up against the far wall, said, "Good job, Benjamin. We appreciate it."

I still felt stuck to my chair. "Can we go now?"

"You can, Ms. Rosso. But we're placing your son under arrest."

He began to read Benjamin his Miranda rights. I watched as Benjamin's look of triumph was replaced by disbelief.

Hernández said, "Ms. Rosso, I recommend you go home, get a night's sleep, then come back in the morning. Your son isn't going home tonight."

# 19

In one moment—that moment when Benjamin wouldn't catch a yawn—Hernández had seen something that trusted friends, including Robert, refused to see.

*Do you feel that way sometimes, Benjamin? Like you can't read people? Or you can, but you don't want to? Stuff just rolls off your back? Other people's needs don't concern you?*

Something was different. Something was *off*. It wasn't that I refused to see. If anything, I looked too hard, with the outline of Ewan's face forever in the back of my mind.

And then again, Ewan had been so extreme, so recalcitrant, so determined to seek out trouble, that anyone else seemed comparatively stable and empathetic. Knowing Ewan helped me see. Knowing Ewan made it impossible to see.

Teachers, doctors, and friends knew that Benjamin provoked other children into fights. They agreed he was mouthy or glib. But no one was ready to give it a label, not even the child-development specialist I brought him to when he was eleven. I'd told Curtis that Dr. Adelman wasn't a "good fit" for us. He never asked what she said or refused to say about my son's personality and behavior.

Her name was Raveena Adelman, a sixty-something woman with a bright silver bob and reassuringly refined clothes, and she had just signed on as my undergraduate thesis advisor. After reading a journal article she'd written about conduct disorder, I asked if she'd be willing to meet Benjamin, and she agreed. I remembered sitting in the campus café because her office had no reception area, opening the detailed form she asked me to fill out, while she met privately with Benjamin. *Grandiosity, Lying, Manipulation, Remorselessness, Unemotionality, Impulsiveness, Irresponsibility, Thrill Seeking.*

It was hard to be honest, but I chose to be. Not many parents are, I learned later, as a graduate school student. Given this sort of checklist, many parents just leave a psychologist's office and never come back. But I stayed. I checked the boxes and in longhand, I wrote out my concerns, even going so far as to mention the fact that my own brother was serving time in prison and had been aggressive, charming, and manipulative from a very early age—a real terror, not just a "handful" or a "growing problem," as teachers often called my son.

After Dr. Adelman had spent an hour with Benjamin, she'd sent him to the waiting room, took a long moment to resettle her jewel-tone pashmina scarf around her broad shoulders, then asked me to stay behind to discuss certain behavioral episodes. I treated her questions like the most important exam I'd ever take.

"Does he mistreat animals?"

"We don't have pets. But that's because we've always lived in apartments that don't allow them."

"Is he aggressive with siblings?"

"He's an only child."

"Does he wet the bed?"

"No. But isn't bed-wetting involuntary? Do researchers still think that matters?"

I wasn't pushing back. I honestly didn't know.

"Not much, but we still ask."

"Has he ever stolen?"

"Not that I'm aware of."

"Does he light fires?"

I'd played with matches and lit fires as a kid, just as I'd shoplifted, but I'd spent a lot of time alone, especially after my mother died. From that day on, I knew what it was like to feel uncared for, and I did everything I could to spare Benjamin that feeling. I rarely left him alone for long. He spent nearly all his time either in school or day care, or with me. There were exceptions of course—the day of the sledding accident, when his friend broke his arm, came to mind—but not many.

Raveena steepled her hands below her strong jaw and gave me the sort of smile you give a mother who worries too much.

"I understand your concerns. But in Benjamin's case, certain personality attributes haven't developed into alarming behavioral problems."

"Except at school."

"Yes. But that's not uncommon. Didn't you say you're rarely in an apartment for longer than a year or two, and that he's had to change schools several times? That upheaval alone can explain conflict with other children and difficulties fitting in."

"But you do see it," I'd insisted, not wanting a damning answer but needing something—truth, advice, confirmation.

"I see something. But I wouldn't want to say anything prematurely. Psychologists and pediatricians aren't miracle workers. Not only are we unable to fix everything, but we use inadequate labels more often than you'd assume. I'm sure you've heard the term FLK?"

That meant "funny-looking kid," a cryptic, impolitic term doctors sometimes wrote into juvenile patient records when something seemed off—more often physical, but not always—and they couldn't pinpoint the problem.

Dr. Adelman said, "I wouldn't apply the conduct disorder label to Benjamin. You need to realize, Abby, there are children who get into much more trouble than your son has. Vandalism, substance abuse, extreme aggression. Granted, lack of parental supervision and other aspects of the environment, even poor nutrition, can exacerbate problem behaviors, whereas a positive environment can both mitigate and obscure."

Not prevent, only mitigate. Not eliminate, but only *obscure*. She seemed to be saying I was hiding Benjamin's true character by being a half-decent mother. But she wasn't promising that my adequate parenting would be enough.

Dr. Adelman added, "Later childhood and adolescence is when you may know better, unfortunately."

"You're saying I have to wait until he's a real problem before I know he has a real problem?"

She smiled again, pushing her scarf back over her shoulder.

I was beginning to dislike that needy, slippery scarf, and the bob so razor-sharp perfect she must need to trim it monthly. "And even then, you might be frustrated, because it's only in adulthood that certain labels can be applied."

"So what do I do now?"

She sighed. "Focus on stability?"

Of course I tried to give my son stability. "That's it?"

"And beware of self-fulfilling prophecies."

I ended up switching thesis advisors a week after that meeting, frustrated that the woman who wrote persuasively in a scientific journal gave me nothing but wishy-washy advice in person. It was my first indication that studying psychology wouldn't necessarily help me, especially when problems were close to home. If anything, the field would taunt me with the false expectation of definite answers.

Now, finally, Benjamin was a teenager. Now, finally, he was in trouble. But as people like Robert tried to remind me, using the least jargon possible, all adolescents are temporarily crazy. My first year at Summit confirmed that. The same kid who seemed stable one moment could do something unpredictable or unkind the next. Izzy's promiscuity and manipulation. Sidney's poor judgment, allowing a stranger into her house—unless, of course, he wasn't a stranger, but I wanted to believe he was. They were the "normal" kids, and they tested boundaries and made poor decisions all the time. And the boys? They were less caring, less reflective, more risk-taking. Benjamin wasn't entirely different from his male peers.

If I went back to Dr. Adelman now, she'd tell me to wait another ten years, until Benjamin's prefrontal cortex had finally matured. But she didn't have my memories or my deep foreboding. And one last thing—she didn't have children. When I discovered, just after graduating, that our college's so-called childhood expert had never parented anything more than a cat, I deleted her phone number from my contacts.

I barely slept that night, but when I nodded off on the couch, from six in the morning to about seven twenty, I had nightmares. I woke with a stiff neck and bleary eyes, imagining how much worse it must have been for my son, cold and alone in a jail cell.

The legal aid number I'd called the night before got back to me with a low-cost lawyer named King who agreed to meet me at the station. I called Curtis and left him a voicemail, asking if he'd decided whether to take on Benjamin, and I told him why it mattered now, more than ever. Then I drove back to the police station, ready this time with a change of clothes for Benjamin, and deodorant and body spray under the assumption they wouldn't let him shower and it would make him feel better. With snacks, including three cold toaster waffles. Also with a paperback—first I picked Stephen King, then worried that looked incriminating, so I swapped it out for a YA novel by John Green. I had no idea if they allowed juveniles in custody to have some way to pass the hours.

Upon arrival, I was made to wait ten minutes before being shown into the interview room. Benjamin was seated at the farthest chair, shoulders slumped, hair uncombed, staring at the opposite wall. He didn't make eye contact with me. Hernández was there, as was another tall white detective named Timothy Price and a Black man in a baggy suit who reached forward to shake my hand.

"Ralph King from Lincoln State Legal. I've already had the pleasure of meeting your son, Ms. Rosso. How are you doing?" Before I could answer he said, "Let's get started, shall we?"

Detective Hernández told Benjamin they needed to go over his statement one more time, especially about the last day of Izzy's life. The detective read the statement and began to ask his first question, about why Benjamin had stopped at home just prior to going to Izzy's house.

I fully expected Benjamin to say something ill-advised when King interrupted.

"My client won't be answering any more questions."

Hernández tried again, followed by Price, but the answer was the same.

"My client won't be answering any more questions. I think we're done here?"

Barely five minutes had passed. King pushed back his chair, shot Benj a serious look, then asked to meet me outside.

"They haven't made a formal charge and I don't think they're going to. Not today. As for Hernández's pushy tactics and Benjamin's unfortunate comments, those can be handled with a motion to suppress, but we're nowhere near that bridge yet. I know they're planning to reinterview some of Benjamin's classmates, and I don't doubt they'll show Benjamin's photo to staff from the motel where Izzy's body was found and talk to anyone else who might have seen him that day."

"How worried should I be?"

"Well, let's see. They've got motive. They'll be looking for means and opportunity. If they can confirm he was with her at the motel, you'd be justified to worry."

He was a straight shooter. I appreciated that, even if his straight shooting made my throat constrict.

"On the other hand," he continued, "they haven't mentioned a warrant. They don't have his phone or laptop. I'd call it fishing except they haven't even bothered to cut bait. Best bet is they're trying to show someone they're on the case when in fact they've got nothing to go on."

*Trying to show someone.* The Mayfields. The Scarlattis. And the other wealthy families who ran this town and wanted to know their daughters were safe.

"Okay," I said, expelling a deep breath. "Good."

"One other thing," he said. "You're a psychologist?"

"A high school counselor. Master's in psychology."

"Your boy ever been in therapy?"

"I'd like him to start. I have a therapist in mind, but he may not be available long-term."

"Long-term thinking is for later. Right now, it would be helpful to show you've done your duty as a proactive, responsible mom. You know he's under stress. You don't think he's done anything wrong but you've gotten him help. Even if he's telling the truth, I can tell he's a defiant kid—that much was clear from my first ten minutes talking to him."

"But won't therapy confirm that he has a problem? Wouldn't that prejudice a judge against him?"

Ralph King held my glance.

"I see what you're saying. But first off, half the teens in this town have been in therapy, even the ones whose only problem is not eating all their broccoli when they were toddlers. And second, narratives form. Your guy starts to put together a certain picture about Benjamin, and anyone else will be playing catch-up. It's generally better to have your own team well assembled before you go to court, if it comes to that."

"Got it," I said.

"And for extra credit, if your guy can teach Benjamin when to keep his mouth shut, that would be worth a lot."

King went back into the interview room. Ten minutes later, he came out with a phone to his ear, loosening the knot of his red tie as he hurried toward the parking lot. He mouthed, *Call you later.* Then, to my astonishment, Benjamin walked down the hall, shoulders slumped, no handcuffs, with Hernández following several feet behind.

The detective said, "Go home. Get some sleep. We'll be in touch with more questions."

I was still holding my sorry grocery bag with the plastic-wrapped waffles, deodorant, body spray, a paperback, and an orange. I held it out to Benjamin and he took it, moving past me to the front doors. He pushed on one but it didn't open. A flutter of claustrophobia tightening my chest. Those bars on my foster home windows. The security at the prison where I visited Ewan for the last time, seventeen years ago.

Finally, we heard a buzz. The door opened.

In the car, I said, "You weren't charged. They said they're continuing the investigation."

"The lawyer explained." He opened up the bag and pulled out the toaster waffles. "Thanks."

"You're welcome. They're cold."

"That's okay." He closed his eyes as he chewed. "Nothing

like being locked up in a freezing-cold prison cell to make a toaster waffle taste better."

I didn't mean to laugh, but I did. Grateful for this tiny ephemeral moment of normalcy. Trying to remind myself: Life isn't all one thing or another.

"They're good. Try one." He passed me the plastic bag. "We don't want you fainting again."

"How do you know I didn't eat breakfast?"

"Because I *know* you."

I took a waffle, took a bite, and with a dry mouth, I chewed. Because I could. Because he gave it to me. Because we were in this together. Happy just because my boy was eating. Happy because he did, indeed, know me.

Then I remembered the apartment as I had left it a half hour ago. Turned upside down, like a tornado had passed through.

Still chewing, Benjamin said, "Can we get going?"

We were down the street when I asked, "You meant what you said, about the beater, though? Because that narrows it down. If there's a janitor at the pool, they can question him."

It made sense to me. Someone else. A man. Maybe the janitor. Someone old enough to buy alcohol. Young enough to be stupid. The sort of person Izzy would have been curious about, an opportunity for experimentation and rebellion.

"I don't know how many crap cars visit that lot, actually," Benjamin said. "Maybe there are two. Maybe there are ten."

"But you were telling the truth to the police, about what you heard? Because this could be the most important clue they've got."

He turned to look at me. "Are you going to believe me?"

"Of course."

"No really. I don't mean, 'I'll believe if it's convenient.' I mean *believe* believe."

"I will."

But he'd see, soon enough. I'd held it together as long as I could, the finger in the dike, but too much time alone last night, reviewing everything Benjamin had said and not said in that interview room, had weakened the walls I'd built over the last twenty-four years. I knew and I didn't know—and not just about him, but about everything. At home, he'd see the proof of my shattered mind. He'd see that I'd betrayed him.

I patted the steering wheel like it had just occurred to me. "We should . . . go to breakfast."

"I just ate two waffles. I stink. I want to shower. And sleep."

"After breakfast."

"I didn't just get a good report card. I was *arrested*. No one celebrates being arrested."

"No, but—"

"Is that what your parents did when your brother was arrested? Take him out to Denny's?"

"I don't want to talk about Ewan."

"That's your answer. He isn't relevant."

I shook my head. Another lie. Ewan had never been more relevant.

"You left your phone home on purpose," I suggested, changing the subject, "because you knew they'd find those angry texts."

Benjamin shifted several times in his seat, pushing away

the chest strap. I didn't expect him to say any more. "Actually . . ."

"Yes?"

"Actually, I didn't want them to see a naked photo I had of Izzy."

I tried to keep my eyes glued straight ahead, so he wouldn't see the shock on my face. "A photo she let you take?"

"No. It was going around school. I just saved a screenshot."

"That's why Hernández mentioned blackmail. He already knows."

"He's an idiot if he doesn't. I'm sure Manny mentioned it to him."

"And that's what Chandra was talking about. Jesus, Benjamin. So multiple people know you had that photo. Were you blackmailing her?"

"*Mom*. Really?"

"Then why, Benjamin?"

I risked glancing over but it didn't help. He was staring hard over his right shoulder, out the window.

"To keep Manny off my ass. He knew I had a copy in several places. Izzy wasn't even embarrassed when that photo got passed around school. She was proud of her body. She liked to show off her tits."

"*Benjamin—*"

"And she was smart. She knew it was a good way to deal with assholes. Tell them you don't care and they'll find someone weaker to take down."

I muttered, "Easier said than done, speaking as a girl. So what happened with Manny?"

"He had a heart attack. He threatened everyone with what he'd do if they didn't delete it. He tried threatening me and I told him the whole point was I wouldn't delete it. I'd only forward it to more people if he tried to beat me up."

I nodded, digesting.

"I saw your face just now," Benjamin said. "I tell you Manny thought he fucking owned Izzy and you're like, *Okay, hmmm*, and I tell you that Manny wanted to beat me up over a girl and you're like, *Yeah, that makes sense*, and I tell you Izzy liked to show off her tits and you freaked out. But they're just tits, Mom. They're tits!"

"They're breasts. On a girl who is now dead."

Red light. When it turned green, I said, "I guess if you delete the photo, they'd still find it—if they get a warrant for your phone."

"Guess so," he said, sounding curiously unbothered.

I cleared my throat. "Well, I hope some of this has taught you a lesson."

He laughed under his breath. "Hell, yeah. Be careful what you put on your phone."

"Oh, Benjamin." I risked another glance in time to see a smirk flit across his face. I felt sick. "That's what you learned? Really?"

"But it was still good advice to keep the photo."

"Good advice from who?" I asked.

This time, he didn't answer.

When my phone rang, I looked for a spot on the shoulder where I could pull over.

"What are you doing?" Benjamin asked.

"Phone call."

"You never pull over." He looked behind us. "This isn't even safe. You could have found a parking lot, at least."

"This could be your lawyer. I'm not waiting."

But I'd already seen it was Curtis. I waited for the call to go to voicemail, then I started texting.

*On the way home with Benj sooner than I thought.*

"Like you tell me? 'Texting and cars don't mix'?"

"It's the psychologist we met at the pool. My old professor. I told him the police held you overnight."

Benjamin sounded disgusted. "Why did you tell him?"

"The same reason I called the lawyer. For backup."

# 20

Driving the rest of the way to our apartment in silence, I thought about Ewan's trial.

I'd spent most of that day sitting in the hallway outside the courtroom with a book I pretended to read, ignoring the stares of passersby and a lone security guard positioned in front of a different courtroom door, about fifteen feet down the hall. What was the book? *Tiger Eyes*? *Perks of Being a Wallflower*? I couldn't remember, maybe because I wasn't paying attention in the first place. I was only staring at the book open on my knees, the polished wood floor beneath my Tretorn tennis shoes, the big oak double doors across from me, and to my right, a little ways down the hall, the drinking fountain and the security guard. The whole time, thinking: *My brother shouldn't be paying for what Grant did.*

Anytime my mind wandered to thinking about what, exactly, Ewan *had* done, I yanked it back like a bad dog on a short leash, and told myself: Grant made all this happen. Grant drove too fast. Grant drank too much. Grant wrecked the car. I loved my brother. I needed my brother. I didn't care that Grant was dead.

"You sure know how to stay good and quiet," the security guard said.

I didn't acknowledge him.

Ewan was sent home, pending sentencing. That night, Martha started rage cleaning as she'd done many times before, following arguments with our dad. She'd drink heavily and bang around like a martyr, swabbing the floor, reorganizing cupboards, or emptying the entire refrigerator, sometimes without putting everything back. Coming downstairs to a kitchen counter of warm margarine, questionable mayonnaise, and spoiled lunch meat was nothing new.

This last time, she'd been more worked up than usual. Ewan wouldn't be with us for long. I didn't know if Martha was just upset or actually nervous with my brother back in the house. But *I* was nervous. I didn't think Ewan would let her get away with turning him in. I didn't think he'd be careful, either. If he went looking for revenge, everyone would know it.

The morning after Ewan came home to us, I woke to the smell of pine-scented floor cleaner, overpowering even from the second-floor hallway. I listened but didn't hear anyone awake. I went back to my room another hour until I heard my father's footsteps down the hall, down the stairs, and into the kitchen. And then I heard him howl.

I was told she'd hit her head on the sharp corner of a countertop. Maybe she was still alive at 1 A.M. or 3 A.M., but by 8 A.M., when our dad found Martha, she was cold. Then the ambulance came. And then, once again, the cops.

The cops searched the house, especially Ewan's room. They left my room alone, including the drawer where I'd put the underwear Ewan brought home the night of the accident. That souvenir had no bearing on Martha's death, but still, Ewan didn't need the cops to ask questions about the car accident all over again, or to go looking for some girl who might have a bad story to tell.

They took Ewan in for questioning a second time, and then they let him out again. They interviewed me, too, for the first time—no longer honoring me with the wide, polite berth they'd given me after the car accident. I told them about Martha and her late-night cleaning habits. They said it was odd how much floor cleaner she used, and it seemed to be mixed with something else even more slippery, maybe another kind of detergent. I shrugged and told them I didn't know anything about that. I didn't clean a lot. I just stayed out of my stepmother's way.

They asked, *Was your brother mad at her, for turning him in to the police?* I told them that my dad and my stepmother both spoke to the police—not just my stepmother. They'd done it the morning after the accident, as soon as they'd discovered blood on Ewan's unwashed jeans and bits of broken glass in his rolled-up cuffs. They got him to admit he'd been involved in a collision, though he refused to describe it. They marched him off to the cops, thinking they were forcing him to develop a sense of right and wrong. They had no idea a person had died, and even less of an idea that Ewan would go to jail. So yes, he was mad about it. But at the same time, he wasn't acting berserk.

To the cops I said, *Not really. He's pretty calm most of the time.*

Later that year, when Ewan had been sent away and we were down to just the two of us, my father hated being home. For dinner we'd go out to a cheap Greek diner where he would linger with the newspaper, smoking and reading until it was obvious he couldn't ask for yet another decaf refill. In the car, he'd be silent—no radio, even. One more smoke, the car filling with a foul haze. Sometimes, he'd miss the turn to our street or we'd end up clear across town, where he'd suddenly come to his senses and claim he was heading for a mini-mart to buy more smokes. I never thought it was dementia. I just thought he wanted one more excuse not to go home.

Opening the door to our house, he'd say, "After you."

Every time I stepped inside, I had that feeling of being on the edge of receiving bad news or some kind of punishment—maybe even a just one. I'd scoot across the dark entryway and dart up the stairs to go to the bathroom and then directly to my bedroom, avoiding any glimpse of the kitchen. I didn't think my brother had broken out of jail and was crouched next to the cupboards, ready to exact his revenge for being singled out as the family's only bad seed. I just worried there was something down there that I didn't want to face.

I felt that way, still.

"*Mom?*" Benjamin asked in a low, astonished voice, as soon as I unlocked the door and pushed it open. "Did someone break in?"

I started toward the kitchen.

"*Wait,*" he said, and my heart pinged in response to his concern. "Someone could still be here. Go back outside."

He ran across the living room, to our only hallway closet,

and he pulled out a baseball bat. It was exactly what my father would have done.

Regretfully, I called out, "It's okay. You don't need the bat, Benjamin. No one broke in."

From inside his bedroom, Benjamin howled. I closed my eyes, letting that betrayed sound work its way into my bones. I waited for him to come back and ask why I'd gone through every drawer. Why I emptied his backpack out onto his bedspread, not bothering to cram the detritus back inside. Why I pulled flannel shirts off their hangers, digging into front pockets.

*Because I only know half of the story, Benjamin. I don't want to find another trophy, but I have to look. Something that might have belonged to Sidney. Something else that might have belonged to Izzy. Because it's what troubled people do, sometimes. They keep things, to remember.*

Even now, after everything he'd said in the interrogation room and on the way home—everything he'd admitted to me—it still didn't add up. He was feeding me some information he knew would upset me, like the confession about the Izzy photo. But he was still keeping me in the dark about the important things. I could sense it, because I'd kept people in the dark, too.

When I got to his bedroom, he was sprawled across the bed, clothes and shoes still on, one corner of the bedspread pulled over his face. He hadn't even bothered to push aside the backpack contents, which now spilled onto the floor.

"Benjamin," I said. "I had a reason."

He didn't move.

"Benj. You haven't been telling me the whole truth."

He rolled over and whipped the bedspread off his face. "I haven't lied! I haven't told you everything, but I haven't lied. There's a difference!"

I inhaled deeply, waiting for him to say more.

He glared at me. "You, on the other hand. I didn't even know I had an uncle until I was, like, thirteen years old."

"There's a reason for that."

"And you take away mail that's addressed to me. You can't stop me from writing to him, you know."

My face flushed hot. But finally, we were talking about it. We should have talked about it before, but there was nothing harder for me than saying Ewan's name, and once we started, he'd be with us all the time—an outline of a person, filling in with details I wanted to forget. Becoming real. Becoming a threat.

"*Have* you written to him?"

He didn't answer.

I suppressed a growl of frustration and I tried to remember what it felt like to be a teenager. The constant temptation to use any bit of control you had—to dissimulate, to hide things, to take perverse pride in the little power you had.

"I planned to tell you everything when you turned eighteen. Until then, he isn't supposed to write to you."

"It's not a law. We're family. You can't be home every time the mail comes. There's nothing you can do about it."

He was right about that, because I'd tried. I'd even asked Robert, who explained that prisoners have lots of rights when it comes to mail, especially the outgoing kind. He told me I could make a special request to the warden, and I tried, but my letter got no reply. Correctional facilities were more concerned with monitoring incoming mail for contraband.

I walked to the foot of Benjamin's bed. "Is he asking you to send him something?" My mind raced. "Or *do* something?"

When Benjamin still didn't answer, my entire body flamed with rage. This was why my last visit with Ewan, in prison, was just before Benjamin was born. Ewan had been away for six years at that point. I didn't worry about Ewan's effect on me, but once I found out I was pregnant, I realized I had someone else to care about.

"He'll manipulate you," I said, trying to keep my voice low and steady. "He loves doing that, and he's good at it."

"You think I'm stupid?"

"I think we're all stupid at times. Especially when we're young, or afraid. It's how people get into trouble. You do one thing, and then another, and before you know it . . ."

I remembered Benjamin's cryptic comment on the way home. Now it made all the sense in the world. "He was the one who gave you advice. To keep the photo of Izzy and use it to threaten Manny."

Benjamin sat up and pushed away the closest pillow. "How many times did I get beat up in Waukegan?"

"I don't understand."

"How many times did you have to come to the principal's office?"

The answer was three. And he got the blame, every time, whether he'd been the first to provoke a fight or simply unable to resist provocation.

"How many times did I get beat up at Summit, Mom?"

"Different kids."

He scoffed. "Zero."

His eyes narrowed to angry black slits.

"Well, look where taking a convict's advice has gotten you—*outside* of school, in the real world. The world where you'll be living for most of your adult life. *If* you're lucky."

His expression didn't change.

"I'm going to ask you one last time. Did you hurt Izzy or Sidney in any way?"

He stared at me, eyes dark and dry.

"You don't deserve to keep asking me that. You're a liar and a hypocrite. You're mean to your own brother. You think everything's black and white. I'm not talking to you. We're done."

*We're done?* I'd laugh if I wasn't close to crying.

"I'm trying to protect you, Benjamin. Even if you've done something very wrong."

It was the first time I'd said it out loud.

# 21

Thirty minutes later, Curtis showed up. I'd texted him a long message about the lawyer-approved intervention needed for Benjamin, but I hadn't expected him to come right away, after everything he'd said about being unavailable. I didn't even know how he had our address.

"Still getting moved in?" he said after I opened the door, making his way past several empty moving boxes, hands occupied with a stack of take-out containers.

"Not exactly."

We settled in the kitchen, under too-bright fluorescent lights, and divided up a pad thai and green curry, leaving a second pad thai untouched for Benj, still in his room. The apartment's chaos was plain.

"This was kind." I gestured to the food. "Should I call Benjamin to come out here?"

"Not yet. Like they say on the plane, put on your own oxygen mask first. At least have a few bites before we talk strategy."

"Okay," I said, forcing myself to swallow two mouthfuls.

He set his fork down after a moment, watching me. His eyes were warm and patient, but inquisitive, too. It was hard to keep eating when I could feel him studying me.

"Let me just say," he started slowly, "that when we first met, I noticed that you seemed to be coming out from under the long shadow of trauma. I didn't know what it was, exactly, but I saw something."

His comment jarred me. We were here to talk about Benjamin. Still, I knew he was prying because he cared.

"I was in foster homes as a teen," I said, matter-of-factly. "I never expected to go to college. By the time you met me, things had turned around. I was doing better—I'd like to think I had some confidence—but I might have been feeling out of place. If that's what you saw."

"Hmm," he said.

He took several bites of pad thai, chewing thoughtfully.

"One thing that concerns me," he said, "is that you don't allow your past to color this situation with your son. Because that's the really important thing, right? Your son was arrested. They may decide to question him again, or charge him. That should be the focus. Not catastrophic fears rooted in the past. Just facts."

I nodded. Facts. But whose?

I told Curtis about the police interrogation, trying not to sound overwrought as I recalled the details unearthed, the puzzle pieces that still didn't fit.

"Benjamin claims he hasn't lied," I said. "In fact, he thinks I'm the big liar in the family."

I tried to laugh, but it came out sounding hollow.

Curtis got a faraway look. "I don't doubt he believes in

his own superiority. His own morality. And your brother, was he the same way?"

I frowned. "My brother?"

"The one in prison."

I touched the back of my hand to my forehead. I pushed my fingertips against my hot eyelids. God, I'd had so little sleep. Ninety minutes this morning. Four or five nights of broken sleep, before that.

"Did I already tell you about Ewan?"

"You still haven't eaten much," Curtis said, nodding at my plate of sticky noodles. "Too spicy?"

"No. I can't eat."

I looked past Curtis to the living room and the mess I'd made. The worst part wasn't just that I looked under my son's mattress and in his messy box of shaving stuff under the sink. The worst part was that after an hour of semi-logical searching, I started upending boxes and digging through drawers like a madwoman. I opened ancient CD cases, looking for the twinkle of an earring. I dug through pockets in search of hidden love notes or folded twenty-dollar bills that hinted of illicit arrangements. Half the time I wasn't even thinking of Benjamin. I was thinking of all of them. The boys. The men. The ones I wanted, the ones I feared, the ones that split my life in two. Had I really talked to Curtis about Ewan?

From the hallway, Benjamin cleared his throat. Curtis rose halfway from his kitchen stool, grinning. "Glad you're coming to join us! We've got an entire pad thai for you."

Benjamin slinked in slowly, served himself, and took a seat on a kitchen stool, which surprised me. I thought he would escape back to his room or the couch.

After a few awkward minutes during which every fork scrape was audible, Benjamin said, "So you've heard we have a convict in the family."

Without looking up, Curtis said, "Not so unusual, given incarceration rates in America. You like to keep in touch with him, then?"

Benjamin looked down at his own plate. "Would that be a problem?"

"Not for me. It might worry your mom, I imagine, if she's left out of the conversation."

"I'm done having conversations with my mom. Ever."

I pushed down the hurt, trying to focus on the good thing that was happening, even if I wasn't the one steering it.

"That's okay," Curtis said, glancing up quickly, then down again, like he was doing his best not to frighten a skittish animal away. "Most of us go through phases where we can't talk to our parents. It's the reason we find other people—friends, mentors, adults we can trust. I imagine you don't have many men in your life that you can talk to?" He smiled warmly. "Ones who aren't behind bars?"

"I don't want a therapist."

"Well, that's convenient, because I don't want a client."

Benjamin looked surprised.

My phone buzzed in my pocket. Robert. I let the call go to voicemail.

Curtis continued, "*However*, I've heard about your run-in with the law, and it's not unlikely that they're going to subject you to some psychological tests, if you're formally charged. It's in your interest to have a friendly expert conduct those tests first, or at least to develop some opinions about your state of mind and your ability to accept guidance. Your mother already told me that your lawyer agrees. He says these next few weeks matter. Some record of treatment, no matter how brief, and some signs of cooperative behavior could go a long way."

Curtis waited for Benjamin to nod, adding, "Impressions matter. And the first label often sticks. I'd hate to see another therapist label you."

"So that's what you're offering. To *label* me."

My phone buzzed again. Texts now. Incoherent fragments with misspellings intact, because Robert disabled his autocorrect. I recognized the rhythm. He was drunk.

"What I'd like to do first," Curtis said to Benjamin, "is just talk. Privately. No agenda. About anything you'd like to talk about."

"Meaning without my mom."

"*Completely* without your mom."

I swallowed hard, trying to loosen the lump in my throat. Benjamin needed to see me calm. I could do this for him. I had to.

When Robert called again, I hesitated before darting down the hallway into the bathroom. Door closed, I answered, "Jesus, Robert. Again?"

"What do you mean, again? I've never been fired before."

"You didn't tell me you were fired."

I couldn't believe the department would get rid of him for borrowing a diary. Cops shoot innocent people without getting fired, at least not immediately.

"Whose voice was that in the background?" he asked.

"Have a few more beers, go to sleep, and call me next

week when your bender is finished and you've talked to your union rep."

"Do you have a man over?"

"Oh, Robert. For fuck's sake. That's none of your business!"

"You worry too much about Benjamin, Abby. Even if he spent a night in jail. That's just . . . it's okay, Abby."

"I agree. It might scare some sense into him. I think he's going to be okay. We're all going to be okay."

"So, you don't need me now."

Here we go. The knight in tarnished armor.

"No, I don't need you at the present moment. We'll be okay. And you're going to be okay, too, Robert. Take care."

I felt bad the moment I disconnected, but I also knew we'd have a better conversation once he'd sobered up.

I shook off my irritation, peed since I was already in the room, washed my hands, and looked in the mirror. Limp hair. Bloodshot eyes. Shiny nose.

Opening the bathroom door again, I heard nothing. I assumed it meant that Benjamin had closed the communications spigot and returned to his bedroom. Instead, when I came out, he and Curtis were still sitting together amicably, finishing their plates of Thai food.

"Sorry for the interruption," I said.

"Nothing to be sorry for." Curtis stood up and carried his dish to the sink, where he washed it without asking, then stacked it to dry. Just when I was about to tell him to leave his pop can he rinsed it out and opened the cupboard beneath the sink. "Recycling in here somewhere?"

"The cardboard box next to the detergent."

"Good." He turned and smiled. "Time for me to go."

At the door, he said, "Can you bring Benjamin to my office tomorrow at noon?"

I looked back over my shoulder, expecting a protest, but Benjamin was studiously ignoring me, eyes on his plate.

"He agreed," Curtis said, intercepting my glance.

"Wow. That's . . . something."

"And given that I need to be up in Wisconsin with my father in two weeks or so, we can do some daily sessions, for as long as they're helpful."

The skeptic in me expected Benjamin to resist after the first session, but I kept it to myself.

"He also agreed not to write to his uncle for the time being. A letter in the wrong hands could suggest something unsavory. Appearances could matter, especially if Benjamin ends up in front of a judge."

"So he admitted to you he was writing to Ewan. You must have the magic touch."

I glanced over at Benjamin, but he seemed intent on pretending that he couldn't hear us.

"That's plenty of progress for our first conversation," Curtis said, smiling. "Get some rest." He pecked me on the cheek—a pleasant surprise. "Plenty of time left in the day. Chance to tidy up the place."

I tried to hear that comment as intended—advice, not rebuke. I whispered, "One last thing. *I'm not sure how much you charge.*"

"We'll figure it out. By the way, don't forget to apply for the Grove summer position—if you want it, that is. I looked at your CV on LinkedIn this morning, and I'm sure you'd have no trouble getting the job."

"You looked at my CV?"

"Just in case I could help." He lowered his voice. "Not a good idea to have your physical address uploaded to a publicly visible CV, by the way."

I couldn't believe I'd made that mistake. But I'd been distracted all week, updating my documents and doing a half-assed job search—and that was before last night's arrest.

"That's how you knew where we lived."

Curtis nodded and gave me one of those half winks so fleeting I wasn't sure if I'd imagined it. "The bigger mystery is, how did I know you like pad thai?"

Trying to match his playful tone, I said, "Everyone likes pad thai."

He leaned into my ear. "It's good to see you smile, even if you're faking it."

# PART II

# 22

I had a friend in grad school—Marta, from Colombia—a single, middle-aged student who had a teenage daughter. At the end of our first semester, Marta's daughter, Camila, was sent to an inpatient hospital program for anorexia, a condition Camila had suffered with since the age of eleven.

I remember asking Marta if she was doing all right, assuming that this latest turn was creating stress at the worst possible time, just as she was facing our first exams and term paper deadlines. But Marta surprised me. She said that the moment her daughter was checked in to the program, she felt better than she'd felt in years, even though Camila was at her lowest weight and Marta had urgent concerns about kidney and liver damage.

"I was just so grateful to have someone else in charge," she told me. "I could finally trust someone else to be watching and weighing and asking all the questions Camila hated me asking. Her life and her future had been in my hands, every minute for months. A person can only take that for so long."

I'd always thought I'd understood hypervigilance, but I

understood it even better now. I couldn't last an hour without thinking of Izzy and Sidney or googling for any news about the police investigations, and in between those moments I couldn't stop listening for a knock at the door. The sound of a closing car door inevitably sent me racing to the window, sure I'd see several patrol cars had pulled up—lights off, stealthy, ready with a warrant and a reason for carting Benjamin away, perhaps permanently.

But things would get better. Finally, I had help. Finally, *we* had a new routine. It started every day with a drive to Lake Forest.

"How'd it go?" I asked Benjamin after picking him up at Curtis's office.

He shrugged.

It was the same reaction I'd gotten since day one, but now we'd made it through three and he was still attending afternoon therapy sessions without protest.

"Talk about anything interesting?"

"Not really." He shifted in his seat, turning toward me, as if something had just come to mind. "Actually, we talked about how weird it is when people get fixated on things."

"Like what?"

He was smiling.

"Go on," I said. "Tell me."

"I told him about the time you came home barefoot, going on about some girl."

I didn't think Benjamin had noticed, especially given the larger drama happening that evening, when Robert had picked him up for breaking and entering.

Benjamin said, "I told him how you gave her your shoes."

"Because she didn't have any."

"And how you took a photo of her and kept staring at it."

I nodded. So this was how Benjamin was using up at least some of his time, evading more pertinent and personal issues.

"Can we go now?" he asked.

The car was running but I hadn't backed out of my parking spot on Curtis's long gravel driveway.

"In a minute. Did Dr. Campbell analyze my . . . what did you call it. My fixation?"

"That's confidential."

I laughed. "Confidentiality runs the other direction. He owes it to you. You don't owe it to him."

I had a feeling Benjamin knew that. He was just being a smart-ass.

I wasn't going to overthink why Benjamin had brought up something so tangential, either to Dr. Campbell or to me. His new therapist would get wise to his deflection tactics.

I could deflect, too. I said, "Dr. Campbell's got a nice place, doesn't he? Three buildings."

I looked past the spruce-green signboard with Curtis's name etched in golden script next to the twin outbuildings. One of them was Curtis's two-room office. The other was slightly larger, with clerestory windows up high near the roofline and a welcome mat at the side door. A mother-in-law apartment, maybe. Farther back on the lot, the main house was bigger, but not too big—a historic property, built before the days of McMansions, with ivy-covered stone walls.

"Those smaller buildings are called carriage houses," I

told Benjamin as we pulled away. "From the days of horses and carriages. Pretty amazing, huh?"

Evidently, Benjamin was not amazed. This time he didn't even bother to shrug.

Curtis hadn't been much more talkative. He'd briefly acknowledged my presence each time over the last three days I walked Benjamin inside. His expression looked relaxed, content, even gratified. I'd spent years learning to read the faces of day care staff and teachers. Even when they said something nice about Benjamin—*So smart! So articulate! He certainly is ready to share his opinions with others*—their smiles showed a degree of strain. Not in Curtis's case, though. Things must be going well.

I rolled down the window as we passed a fence-bound pasture that faced Curtis's long driveway. Behind it, a chestnut-colored horse raised its head as we passed, whinnying. Therapy with a view. Here, one could almost imagine that life was beautiful and Benjamin would never see the inside of a police station again.

"Oh," Benjamin finally said, halfway home. "Dr. C did have one message for you. He said you should take me for a hair trim."

"*That's* the message?"

Benjamin's hair was short enough, not much past his ears. I thought it looked cute when the bangs got a little scruffy. He was neater than a lot of Summit boys.

"Yeah, he said it looks better. He said it wouldn't hurt if I dressed nicer, too. In case the police talk to me again."

"Did you give him reason to think they will?"

But the pipeline had closed, at least until we had passed

downtown Pleasant Park. The last of Main Street's shops and restaurants were in my rearview mirror when he said, "You never told me how you got pregnant."

I shook my head once, like I'd just felt a fly buzzing around my ear.

"Sorry," I said. "You surprised me with that one. Let's see."

There was construction ahead of us, just where Green Bay Road met our neighborhood. A pothole brigade.

"When you were thirteen, I did tell you about your father. I mean, I told you I didn't know who your father *was*."

With acid in his voice he said, "One-night stand."

"Yes, sort of." *Zero-night stand* was more like it. I was drunk, screwing with a man who'd bought me drinks and was even more intoxicated than I was, in the grungy bathroom of a Clark Street bar. Did anyone want their kid to know they'd done such things? "I didn't get to know him well. I made a mistake. But you, Benjamin, were not a mistake at all. Not one little bit."

"Is that what you told people? That you fucked a stranger but somehow, I wasn't a mistake?"

I paused. Breathed. Smiled at the construction worker who had just turned his stop sign around to "slow."

"I told them, from the very start, that I planned to have you. And life went on from there."

He made a doubtful huffing noise. I made the turn onto our street. I could feel him staring at me, hard.

"You don't talk about your parents."

"I'm sorry you didn't get to know them. My mom died when I was eight. My father had dementia and was institutionalized by the time I was fourteen."

"But you had a stepmother, right?"

"Not for long."

He said something under his breath.

"I'm not avoiding the question, Benjamin. I just didn't get along with her very well. Nothing more to say, really."

He turned toward me, staring. "The evil stepmother trope. That came up in my lit class. Cinderella. Snow White."

I laughed. "I guess I'm a walking cliché."

"I hate when you do that."

"What?"

"Laugh when you think something isn't funny."

I parked at the curb. "Where are these particular questions coming from? Were you talking about your grandparents in therapy?"

"No. I was talking about you."

I glanced over. "You mean, about you and me? How we communicate?"

"No," he said, stony gaze diverted to the windshield. "Just you."

For the rest of the day while I web surfed, looking for new jobs and cheaper apartments up and down the North Shore, Benjamin remained behind his closed bedroom door. I knew, from the sound of the hectoring and lecturing male voices, that he was watching videos—never quite loud enough for me to hear.

He had earphones. Listening unplugged was a purposeful choice. He wanted me to know—and yet not know. He was spending hours listening to things I'd find objectionable, things that would worry me if I could make out more than scattered words, but it wasn't the words that mattered so much as the tone of anger and grievance.

When Robert called, I picked up and then almost immediately wished I hadn't.

"I stopped by your place at lunch, in case you wanted to get a bite."

"I wasn't home."

"So I noticed."

I'd never liked the idea of a man cruising regularly past my house, even when we'd been dating. "You know I prefer people to call or text first."

"Yeah, well, I happened to be nearby. With a lot of free time on my hands."

"Speaking of that. Doesn't your department have to do some sort of investigation before they can decide about your job?"

"They can if they want. I resigned."

"*I* see. You quit before they could terminate you. It's getting clearer now."

"They don't want me, Abby. They haven't wanted me for a while. And if they don't want me, I don't want them."

I wasn't sure I believed him. Robert would have been giving up an awful lot by voluntarily quitting. The conversation flagged until he started asking about Benjamin's therapy.

"Every day, huh?" he asked. "Is that normal?"

"Who says I've been taking Benjamin every day? If you've been driving by my apartment over and over—"

"I put two and two together. You've been too busy to return most of my texts."

"I don't like feeling watched, Robert. I've told you that."

His tone grew serious. "Hey, did Jack Mayfield ever bother you again?"

"No."

"Good."

But I detected some disappointment. Without another person bothering me, Robert didn't have enough reasons to insert himself back into my life.

He asked, "You gonna give me any hint how Benjamin is actually doing?"

"I told you. He's going to therapy. He's getting up on time. He's not resisting. Not even complaining, actually."

"So that's good, right?"

I felt around in my body for some way to explain. "Not if he's only using the time to find new ways to needle me." But that wasn't right, either. Not just *needle*. He was digging.

"Doesn't the doc need to tell you what they're talking about?"

"Absolutely not." It was something I had prepared myself for as a high school counselor. Parents nearly always want to be kept in the loop, but they have no right, and on top of that, allowing kids to develop autonomy is often one of therapy's primary goals. "Confidentiality applies even to minors as long as there's no threat of harm to themselves or others." I quickly added, "No *current* threat. We're not narcs, in other words."

"Sounds pretty dumb to me."

"Robert, I've got to go. But I'm sorry about your job. Really."

In a gruff voice, he mumbled. "Thanks. Hey listen—"

"Hey listen," I said back, intercepting him before he tried inviting me to dinner. "I need to call the lawyer."

It was nearly 6 P.M. when Ralph King returned my call.

"Did you see the news on channel seven?"

He gave me the short version: The police chief and the Scarlattis were pressing for public information about any man who might have been seen with Izzy at the Blue Moon, where she had died. The Scarlattis had no patience with the police department's policy so far, of keeping a lid on many of the case's details. They wanted the public to know and to start helping.

"Are they saying exactly how she died?"

"They're talking drug-induced homicide, with no clarification on intent—in other words, whether it was on purpose or an accident. But they haven't named the drug."

"It was something she had an allergy to. The family told Dean Duplass, just like they told her about the phony suicide note. I heard it from another teacher."

"Telephone game," he said briskly. "You see the problem there? When the police share that info, I'll believe it. For now, we should focus on the next likely development that could involve Benjamin directly."

There was a motel maid, he told me, who'd heard a man's voice coming from the room where Izzy died.

King said, "I wouldn't put it past the detectives to do a sort of voice identification lineup."

"How does that work?"

"They'd ask Benjamin to voluntarily come in and record the words the maid said she heard, then ask the maid if the voice sounds familiar." I started to object but he interrupted, saving me from a rant. "Don't worry. We're not doing it. Voice testimony is even less reliable than eyewitness testimony. I just wanted you to know what they've got so far and what they haven't."

"If they're so interested in sounds, are they doing anything with the car sound Benjamin described?"

"The dragging tailpipe?"

"That isn't how he described it."

King seemed annoyed with my correction. "I can't say that they are, but listen. You are not obligated to pursue any information or form any hypotheses. Let the police find their suspect. Your son hasn't been charged."

"Yet."

"In the meanwhile, how's Benjamin doing? Learning some manners? Getting in touch with his softer side?"

Everyone wanted to know how my kid was doing in therapy, even the people who seemed to think therapy was a touchy-feely waste of time and money. I didn't have a simple answer for King, so I lied.

"He's doing great."

"Good. Maintain a low profile and keep your boy out of trouble. It could be a long summer."

When I got off with Ralph King, I did what I should have done a week earlier. I dialed up Grace, the Summit secretary.

"Looking for a time to pick up your monstera plant?" she asked in a sunny voice, as if I'd left my job voluntarily.

"If you like it and you've been watering it, it's yours." I thought of the other things I'd left behind—the comfy blue chair, some books. A lot of the staff took time off in late June. If I waited until then, I wouldn't have to run into many familiar faces. "By the way, everything fine with you and your family? Summer plans?"

"I'll be taking my break on July first, but I spend most of that time alone."

"Doug doesn't get vacation?"

"Heck no. He's got more summertime business than he can handle."

Doug was a foreign and luxury sports car mechanic. That's why I was calling. "This is going to sound strange, Grace, but Benjamin heard a noisy car—maybe a beater—without seeing it. It had a hard time starting up, and then it kept making a repetitive sound. The owner of that car matters, if we can find him."

"Is this about the girls?"

"Yes," I said, trying not to sound tense. "Do you think if I called up all the mechanics in our area and described the sound for them, they might be able to recall if any old car came in for a repair in the last couple of weeks?"

"Gosh. No idea. But you could go to YouTube. There are all kinds of automotive sound libraries and diagnostic videos on there. Car owners are pretty fanatical. If it's a beater and the person is a DIY kind of guy, he may not have gone to a mechanic. What'd the car sound like?"

I tried to remember Benjamin's exact words. "Like a typewriter."

"That's called tappets. A lot of engines make that sound. Not low-value beaters, exclusively. Fancy vintage cars, too."

"That's fantastic. Thanks, Grace."

"Doug can confirm it. You want him to call you, or the cops?"

"He'd call the police directly?"

"If it helps the girls' families. Of course."

"That would be incredible. Ask for Detective Hernández or Wood. You can mention that I was the person who asked about the sound, and he'll understand why. But I'm sure they'll be happier to hear from Doug than from me."

Not a beater, necessarily. It could even be a fancy vintage car. More suspects. More possibilities. Ralph King thought that sleuthing was none of my business, but if no one was going to ask the right questions, I had little choice.

On my worst days, I'd been a fool, hiding information in a confused panic. But I could make up for that, as long as I believed Benjamin had done nothing wrong. If he had, Curtis wouldn't be looking so relaxed and upbeat each time I showed up to collect my son. I had to cling to that assumption. For now, I had nothing else.

# 23

I was making French toast on Sunday, a day with no therapy sessions scheduled, when Benjamin emerged from his room and asked me to drive him to the pool. I had a spatula in one hand, my phone in the other, scrolling the news with my thumb until I suddenly stopped. There she was. The girl I'd seen on Green Bay Road.

"Mom," Benjamin said. "Smoke."

I pulled the pan off the burner and shrugged my shoulders up to my ears, sure the fire alarm was going to go off any second. In our last apartment, it would have.

"Can you open all the windows?" I asked Benjamin.

He ran around levering and waving his arms. I turned the hood knob, trying out the fan for the first time since we'd moved in. It whirred and rumbled, emitting the faint smell of mouse droppings, but it did little to eliminate the smoke.

Benjamin came back to the kitchen several minutes later. "The good news is we won't go deaf. The bad news is the smoke detector doesn't work. The batteries inside look corroded."

"Right," I said, looking around for a pen to add to the chore list on the fridge.

My phone was still in my hand. *Arlington Heights woman reported missing. Veronica Lynn Lovell.*

"So?" Benjamin asked.

I was reading about where she'd last been seen—at a sports bar out in Fox Lake, far to the northwest of us. I tried to remember what he'd been asking me. *The pool.* "You want to swim?"

"Not to swim."

I didn't understand. "You don't play tennis. We don't even have rackets."

"No. Just to see it."

"The *pool*?"

"The parking lot. The front of the building. Can you drive me or not?"

"Of course I can."

I looked back at my phone.

"She's the same girl as that picture in your phone," he said, looking over my shoulder.

"I wasn't sure."

"Yeah, it's her."

He seemed mildly interested at best.

After I finished cooking, I opened up my photos and toggled back and forth, comparing the girl's picture to the news photo. Then I phoned the nonemergency police line. A woman took my message, though she didn't seem particularly interested, especially when I told her how long ago I'd seen Veronica.

After I got off with the cops, I ate two pieces of French

toast, all while watching Benjamin from the corner of my eye. He was sitting on the edge of the couch, tapping one knee with a pen as he stared out into space, with one of his notebooks sitting next to him, unopened.

A third piece of French toast was on my plate, but I'd lost my appetite.

"Ready," I said. "And make sure you have your wallet. You can drive."

The practice driving put him in a good mood, and he nodded his head to a song playing through the outdated car radio, despite an occasional crackle from the frayed auxiliary cord hooked to Benjamin's equally outdated phone. But as soon as we approached the Dartmoor Club sign, his body language changed. Sitting more upright, with his chest close to the steering wheel, he maneuvered around the parking lot, tracing its perimeter. The entire lot was easily in sight of the pool's front doors.

He crept slowest at the lot's northern end, where there was a partial roof structure casting desirable shade onto one section of parking spots. Five of the spots were marked DIAMOND CIRCLE, probably for some upper level of club membership. At a greater distance from the front of the building, five of the spots were marked STAFF.

Finally, he pulled up to the half-circle drive. He idled. Then he turned the music back on and drove away. I'd been so absorbed trying to understand what he was looking for that I hadn't even registered when the radio had gone silent.

I was about to ask when he cut me off. "I need to think, Mom. Don't talk." Softer, he said, "Please."

I obeyed. In any case, I felt I already knew: He was trying to remember that day with Izzy—the day he'd heard but thought he hadn't seen the car that picked her up. Either that or he was doing an expert performance, showing me he was trying to remember.

Or maybe he was picturing what he'd say if the cops arrested him again—maybe even in connection with a new community concern. A girl had gone missing. Maybe it had nothing to do with Izzy or Sidney, but there must be pressure to prove that the police weren't asleep on the job. I found myself thanking heaven that the Arlington Heights girl had gone missing from a sports bar nearly an hour away, and then feeling the wrongness of seeing every piece of possibly crime-related news only through the lens of my own child's perceived guilt or innocence.

I said nothing else on the way home. But that evening, on the pretense of running to the store for milk and with that strange parking lot tour still on my mind, I drove around Pleasant Park, trying to count all the beaters (not even one) and the vintage cars (surprisingly many) in our town. I drove past a used-car lot and two different specialty car mechanics. I did several loops around our downtown district, then I drove to the library, past banks, a pet-grooming shop, a high-end toy store, and a fancy hair salon, and then finally to the train station, where various gleaming cars idled, waiting to pick up passengers from the northbound commuter train.

Next, I drove to Summit, where I felt my heart drop down into my stomach at the first sight of the electric signboard, which bore Sidney's and Izzy's names followed by some digital hearts. At the base of the sign, a small memorial had taken shape: teddy bears, cut flowers now wilted by the heat, and a few framed photos. I got out of my car and walked closer, crouching down to study the largest framed photo. In it, Sidney and Izzy were seated at a Halloween party, with their arms thrown around each other and red Solo cups at their feet. Sidney was dressed as an angel. Izzy was dressed as a devil, with plenty of cleavage showing. *A little on the nose*, I thought, but I was grateful Dean Duplass had allowed students to leave whatever they wished.

In my purse, I had an organic dark chocolate candy bar I'd bought as a treat while picking up the milk. I left the chocolate sitting flat on the grass, an inch away from one of the picture frames. Then I drove home. The whole time, I kept my window down, listening as hard as I could for the telltale sign of an engine making the tappety sound as it started up or idled.

In an hour of driving, I never heard a thing.

I hadn't visited Willa in person since losing my job. I had no excuse to stay away now, especially since Curtis had started meeting with Benjamin for longer sessions—two hours instead of one. That gave me time to run up to Winthrop Harbor, chat an hour, and come back just as the session was ending.

When I dropped by that Monday morning, she was sitting in her yard with two metal lawn chairs already unfolded for us. We hugged, longer than we had in a while, my arms tight around her curved back. She was getting shorter, her arms and legs spindlier, although the only effect of aging she mentioned regularly was her hair, which she'd stopped dyeing during the pandemic. Once it was safe to visit, I'd come by regularly to help give her hair rinses to make the silver outgrowth look more vibrant.

"I'm still thinking about going back," she said as we settled into our chairs with iced tea. I knew immediately what she was talking about, because she mentioned it nearly every time I saw her.

"I think your hair looks beautiful that color. And I like the shorter style."

"Poodles. That's what your mother and I thought of women who looked the way I look now. She would never have let her hair go gray."

I had no idea. I'd frozen my mother's image at the age she died, forty-two—the same age I'd be in just a few years.

Willa said, "They used to tell us that older women should never have long hair. And by 'older' they meant over thirty."

"I think you should wear it however you like."

"What they didn't explain is you get my age and you don't want to deal with clogged sinks. It's a practical issue."

Willa took a drag on her cigarette. Each time she did, she slitted her eyes nearly shut, the deep wrinkles running across her tanned skin all the way to her hairline. Then she exhaled, grinning broadly, the pleasure of her vice undeniable. I had to resist the temptation to ask for a cigarette, even with the proof of its damaging effects in front of me.

I told her, "Ewan has been writing strange, creepy letters to me and Benjamin. Unfortunately, Benjamin has written him back, at least once."

Willa set her cigarette in an ashtray emblazoned with the

logo of Bally's Casino before turning to me. She took my hand in hers.

"Abby, I'm so sorry. Maybe it's my fault."

"Of course it's not."

"Maybe it is. The last time you dropped him here to mow the lawn, he asked me if I had any photos of your brother, and I lied and said no. I didn't want him thinking about your brother. And I didn't want to mention it to you, either. I knew it would upset you."

"I understand. There's more I need to tell you. Maybe I should get us fresh teas, first?"

I had to watch the clock once I came back from her mobile home's tiny kitchen with topped-up glasses. I still had a lot to explain—about Sidney, Izzy, my suspension, Benjamin's arrest.

"Which brings me to my awkward request. You once said I could always come to you in an emergency. For a loan. Well, I've got Benjamin in therapy for the first time, and—"

"Say no more," she said, popping out of her chair. When she came back, she had a burgundy faux-leather checkbook.

The quickness of her response had surprised me.

"I feel terrible about this—"

"No," she said, starting to make out a check with a shaky scrawl—two thousand dollars—even though I hadn't mentioned a figure and I couldn't imagine a woman like Willa could afford that much.

I accepted the check and hugged her. She hugged me back so long and hard I could feel the vibration of her chest into mine with each raspy breath.

When she let go, she said, "I never wanted to say anything,

especially when it came to Benjamin. I knew it wasn't my place. But I'd always hoped you'd get him the help he needed."

"It's too much."

"It isn't. I've been waiting for you to ask."

*Waiting how long?*

I felt rattled by her generosity and even more, by what lay behind it. An older woman's trust in me. Her equal mistrust of my child, brewing for longer than I could have guessed.

I thanked her, took my glass into the mobile home, and came out again, with a final rushed minute for one last hug and more thanks of confused gratitude. I was about to go to my car when she said, "Did you hear about that missing girl? She's from your area."

"West of us," I said. "Arlington Heights."

I didn't mention that I'd seen the girl much closer to our home, between Pleasant Park and Lake Forest. It seemed like planting a seed of suspicion or concern that didn't merit planting.

Willa said, "The poor parents are furious because the police aren't taking it seriously. They say she's not a runaway. Wonder if it has something to do with those girls from your school."

"No idea. Doesn't it seem like there's suddenly all these crimes against young women—all from the North Shore?"

Willa had eased back down into her lawn chair. She lit a fresh cigarette. "Not at all. It was much worse than this, before your time. Not just the North Shore, but northern Illinois, southern Wisconsin. Your mother and I used to talk about it, though she always reminded me not to talk around you and your brother. She didn't want you to be scared."

"When was that?"

"If she thought Ewan shouldn't hear, he must have been only twelve or so. A year before she died. So you would have been . . . seven?

"But then the numbers started coming down," she said. "Or at least the number of dead girls found. I suppose there were still runaways and unaccounted for missing persons after that, but not bodies. These things must come and go in waves."

I checked my phone. I apologized again for the morbid topics. I thanked her again for the loan. I gave her a tight hug, squeezing her warm, round birdcage of a chest, sorry when I had to let her go.

When I got to Curtis's office, I was several minutes late, but Benjamin wasn't ready yet. That was a first. I waited in the car until it got too hot. Then I got out and wandered toward the shady side of the mother-in-law apartment, where some unwatered azaleas were browning and shriveling in the heat. I looked around for a hose, and finding none, peered into the window instead. On tiptoes I could make out a room empty except for a collection of free weights and kettlebells. So, it wasn't being sublet to some prim elderly lady, as I'd assumed. And then again, I'd never seen another car or anyone coming and going.

A car door opened with a rusty creak, then slammed shut. Benjamin was done with his appointment and waiting for me.

"How'd it go?" I asked after I buckled in.

He pushed a piece of paper into my hand.

At first I thought it was a bill. Instead, it was a handwritten note on cream-colored letterhead: *Benjamin mentioned that a detective brought up the possibility of using hypnosis to retrieve a memory but he's nervous about the process. I have client calls all afternoon but I'd like to phone this evening if that's okay? Thank you. Curtis.*

"This is great," I said, backing out, windows still down. "He must think hypnosis can help you remember the car that picked up Izzy at the pool. That's why we went there the other day, wasn't it?"

"I told you. I told everyone. I didn't see the car."

"I'm not questioning your honesty. I just wonder if you've forgotten. It happens." *Maybe especially when you're distracted by a girl stepping out of her underpants.*

I heard Benjamin sigh and shift, bringing his knees up against the glove box, when he could simply move the seat back and have more room. Sometimes, I thought he liked to pretend he was one of those tall, gangly teens who simply wouldn't fit anywhere. "I think you should try it. There's nothing to be worried about. It's a myth that you lose control or do things against your will."

"Then what's the point?"

"You're suggestible. But only in a way that you want to be suggestible. That's why it can be helpful for entering a deep enough trance for remembering lost details—and other things too. People have used it for chronic pain control, quitting bad habits, managing anxiety . . ."

"If it's so great, you try it."

I looked over. He wasn't scowling or glaring.

After a minute, I said, "Okay. If it would make you feel

better knowing I tried it first and didn't end up flapping around like a chicken, then I will. I'll ask Dr. Campbell to hypnotize me. It's a deal."

From the corner of my eye, I could see his half smile.

I'd reached the end of the white fence, where we normally turned left onto a larger street that led us back toward Green Bay Road.

"Look at that," I said, feeling lighter already. A small lane ran behind the horse pasture, into a deep stand of woods, toward a sign I couldn't read from this distance. I drove slowly, wheels churning gravel, until the font became legible.

GROVE ACADEMY, EST. 1936.

The dense canopy of trees enclosing the road made it look like an enchanted tunnel. We crept forward, my foot completely off the gas until the road branched. A sign indicated dormitories to the left, main buildings to the right. Around a bend, the shadows parted and a red roof appeared, fronted by a half-circle drive. One side of the main building sloped up like the prow of a ship, decorated with stained glass.

"I applied to work here, three days ago," I told Benjamin. "I knew the school was nearby, but I didn't realize it was this close to Dr. Campbell's office."

"Yeah, he says the office and house came with the teaching job," Benjamin said.

"That's a great perk."

The oaks here were taller than at Summit, with thicker trunks and gnarlier branches. They reminded me of some black-and-white photo I'd seen, taken in France. All of the signage, I noticed, matched Curtis's gold-on-green professional clinic sign.

As we watched, a nun in a black habit and thick-soled white running shoes exited the front door, saw us waiting at the bottom of the drive, and waved before continuing to her red Volkswagen Golf.

"Look at that, Mom," he said. "Even a nun has a cooler car than you have."

I smiled. "Cooler shoes, too."

After a moment, he asked, "Are most of the kids who go here Catholic?"

"Only about half, according to their website. Plus they went coed last year. That could be convenient, if they offered a tuition waiver for staff family, the way Summit did."

I waited for him to object. When he didn't, I said, "I don't think I'll get it, though."

"You might."

The day's peace offering.

# 24

Most evenings, we had the television on, though Benjamin paid only half attention to the programs I liked. He'd get up from the couch often, as he always had—restless, scrounging for snacks or taking longer than expected in the bathroom, where he was probably watching his own videos or scrolling. That night, he was more restless than ever.

"Don't pause it," he said, getting up from the sitcom we were watching.

"I don't mind."

Usually I did mind, but things had changed. I couldn't focus. My mind flitted back to Summit, back to Sidney or Izzy. While Benjamin was out of the room, I googled statistics. What kind of date rape drugs are most often used? How many women reported having drinks spiked sometime in their lives? Awareness was widespread, and even so, 8 percent of college women had reported being drugged, an article said. Almost 3 percent of college women reported drug-facilitated sexual assault.

I kept looking for stories that matched Sidney's and Izzy's, but what I came across the most were girls and women drugged at parties, in bars, at travel resorts—as well as articles telling what women should do to keep a better eye on their drinks. *Right. Leave it to the victims.*

It wasn't really just about drinks, other articles agreed, or about the wide availability of drugs, either. It was about consent.

Izzy had been the one to remind me what a recent concept that was. The subject of *SNL* jokes in the 1990s. A commonplace topic by the time I was in college. And now? Maybe things were backsliding or even reversing, as things all too often seemed to do. Maybe men were just tired of asking. Tired of waiting. Maybe it was more of a turn-on to see women as they often appeared in bad porn—as the recipients, willing or not willing, of whatever a man decided to do to them. Maybe for a certain breed of man, inexperienced or confused or full of loathing, "not willing" was even better, as long as there was a way to ensure he'd have control of the situation.

Benjamin still hadn't emerged from the bathroom. No sound of flushing or running water. I opened an incognito window and quickly typed *murder date rape drugs.*

I flinched at the first search result. According to a UK headline, an east London man named Stephen Port had murdered four men he'd drugged. *Obsessed with date rape drug pornography*, the article read.

At least one of the victims' deaths was ruled a suicide—no investigation conducted—because the police simply assumed. Dead body. Drugs in his system. A suicide note nearby. But the note hadn't been written by the victim. It was written by the killer. The killer's landlord was the one to read about multiple murders and notice the connection. Still, the police ignored the landlord. Port was given free rein to continue doing what he wanted to do.

*Why*, I wanted to know. But I couldn't find any quick insights into Port's psychology. The search results were overloaded with articles about the police's baffling mishandling of the case.

While walking her border collie, a woman found one of the bodies in a churchyard. She called the police. Several weeks later, she found a second body in the same spot. She called the police again. *I am the same woman that found the other body a few weeks ago . . . and I have found another young boy.*

And still, even with bodies dead from the same apparent cause, in the same location, the police didn't interpret the deaths as murders—and certainly not connected murders. With idiocy like that, it was easy to imagine why serial killers remained uncaught.

As soon as the thought struck, I regretted it. *Uncaught.* That was terrifying. *Serial killers.* That was worse. A predatory killer who murders again and again—the stuff of horror movies and sensationalist tabloids and TV shows. It seemed so . . . 1970s. As outdated as an avocado-colored refrigerator or a macramé wall hanging.

But Port had killed his victims in 2014 and 2015. He wasn't one of those California sadists picking up stray bell-bottom-wearing hitchhikers. He was someone of my generation, using a dating app to find his victims. He didn't need to drug or deceive them into following him home. They expected sex, most likely. But that wasn't enough for him. He was in pursuit of a particular experience.

Port's description of one of his victims: *like a rag doll*.

Part of me wanted to pretend I couldn't imagine such a man—never mind the person who'd killed Izzy or Sidney. But of course I could. It didn't take a psychology degree. I'd known my share of aggressive, empathy-deficient men with fragile egos and short fuses. I had no trouble imagining them as serial domestic abusers. But take that self-entitlement and penchant for abuse, then add a warped sexual fantasy . . .

I heard footsteps and rapidly closed the window on my phone. Benjamin chuckled at the scowl still visible, evidently, on my face. "Irritating text from your ex-boyfriend?"

"Just . . . news," I said, trying to banish the images in my head. "Politics."

Benjamin looked around without sitting. He gestured at the paused sitcom.

"I don't really want to watch anymore."

"You sure?"

He picked up his socks from the floor.

"Thanks," I said.

He was doing that more often lately. Picking up his socks. Flossing his teeth.

The hair trim Curtis had suggested for Benjamin last week—that was something a detective or judge might notice. But not the socks. Not the used floss in the garbage can. And certainly not the made bed, sheets tucked in and pillow centered with perfection. Wasn't there some Navy SEAL who gave a commencement address about that?

A mother couldn't complain. Only wonder.

"I'm turning in," Benjamin said, though it was only nine o'clock.

"Okay. Good night."

I'd given up on the Netflix program and gone into the kitchen, hoping we still had some ice cream left, when my phone rang. Robert.

"I need a cop's intuition here," I said, a few minutes into the call. "Do you think the police are doing everything they can? I mean—two local girls. And did you hear about the twenty-year-old who went missing? That's the girl I saw, on Green Bay Road."

"Let it go, Abby. My hunch says that girl has nothing to do with Izzy or Sidney. You can't begin to imagine how many people go missing."

"How many?"

"Over twenty years in Chicago, hundreds of thousands."

"Not *hundreds* of thousands."

"Look it up. Most of them are cleared as noncriminal cases, but that still leaves a lot of missing people. Girls and women, especially."

"There could be a killer out there, preying on young women. They should have more leads."

"Forty percent of homicides go unsolved."

"But not in wealthy communities with parents pressing for answers, I imagine."

"They never found the person who murdered Harper McKibben, and she was a Winnetka girl, from a posh local family. Nannies and private schools, the whole bit."

I'd never heard the name, but it still sent a shiver through me.

"What happened? They just gave up?"

"They never really close a case like that, but they pretty

much stopped dedicating significant resources four or five years ago."

"Anything similar between that case and the Summit girls?"

"Not at all. The McKibben case was hardcore. Seemed like a pro. Rape, bondage, blunt head trauma, disposal in a ravine. She was probably picked up by someone she trusted after her family's private driver didn't show up at the train station. Middle of the day. No drugs or alcohol involved. No private home or motel. No witnesses."

"It's unbelievable what people think they can get away with. Where was the McKibben girl found, exactly?"

"Fourteen miles north of her home." That put the location only ten or so miles north of Pleasant Park. "But it was even closer to the train station where she was picked up—only a couple of miles. That's the thing about killers. They're generally stupid. They don't travel too far."

I thought of the Stephen Port case again—multiple bodies found dumped close to Port's apartment. Reckless behavior. An allegation of rape already on his record. And even so, he avoided the police's notice.

"I should know this stuff. Can you recommend a book?"

"I'll give you more than a book. I'll bring over my files."

"I don't think you should be showing me confidential files."

"What, you think I can lose my job twice? Anyway, it's all public. From back when I was studying to become detective." He laughed bitterly. "I'm surprised I haven't shredded it all. It's mostly FBI stuff, plus some Wisconsin and Illinois maps I marked up. Cluster maps. Kill sites. I'll have to dig it out of the basement. Half of the boxes down there aren't worth keeping."

It sounded like awful stuff. The last thing I wanted to read. "As soon as you get a chance," I said.

Robert's call had left me with an uneasy feeling I couldn't shake. I emptied the cheap vanilla ice cream carton of its last two spoonfuls of freezer-burned goop. I took the garbage out, came back and closed the apartment blinds, then checked twice to make sure the apartment door was locked.

I wasn't sure why I needed to see Harper McKibben's face, but I did. In the first online photo I found, she looked younger than the Summit girls by two or three years and childlike compared to Veronica Lovell.

Harper was short, with braces, heavy brown bangs, and splotchy skin, and in the news photo she was wearing a school uniform that was more traditional than Summit's. Dark green-and-black plaid skirt well past the kneecaps, white button-down blouse, white thick-cabled knee socks, penny loafers. The word *homely* came to mind—shame on me for thinking the word, as if it mattered, though for the detectives it probably did. One killer targets a certain kind of girl; another chooses a different one.

The same question in both cases—what drives a man to do something like that? Because it was a man, surely. I didn't need a criminology class to know how women more often killed: furtively, without a man's bold assumption that he'd never be caught. I couldn't imagine any person who'd want a career dedicated to parsing the contrasts. In any case, the Harper McKibben murder was already seven years old. No overlap, I told myself again, wondering if this should make me feel better or worse.

I felt a sudden, desperate impulse to drink. To call Robert to come over with his gruesome box of files and open up one beer after another until I understood why men did what they did or was drunk enough to stop asking. I was close—oh, so very close—and then the phone rang, and it wasn't Robert sensing my weakness. It was Curtis, calling as he'd promised.

He said, "I'd like to see Benjamin for three hours tomorrow, if that's okay. Starting at nine?"

"That's fine. I'll drop him and do some errands."

He reminded me, "And I wanted to follow up on the hypnosis idea."

"Yes. I talked about it with Benjamin after seeing your note. He seems curious, but he challenged me to go first."

Curtis laughed. "Has he been challenging you more in general, since the sessions started?"

"In small ways—very visible ways—he's behaving better. But in other ways, I feel like he's testing me, like he wants to prove something."

"Or maybe just to know something. Your son is a curious boy."

*Not usually*, I wanted to say. I'd spent my whole life with Benj without him being curious about anything related to my life.

"I'm willing to be hypnotized, if it will help," I said. "I was thinking we could do a session focusing on smoking cravings."

"You still have them?"

"Unfortunately."

Curtis hesitated. "Hypnosis isn't usually a one-off treatment."

"I know. I'm not expecting stellar results. It's just to show Benjamin there's nothing to worry about."

"I'll tell you what. We'll have you do a session, and then we'll back off and see if Benjamin feels confident enough to try hypnosis next week. Between now and then, I've got a long list of moving errands."

"Could I do any of the errands for you, during Benjamin's morning session tomorrow?"

The line went quiet for a moment.

"Boxes—I need two dozen, medium size. Printing. I already moved my good printer up to my father's house. That was a mistake. I'm in the middle of a big edit and I need to see it on paper."

I smiled. "I can do boxes. I can do printing."

"It sounds like we have a plan. And one more thing. You mentioned Benjamin's soccer accident. He had brain scans done? I'd like to see those, if possible."

Concussions could affect behavior. But Benjamin's concussion had happened a long time ago. "Do you think his accident caused a personality change?"

"Doubtful. The scans are just useful for looking for biological indications of certain preexisting disorders. Obviously, new scans might be a good idea, but let's hold off for now and see what we get from looking at the old ones. I've stepped away from active research, but my Menkoka Institute team gives me access to plentiful comparison data with my patients of his type."

"And what types are those?"

"We'll talk about that soon. Scans first. Then I have a few more tests I want to do."

# 25

The next morning, before inviting Benjamin into his office, Curtis gave me a thumb drive. I was at a Lake Forest print shop, about to do the chore he'd assigned me, when I saw a young male employee tape a hot-off-the-presses flyer in the front window: *Veronica Lynn Lovell, age twenty, last seen at the Dugout sports bar in Fox Lake, wearing long-sleeve white shirt, jeans, low-heeled black boots. Fairy tattoo on lower back.*

"The missing girl," I said.

"Yup," he said, uninterested. "Family is emailing them everywhere."

"How long will you keep it up?"

He frowned at me. "I don't know. Until she comes home safe, I guess."

"Right," I said. But I knew that wasn't true. If it was, there'd be missing-woman flyers all over the place. Robert had challenged me to look up the number of girls and women who went missing in Chicago, just for starters, and I had. The statistics were galling.

I hadn't been able to find numbers specific to the North

Shore, but I thought about what Willa had said—that she remembered a big upswing in girls and women going missing in our area and well beyond it, into southern Wisconsin, years ago. Local detectives probably wouldn't see Veronica Lovell's disappearance as part of that old trend, and why should they? No one even knew if Lovell's disappearance involved foul play.

The flyer had a scan code that took me to a Facebook page started by Veronica's family. I read posts left by many people who had seen Veronica more recently than I had, as well as friends eager to vouch that she wouldn't take off for no reason. She'd just accepted a park district job in Libertyville. She'd just signed a new lease at an apartment complex and she was going to be the maid of honor at a wedding in July. No one mentioned arguments with a boyfriend, which made me doubly glad I reported that when I phoned the police, just as one breadcrumb among many. But then I saw a post from someone who was among the last to have seen Veronica.

*We all went for drinks at the Dugout. Veronica was feeling sad because her boyfriend Justin left two days ago for his new job in Boston. I should have stayed, but V was talking to a bartender she knew and seemed determined to make a long night of it, at least through the karaoke. I'll never forgive myself for letting her stay.*

So, the boyfriend was in the clear. I scrolled until there were no more posts or comments to read. Twenty minutes had passed since I'd walked in the door and I hadn't even made my own copies yet.

I took the thumb drive and inserted it into the printer. Multiple file names showed up. I scrolled down through a list of what looked like surnames—clients, possibly. Curtis wasn't being cautious, handing over client info on a thumb drive. The crisis of caring for his father and closing his practice in a hurry may have made him more mistake prone. Then again, if he'd hired a personal assistant, he would have had to trust his documents to someone. I wasn't his employee, but I was the next best thing, a colleague who knew the rules.

I kept moving down the list alphabetically, pausing for a moment when I saw Rosso2024. That was our name. A file on Benjamin. I looked over my shoulder. How easy it would be to press Print and get a preview of conclusions Curtis might not share for several more days or weeks, in addition to notes he might never share at all.

But that wouldn't be right.

My finger hovered over the printer control screen. I pushed the down-arrow button. Rosso2024 disappeared and the alphabet continued, until I was at the very last file: WBL52024. It was the *What Boys Learn* draft he wanted printed. I selected two-sided copies, pressed Print, and took a step back, listening as the printer hummed, satisfied with my selection.

"You didn't have to clear your whole day," I said two hours later, as Curtis directed me to relax in the hunter-green armchair opposite his. "You already spent the whole morning with Benjamin."

"Quite all right. Besides, while I'm with you, he's occupied and there's less for me to pack tonight."

Movers were on their way. Curtis was only a little behind the schedule he'd promised his ailing father. He'd be putting half of his belongings in storage and the other half at his father's place, in Fond du Lac. While we were occupied, Benjamin could finish the job of emptying some filing cabinets and boxing up some old vinyl records in the main house.

"He really is helpful, you know," Curtis added.

"With other people, especially."

I didn't remind Curtis that I'd discovered Izzy's underwear precisely because Benjamin hadn't unpacked his own clothes. We hadn't revisited any of those specifics—the underwear, whether Benjamin understood how to treat women kindly, why he shouldn't communicate with Ewan. Those were still privileged conversations.

Curtis rested his legal pad on his knee. He gazed into my eyes. "You're sure you won't reconsider my offer to take Benjamin for one special day out?"

It was the first thing he'd asked when I walked in for my afternoon session, just after I handed him the print job along with a check I'd made out after depositing the loan from Willa, though he tried not to accept it. He hadn't given me a bill, but he hadn't said the sessions would be pro bono, either.

*We'll tally it up later.*

*Then this is a down payment.*

Curtis's new request confused me. Here was his manuscript, a reminder of his deadline problems. The movers were coming but he was still getting things boxed up. He'd mentioned his father twice since I'd sat down. There couldn't have been a less logical time for Curtis to take Benjamin to the pool, then to lunch, and finally to an auto show in Kenosha and perhaps dinner after that.

He insisted. "It's a fitting reward for all he's done."

"I think it's too generous. He's only helping you pack a little."

"By 'all he's done,' I meant compliance with our sessions. Good behavior should be rewarded."

"He's never been all that responsive to rewards."

Curtis smiled. "Then perhaps you've offered him the wrong kind."

I looked down at my hands, rubbing them in a manner I hoped appeared thoughtful. In truth, I was anxious about offending Curtis, given the way he'd prioritized my son's needs.

"With the heat wave coming, I thought I'd take Benjamin to the beach. I need to keep finding new ways to spend low-pressure time with him. But thank you."

A long silence followed. Curtis got up from his armchair and went around his desk, where he opened a drawer and busied himself with something—pulling out microcassette tapes, it looked like, until he'd found one that satisfied him. Even then, he kept delaying, his face averted. I *had* hurt his feelings. Since Sidney's death, I'd questioned the number of times I found myself missing our regular chats. But I also knew that attachment to clients—a "positive therapeutic alliance"—is both expected and necessary for client security and growth. There was no reason for me to question the bond Curtis had formed so quickly with Benjamin.

"How's the tea?" Curtis asked.

"It's good."

I took another sip—chamomile. Extra honey, and a little hot for a summer day.

"You seem nervous about this."

"I'm sorry."

"There's the apologizing again."

I settled deeper back into the chair. "I'm trying to relax. I really am."

"You don't have to try. You have to stop trying. That's the wonderful thing."

I took another sip and set the nearly empty cup on the pretty side table next to my chair, scooting farther back into the soft upholstery. "Okay, I'm ready now. No more messing around."

"Good." He came back to his own chair and squeezed the clicker in his hand. The lights dimmed. "This will be similar. It's really just a question of deep relaxation. You can compare this to a nap, or to a flow state. Whichever you prefer."

"A nap sounds easier. 'Flow state' sounds like I have to perform."

"That's a good insight. Then let's call it a simple nap, except you're still awake. We could also call it a deserved vacation."

I kept waiting for Curtis to start the hypnosis—not with a swinging pocket watch, of course, but with some other image sequence that spoke specifically or metaphorically to what I needed to do. Shed a bad habit. Discover some internal strength. Feel relaxed and without longing.

Instead, he focused on smoke, which surprised me. But maybe that was the point—to realize I could smell it, watch it—and all without needing to pick up a cigarette.

"You can still see it, spiraling upward?"

"Yes."

"And the smell?"

He kept talking in a calm voice that got lower and breathier by increments.

"Where are we, exactly?" I heard Curtis say. "What does it feel like, now?"

It was hard to focus on the words. A wave of sleepiness was washing over me. Clearly, this hadn't been the right day to try.

"Where are we, Abby?" he asked again.

"The river. The trail, next to the river."

"Very good," he said warmly. "What season are we in?"

"Summer. It's always summer."

"Always summer?"

"When things happen. Parties. Other things. It's warm. Like—body temperature. Like I'm swimming through the air. It's hot but it's dark so it's not too hot. Just . . ."

He interrupted, talking in that way that people do at parties when you're drunk and starting to nod off. You pretend to listen. You do your best. If only they'd understand.

"That's fine, Abby. Just follow the river . . ."

"The lights."

"The lights. That's fine, too. Are they reflections on the water?"

"No."

"Are they stars?"

"Headlights."

"Good, Abby—"

"Shit."

"You're okay, Abby."

"I'm not. I feel dizzy. I need to . . . be sick."

"It's okay to be sick."

"No, it isn't. And we have to leave. They'll leave without me. They know I'm underage."

"So, let's walk back slowly. Back to the—"

"But he's here. And he's angry."

"Your brother."

"He's angry because I didn't do what I was supposed to do. I see him looking at me. I'm trying to pull up my underwear but they're wet. I don't want him to see."

"Is this still your brother, or someone else?"

"And I still need to be sick. I know Grant's coming. But Ewan's trying to protect me. He has to. He will."

I opened my eyes suddenly, squinting to find a clock, but there was no clock.

Curtis looked up from behind the small desk at the back of the room, where he was scribbling notes with one hand and punching the button of an old-fashioned recording device with the other. The last time I'd looked, he'd been in the armchair opposite mine.

I asked, "Do we need to start over?"

My foot had gone numb from being tucked under one leg, and now I shook it out, wincing at the pins and needles.

"I'll be with you in a moment," he said, still writing.

There was nothing to look at. No artwork on the wall. No diplomas. The office packed up, or nearly so. I felt suddenly emotional—abandoned, or about to be. I jammed the heels of my palms against my eyes.

A heavy mechanical thunk echoed from beneath his desk. One of those old-fashioned Dictaphone devices. The last time I saw one was in my father's office. He'd record memos on the weekend, then bring the tiny cassette tapes to work for his secretary to transcribe.

"I've stopped the recording," he said. "Our time is up. Do you feel refreshed?"

No, I felt soggy and gross and vulnerable, like I'd been dragged along a muddy trail.

"But that was only a couple of minutes."

He looked at his watch again. "Close to an hour."

"Did I fall asleep?"

"No," he said pleasantly. "Did it feel like sleep?"

"Maybe."

"Well, that was the suggestion we both initiated, when we talked about 'nap' versus 'flow state.' You elected for the sensation of a nap."

"So you're saying I chose not to remember the last hour."

My stomach cramped. For a second I thought I might actually vomit. I looked around for the teacup, thinking a swig of liquid might settle my stomach, but Curtis had already cleared it away.

"You talked about being nauseated during the hypnosis—something brought on by a memory. I see that sensation has carried over. It'll pass, if you let it."

Why wouldn't I let it? He was saying the nausea was in my head—which I suppose it was. The nausea, and the anxiety, and a feeling of imminent doom.

I said, "I don't think I did so well. Something went wrong."

Curtis capped his pen and left the desk, taking the armchair opposite mine. "If you mean that you encountered some stressful memories, that's normal. We navigated them together, Abby."

"But I don't remember the navigating. Most people who get hypnotized have at least a vague recollection, so I've read—"

"Yes," he interrupted, firmly. "Most people. But then there are the other ten percent." He leaned forward, elbows on knees, fingers steepled. "I'm going to speak to you not as therapist to client, but as peer to peer. Psychology is a science. But it's also an art—"

"I missed something, Curtis," I interrupted, panic rising. "I feel like I was swallowed by the darkness and I missed something."

"You didn't miss anything." His tone sharpened. "If you keep saying that, you'll come to believe it. You were not unconscious, Abby. We were engaged in a dialogue."

"But I don't remember."

He looked disappointed. "I recorded the session. I'll transcribe it. You can request a copy."

I decided to take him at his word. "Yes, I'd like that copy."

"I'll get it to you in a few days." His expression softened. "I'm a lousy typist, remember? But I insist on doing the therapy notes myself. It helps me review and find new ways into the problem."

"Problem," I repeated back, hoping he'd explain.

"And anyway, it's better for you to have a little time to process first, before you read the transcript."

I didn't know how I could be expected to process what I couldn't remember. "You said there was a problem?" I asked again.

"Your guilt around the experience. That night with your brother, near the forest preserve. And the man named Grant. Driving down the road. Picking up the girl. The accident."

I remembered underwear and shoes, so I knew a girl had been in Grant's back seat, but I hadn't seen her. I found it hard to believe I'd tell Curtis about her, or the accident. I'd promised Benjamin that a person wouldn't do something or say something against his own will under hypnosis, but somehow, I had.

I said, "Most of the night was a blackout for me."

Curtis was studying me intensely.

I said, "Ewan could have helped Grant. At least he could have tried."

"But you feel guilty, too."

"I don't think so."

He lifted an eyebrow.

I said, "Maybe this was a mistake." As soon as I said it, I heard Izzy's voice. *Well, this was a mistake.*

"I thought we were going to work on cigarette cravings," I said.

Curtis's expression didn't change. I could fill in what he was thinking: *Your mind went where it needed to go.* But I didn't believe that. There was no part of me that wanted to think about Ewan and Grant again. No part of me that wanted to tell Curtis about that night.

"I'm not sure what I should tell Benjamin about this process," I said. "That was the whole point of this. I guess I could tell him it was fine. Strange, but fine."

"Tell him a lie, in other words, from your perspective?"

"Not exactly."

"But it's obvious. You didn't feel in control of the hypnosis. You claim not to remember everything we talked about. You seem tired, disappointed, anxious. Those aren't strong endorsements."

"Maybe I'm just one of those people who can't, who doesn't—"

"Nonsense," he said, with uncharacteristic harshness. "You

accepted hypnosis easily. You were almost *too* suggestible. To me, that suggests PTSD or dissociation. Maybe you're just regretting the potential consequences of what you shared."

*Consequences?*

"But therapy is a confidential space," he continued. "There's no reason for me to report anything you recounted—not to law enforcement or anyone else."

"I don't understand."

He pursed his lips.

"No really, what do you mean by that?"

"Let's forget about this session. I agree that it didn't go well, and without multiple sessions and a long-term plan, hypnosis is little more than a party trick."

"I don't want to forget about it." I moved to the front of my chair and sat up straighter, trying to clear the fogginess from my head. "I wasn't trying to be hostile. I'm just confused."

He pressed the tips of his fingers against his mouth. Like he was thinking. Judging. Deciding.

"Abby," he said after a moment, with perfect calm.

"Yes."

"This wasn't useful."

He opened a desk drawer, placed his notepad and pen inside it, and closed the drawer firmly.

"Do you still want me to bring Benjamin in again, tomorrow at nine?"

"Of course. I would never forget about my obligation to Benjamin."

"Thank you."

"Don't thank me, Abby."

I didn't know what that meant, either.

# 26

When I got home, I had good news in my inbox. Grove had selected me for the summer trial position: six weeks working with international students who were considering boarding school in the fall. That position could lead to a full academic-year job. Sister Lucretia told me they'd been waiting for the recommendation from Dean Duplass, but they'd decided my other letter of recommendation was sufficient.

*Other letter.* It couldn't have come from anyone other than Curtis. He'd vouched for me.

In practical, objective terms, I felt better. Less worried about money. Less certain that no school would ever hire me again. I had a place in a community. Benj and I both had a place.

But it all felt like someone else's good news—as if I'd received a phone call from a friend, and I was having a terrible day but I couldn't let my mood overshadow the friend's good fortune. Better to congratulate her, and to keep my dour mood to myself. If I ignored it, surely it would go away.

I could actually see myself, as if from a distant position in the corner of the room. I watched myself going through the motions of making dinner, starting a pot of jasmine rice, opening and closing the freezer, pulling out a fresh head of broccoli. I watched myself slice vegetables and move from place to place inefficiently, still remembering my old apartment's layout, forgetting where I'd put the five-spice powder or the sesame oil—all with a vacant expression and sagging shoulders. Is that how I really looked?

"Chicken and broccoli, extra spicy, two minutes!" I called out to Benjamin, in his room.

Is that how I really sounded?

It had to be the hypnosis, making me feel this temporary sense of distancing. I hadn't emerged completely from the trance Curtis had facilitated. Maybe I was, in fact, one of those people who is all too suggestible. Someone who wasn't tethered firmly to reality.

"I hope you're hungry," I said as I scooped rice. I set out forks and chopsticks, since sometimes Benj liked to use both. Instead of bringing everything over to the living room coffee table, where we all too often ended up, I served the food on the kitchen peninsula.

With perfect timing, he slid onto a bar stool just as I was setting bottles of sriracha and extra soy sauce within arm's reach.

"Smells good," he said.

He'd come to dinner wearing a red and navy blue–striped rugby shirt I didn't recognize.

"Thrift store?" I asked. "I don't remember that one."

He didn't look up. "Dr. Campbell gave it to me. The

person who lived in that separate apartment left a bunch of stuff behind. He was going to donate the clothes to Goodwill but he offered me some shirts."

I made a face. "He just gave away the person's shirts?"

"They moved out!"

I couldn't shake it off. The weird part wasn't just the clothes, it was the fact I didn't remember Benjamin leaving Curtis's carrying anything.

"This was today?"

Benjamin laughed, eyes still down on his food. "You were pretty loopy coming out of that hypnosis."

"I guess I should have let you drive, then."

"Yeah, I guess you should have."

I no longer wanted to talk him into trying hypnosis, but I didn't want to prejudice him against it, either. "It did feel a little strange, but mostly it made me sleepy." I looked down. "And hungry." I'd already inhaled half of the food on my plate.

He shook his head. "Still not into it."

"Okay," I said. "That's fair."

We were halfway through eating when the sound of a funky bass scale started up from below us. The vibrations rattled the glasses in the nearest cupboard. When a magnet fell off the fridge, Benjamin laughed.

"You've been stuck in your room a lot, lately," I said. "I never wanted you to feel like a prisoner this summer. Didn't you say David offered to teach you guitar?"

"Yeah."

"But you don't want to accept because he's too much of a stoner? Because I know that part already."

"No, because when I go down there, he usually has a few other guys over, and I don't like what they're into."

"Video games?"

"Nope."

I waited what felt like a reasonable amount of time. When he still hadn't volunteered any hints, I said, "I know David smokes a lot of pot. I hope they're not using other drugs down there."

Benjamin shrugged. "No. Just watching porn. I don't like it."

I couldn't tell if he was being honest or just telling me—a woman, his mother—what he thought I wanted to hear. Maybe he could read my skepticism because he added, "Dr. Campbell says that's good I don't want to watch porn with them. He says they're asking for problems."

"Because they're watching porn . . . in a group?"

"Watching too much at all. He says most guys watch so much that when they finally have real sex, like on a regular basis, they can't get it up without acting out what they've seen in movies. Like they don't even feel comfortable with a real body."

*A real body.* The phrasing seemed odd, but maybe he was just trying to avoid saying "a real woman" or anything non-inclusive.

"So," I treaded carefully, "Dr. Campbell is anti-porn."

"Pretty much. Not because he's worried that it's not fair to women or something. It's because he thinks men get messed up. They live in fantasyland for so long, they get addicted to fake sex. Sometimes they can't perform."

He must have noticed my eyebrows lift in response to the last word.

"I was trying not to say 'fuck,' Mom."

"Thank you." I took a few more bites. "Do you want to hear my opinion, as a woman?"

"Do I have a choice?"

"You do."

He smirked. "Fine, tell me."

"I think violence against women has been normalized by pornography. So even if it's one way for people to learn about sexuality, it comes with a cost."

The conversation had run its course. But he didn't look particularly irritated or nervous. He just looked like he knew this wasn't an extended conversation to have with his mother. We'd tried. We were getting somewhere.

"I'm just glad," I said, "that you're comfortable talking about sex with Dr. Campbell. It must be hard not to have men around to talk to about these things."

Benjamin's plate was nearly empty and he was shoveling fast.

"Change of subject," I said. "Grove sent me a contract for the summer. I'm going to sign, but they're already hinting this is a first step toward a fall job, and I want to know in advance. If you wouldn't consider going to school there, it's a no-go for me." I start listing pros and cons, telling him about Grove's state-of-the-art science lab and multiple foreign language options, including Japanese. "Eighty-five percent girls for now, even though they're recruiting boys heavily. Maybe the girl-to-boy ratio is a good thing?"

He cracked a smile. "Must be easier to get a prom date there."

"Okay," I said, feeling a bubble rise in my chest. "So,

you're not entirely against it. Not that I have the job yet. But that's good to know."

A cool breeze was blowing in from the open window. The stir-fry was tastier than anything I'd made all week, probably because I made an effort, using fresh broccoli instead of frozen. We were having the most normal conversation we'd had in weeks. The strange, dislocated feeling I'd sensed was dissipating, perhaps no more complex than hunger.

Benjamin went to the fridge and brought back two flavored waters without asking, as well as some paper napkins.

"Thanks," I said, setting down my fork. "I want to talk about one topic we haven't really settled, and I know it may be coming up in your therapy."

Benjamin stiffened, but I kept going.

"It's about my brother. I know it must be hard for you to understand why I throw out his letters and don't want you to communicate with him. But you need to know. Ewan did bad things that landed him where he is now. He's not a good person. But even more important, he won't ever *be* a good person. I'm sorry for not explaining that."

Still, nothing. Benjamin had never been good at offering or accepting apologies.

"If he'd played his cards right," I said, "he could have been out of jail when I was still a teenager. He could have started over. We could have finished growing up, together. But he's done even worse things in prison. Fights with other prisoners. Attacks on guards. He assaulted a dentist so violently the poor man was left with brain damage. Can you imagine that? Attacking a stranger who is only trying to help you?"

Benjamin ignored the question, eyes focused on his food.

He looked angry. Some of it was about Ewan, without a doubt, but I wondered if he felt resentful about other things we hadn't yet discussed. "Are you mad that I'm not letting you go out for a special day with Dr. Campbell, up to Wisconsin?"

He lifted his head, brow furrowed. "What the fuck?"

"He didn't mention it to you?"

From his smoldering expression, I could tell that he hadn't.

"You can't keep me home every goddamn minute," he said. "When I get a car, I'll go wherever I want. And I won't need a stupid therapist to take me. I can do what I want. I can visit anyone I want."

From below came another bass riff. Less charming this time.

"Visiting Ewan would be a bad decision. You can't do it now—not at your age—and I don't think you should do it later, either. Once he gets to know you better, he'll find ways to manipulate you. When you wrote him back—"

"Once. Just once."

"Thank you." I slapped my palm against the countertop, harder than I'd meant to. "At least you're finally admitting it!"

"I told him we moved, and I mentioned a few things about school. That's it."

"But that encouraged him, don't you see that? Protecting you from him is something I take very seriously. So when you wrote back to him, I felt . . . well, I guess *betrayed* is the word—"

"Betrayed?" Benjamin dropped his fork onto his plate with a clatter, sending grains of rice flying. "*You* felt betrayed? You invaded my privacy!"

Quietly I said, "Okay." I took a deep breath. "Okay. We

both need to calm down." I'd been holding up my hands, palms out, directing him to relax. I lowered them and waited, watching to see if he was calming down, too. "Benj, I was just a little worried—"

"You weren't 'a little' worried." He shaped the scare quotes with his fingers. Then he reached down for the edge of his plate, looking up to double-check I was still watching, and flipped it violently across the peninsula, missing me by inches.

I shrieked as the plate shattered on the kitchen floor.

He shouted, "You think I'm a murderer!"

I jumped off the stool. Flecks of food and sauce had sprayed onto my feet and lower legs. Broken ceramic everywhere.

He jumped up, too, but he was on the opposite side of the peninsula, clean and spared. His face was beet red, a thick cord of purple pulsing at his neck. "How am I supposed to live with someone who thinks I killed Izzy? Or Sidney?"

I stepped backward, palms up again. "I don't think you killed them."

"Or made them kill themselves! You're sick! You hate me! You shouldn't be my mother!"

My voice trembled. "Calm down, Benjamin."

"You just sent me away. To talk to a shrink."

I kept my voice low. "But you like him."

"Better than *you*."

"Benjamin, I love you—"

"Oh yeah? Like the way you still love your brother? The way you were willing to just cut him off and throw him away?"

I whispered, "Because he isn't a good person. He isn't safe."

"Well maybe I'm not good or safe."

"You're just parroting me now. This isn't a conversation."

"I didn't *want* to have a conversation. I don't forgive you. Not for thinking I'm a terrible person. Not for going through my stuff. Not for cutting me off from family. Not for making my life even worse than it already was."

He balled up his fists, closed his eyes, and screamed at the top of his lungs. The bass coming from below us stopped.

"Shhhhh . . ." I start to say, but it only set him off again.

"Don't fucking shush me!"

Someone could call the police. They could pick Benjamin up. They could use this as proof that he was violent. He'd be a suspect all over again. All because we lived in an apartment with a downstairs neighbor and thin walls. We weren't allowed bad days. We weren't allowed secrets. We weren't allowed mistakes.

I took another step back. He took a step forward. "I'm not a baby!"

I moved closer to the front door, tripping sideways over a big plastic jug of laundry detergent we kept against the wall. The doorknob jammed into my hip. I groaned, then cupped a hand over my mouth and thrust the other hand out, trying to keep Benjamin at a safe distance.

Things had been getting better, so I'd thought. But now I was leaning back with the memory of Ewan's fingers around my throat, lifting me off the ground. My own brother, choking me. Which wasn't even a major shock at the time. It was just something Ewan did. Something I'd had no choice but to tolerate, because I had no one else.

If anyone came knocking now, I'd need to explain. The shouts were from a movie. I flattened my back against the door, both hands up, ready to protect myself, while my brain turned cartwheels, trying to imagine how I'd protect *him* if the police came.

I held my breath until Benjamin stalked off to his bedroom. Even after the door shut, I was still holding it.

# 27

The week before we moved to Pleasant Park, about one year ago, Benjamin and I spent time driving around the North Shore, checking out apartment listings we'd seen on Craigslist. At one point, we'd taken a wrong turn down a small lane, all the way to its dim, shadowy dead end. The dense oaks overhead, never mind the long driveways leading to hidden, widely spaced houses on both the left and the right were proof that we were in the wrong place.

"Maybe the apartment is in someone's basement," Benjamin suggested, helpfully.

"These kinds of people don't rent out their basements," I said. "Trust me."

We turned around, and now we were heading east, squinting into the dazzling late-morning sun that was shining through the dappled leaves and painting the road in irregular splotches and stripes, the contrast so strong it made everything look briefly monochrome. I had just started to adjust my sun visor when Benjamin shouted, "Stop!"

A green MINI Cooper was in front of us—backing up,

actually, so fast they almost rammed our front bumper. Brake lights blazed red. A teenager stuck his head out the open driver's side window. Someone else was on the passenger side—another teenager, looked like. The driver steered far left and accelerated quickly, speeding away, and now we could see why. There was something in the road—the obstacle they'd driven around.

"They hit it," Benjamin said, sounding disgusted. "They hit it and now they're leaving it, like it didn't even happen. Rich assholes."

We both got out of the car and approached silently, with caution. The deer was dead, I thought. I hoped. But then I saw it lift its head, one eye rolling back, terror visible.

"It's suffering," I said. "I'll have to call someone."

I ran to the car, grabbed my phone, and stepped out again, shielding my eyes from the sun while I listened to the nonemergency police line's phone tree. I'd just gotten connected with a human being who told me I should have called 911 after all when I looked over in time to see Benjamin walking from the road's shoulder. He was carrying something large in one hand.

I hung up the phone.

He took another step into the road.

"Stop!"

He was standing over the deer. Arm raised. Rock still in his hand.

"Benj, no!"

I hurried over. The deer's ribs were moving in and out like a bellows as it panted, that one eye still rolled partly back, nostrils flaring as the deer tried to move its head enough to keep us in view.

Benjamin glanced toward me. "Why?"

I stepped closer and touched his arm. Reluctantly, he lowered it.

"Someone from the highway department will come out. They'll handle it."

"I was handling it."

"I don't want you to handle it."

I got on the phone again. I could still see him, crouched even closer to the deer. It was too tired to lift its head now, but its ribs were still moving.

"They've got someone on the way. Come back to the car."

"Look," Benjamin said.

"I don't want to look."

"You're going to miss it."

I didn't want him to spell out what *it* was. I didn't want to witness his gruesome fascination.

"One minute," he said.

I felt like I was walking in on a boy touching himself, discovering new things about his own desire.

Turning away, I asked him one last time. "Please come back to the car."

I hadn't thought about that day since it happened. I assumed my subconscious pulled it up into my dreaming brain now because I went to bed upset about the fight with Benjamin. In my dream, he was completely calm at first, the way he'd been that day with the deer. But when he wouldn't come back to the car, I approached him and reached out for his forearm again, wanting him to drop the rock and come with me. Instead, he turned and grabbed my wrist.

Dream Benjamin went from calm to raging in a flash, and I lifted a protective arm over my head, trying to shield myself from his arm and those fingers, long and white with tension, clutching the rock. My mouth was open but I couldn't scream. My back was bent, aching with the effort of leaning away, every muscle straining, my eyes so wide the tension wrapped around my skull.

I woke up, soaked in sweat. My back hurt. My head ached. The back pain was due to my shitty mattress. The headache was due to stress, or maybe a continuation of the strange grogginess I'd felt since the hypnosis session.

I found a better position and went to sleep again, and this time I dreamed I saw the UK killer, Stephen Port, gently carrying a body in his arms across a quiet road and into a cemetery, where he laid it down next to another body. At least I thought it was Port, just as I thought the bodies he was carrying were dead. I hoped they were, but I must have started doubting, because I followed him, needing to be sure. When I got closer, I saw that the eyes of both young men were open—if they were in fact men and not young women. Everything in the dream was changing. One victim's mouth was parted, pink tongue tip just visible. The other victim's nostrils were flared and quivering. Neither of them were dead quite yet, after all.

In the dream, I kept calling after Port, trying to get him to turn and look at me, but when he finally did, I saw it wasn't Port. I felt mad at myself for not recognizing him before—his dark hair, his gait, his posture. I looked into his eyes, feeling no shock, only deep sadness.

I looked around for a rock. I held it out to the killer. I said, "But no more after this. Then you have to stop."

# 28

The next morning, Benjamin climbed into the car, silent as usual.

"Buckle up," I said, gratified when he complied quickly, then annoyed at myself for being appeased by so little.

The whole morning was reserved for another of Benjamin's extra-long therapy sessions. I had a lot that I needed to tell Curtis—about last night's hostile outburst for starters. But when we arrived and tried his office door, it was locked. I walked to a side window that looked into the dim waiting room area, tapping on it with a key.

Curtis's car was missing from the gravel drive in front of the main house. I peeked in a window covered with a gauzy white drape, rang the bell, and listened for the sound of footsteps. I was heading to the mother-in-law apartment, in case he was in there packing or storing boxes, when I heard the crunch of wheels on gravel. I looked in time to see the white blur of his SUV speeding past the far side of the main house, where he generally parked it, to some place in the back, out of sight.

A minute later, Curtis advanced toward me, looking haggard. He was wearing jeans and a blue chambray shirt rolled up at the sleeves. His hair fell heavily over his forehead, uncombed and a little greasy. He raised a hand in greeting and strode at a diagonal, toward the office door. Key in lock. Door open.

From inside, he finally turned back, fastening a smile onto his shiny face.

"Apologies," he called out too loudly, the way you do when you're shouting across the lawn to a neighbor and don't want them to come any closer. "Emergency with my father. I drove as quickly as I could. Didn't want to keep you waiting."

Fond du Lac was two hours away. I hated to think of him speeding the whole time, just because we'd clogged up his schedule.

Benjamin said the first appropriate thing. "We can come back later, Dr. C."

"Nonsense. Come in." He gestured with a beckoning finger to Benjamin, then held up his hand, stopping me from stepping forward.

"If I could just speak with you first," I said. "Last night. Benj and I. We had a—"

"I'll ask him about it," Curtis said.

Benjamin had already slipped into the inner office, leaving Curtis standing at the half-open door, facing me.

"Please," I said. "Just a moment."

Curtis ran a hand down his shirt, smoothing it. He looked up, his smile a tense rictus.

"All right. What is it?"

"We had a conversation. The subject of my brother came

up. I said some things. And then suddenly, Benjamin got very angry."

Curtis was frowning now. "Suddenly?"

"Yes, he threw his plate and stalked after me. I thought . . ."

But there I stopped, trying to be as truthful with Curtis as possible. It wasn't so much that I thought Benjamin would physically attack me. Not at *that* moment. Not exactly. But someday.

"Is this a new behavior?"

"No. He used to lash out when he was younger. Thirteen, fourteen. I chalked it up to hormones." When Benj was younger and smaller, it had seemed like a pathetic temper tantrum. Now that he had the body of a nearly grown man, it was much more frightening. "In the last two years, he'd gotten his temper under control—until last night."

"It won't happen again," Curtis said.

*Won't happen again?* It was an odd thing to say. No therapist could make a promise like that.

"I hope not, but of course—"

"It won't. Put it out of your mind."

Maybe Curtis realized how illogical and overconfident he sounded because he adjusted his tone.

"I'll talk to him about it, Abby. Now, if you don't mind." He gestured toward the closed office door, behind which Benjamin was waiting. "We'll cover all of it, and if you have any other concerns, I'll be ready to listen. Come back in three hours."

I studied him again—the sweaty, floppy hair and rumpled shirt. The atypical jeans, one leg marked with a black grease stain. He looked like a man pulled in too many directions.

I was responsible for that, as one of the people pulling. Thank goodness we'd already dispensed with the idea of him spending a full day out with Benjamin.

"Can't I help you with anything? Walk your dog, at least?"

Curtis looked baffled.

I reminded him. "Sammy. Your dog?"

"Oh," he sighed. "I made the tough decision to turn him over to my ex-wife and my daughter, as long as I was within hailing distance of Green Bay."

Green Bay? I thought he'd only driven to Fond du Lac. No wonder he was exhausted.

"Is that where she lives now, your ex-wife?"

He sidestepped the question. "I'll be traveling too much this year and next. Father. Book tour. Sammy's better off."

He nodded—subject closed—but the fatigue on his face was plain.

"I hope you get some leisure time soon," I said.

"Yes, but I never like to leave things unfinished. I'll make the most of the time Benjamin and I have left."

He closed the door.

I'd just pulled into the Starbucks nearest Curtis's office, to pass the time before I was due to pick up Benjamin again, when my phone rang. I half expected to see Curtis's name on the caller ID, asking me to return early to retrieve my son. Maybe he'd come to the conclusion that he was too busy and tired for such a long session, after all.

Instead, it was Willa.

"Hi," I said. "Are you okay?"

"Fine. Did you hear the news?"

"No," I said, my mind going to the darkest place. Another victim. But Willa's tone was too bubbly for that.

"They've found the killer."

"They've arrested him?"

"They don't have to." She squealed with barely contained excitement. "He's already dead. He crashed his car, and police found stuff inside. Zip ties and blindfolds, his phone, with compromising photos of Isabella and Sidney. Wait, I'll hold the phone up to the radio."

The voices were too garbled to be decipherable. I waited for Willa to come back.

"He wasn't a high school student, was he?" I asked her.

"No. Twenties."

"Local?"

"No. Out of state."

The older man. Not from Pleasant Park, not even from Illinois.

"Any mention of the kind of car he was driving?"

"An MG."

Vintage car. *Tappets*.

Willa added, "Crumpled like a cheap little tin can. Any normal car would demolish a little two-seater like that."

By normal, Willa meant something big. She'd been begging me to buy a giant gas-guzzling SUV for years now, for "safety's sake."

"Get your radio on," she said. "They're still talking about him."

"That's okay, I'm looking up the details online. We should get off and I'll call you back tonight."

But she was too hyped to hang up. "They found more

of the drug that Izzy had an allergic reaction to. Tablets of something. *Cata*-something."

My blood froze.

"Catapres?"

"Maybe."

That was a brand of antihypertensive. I took the generic version. Clonidine. Catapres. Practically identical.

"It's common. Are they saying Sidney was dosed with the same drug?"

"They mentioned a 'benzo' something and opioids, not much but enough to do the job, ground into powder and dissolved in a bottle of prosecco."

"Geneva's sleeping pills and pain pills. But they didn't mention clonidine, in Sidney's case?"

"What am I, a pharmacist?"

"No. Sorry. I'm just trying to understand."

I pulled out the laptop I'd brought in order to look at the Grove summer contract. From the parking lot, the Wi-Fi recognized I'd been here before and connected automatically.

As Willa talked, I opened a window and located photos of the scene. None of the big outlets near us—the *Chicago Tribune*, or even the *Lake County News-Sun*—had run anything yet. But there was a Madison, Wisconsin, news article with a photo of a crashed car, an open trunk with duct tape, zip ties, garbage bags, several dark green fleece blankets, and a close-up of pills. I enlarged the photo on my screen. They weren't the same as mine. Different color, different letters on the tiny tablets.

I googled quickly and without satisfaction. At home, I could look up the drugs in my *Physician's Desk Reference*.

"Anyway, the sicko's dead now," Willa said. "Skidded off the road and rolled over. Good thing the evidence was in his car."

"Good thing," I said, still taking it all in. Evidence. Phone. Photos. Pills. And of course, they'd have no trouble matching his DNA, especially in the case of Sidney, if he'd been the one to have intercourse with her, as the news reports suggested.

I looked back at the article. The accident had taken place in Janesville, south of Madison—a hit-and-run, tire tracks clearly showed. A drunk driver possibly; the common tire brand and paint color left at the site of impact were both unfortunate, in terms of pursuing leads, although the police pledged to try. What did it matter? He was a bad man. The killer had been found—and not just found but stopped, forever.

I re-skimmed the Wisconsin article. *The driver was a former resident of a juvenile facility near Madison.*

I googled those last four words, and several facilities showed up. One of them had Menkoka in the title. The name rang a bell.

"I should get off," I said to Willa.

"Okay. Have a good one."

The first article had provided the driver's name—Christopher Weber. I searched and found another short item from a Wisconsin news outlet. Weber was twenty-two. He had aged out of a juvenile correctional facility for the mentally ill and was supposedly rehabilitated, but as a commentator noted, *Most of these kids are never fully rehabilitated.*

Ewan had been placed in a psychiatric treatment center at the age of eighteen, but he was moved to a regular prison at the age of nineteen. That's why Menkoka sounded familiar. It was the only facility of its kind in our area that worked with extremely difficult youth offenders. It was the place Ewan had spent some portion of a year—barely six months—prior to aging out.

I had twenty minutes left until I needed to get back to Curtis's office and pick up Benjamin. Still, I kept searching. Weber. Born in Milwaukee. One website already had his photo up. Handsome, clean-cut, sharp nose, small mouth, dark close-set eyes. Like they always said: *normal*. And a little too young to be a likely suspect in other crimes, like the murder of Harper McKibben.

All the proof of Weber's involvement was there, even zip ties and blindfolds—not that he'd used those things on Sidney or Izzy. But maybe he planned to use them on another victim, his next time.

Now there would be no next time. A more ideal resolution couldn't be imagined, and yet I didn't feel satisfied. I felt confused—by everything that made no sense, by everything that made *too much sense*.

And what about the missing girl, Veronica Lovell? She was never mentioned in any of the news stories. What about the possibility of other girls, other women?

I texted Robert: *Check the news. Police think they've found the killer. His name is Christopher Weber.*

I hit Send and then stared at my own text. *Think they've found.*

I wanted to take it back. To delete that word *think*.

# 29

I was ill at ease, sitting down with Curtis in his office a half hour later. He'd dragged in a third armchair and it was a snug fit.

"You're welcome to stay," Curtis said to Benjamin. "There's nothing I'm going to say to your mother that I wouldn't also be willing to discuss with you."

"I'd rather not."

Today we'd be doing the full debrief Curtis had promised and I knew that once we dug into the details, little else would seem to matter. Not wanting to forget, I rustled in the inner pocket of my laptop bag for the thumb drive, past several other thumb drives, coins, and lip balm. Curtis took it and slid it into his pocket with barely a nod, eyes still on Benjamin.

"I agree with Dr. Campbell," I said to Benjamin. "You're old enough to hear whatever he has to say." Benjamin was looking down at his hands on his knees. "Or, if you prefer, you could go sit in the car." I pulled the keys from my pocket. "Just don't—"

"Go anywhere," Benjamin completed my sentence.

"Obviously." He directed his irritated gaze to Curtis. "See how she doesn't trust me?"

Curtis smiled. "If she didn't trust you at all, I don't think she would have handed you a set of car keys."

When we were alone again, Curtis said, "Thanks for bringing me a coffee." He picked up the thin brown envelope of MRI scans. "We have a lot to cover—"

"I just heard some important news that will factor into Benjamin's case. They found the person who is responsible for the deaths of Izzy and Sidney. Evidently, he was a former inmate of an institute for troubled teens near Madison."

"I know," he said, taking a moment to adjust the coffee sleeve and take an agonizingly slow sip. "The car wreck happened in the middle of the night and the institute was informed by law enforcement within hours. They contacted all researchers and former staff, knowing we would get 'gotcha' calls from the media."

"So you worked there, at some point."

He looked at me with a bemused smile. "I've mentioned it to you. It's the preeminent institute of its kind in the country. My affiliation is in my bio. It's no secret, Abby."

"Were you . . . shocked?"

"Shocked that a psychopath would engage in high-risk behaviors that would lead him to drive his car off the road?"

"Another car was involved."

"I would assume that Christopher was a reckless and aggressive driver. Maybe he pissed somebody off. It's all part of the profile. Shall we get back to today's priority? Let the authorities be happy that there's one less recidivist psychopath in the world."

I was taken aback by both his brazen attitude and his word choice. "I didn't expect you to call him a psychopath."

"We both know it's a problematic word, but we also know what it means. Antisocial personality disorder *with psychopathic traits*. The institute wasn't founded to serve that kind of person per se, but that does represent our population. We do extreme interventions with violent, intransigent individuals. None of it is secret. We get a lot of press."

His sober expression failed to mask his pride.

"I know you can't talk about him in detail, because he was a client. But why do you think he picked Sidney and Izzy? Was it just about sex and then his plans went awry, or do you think he planned to kill them from the start?"

"Theoretically? People like Christopher explore fantasies and decide when they're ready for fantasy to become reality. We often see that with serial killers."

"The newspapers didn't label him a serial killer."

I was still resisting that phrase and all of its tawdry associations.

Curtis shrugged. "He died young. Two known victims. With more time there would have been others."

He was speaking matter-of-factly, just as Robert spoke about criminals. It bothered me more than it should.

"Anyway," he said, "it's a common pattern. Those first flawed kidnappings. The break-ins that stop short of murder. The not-quite rapes, especially in the case of a tentative individual without a lot of real-life experience, where women are involved. Even for those killers motivated by sexual gratification, there's a lot of variety."

I didn't want to know about all that "variety"—didn't

want pictures forming in my head that might never go away. I only wanted to understand about Christopher Weber and how his and Curtis's paths had first crossed.

I said, "I didn't know you work with incarcerated psychopaths."

"*Worked*, for the most part. Past tense. I planned to mention the institute today, when we go over Benjamin's test results. But he's not a good candidate for the youth treatment center. He wouldn't be admitted, because he isn't already in juvenile detention. The institute only has room for a few dozen—"

"*Benjamin?*"

Curtis tapped a finger against the MRI envelope. "Abby."

I'd been holding a nearly empty paper coffee cup between both hands, squeezing so hard I dented it.

"Talking with parents is the hardest part," he said. "But the pain is usually short-lived, and it's followed by relief, because the good parents—the ones who show up for appointments at all—already know. They may not know the correct terms to use. But they know."

"Aren't parent interviews essential to the diagnosis?"

"Benjamin supplied more than enough information. He was willing to be frank about school fights, in particular, as well as the impulses he has felt but not acted upon." He paused, letting me absorb.

"Impulses," I said.

"Now, Abby. We all have impulses."

I sat back, directing myself to say less, to listen and be patient.

"I needed to earn Benjamin's trust and get to the point

where he could report with some degree of honesty. And I needed to build up the timeline. I knew you'd feel better if I relied on more than just the PCL: YV."

I knew the sequence of steps, all of the boxes that needed to be ticked. It wasn't enough for a child to exhibit grandiosity, pathological lying, failure to accept responsibility. It wasn't enough to know a child took excessive risks or constantly required stimulation.

"But he isn't on probation or parole," I pointed out. "He hasn't had multiple brushes with the law. That's practically a requirement of the diagnosis you're suggesting."

"Not multiple brushes," Curtis agreed. "Not *yet*."

I thought back to Ralph King's certainty that I should get Benjamin into therapy, his confidence that we needed to "shape the narrative." But Curtis seemed to be heading toward a narrative—a specific diagnosis—that would look very, very bad, if a prosecutor ever discovered it.

"I know what you're thinking," Curtis said. "You want to know the truth about your son, so you can guide his development. But you don't want him to be stigmatized."

"Stigmatized is the least of it."

"But we both know that because of his age, we can only say so much. That's a good thing."

My distress must have shown on my face, because he tried again to reassure me. "You were frustrated with the session you had with Dr. Adelman because she didn't give you hard answers. I'm guessing she would have mentioned conduct disorder."

"She wasn't ready to use that label."

"Or the one that sometimes follows, yes, if the behaviors

persist?" Antisocial personality disorder, he meant. "Don't worry. I'm not ready to use that label, either. Certainly not on any forms of documentation that could surface easily in the event of a negative future event."

*Negative future event.*

I nodded, if only to urge him to go on. I needed to know everything. Once I knew, I could help. *We* could help. If I didn't believe that, I'd chosen the wrong profession.

"Let's continue," Curtis said. "We're not talking fate here. But we are talking about a poorly stacked deck." He opened the flap of the MRI envelope. Inside were the images of Benjamin's seven-year-old brain, the one I'd thought was perfect, aside from a soccer concussion. "Early onset is a key element of accurate diagnosis, and we do see signs in Benjamin's scans, unfortunately."

He pulled out one of the images and began pointing to various features. I'd never studied this area of neuroscience. They didn't have MRI scanners in the high schools where I'd always planned to work.

"We can see reduced volume in the amygdala, just to start." He paused to see if I was still following. "You're quite lucky to have these scans as a baseline."

Lucky? I felt sick.

He said, "I thought you'd feel better seeing the biological origin. It can make a parent feel less directly responsible."

"Curtis, I *am* responsible. He has my genes. He was shaped by the fetal environment within my womb. I didn't beat him or ignore him or warp him in some other despicable way, but I *made* him."

Never mind, I thought, that any seven-year-old's brain

would have been shaped by nature *and* nurture. The perfect parent might have modified seemingly innate tendencies. More enriched learning opportunities. More socializing with others. More love. More discipline. Better food. Better toys. Brighter sunshine. All of it!

"Let's talk about his assets," Curtis said after a respectful delay. "In many ways, Benjamin is the very opposite of my Menkoka research subjects. Goal setting, for example. Benjamin excels at that. Intelligence: no problem there. Impulse control, however . . ." Curtis held out a level hand, seesawing it. "Sometimes very strong, sometimes not. But that's something we can work on."

I was waiting for more good news, trying to hold back from taking my own turn listing Benjamin's positive behaviors. He was protective, sensitive, and dutiful—at times! And yet we were here because of the other times. Those brief, regrettable moments that could change a life's trajectory.

"Has Benjamin told you something specific that the police need to know?"

Curtis looked taken aback.

"You're upset."

*Of course I was upset!*

"The answer is no," he said.

I wanted to believe him. There was no reason *not* to believe him.

Except, of course, for the rules of confidentiality. The question wasn't whether Benjamin had been a threat—to Izzy or anyone else. From Curtis's logical and legally defensible perspective, the question was whether Benjamin was a threat *now*.

Curtis smiled, and this time, it was a relaxed smile, open and sincere, even ebullient.

"Abby, you can't believe how frustrating it is, working day in, day out with psychopathic boys who are . . . may I be frank? . . . stupid and impulsive. They don't try to evade most negative consequences, because they simply don't care. Sometimes, you can reward them—a candy bar here, a video game there. But you can't punish them. To find a young male subject with psychopathic traits who will actually *listen* and *learn*, that's nothing short of remarkable."

I sat back in my chair, stunned.

*Psychopathic traits.* We might as well have been using the single-noun term. *Psychopath.* My son, a psychopath.

Not yet a psychopath with a long criminal record. Not a psychopath whose every behavior was a flagrant violation of societal norms. But that was only on account of his youth. With time, there'd be more opportunities for bad choices and even worse influences.

In a shaky voice, I said, "I'm grateful for your candor, Curtis. I really am. But I thought you weren't prepared to apply that sort of label."

"I didn't say *antisocial personality disorder with psychopathic traits*. We already agreed that's not a diagnosis for anyone under eighteen."

"But . . . traits."

"Traits!" he called out. "Traits! Traits! It's not such a scary word. It shouldn't be." He was still smiling. "I'll be honest, Abby. Many of my clients frustrate me. I can't cure them, given the nature of the pathology. I can't sufficiently mentor or mold them. At Menkoka, two-thirds of our released juveniles commit crimes again, and we're supposed to be happy, because it's not the ninety-eight percent recidivism we see in the general psychopath population. But that still means the *average* Menkoka resident is an abject failure."

I tried to keep focusing on his words, instead of rushing ahead into the future—trying to determine how we'd find a new therapist, wondering what sort of interventions had been shown to work, if there was a developmental window that closed during adolescence, and how I could make the most of the time left.

"Benjamin is different," Curtis said, pulling me back to the present. "Give him a chance, Abby. Give *us* a chance."

"I'll need some referrals. I have to help Benjamin transition to another therapist he trusts. I'm indebted to you, for all you've done. But you're leaving town soon, to be with your father and work on your book."

"Yes, *but*. Let me think on it, Abby."

Curtis's lengthening silence told me that our meeting was finished. No more diagnostic revelations. No more claims for the efficacy of treatment. I stood up, feeling numb, and only remembered as I neared the door that Benjamin had no idea the police had found their man.

"I'll show him the news about Christopher Weber when we get home. I'll tell him it's all over. But he might need to process it all with someone. Will you talk to him, tomorrow?"

Curtis nodded. "Of course. But you have to realize—he won't be half as relieved as you are. Benjamin always knew he was innocent. *You* were the one who doubted."

# 30

The day after Curtis talked to me about Benjamin's diagnosis, I met with Dean Duplass, who said the school would be giving me two weeks of compensation as an apology for my confusing dismissal and for replacing me as the summer skills counselor. That afternoon, I returned my signed contract to Grove and got an email outlining the summer schedule. The killer had been found. The police didn't seem interested in talking to Benjamin anymore. My life was being mended, one piece at a time. So why did it still feel so tattered?

On Friday, I drove Willa to a Home Depot so she could look for a replacement screen door for her mobile home. When news about the criminal investigation came on the radio, we stopped chatting to listen. The reporter explained that Weber's car was frequently spotted around the North Shore. Briefly, the twenty-two-year-old worked as an assistant in a mechanic's shop, where he spent his free time fixing up the ailing MG he'd bought for a few thousand dollars. Then he got a stint as a pool and tennis club janitor, but only for about six weeks.

"At Dartmoor," I said to Willa. "I don't know why they won't name the club. That's where he worked. That's where he met the girls."

The newscast carried on with the expected quotes from the few people who were willing to talk about Weber—how normal he was, how unexceptional.

"Yada yada," Willa said. "You said Sidney's mom had a pill problem. Maybe he was her dealer and that's how they met. And if he worked at the pool, he could have delivered them right to her lounge chair. Nice, right?"

"Maybe." I sighed. "But then again, if he had such a good supply of fun drugs, what was he doing giving Izzy something so weak? The pill she took was a mild sedative. They're not common date rape drugs. Unless he knew she had that allergy—and how would he?—he would have tried something different."

The news had transitioned to music. Willa turned it off, then twisted further in her seat to face me. "What are you talking about?"

"I'm not saying he wasn't in the motel with her. I mean, he took inappropriate photos. And he was obviously thinking of doing something violent, something that required subduing his victims, given all that stuff in his car. Wouldn't he have given her something stronger, if he meant to knock her out?"

"What's gotten into you?"

"Nothing."

Willa narrowed her eyes and pursed her lips, deepening her wrinkles. "So what if he didn't plan to knock her out? Maybe he just wanted to relax her enough to go along, and he thought she would, unlike that other girl."

"But isn't that a different criminal profile?"

"Different criminal *profile*? What are you, now—one of those characters on those TV crime shows, with the wall of pictures and string?"

"You watch those shows, not me."

"That's right. I do. And let me tell you—some guys tiptoe into the shallows first. So maybe Izzy was the shallows."

"Okay," I said, trying to ground myself again. Dr. Campbell had said the same thing about a hesitant and inexperienced killer like Weber. He hadn't refined his methods yet. On top of that, he'd chosen a compliant victim. He might have thought he didn't need strong, fast-acting drugs, necessarily. "You're right. It makes sense."

Willa touched my shoulder. "Abby. What's up with you? Everything all right at home?"

# 31

The Weber news should have removed a burden from Benjamin's shoulders, but he seemed to struggle under an even heavier weight now. He roamed the apartment with an awkward, stiff posture, like he was expecting someone to jump out from a closet. He was neither hot-tempered nor sassy nor completely silent but something else entirely—cautious and brooding. Like he was still waiting for the other shoe to drop.

I knew that feeling. It summed up most of my adolescence.

Two days had passed since I found out about the identity of Chris Weber. One day had passed since Curtis spoke to Benjamin about Weber privately. After I got home from shopping with Willa, Robert stopped by to casually congratulate Benjamin and ask if he wanted to go for a drive—something I encouraged, just in case Benjamin wanted to confide something to Robert that he wouldn't say to his own therapist. None of it persuaded Benjamin to open up. He returned to his bedroom, telling me to let him know when dinner was ready.

"Not pizza, if I get a vote," he said, just as I'd pulled the Giuliano's menu flyer from the fridge.

"You want to make some pasta and homemade sauce, together?"

"Not really."

But he didn't sound rude about it, just fatigued.

Since he was stopping by, Robert had brought the box of criminology files he'd mentioned, so we could look through them together. I grabbed two beers from the fridge and told him we could make tacos, the boring kind. Ground beef, hard-shell tortillas, a packet of spices.

"Nothing boring about that," Robert said. Would I ever date someone with more refined tastes?

I took out the ground beef and put it inside a Ziploc and then into a pot of cool water to defrost, since our microwave's defrost function always ended up cooking the meat into a rubbery gray mess. Back in the living room, I started to pull the files from the box and lay them out on the coffee table. "Just from what I've read online, I've started to have nightmares."

"You still want to look, then? The Mayfield and Scarlatti cases are closed."

"But what about Harper McKibben? What about Veronica Lovell? What about all the other women who are still missing?"

Robert whispered, "*Tell me you haven't gone nuts. You're not still worrying about Benjamin.*"

"Of course not. Not in the way you think."

"Thank god, because he wasn't even born when half this stuff happened."

I rolled my eyes. "I know that, Robert."

"Then?"

"Let's just say my view has expanded. The world's a more violent place than I thought. It's the world in which Benjamin will be living and I need to understand it."

That seemed to satisfy him. I would have told him everything if I had more than just a feeling, too shadowy to pin down.

"Suit yourself. As long as you skip the photos, this stuff is actually pretty dry. Half of it is numbers and tables and stuff."

Robert started with a simple graph. "This is the first one that got me thinking."

The graph showed the changing behavior of over fifty known serial killers over time, according to how many victims they had murdered. One line tracked the distance killers had traveled from home in order to kill—never very far. The other line tracked the distance killers had traveled to dump bodies—an average of fourteen miles. The more victims a killer had—the longer he'd killed, in other words—the less he was willing to travel in order to kill or dump.

"It's like I've told you. Killers get lazy," Robert explained. "And cocky. The longer they're not caught, the more they become convinced they never will be. And sometimes they seem to take extra chances on purposes, like it's fun. You know you see serial killers taunting police in stupid movies? It's not stupid. Many of them do that. They seem to need stimulation, whatever the cost."

"So, the FBI already has that figured out."

"Yeah, but we don't have the same sort of stats and graphs for every part of the country. And we can't pin down the patterns for the cases where we don't know the killer—or even if a woman *was* killed. Add in unsolved crimes and missing women, and everything gets a lot more complicated."

He showed me some maps he'd made on his own for murders from our area, confirming the same general patterns found among well-known serial killers. In cases that seemed connected, even if the killer was not identified and arrested, the pickup and disposal sites got closer and closer over the lifetime of the person assumed to be responsible.

"How about these?"

I pointed to some other associated dot pairs that got farther apart over time.

"Those are cases where the early crimes—especially the very first killings—are haphazard, less planned, carelessly executed."

"Like Christopher Weber's."

"We'll never know if he would have gained enough self-control to become more careful over time."

"So some of them do become more careful."

"A smaller subset, and obviously, we know the least about them, because in many cases, they're never caught."

I saw a margin notation for Harper McKibben along with the color-coded dots indicating where she was picked up, not far from her home, and where her body was found.

"You didn't mention that she was part of some serial killer spree."

"Not an identified one. But if she was a first, she was a surprisingly clean and disciplined first. If that person kept killing—as a few FBI reports have hypothesized—it just means that particular killer did an even better job later."

"Better how?"

"Better choice of victim. The person is never missed. Or better choice of disposal site. The victim is reported missing but never found. Either way, it can't get definitively logged as a homicide."

A half hour later, I checked the meat. It was still frozen. Screw it, I'd order pizza after all, as long as they would deliver. I got us two more beers.

"Now I understand," I said to Robert. "You really wanted to be a detective."

"Yes, I did."

"I hope you haven't blown your chance. I didn't realize how many monsters are out there."

"Downside of being a cop. You know the worst that people can do. It gets in your head."

I studied the maps some more.

"Willa mentioned to me that we seemed to have an increase in murders of women during her lifetime. I was a kid, so this was maybe twenty-five or thirty years ago at most. Late '90s onward."

"Not a lot of people pick up on that. I think it's one of those tunnel vision things. For a long time, people assumed your average quiet white guy wasn't the kind of person who would murder. But then we had the golden age of serial killers—'70s through about 2000—and the thinking reversed. The quiet white guy became the prime suspect."

"Right. So?"

"And in our area, it wasn't just the quiet white guy. It was the gay loser who targeted vulnerable young men. We had John Wayne Gacy, doing his clown thing in the '70s—that was the Chicago area. We had Jeffrey Dahmer, the Milwaukee Cannibal, in the '80s up until '91. These guys were weird as hell and dumb as stumps. Only people dumber were the cops who didn't catch them.

"Both men died in '94. Two terrifying murderers, out of everyone's hair. Before, detectives didn't understand about men preying on men. But after Gacy and Dahmer, that's what they started looking for, if they looked for anything at all. Like I said, a lot of people thought the age of serial killers was over."

"So now there was a new kind of tunnel vision?"

"Yeah, and a lot of self-congratulation—like police and FBI finally knew what they were dealing with. Which only continued in the 2000s. Like Willa told you, there seemed to be more killings of local women in the late '90s, but then that wave passed, too. Supposedly."

"I get the sense you don't think it really passed."

"I think we started finding fewer bodies. And the ones we found didn't seem connected in ways anyone could figure. But maybe that's because we weren't dealing with killers who were as dumb as Gacy and Dahmer."

"That sounds ominous."

I turned over the pizza flyer to use the blank side on the back for scribbling notes. "Where's that table that shows the dates victims disappeared?"

He dug through a folder and pulled out several photocopied pieces of paper. "Which counties you want?"

"For Illinois, Lake, and McHenry. For Wisconsin, whatever is just north of there."

He pulled out three tables: Kenosha, Racine, and Walworth. "And I'll give you a couple extra counties farther west. Not a lot of disappearances, because the populations are smaller, but an increasing number of disposal sites, starting in . . ." He flipped through loose pages until he'd found the right one. "Maybe twenty years ago."

It was going to be a bigger job than I thought. I fetched my laptop and opened a spreadsheet.

I said, "These were disposals of bodies from . . . ?"

"Closer to us. North Shore and north to the border. Some from Kenosha-Racine."

"And where did the disposals cluster, before then?"

"Closer to where the girls and women were picked up."

"So over time, bodies were being disposed farther away, which isn't part of the national trend or anything like that graph you first showed me."

Robert laughed. "Maybe gas prices were going down."

"Well, were they?"

A minute later he looked away from his phone and back at the papers spread across the table. "No, they were going up. At least until 2009, gas was a little cheaper, but then it started climbing again."

The maps were a confusing mess of multicolored dots, the margins crowded with names and codes. I needed to see it all chronologically, organized in a way I could re-sort each time new data was added, until the patterns became clearer.

It took longer than I'd expected, the two of us busy using Google Maps and paper maps, me telling Robert to pause as I sorted rows and made room for another girl last seen at a highway rest stop, a girl gone missing from a party held on a farm, a girl who'd gone canoeing with someone she met in a campground, a girl who'd called a rideshare service but was gone by the time the driver arrived. And those were just the ones who'd later be found dead. We had to consider the ones who had never been found, whether the cops considered their cases open or closed.

Robert put the ground beef back in the fridge and called for pizza. The pizza came. Benjamin ate in his room, watching YouTube videos, and I didn't dissuade him because I didn't want him to ask what we were doing.

Over the next hour, I made additional spreadsheets, focusing on the few cases in which the killers were known.

"Let's add Veronica Lovell, too."

"That seems like bad luck."

I added her hometown and the place from which she'd disappeared: twenty-eight miles apart.

Robert said, "We don't know the 'point of fatal encounter,' if there even is one in her case. All we know is where he snatched her—Fox Lake. If the person was being careful, he'd live more than three miles from there."

"Doesn't narrow it down too well, does it?" I drew an imaginary circle with my finger.

"The more careful he was, the less it narrows it down. The radius just gets bigger and bigger."

"So the question—if you were looking for her—is to figure out how careful this particular man is." I studied the first graph he'd shown me and the spreadsheets we'd made together. "You told me most killers get less careful. But it looks like in our area, they got more careful starting in the early 2000s and really careful from at least 2010, at least in terms of how far they traveled to find a victim and dispose of the body." I looked at the spreadsheets again. "What changed?"

"Netflix?"

I elbowed him.

"I'm not kidding. Between streaming true crime and using the internet, it's easier to learn how to avoid getting caught."

"It *should* be easier. But you already showed me. The most notorious serial killers get more reckless over time. Except, not lately." I pointed to the nearest map on the table. "Not where we live."

# 32

On the weekend, Curtis had no sessions planned with Benjamin. Their final session would be on Monday. I had mentioned to Curtis that we'd be attending Sidney's funeral over the weekend, and I mentioned it again to Benjamin on Friday night, after Robert left.

"Perhaps something to discuss, on your final day with Dr. Campbell. Thoughts, feelings."

"*Perhaps*," Benjamin said, imitating me facetiously. But then his tone changed. More quietly he said, "*If* I go to the funeral."

"I think you should."

"Sidney wouldn't have come to mine, if I'd been the one who died, and Izzy—no way."

I got up and took my plate to the sink. "Wow. You really didn't like Izzy, did you?"

"I did like her. I liked her a lot."

I turned back toward him, surprised by the sincerity in his voice.

"She wasn't full of shit, Mom. She would have hated

funerals, especially the kind where people who don't even know you come all dressed up with those big sunglasses, getting weepy and putting on a show. I'm sure she hates the teddy bears and shitty cheap stuff people are leaving next to the Summit sign. She hated people who bragged about where they were going to college or for their next fancy family vacation. She hated liars and she hated . . . she hated . . ."

He stopped mid-stammer. I averted my glance discreetly, not wanting him to jump up and hurry away.

"You're right," I said, turning back toward the dishes, wishing I could hug him but knowing he wouldn't let me. "That's the impression I got of Izzy, too."

Benjamin was home, still sleeping in on a Saturday morning, when I hit the secondhand boutique in downtown Pleasant Park that had the best selection of affordable work clothes. I wanted to look right for my Grove job—a little dressier than I'd been at Summit, at least until I saw how the other teachers dressed. Maybe I'd find some black flats that would double for the funeral and for work. I had to get used to leaving Benjamin on his own. After all, I'd be occupied at Grove for the next six weeks. He wasn't a child anymore. I needed to trust him.

I was on the way home, listening to public radio, when the top of the hour news announced that Veronica Lynn Lovell had come home. She was alive and well. Shaken but well.

I ran in the door to turn on the television, hoping to get more details. I was aiming the remote when Benjamin came out of his room, scratching his taut midriff, and headed toward the bathroom. Over his shoulder he called out, "Missing girl, right?"

"How'd you know?"

"I just read it online. Freaky story."

"What's freaky about it?"

But he was already behind the bathroom door, and I gave up on the television and opened my laptop instead.

Veronica had fallen sick suddenly in a bar many days after I'd seen her on Green Bay Road. She didn't remember the fact that she'd called an Uber and failed to meet it outside or that she'd accepted a ride from someone else who came to her aid. She woke up once in the car, where she was laid out in the back seat, but the only thing she remembered was a calm voice from the front promising she was almost home.

She woke blindfolded, still dressed, in a house or apartment. No memory of being carried inside. No sounds of neighbors. When her blindfold was removed, she saw black garbage bags taped over the windows, a wall-mounted television, a queen bed with gray blankets that crinkled due to the plastic sheeting that was under the linens.

At no time did the stranger touch her. He didn't drug her again, either, if he'd been the one to do it at the bar. He entered the room only once each day, with a balaclava over his head, loose black clothes that obscured his build, and disposable blue latex gloves over his hands. He told her she was being monitored by a camera around the clock. The room had a mini-fridge stocked with sandwiches and water, with access to a small, adequate bathroom with motel-type soap, paper towels, and no windows. The TV was hooked up to several streaming services. The remote, like the bed, was plastic wrapped. When the man spoke, he used a high, artificial voice that didn't sound like anyone she knew.

The most frightening moment, Veronica's parents relayed in a clip of a TV news report, was when the unknown man told the twenty-year-old she was being moved to a new location. She thought she was being trafficked somewhere else, into the hands of someone less gentle or conscientious. For a long time after she was brought out to the car, blindfolded and with her hands tied, she could hear a vacuum running in the house or apartment they'd just exited, and once he entered the car, she could smell bleach.

Then they started driving. At least an hour. The car stopped. The man let her out onto the road shoulder, still blindfolded.

"The plan changed," he said. He snipped the plastic ties at her wrist and told her she could count to one hundred, then take the blindfold off.

The reporter asked Veronica's mother, "Do you believe Christopher Weber was the one who took her?"

*Weber's car was a two-seater MG*, I thought to myself. The news story had already described Veronica reclining in a back seat. On top of that, Weber was dead.

But I was criticizing too soon. The reporter prompted, "Not the one who let her go, because Weber died days before her release. But could he have left her with a partner, and that's why the plan changed, once Weber crashed his car?"

"She thinks it was all the same man."

The reporter looked disappointed. "But she couldn't see him."

"But she could hear him. She could smell him."

The reporter started to turn away, ready to wrap up her commentary, when the mother added, "That's the only reason we're talking about this. Because whoever did it is still out there. People should know."

The reporter asked Veronica directly if she had anything else to share. Had the man said anything else before driving away? The mother threw a cautioning glance at her daughter, like she didn't want her to answer. But Veronica, who hadn't spoken once during the interview, lowered her mouth toward the microphone. "Kittens must catch their own mice."

"Kittens?" the reporter asked.

"That's what he said."

# 33

Izzy's family had chosen to have a small, family-only funeral shortly after her death, but Sidney's family waited. Some people said it was because they refused to bury her until the coroner had returned every last organ and tissue sample. Or maybe it was only that Geneva had left Pleasant Park for several weeks, perhaps to dry out somewhere and regather her strength.

Either way, the delay and desire for belated resolution resulted in a funeral so large that it was nearly impossible for anyone but family members to gather close enough to hear the priest or speakers who followed. The cemetery, located just a few blocks from downtown, was bordered by quiet streets on all sides, and every one of those streets was backed up with black town cars restlessly circling until the service ended.

I had walked from home, aware of the parking challenges, and now I remained at the back, head bowed, trickles of sweat running down my spine, my long-sleeved black blouse clinging to my damp back. I hadn't known how to dress for a sweltering funeral. Some people had brought umbrellas for shade rather than rain—a good idea that hadn't occurred to me as I'd hurried out the apartment door, asking Benjamin for the third time if he wanted to come along. He hadn't.

I told myself that was okay. You couldn't force a kid to grieve publicly. You couldn't force a kid to grieve privately, for that matter. Even now, he expressed only anger at the girls, but especially Izzy, and then only tersely, blaming her for falling for a guy like Christopher Weber. I believed, now, that he missed her. He was just mad at her for being dead. It was one way to care—being angry. It was better than feeling nothing.

Standing apart from the crowd, so far from the grave site I was nearly backed up against the wall that bordered the cemetery's western boundary, I thought about Sidney's interest in psychology and imagined how she might have started talking to Weber at the pool, where he'd briefly worked. The latest news reports had hypothesized about Weber's agile deception as the key to attracting two underage girls, but I felt almost certain Sidney was drawn not to any lie but to the truth—that he had a criminal record and a troubling but intellectually interesting diagnosis. I imagined him striking up a wounded pose, lamenting his inexperience with women, due to the years he'd lost to incarceration. She might have convinced herself that she could cure him of any residual antisocial tendencies, maybe even keep him from taking the quick on-ramp to incel misogyny. The last day of her life, when she let him into her house, she must have thought she was helping him, still.

I imagined him arriving with a sob story—that Izzy no

longer wanted to see him, which would have made Sidney feel guilty, since she was the one who'd warned Izzy not to become romantically entangled with a psychopath. Or maybe he fed her an even less factual, self-aggrandizing version—that he was taking Sidney's advice and no longer seeing Izzy of his own accord. Maybe they'd pulled out their phones to compare text messages, Sidney sincerely worried about Izzy and Weber only pretending to be, searching together for clues to her silence.

If he was a master manipulator, he could have shown Sidney proof of the breakup texts he'd written—texts Izzy wouldn't have seen, because she was already dead. If he'd watched Sidney open her own phone, he would have had the passcode for later, so that he could type the cryptic text to Geneva that others would interpret as a suicide note.

My imagination had gotten away from me, but I kept following it. I could picture the small-eyed, dark-haired Weber I'd gotten to know from news photos, asking Sidney to go downstairs to the massive Mayfield kitchen and find them something fun to drink. While she was gone, he could have hurried to Geneva's master bathroom, to rustle through her drawers and cabinets for pills he could smash up, ready to dribble into the prosecco bottle when Sidney wasn't looking. He'd sip his first glass and pressure Sidney to drink all of hers, then accept a second glass from the tainted bottle.

I felt a hard lump in my throat, imagining the bitter taste of that fouled wine, wondering if Sidney objected or went along, trying to spare them both the embarrassment of outright rejection. *Drink with me, and then I'll leave. Have a second glass and I won't come closer. Take your shirt off, and I won't touch you. Let me take a photo. Drink again. Don't reject me. This is helping. I need this. You promised this. You have to.*

His prints would be on everything—the phone, the bottle, the bathroom counter where he smashed the pills—but if the detectives weren't smart, if they believed the suicide setup, if they'd dealt with precious few murders in this safe, upscale community, then police wouldn't necessarily dust for prints—not right away. Weber's cockiness had led him to make bad choices, but the police department's ineptness had let him get away with those choices, at least for a while.

"Abby?"

I swiped my eye dry and turned in time to see Rita, from Summit.

"Oh, hi," I said with a shaky smile, accepting her sideways embrace. "Good to see you. It's been too long."

"Are you on Team Jack or Team Geneva?"

When I shook my head, confused, she clarified, "Drinks here in town with the mother's crowd or in Chicago at the dad's bar?"

"Neither. But I did want to express my condolences, if I can catch Geneva."

Rita gestured ahead of us, where a fast-moving mob of black surrounded a small blond figure. "Good luck."

Geneva was almost to a black car parked at the curb when I heard a familiar voice say, "Anything I can do. Anything at all."

I sidestepped two elderly people in time to see Curtis kissing Geneva on both cheeks while she gripped his hands. "You've already done so much. Jack and I failed you."

"Of course not," he said.

As her petite head disappeared into his chest, several onlookers discreetly stepped away, realizing this would be more than a quick, obligatory hug. When they separated, Geneva's face was slick with tears. A moment later she was hustled into the car's back seat by a younger woman. I'd lost my chance. In any case, I was too surprised to speak. Curtis had never said anything about knowing the Mayfields.

I was surprised, halfway down the block, when I heard Curtis calling for me to wait up.

"Going home?"

"Yes."

"Your car—?"

"No, I walked. I knew the parking would be tricky."

He caught up and gripped my elbow—a touch that gave me an unexpected electrical zing.

"Those shoes can't be the best for a long walk."

"They're all right."

"Nonsense," he said, pointing to a bright orange sports car parked on a small paid lot across the street. "My car. I'll drop you."

The first surprise, or rather second, coming after the Mayfields revelation, was that Curtis had a flamboyantly decked-out metallic orange Jaguar; his plain white SUV was in the shop, he told me. The next surprise was that he suggested lunch at Ray's rather than heading directly home.

"Funerals hit me hard," he said, uncharacteristically frank. "Maybe it's because I expect the next one to be my father's."

"And it's gotta be harder when you know the family."

He took my pointed comment in stride. "Now you know.

Jack and Geneva were among the last of my client couples. I think my own divorce extinguished my brief zest for marriage counseling, so I returned to my specialty, helping young men."

More candor. Was this flirtation or simply a softening, now that we were away from his office?

"I remember at the pool, when I first told you I lost two students," I said. "You gave no hint of knowing either one."

"How could I?"

True. I didn't know why I felt like I had some right to understand his connection to the Mayfields. To change the subject, I said, "Benjamin didn't want to come to the funeral."

"No point in pushing someone when they're not ready. Forcing kids to mourn the way we do is just another way to encourage deception."

We caught a yellow light on Main Street and as Curtis brought the Jag to a smooth stop, I said, "You would have zipped through that if I weren't in the passenger seat."

"Absolutely," he said, with a deep belly laugh. There was the Curtis I hadn't seen since the pool, or maybe since college. Completely unguarded.

"I hadn't pegged you as a sports car guy."

"Bought it seven years ago during my midlife crisis, post-divorce. Typical, right?" He reached across to tap my knee. A second zing. I snuck a sidelong look at his face—the dark eyelashes framing kind eyes that first attracted me, years ago.

"If the worst thing you did was buy a fancy car, I'd say that's pretty good."

"You're assuming the best. That's generous." He glanced

over, smiling. "I did some healthy things, like losing the weight. I did some foolish things—indulging appetites long suppressed, one could say—as divorced men sometimes do." He ran his fingers around the leather-covered steering wheel for a moment, eyes on the road. "I could have sold it, but the car's a souvenir in a way. A way to remember. We all have those less stable times in our lives, but they pass."

"Self-compassion is important," I said, but he didn't seem to hear.

By the time we were seated at Ray's, Curtis's warmth had spilled over into uncharacteristic abandon. Maybe it was the effect of the funeral, as he claimed. Or maybe the stresses of work and family had pushed him past the point of compartmentalization. As we sipped our first glasses of red wine, he talked about problems up in Fond du Lac.

"Father's estate is completely unmanageable. The house has eight bedrooms, he refuses to install a chair lift or restrict himself to the main floor, when he easily could. And the lawn, the gardens. Ridiculous. Of course, as a former doctor himself, Mattathias Curtis Campbell—"

"Mattathias?"

"Yes. Mattathias—daunting name, isn't it?—has little interest in knowing what his son thinks about progressive dementia and the fact that he's taken more falls in the last month than in the last three years."

Curtis filled me in on the all-too-familiar pattern. No siblings; a father who had become difficult with nurses and housekeepers.

"For a while I felt good helping Dad get through this next

stage of his life, and I was particularly grateful he was well enough to avoid a nursing home. But now I just worry all the time. We fight. He's gotten mean, in a way he never was before. Petty. Selfish. I know it's just his brain changing. I don't want to admit it . . ."

He trailed off. The waitress brought a new carafe of Chianti to the table. I hadn't noticed that we'd emptied the first one. "But here, let's toast to friendship. I know you understand exactly what I'm going through." We clinked, and then I let him talk me into staying for a late lunch to soak up the wine we were both drinking at reckless speed.

The oilcloth table covering was sticky. The breadsticks were doughy. The spaghetti sauce was too salty. And still, I was glad we'd picked Ray's, because it was the only down-to-earth restaurant in town. Robert and I had eaten here many times, and from the dark booth Curtis and I had chosen, I could see across the mostly empty dining room to the two green padded barstools where Robert and I usually sat. He and I came for sports games—Bulls, Bears, Cubs, Blackhawks. No need for deep conversation when there was a goal, foul, or penalty to discuss. With Curtis, by contrast, it felt like I was spending time with a grown-up. No games or distractions required.

"Only a half glass," I said, when he started to refill mine again. "Ladies' room. 'Scuse me."

I didn't realize how tipsy I was until I stood up and wobbled through the maze of empty tables between our secluded alcove and the restrooms. In the bathroom, where I texted Benjamin, telling him not to expect me for a while, I came close to dropping my phone in the toilet. At the sink, I splashed too much, spraying droplets on my blouse.

I patted it dry with a paper towel. Then I peeked between the top buttons to check which bra I was wearing. A light pink one. Not too embarrassing. Relatively new. No stretched-out straps or safety pins.

*You're thinking of sleeping with him.*

I shook my head, balled up the paper towel and tossed it into the garbage. Then I smoothed the back of the skirt, feeling for the high-cut panties that matched the bra. Also newish.

*But you want to!*

It had been years since I'd heard that drunken inner voice, laughing at me, but also daring me.

On the way back to the dining room, I passed the loud bar and did a double take. A man seated at the farthest padded barstool looked like Robert from behind. The same wide back and sloping shoulders. I stopped staring when two men stood up to cheer for a home run, blocking my view.

Back at the table, Curtis asked, "You all right?"

"Maybe I could use a coffee."

When the waitress brought it, I poured in three sugars, then squinted toward the bar section again. Curtis made his own restroom visit and on return, slid into the booth next to me, the sides of our thighs touching.

"Thank you," he said.

"For what?"

"For not leaving once you realized I was falling down a rabbit-hole of self-pity. I haven't talked about my father to anyone else." He drained his wine glass and clapped his hand over mine, pinning it to the tabletop. "A better son would be at his side now."

"You need to leave town. You should, and you will."

"On top of that . . . you and I." He hesitated. "I shouldn't have treated you as a patient—not even once."

He pushed his hair back, leaving a few dark, scruffy pieces standing. He'd stuffed his tie into his jacket pocket and unbuttoned the collar of his shirt, revealing a neck flushed red from sun or drink. I felt a twinge of guilt for liking him in this disheveled and vulnerable state, not that I wanted to see him in despair.

His hand remained cupped over mine. "You knew I was interested that day at the pool. I may run the occasional yellow light, but in every other way, I'm a rule follower. And you and I both know what the rules say."

"Yes, we do," I said, waiting for him to say the next part. *Rules are meant to be broken.*

Curtis squeezed my hand. "The man who took care of Dad's lawn quit."

"Oh," I said, surprised by the change of subject. "Is that a big problem?"

"Dad gets upset when I try to help. If I had a young man with me, it would be different. Dad would see it as giving that young person a sense of direction. He'd go along."

I wanted to get back to our previous unfinished conversation.

"If you're saying that Benjamin could ease your stress by mowing a lawn, then yes."

"Good," he said, releasing my hand in order to slap the table once, triumphantly.

He turned in the booth, eyes on mine.

"I have a serious proposition, Abby. I'd like to take

Benjamin to Wisconsin. Bring him up to the family house. Time for some therapeutic guidance, but mostly it would be role modeling. Work, good habits, the right amount of structure."

I pushed into the far side of the booth to get a little more distance and half turned, just as he had. Now, the booth felt too small, our knees jostling for space.

"You're thinking . . . a weekend?"

"I was thinking about the rest of the summer."

Our waitress appeared, clearing the half-finished spaghetti plates. "More drinks? Room for dessert?"

I slid my credit card into her hand before Curtis could reach for his wallet.

"Just the bill," I said firmly, waiting for her to leave before speaking again.

Before, he'd wanted a special day out with Benjamin. Now he was pressing for several weeks.

"Thank you, Curtis. Really. But there are still things I need to discuss with Benjamin. Things I'm hoping he'll tell me. And I know that takes time. The kind of time you get with a teen when you're not in a rush or trying too hard. Cooking, driving, just sitting around. You know?"

When Curtis didn't reply, I continued. "As for habits and structure, he's got that. He doesn't sleep all day. If it's too late for him to get the lifeguard job, I'll help him find something else."

Curtis's mouth was pinched. He seemed not to realize that his right knee was pressing into my thigh.

I said, "I guess I should be getting home."

"Of course. I'll drive you."

"Actually, considering all the wine . . ." I pulled out my phone, swiping in search of a rideshare icon.

"I'll drive you," he said again.

"Or I could walk."

I set my phone aside, took another sip of my coffee, and looked at his, barely touched.

Noticing my glance, he said, "I didn't have as much wine as you had. And I weigh twice as much as you do, even after losing all that weight." He tapped his flat belly. "You never asked me how I slimmed down, by the way."

"Ozempic?"

"Loneliness."

The divorce. His daughter, far away. "Oh, Curtis."

He took a long sip of coffee, then smiled, but the smile didn't reach his eyes. "That wasn't a bid for sympathy!"

I felt embarrassed for him now. For myself, too. I should have understood. He wasn't maximizing time with Benjamin only for my son's sake. He was trying to fulfill a fatherly role. His daughter—the very same age as Benjamin, he'd told us at the pool. The same birth month, even.

"You've been good for Benjamin," I said. "But . . ."

"But?"

"I'm his mother. He's going through a difficult time. I need to be there for him."

"Even if he doubts your love right now."

"*Especially* if he doubts it."

"And even if he's at a critical crossroads."

"Yes."

"And even if your family history doesn't generate much confidence in reversing a certain pattern . . . ?"

"*A certain pattern*," I said, frowning, wanting him to explain further. "I know you believe that boys need male role models."

He mumbled, "It's not only that."

I kept trying to make eye contact with Curtis, but he refused to look at me now. When he took out his phone, I assumed he was taking my advice and calling a car. But then I heard the whoosh of an email being sent.

He slid his phone back into his jacket. "We used group therapy at Menkoka for a while, but it backfired. The problem with housing and treating psychopaths together is that instead of getting better together, they get worse. They study each other. Learn from each other. How to deceive, manipulate, don useful masks—all while finding reassurance in each other's company. '*That person* got away with such and such moral violation; so could I.'"

Half an hour ago, he'd been venting about his father. Two minutes ago, he was pressing his warm thigh into mine.

"If you're suggesting I'm a bad influence on my son, that's ridiculous."

"I'm only suggesting that it's very important whom Benjamin spends time with right now."

"My son isn't one of Konrad's ducklings," I said, trying to diffuse the tension, expecting him to laugh at a psychology reference.

Curtis slid out of the booth. "I just sent you the transcript from our hypnosis session. I didn't think you should read it before, but I've changed my mind."

"Okay," I said, perplexed by his insistence. "Fine."

I nodded and looked around, disoriented, following him

halfway across the dining room before realizing I'd left my purse under the table. I'd just hooked a finger under the strap when a commotion erupted in the bar section of the restaurant, competing with the noise of the televisions. Curtis's firm diction was drowned out by an even louder, familiar voice, braying with indignation.

Standing up fast, I banged the top of my head on the underside of the table. I closed my eyes for a second—*men*—and then hurried to break things up before someone did something stupid.

# 34

"*Our* place? You had to bring him here?"

Robert stood in the restaurant entryway, a few feet from the bar, blocking Curtis from leaving.

"You're kidding me," I said. "This isn't *our* place, you idiot. It's just the only affordable restaurant on Main Street."

Robert had his shoulders up, knuckles of one hand grinding into the palm of the other. Curtis moved closer, clasping my arm protectively.

In a gravelly voice, Robert said, "I suggest you take your hand off her."

"*You* suggest?"

"Both of you," I said, "chill out."

"It's a good thing I stopped you," Robert said, sizing up Curtis. "How much you both drink? Two bottles of wine?" He pushed back the bottom of his Cubs jacket to reveal the holstered gun at his hip.

Curtis said, "I don't know who you are, but we'd both like you to take a big step back."

Robert ignored the order. "If either of you walk out that

door and get behind a steering wheel, you are going to see blue lights so fast—"

"I'm walking," I said. "Not that it's your business."

"It is, Abby. It definitely is. And you're making a big mistake."

"*I'm* making a big mistake?"

I shook Curtis's hand off my arm, but neither man seemed to notice.

"We're not even dating," I said.

Curtis shout-whispered in my direction, "That's not his business, either."

"I know it's not. But I want to see the embarrassment on his face when he realizes he's making a public stink for nothing."

Robert wasn't cowed. "You shouldn't be letting Benjamin spend every day with this guy."

"So, you *are* watching us. And you're acting like a teenager whose hormones have gone haywire, which is the last thing I need."

"You don't know what you need," Robert said. "Not in this case."

Only two nights ago, I'd spent a perfectly good evening with Robert, studying criminology files, drinking beer, eating pizza—with *none* of this. No juvenile behavior. No jealousy. I had believed, once again, that we could be friends.

I stifled a groan of frustration. "Don't do this, Robert."

Loud enough for the whole bar to hear, he said, "Do what—tell you not to fuck this guy?"

My face flamed. Between the wine in my gut and the anger and humiliation bubbling in my veins, I felt woozy.

"That's enough. Don't call me again. Don't text. Don't stop by. We're done, Robert. We were done before. You just don't seem to get it."

"And *you* don't seem to get that you're being hoodwinked. This guy's misrepresenting himself."

"What are you *talking* about."

"Ask him about his ex-wife. Ask him about the restraining order."

"We're leaving," Curtis said, "and we'll keep your warning in mind . . . officer."

Under my breath, I said, "He's not an officer. He got fired."

The bartender, a maternal older brunette named Sheila, came around the bar in time to put an arm around Robert's shoulder. "Honey, let's get you that refill. And some mozzarella sticks, on the house."

Curtis and I made use of the distraction to slip out the door. As soon as we were down the block, he said, "He implied he'd arrest us for drunk driving. He was impersonating a cop."

"He is a cop."

"*Was*, you said." Curtis turned, furious. "He showed off his gun. He wanted me to think he could arrest me. There's something abnormal about that guy."

Curtis wasn't wrong. But I'd already taken enough machismo. I wasn't going to defend Robert, but I wasn't going to piss all over him, either. I put a hand on Curtis's forearm to slow him down.

"Why did he mention your ex-wife?"

"Restraining order. On the advice of her attorney. Oldest trick in the book."

"I'm not familiar with all the tricks. Enlighten me."

"She was the one who violated the marriage—infidelity, plundering of our shared bank accounts—and when I told her I wanted a divorce, she called 911 and made a false report that I hit her."

We stopped at the crosswalk, waiting for the light.

In a cooler voice, he said, "It was clever, when you think about it. I write about men's issues, I'm a respected psychologist. What's the best way to punish me? Make the community think I'm an abusive partner."

"Did people believe her?"

"She got an emergency protective order. That's the first step. No questions asked. But when we're expected in front of the judge, she doesn't even show up to present her so-called evidence. Too busy off on some pleasure trip with another man, sailing on Lake Michigan. No protective order was granted. End of story."

We crossed the street. Ahead of us was the parking lot, with Curtis's orange Jag in sight.

"You're there," I said, pointing, "but I'm going this way. On foot."

We both stopped, awkwardly looking at each other.

"Thanks for lunch," he said, smoothing down his hair. "I'm sorry it got a little . . . dramatic at the end."

I had the feeling he was talking about the standoff with Robert and the rapid-fire interrogation about his ex-wife, but in truth I was more upset about the earlier part. He'd questioned my abilities as a mother. Made strange references to my family and its multigenerational problems. Compared Benjamin to an incarcerated psychopath who needed to be kept away from other . . . I wasn't imagining it . . . other *psychopaths*.

Curtis said, "I don't mind sharing details of my divorce, if you have concerns."

"Why would I have concerns?"

He nodded, satisfied. "We still need to wrap things up with Benjamin, one way or another. The summer offer is still on the table."

I pictured it literally: a gleaming, very expensive-looking chafing dish—one I had no plans to touch. Local therapy sessions were one thing. An entire summer away was another. Still, I thanked him.

"You're welcome. Please bring Benjamin by, tomorrow."

"I will."

"It may be one of my last chances to see him for any substantial period of time."

"Yes. I'm aware."

"And Abby, it's time for you to read that transcript. Don't put it off."

# 35

The suburbs closest to the Wisconsin border were where I spent the most normal years of my childhood, back when my mom was alive and we lived in Winthrop Harbor, close to where Willa lived now. I didn't take Benjamin there often, and yet there was easier access to Lake Michigan from places like Zion. The public beaches weren't especially beautiful, but the swimming was free and by late afternoon—tipsiness from the wine at Ray's converted into a dull headache—it seemed a much better place to be than our stuffy apartment. Benjamin always preferred the pool, whereas I preferred this, an escape from the judgmental eyes of our Pleasant Park neighbors, even if the coarse yellow sand was spoiled by cigarette butts.

When we arrived with our towels, Benjamin nodded to the squat concrete building visible at the shoreline, just to the north. "Is that really a nuclear reactor?"

"Sure is."

"Does that mean there's radiation in the water?"

"Makes it a little warmer."

Benjamin's eyebrows went up.

"Kidding. You think the fine communities of northern Illinois would let us swim here if there was anything wrong with the water?"

I chose not to tell him about the long history of toxic pollution precisely where I—and he—had grown up. Even my father, who'd enjoyed fishing for coho off Waukegan piers knew to release every fish he caught.

Benjamin pulled off his T-shirt. "No point waiting."

"Hold on," I said. "I need to ask you something."

I reminded him about Curtis's offer to take him away to his father's place, where Benjamin could do chores and help out.

"Yeah, so?" Benjamin asked.

"Would you like to do that?"

"No, I'd like to do what other Summit kids are doing. Go to California for screenwriting summer school. Go to Italy for mountaineering."

"I can't send you to California, and I can't send you to Italy."

"Surprise, surprise."

"So? Would you rather earn some money helping Curtis?"

"Yes, if I have no other choice. I'd prefer to go somewhere and see something new and earn some money, instead of just boiling inside our apartment. Of course I would."

Of course he would. Why had I asked him if my gut told me he shouldn't go? Maybe I was hoping for an out—an act of resistance on Benjamin's part, so I wouldn't have to be the one to say no when Curtis asked again on Monday.

"Enjoy your swim," I said. "Don't go too far out."

"What's too far?"

"I don't know. Farther than I can see you."

He exhaled through his nose, aloof superiority audible in that little puff of air. When he was younger, fart noises were the thing. I missed those playful noises now. Someday, I might even miss moments from this summer, as difficult as it had been so far. Children grow up too soon. Even the challenging ones do.

There was my answer. I didn't want to send Benjamin away, even if he wanted to go, and even if it might make my life temporarily easier. I couldn't let him go away with someone I didn't know well, even if Curtis was well-intentioned. My gut was telling me, loud and clear. I couldn't afford to make even one more mistake with Benjamin. He would have to be mad at me on Monday, if Curtis offered again and I refused. We'd both live with it.

"Benjamin," I said just as he stepped away from our towels.

"Yeah?"

"You're a good swimmer. I trust you. Just be careful."

After he'd waded into the water, I pulled a folder from my tote bag. Inside it were some FBI technical papers from Robert's files. All weekend, I'd kept sifting through materials, trying to shake off the inexplicable perception of a continuing threat, even with Weber dead and Veronica Lovell released. That strange line from the news interview came back to me now. *Kittens need to catch their own mice.* Who were the kittens? Who were the cats?

I read another FBI report, one meant to dispel popular myths. Serial killers, it said, are not always single, dysfunctional loners. Serial killers are not all white males. Serial killers do not want to get caught over time, even though they do tend to get careless following years of getting away with their murders.

I knew those things already. *What else?*

My next homework assignment was even less pleasant. Curtis had sent me the hypnosis transcript. Squinting at the dim screen, I opened and began reading.

First, it was easy to take in. Curtis had typed everything he'd recorded, even our banter at the beginning of the hour. Within half a page I was no longer on the Zion beach, reading a dim screen. Not in Curtis's office, either. I was at the forest preserve not far from here, reliving it all again. Age thirteen. With my brother and his friend. *Grant.* A name I'd rather forget.

I read about getting drunk, needing to vomit, needing to pee. Ewan following me. His taunts and his violence. The way that I accepted all of it and still looked up to him, no matter what he threatened. The way I never knew when he was being serious or simply teasing. Those moments I never saw coming. His hands around my neck, lifting me off the ground.

The transcript matched my conscious memories. The main difference was the level of detail. The sensations hit me like waves. The heat. The sound of cicadas. The smell of the muddy creek.

When I got to the moment when I was walking through the woods to the next trailhead, where I fell asleep or passed out, waiting for Ewan and Grant to pick me up, I saw there were still many pages left to read. My eyes flitted across the screen. A trickle of sweat ran down my neck. These were the parts Curtis didn't want me to read—until he did.

*Dogface*. That was Ewan calling out from the open car window. *What the fuck. Wake up.*

The car stopped. Doors opened. Driver's side, passenger side, and then a third door, the back passenger door. Grant yelled, *Hey!* A girl had jumped out.

*Get the fuck back here.*

Ewan was pulling me to my feet, and I looked and she looked back. I didn't understand what I was seeing.

She was young, maybe a year older than me, and thin, and pale. Her bare arms and legs glowing in the moonlight. Her beige bra still on, something balled up—maybe a T-shirt—in her fist. But from the waist down she was naked, and her eyes were wide with fright.

*Hurry*, Grant said to Ewan, who shoved me into the front seat of the car and then climbed over me, so he was in the middle, all the better to yell at Grant.

*You better fucking go after her.*

*It's all right.*

*It's not all right. She's running straight back to where the cop cars were.*

*Naw*, Grant said. And again: *Naw, girls like her don't tell. She's totally fucked-up. Last thing she wants is anyone to know. You're just mad you didn't finish.*

Ewan said, *I don't want your sloppy seconds.*

They continue arguing, even as they pulled out and started driving opposite the direction the terrorized girl ran.

Ewan said, *Way you gave it to her, she's not as scared as she should be.*

Ewan twisted and half crawled into the back seat, squashing me against the door. When my brother settled back into the front seat again, he had the vodka bottle and a pair of girl's tennis shoes that he chucked—one, two—out the open window and into the blur of woods we were passing. Then he levered himself into the back again and came back with something small and white in his fist.

*Promissory note*, Ewan said, holding them up for us to see. *I know where she lives. Met her at a party last summer. I already told her that if she says anything about me, I'm gonna come and give her a lot harder ride than she got, once she's cleaned up and worth fucking again. Something to remember me by.*

Grant said something under his breath but Ewan wouldn't let it go.

*I'm telling you, you damn fucker. You don't know how to handle a girl.*

Grant grabbed the bottle of vodka and started gulping it fast, heavy foot on the gas pedal, driving faster and faster the more Ewan kept ragging on him, telling him his fucking car was no good anyway, telling him he wished he never met Grant with his shitty taste in skinny girls and his piece of shit car and his . . .

But then I'm being pushed hard into the door again, my body suddenly twice as heavy, my shoulder starting to hurt because we are going around a curve way too fast, my eyes flashing open, my hands reaching out automatically toward the dashboard, fingers clawing for something to hold on to.

This, finally, was something I remembered, something I didn't need the transcript for. The centrifugal force. The way I knew what was coming. The way Ewan and Grant wouldn't stop shouting, even then, the speed and the vodka spilling and the sharp curve and then we weren't on the road anymore, we were on the shoulder and beyond it, jolting and jumping and still going, forward, down a steep bank—but at least we were slowing, it seemed like. And then the car rolled.

*Push*, Ewan said.

That, I remember.

*Stop crying push the door open help me fucking push*, until we were able to get out.

But Grant was still in there, folded so far over the steering wheel it looked like it was part of him. Head turned toward us, mouth open, eyes shut. Big black trickle of blood running down the side of his face, dripping from his chin.

Minutes later, Ewan and I had managed to crawl up to the shoulder of the road. From there, we could still see the glint of light on the rolled car, and what looked like rising steam or dust, but only faintly.

*You think he was still breathing?*

*I think so*, I said.

That, I remember.

*Ewan*, I said. *You shouldn't* . . .

*Here comes a car.*

A man pulled up and rolled down his window. *You both all right? Is that your car down there?*

I said, *We're fine.*

Ewan looked at me.

I said, *Tow truck's on the way, and a trooper passed and said he's coming back. Dealing with another emergency. So you can go.*

Ewan stared at me. Surprise in his eyes, but something else. Pride. I'd never seen him look at me that way.

*You sure?* The stranger spoke directly to Ewan. *This looks like an emergency. Your sister looks pretty shook up.*

*Didn't you hear her? She said we're fine.*

I don't know how long we waited there. Even in the transcript, it didn't say. At some point Ewan left my side to walk down to where Grant was, in the flipped car. He came back muttering. He repeated the process a little while later. Then, at some point, he came back to me and said, *Good job, Dogface. You're smarter than I thought.*

We started walking. We got home to our house just as the sun was coming up.

My dad and Martha were fast asleep. Ewan went directly into the shower after dropping his shirt and bloodstained jeans on his bedroom floor. I walked past the foul clothes and straight to his nightstand, where the white pair of underwear was sitting, one leg hole ripped larger than the other.

I remembered the beginning of the night and the very end of it. I didn't remember the girl but I knew that if I left the ripped pair of girl's underwear in Ewan's bedroom, someone could find it and start asking questions. So, I took them.

In the transcript, Curtis asked: *You feel guilty. You did nothing to help that girl. You knew your brother helped capture her and he threatened to assault her later, especially if she reported what Grant had done. Perhaps even if she didn't report it.*

Yes.

*You knew that Grant was still alive and you did everything you could—you and Ewan both—to make sure he didn't get help right away. You assisted in that.*

Yes.

*You actually were the one to suggest leaving Grant without aid.*
*Yes.*
*And then you helped cover it all up.*
*Yes.*
*And did you feel remorse at the time?*
*Not really.*
*No remorse. Not even given the cost of that escapade to two lives—actually, three?*
*Not really.*

There was no way to tell, from the transcript, if Curtis sighed or hesitated or got up from his chair and went to his desk, to mull the problem for a while. But at some point he spoke again.

*When you wake up, I want you to feel refreshed and not distressed. But I do want you to incorporate these memories and reflect upon them from an adult perspective, with calm and compassion, as a person who has moral obligations and responsibilities. You will integrate your younger and older selves. You will not suppress these memories but rather continue to probe and learn from them. I'm going to count backward from ten. When I'm done counting . . .*

That was it.

I looked out toward Lake Michigan, ruffled and blue, and spotted Benjamin's high elbow, rising out of the water, and his head turning to breathe every second stroke. I tried to find some peace in it: the regularity of his swimming, the fact that he had grown from fragile baby into strong, independent young man. All this time, I'd worried he was turning into Ewan. I hadn't stopped to worry that he was turning into me.

I checked myself, trying to feel for the integration that Curtis had demanded. I tried my hardest to remember the parts I had blanked out—the half-naked girl standing by the car, the lie I'd told to the Good Samaritan, the fact that I'd told Ewan we needed to leave Grant and not help him.

I tried harder. White limbs. Beige bra. Later, the scene of the accident, talking to the man who stopped by, Ewan's look of pride.

I tried to put it together, like I was playing with a dress-up doll, but it didn't feel the same as other memories from that night. The camera focus remained fuzzy, the resolution poor.

*And did you feel remorse, then or later?*

*Not really.*

Curtis had peeled me and cut me open. He'd revealed my rotted core.

Ewan had gone to jail not for anything to do with that girl—no girl ever reported a rape that night. He hadn't even gone to jail for anything he did that directly led to Grant's death, like drinking and arguing with Grant until Grant lost control of the car. The charges that stuck were relatively minor—failure to report, obstruction of justice—and even that wouldn't have kept him imprisoned long except for all the trouble he made once he arrived at Menkoka and later, at Bosqueville, where he'd been stuck ever since.

As for me, I never even completed an official statement. Based on Ewan's account, everyone believed I was blacked out for nearly all of it.

What kind of person did what I'd done?

It was clear now, exactly what Curtis had been trying to tell me.

*It's very important whom Benjamin spends time with right now.*

He was right. Curtis had always been right. I was a hazard to my own son. The more he knew about me, the more he'd believe that even the most heinous acts easily go unpunished. He'd already detected hypocrisy. He'd keep digging for it, and then he'd look at his own life and realize there was no reason to play by society's rules. *I* hadn't.

*Don't thank me,* Curtis had said directly after the hypnosis. I didn't want to thank him, it's true. But if he was willing to keep my secrets, it meant he'd be willing to keep Benjamin's, too. That mattered.

The most important thing any mother does for her child is to know when to let go. A better mother would have let go even sooner.

# 36

"So, let me see if I'm understanding," Willa said on Monday evening, our normal check-in. "You have a new job, which might lead to an even better job. You got some unexpected money from your last employer. You have a clean apartment that will stay clean, because you're the only person in it. And you don't need to worry about your teenage son for the rest of the summer."

"Two weeks," I clarified.

It's what we had agreed on when I brought Benjamin over for what would have been their last therapy session but now, since my about-face, represented the beginning of a new therapeutic phase.

Willa asked, "This isn't the psychologist you gave your phone number to weeks ago, is it?"

"Yeah. Curtis."

I'd kept most of the details of Benjamin's therapy from her, as well as his diagnosis, something I didn't plan to tell anyone, ever, if I could help it.

"Wasn't Benjamin trying to get a job at a pool?"

"They told him that members' kids got first dibs. They put him on a list but his only chance will be if another kid quits."

"And does Benjamin think he's going for vacation?"

"No, he knows it's work camp," I said with a weak laugh. "You should have seen Benjamin's face when Dr. Campbell explained everything they'd be doing."

"He's 'Doctor' now. Didn't you just call him Curtis a minute ago?"

"There's some sort of shed to be assembled, aside from the yard work, and Dr. Campbell said he wasn't going to help. He handed Benjamin a printout of the steps, just as a preview, and I could tell at that moment that Benj shares my phobia of assembly instructions."

"He'll figure it out."

"Yes, I'm sure that's the point. Make him sweat. Give him challenges. Plus, he has to take a tech break. No phone for the first week."

"Sounds exactly what every teenager should be made to do. Now tell me about your new job."

I told her about my first day at Grove, working with a group of six Chinese, two Japanese, two Arabic, and one Spanish student, all of them so fluent in English that we'd have no communication problems—or so I thought until the end of the day, when I realized that quiet Min and even quieter Basma had been nodding automatically to hide their complete lack of comprehension. We'd have six weeks to figure it out. Whether or not they picked up on "study skills and college-prep mental health strategies," they'd get lots of English immersion.

"If they hire me in the fall, I won't just be a counselor, I'll also teach a high school level psychology class. And I'll oversee a small team of student mental health advocates."

I trailed off, voice flattening.

"It sounds great, hon. But for some reason, you don't."

"It's been a long time since I've been alone," I told Willa, finally—the truth, but not the whole truth.

After a phlegmy guffaw, Willa said, "For godsake, woman, count your blessings."

The next day and the one after that were the same. Rewarding days with the international students, followed by too-quiet dinners, at home. Curtis and Benjamin had left Monday afternoon. Today was only Wednesday, and I didn't feel used to Benjamin's absence, I only noted it more with every passing hour. Something already felt wrong, and it was more than just a change in routines or an early preview of empty-nest syndrome. I regretted the phone detox plan, though I'd believed at first it would be good for Benjamin. I wanted, at the very least, to know they'd made it to Fond du Lac okay. I'd simply have to wait—four more days, possibly, until Curtis had decided the one-week detox had worked and Benjamin could have his phone back.

In the dim, hot silence of my apartment each evening, I had plenty of time to think. I continued to ponder the details of Harper's murder, and Veronica's snatching and release, and Robert's criminal files, which had managed to convert the landscape of my childhood—northern Illinois, southern Wisconsin—into a geography of bodies lost and found.

I thought about the hypnosis transcript, including all the

parts I hadn't remembered. From there my mind traveled further back, looking for proof of my dark side. But it didn't add up. If I really had antisocial personality disorder, why did I feel so guilty and remorseful about what the transcript had revealed?

And then again, psychopathy was complicated. Now, with more free time, I sifted through some of the latest research online. I read papers that claimed there were different kinds of psychopaths—primary and secondary *variants*, with heterogeneity within each, and primary and secondary *subtypes*, and continuums within each. And there were different personalities and different etiologies, or causes, and quite possibly, someday, we'd all be talking about psychopathy as a spectrum, our assumptions reorganized, as they had been already in terms of autism.

*Spectrum.* Like a rainbow. I tried to find the beauty in that word.

Perhaps Curtis had understood all this. Perhaps it's what he'd meant when he said he wouldn't give Benjamin a simplistic label—and wouldn't have, even if Benjamin were eighteen, the age when the antisocial personality disorder label was sometimes applied. It was fortunate that I'd found a therapist who wouldn't force Benjamin into a box. In time, the research seemed to be suggesting, the boxes and labels would all be changing anyway.

I kept trying to remember how I'd felt when Benjamin first started therapy—that, like my friend Marta, whose daughter, Camila, was in an inpatient program, I could appreciate the feeling of handing over control to another responsible adult, one who knew much more than I did—and on top of that, didn't have my shameful past. I kept trying to locate a feeling of resolution, acceptance, or some kind of optimism. But instead, I only felt a sense of emptiness and foreboding.

I wanted to hear Benjamin's voice. I wanted to see him. I wanted to tell him I loved him. Maybe he wasn't an easy kid to love, but I did, even his wiseass remarks, even his impatience. I had always felt he might grow into his personality, or that he'd find new interests, or a purpose, or love, and all of that would make him feel more comfortable in his own skin, more tolerant of others, so that he'd no longer seem belligerent, only confident. I'd seen that happy, relaxed confidence at times.

I washed the few dishes I'd dirtied—a single plate and fork from dinner, a coffee cup from earlier. The garbage hadn't needed emptying all week—one person, less waste—and I hadn't checked the mail daily since Monday evening. I'd already changed into an oversized nightshirt that went down to my knees. Half dressed and barefoot, I walked around to the side of the house, where the mailbox and garbage cans were.

As soon as I opened the mailbox flap and saw the envelope—the third of its kind in two weeks—I tensed up. But then I told myself: *Ewan can write all he wants to write. It doesn't matter. Benjamin isn't even here.*

I walked slowly back around the house, opened the door, and continued to the kitchen, where I held the letter up to the light. The note inside was smaller than the previous ones had been, not even the full width of the envelope.

I could simply not open it. I didn't have to give him the power of my immediate attention.

And then again, if I never read it, I'd think about it even longer.

I opened the envelope and took out the folded piece of unlined paper. In the very center was the briefest note Ewan had ever written.

*Did it work?*

I turned the note over. That was all of it.

Only three words, all in block letters. Three words that made my heart pound. I wanted to rip up the letter, but I knew I shouldn't.

Did *what* work?

*God damn him!*

I returned the folded note to its envelope, which I left on the kitchen counter. I willed myself to continue with my bedtime routine. I tried not to think about it, but I couldn't stop thinking about it now.

*Did it work?*

The answer came to me in the bathroom, just as I stuck my toothbrush in my mouth. I remembered the day in the car, on the way home from the police station. The discussion about the naked photo of Izzy. Benjamin's assertion that he'd kept it as a way to threaten Manny. His cocky assertion that it had been smart.

*Good advice.*

*Good advice from who?*

Benjamin hadn't answered while we were in the car, but not much later, I'd decided it had to be Ewan.

Advice given, advice taken. Stupid. Enraging. But it was over. At least Benjamin hadn't read this latest note. At least Ewan wouldn't get the satisfaction of an answer.

I finished brushing, shaking my head and breathing hard through my nose.

If it was really over, why was my heart still beating too fast, my chest tight and my vision starting to dim around the edges?

I washed my face and resoaked the washcloth in cold water before placing it on the back of my neck. I walked back to the front door to check one last time that it was locked.

In the kitchen, I took the recently washed glass from the drying rack and filled it with cold tap water. I reached into my purse. I pulled the clonidine bottle out and set the pill on my tongue, hand on the water glass I was about to bring to my mouth.

*Did it work?*

The pill dissolved, bitterness coating my tongue.

It wasn't about the photo of Izzy.

When I felt the glass slip through my fingers, I didn't yelp. I didn't curse. I just stared at the exploded shards and spilled water at my feet. Then I carefully stepped over the mess and proceeded to the far corner of the living room.

My feet were wet from the water. My mouth was abnormally dry. The bitter chalky taste remained.

I looked down to the bottom shelf, at the thick *Physician's Desk Reference*—the book that had gone missing, though I hadn't been able to figure it out at the time. It was back in place now, in the middle of my college psychology textbooks, filling the slot that had puzzled me.

Benjamin had borrowed it. Not after Izzy's death, out of an understandable curiosity to know why she might have died, but before. I couldn't prove that, but it didn't matter.

Because what I did know for sure was that my clonidine refill bottle had gone missing as well. That's why I'd missed several days of doses. That's why I'd passed out in the police station. Benjamin had taken it.

*Did it work?*

Ewan's advice about keeping the photo of Izzy was old news. *Did it work?* was a question about the next step. How to win Izzy over. And the answer was giving her what she asked for. But it hadn't turned out the way anyone expected.

Benjamin had stopped home after the pool. I'd never understood why, and even the police had forgotten in time.

Benjamin was the one who gave Izzy the clonidine, which she didn't take until she was in the motel.

Not to kill her. Not intentionally. No one could have known it would kill her. But maybe to satisfy a request.

*Girls want things. They get things.*

*She was using me.*

But he hadn't meant to hurt her.

Shock rooted me to the spot where I now stood, in the dark living room.

But . . . *Christopher Weber?*

They'd found him and his car. They'd found photos, and pills—the same kind, but not the same brand.

It had all been too neat—the bad guy, not only caught but fatally punished. It had seemed wrong from the start. Because why would he have the same pills? If it was a coincidence, it wasn't a satisfying one, but right now that particular mystery was less important than understanding my own son's troubled state of mind.

I pictured Benjamin how he'd seemed since Weber's

death—if not haunted, at least burdened. Still afraid of being caught. Still struggling with anger—he hadn't wanted Izzy to go meet Weber in Wadsworth—which was easier to deal with than grief.

Because he *had* cared for her. I believed that.

Benjamin hadn't been able to tell me. I knew how it felt to know something that no one else knew.

My troubled, unreachable son.

Carrying a secret he probably thought he'd be carrying to his grave.

# PART III

# 37

## TWO DAYS EARLIER

### BENJAMIN

"You're kidding."

Dr. C is holding open the driver's door of his orange Jag for me.

"Why, you're too afraid to drive it?"

"Maybe." I don't even know if I'm allowed to drive someone else's car without a full license. But fuck. *This* car.

"You'd prefer to drive the SUV?"

That one looks expensive, too, but it has a dented front bumper and scratched hood. The front license plate is missing. I walk around it. Actually, both plates missing.

"We're taking them both up to Fond du Lac?"

"No, we're leaving the SUV in storage, here at the house," he says. Then he looks at me and laughs. "You look relieved."

I'm about to ask Dr. C if he had an accident with the SUV—he never said anything about that even though I've seen him basically every day—but then I have a more interesting thought. "That means we're taking the Jag all the way to Fond du Lac."

He shakes the keys. "Now you're getting it."

So, driving is part of it. Maybe the best part. Once we get there, he's been telling me and Mom all week, I have to work for my "keep." I've brought an old pair of jeans and two paint-stained shirts. A swimsuit, which might be optimistic. His father's mansion might have a pool or it might not, but there's also lakes. Or one big lake. I don't know why I haven't asked, I just don't want to be one of those people who asks question after question, like *What's a dumbwaiter?* I heard him telling my mom something about that so I looked it up. Used by servants to move stuff between floors. Does his father have servants? Then I remember: I'm the servant.

Back home, Mom tried to give me sunscreen and a gardening trowel to bring, but I told her they probably had all that stuff.

Dr. C and I already loaded a toolbox into the trunk. Lots of other random hardware-store stuff—tape, ties, shovel, blue tarp.

"Premium," Dr. C tells me. "Always."

My mom says "cheapest one." Always.

He goes inside the gas station while I'm pumping for him, and I see two girls checking me out. One is pumping gas into a little hatchback and the other has the front passenger door open, digging pop cans and wadded-up tissues from the door pockets, but while she does it, she's looking under her arm to check me out. Okay, to check the car out. Not me, necessarily.

I stand up a little straighter, tense my biceps, squeeze the gas pump, and then immediately ease off, worrying the gas will overfill and spew all over the place.

Dr. C comes out. Sees what's up. He wags a finger at me. I think he's joking about it, with the girls and with me both, but then he comes up right next to me, takes the pump from my hand and says, "In." He's not joking.

I wasn't even looking at them.

He's crabby and quiet all the way to the Wisconsin border. It could be worse. We could be talking the entire way, every minute, which was closer to what I expected, since that's what we do in his office. Talk talk talk.

His phone rings. I'm gonna kill my mom if it's her. We just said goodbye less than an hour ago.

"Matt here," he says, and I'm confused but I make sure I don't look it. It's a real estate agent, I can tell, because he's talking about the house, showings, something about taxes, something about the cracked tennis court—they have a tennis court?—and then he's telling her, yes, it will all be mowed by tomorrow. Front and back. No, he's got it covered.

He hangs up. "Bitch."

This time, I let my expression slip. He sees it and laughs.

"I thought we weren't supposed to say that word."

"Bitch?" He cackles. "Go ahead, you can say it. Say whatever you want." He reels off a whole list—the *c* word and the *w* word and various *s* words. "Just don't say it in the wrong situation. Not in front of a woman, for starters."

He drums on the steering wheel, pleased with himself, and I'm getting up the nerve to ask him how much a Jag XF costs when he adds, "and never text those words either. You already got in trouble for that."

Yes, covered.

"It's not so much what you do," he says, "it's what you get away with."

I'm still working my way up to asking about the cost of his car when he says, "I go by Matt because that's my birth name. Curtis is my middle name. Both are after my father. When I'm in Wisconsin, I like to leave my work identity behind, much as I'm able."

"Oh," I say, put at ease. I don't know. *Ease.* Whatever. He can call himself anything he wants, especially when he's talking to a bitch.

"I see that," he says. I wasn't even smiling yet. Sometimes I think Dr. C can read my mind.

"Matt's a good name," I say. Stupid comment. Not sure why I said it, except that we have a long day ahead. Me, him. Seats the color of a horse saddle. "I'd prefer to go by Ben but my mom says Benj which sounds like slang. Like it's supposed to be short for 'bougie' or something else. I don't know."

"Ben it is. You should have told me that in our first session."

"Sorry."

He speeds up to pass a yellow convertible, then whips back into the right lane. "Don't catch your mother's apologizing disease. It's not attractive. Especially for a man."

I count the number of cars we're passing. After fifty, I say, "You knew my mom in college, and I know you guys went out on a date after Sidney's funeral because she came home from the restaurant a little drunk."

I wait for him to scold me for prying, but he looks calm and curious.

"So?"

"Do you like her?"

"Define 'like.'"

"How many miles are we from your home?" he asks a while later.

I reach for my pocket before remembering I left my phone at home, the way he told me to. No screens for two weeks. He told my mom it would be just one, and he told me if I left my crappy phone at home he'd buy me a new one, as long as I never once whined about being offline. "I don't know."

"Math, Ben. Math."

I look over at his speed. He's doing ninety, but maybe only since we crossed the border into Wisconsin. I didn't see what time we got in the car. But I look up at a sign for Milwaukee exits and I guess. "Fifty."

"Close."

He passes several more cars. Mr. C—I mean Matt—or Dr. Matt—has a killer foot. He taps the steering wheel again, which I now see has tiny holes in it, like a fancy leather glove.

"You know how many miles from home most serial burglars and rapists travel to commit their crimes?"

"Um. No?"

"Three miles." He laughs. "Stupid, huh?" Then he looks over at me. Long and serious. "You'd never be that stupid. Would you?"

. . .

We're coming up to a sign that says MADISON when Matt says, "Not too late."

We pass it before I have time to ask him what he means.

"Still not too late," he says as we approach another sign. "We can get off at the next one and come back around."

I have no idea what he's talking about.

"You ever been up to Bosqueville?" he asks. "It'll add another two to three hours, but driving's the best part, right?"

I know Bosqueville. From the envelopes.

"My uncle's in a maximum-security prison there."

"Ding-ding-ding," he says, like we're on a game show. "Ewan would expect me to drop in, if I was in the area."

"You know my uncle?"

He never mentioned that. Not the first time he came over and talked about my uncle and how I shouldn't write to him, not the time my mom and I had a big fight about it. Not a few days later in session when he asked me, again, how I felt about my uncle and would I want to talk to him after all. Maybe he's pulling my leg.

"I know your whole family," he says. "I knew your brother even before I met your mom. Can you guess why?"

"Because you taught at his college?"

"Your uncle never went to college. He was sent away at the age of eighteen, just two years older than you."

I watch exits come and go—gas, coffee, fast food, gas. Matt keeps veering toward the right side of the road, like he's waiting for me to say something, dropping speed from 80 to 75 to 70 to 60, then retaking the center of the lane.

"I met him at Menkoka before you were born," he says, finally. "And then I met him again when I was visiting

Bosqueville to do some follow-up studies on recidivist research subjects. Boys of mine from Menkoka who ended up reoffending landed in maximum security in a location much less pleasant than our juvenile center. We had enough men of the same profile, all in the same place, that we were able to launch a larger study, including with men who'd never had the advantage of our Menkoka program—those would be the 'controls.' Do you know what *control* means?"

I did science fair once. But I don't answer, and I know he'll go on anyway.

"We found variation between the groups, but not as much as we would have hoped. Certainly not as much as *I* would have hoped. It's a stubborn population. Still, I got to know Ewan and other interesting men whom I continue to visit."

*Whom.* The only other person I know who says *whom* is my English lit teacher.

"And imagine my pleasure," he said, "when I found out Ewan had a sister. Imagine my *extreme* pleasure when that sister ended up in one of my classes. I was tickled talking to her. Noting their similarities, their differences—not that I let her know I'd talked to Ewan. And then I found out she had a young son."

He takes one hand off the steering wheel and places it over his heart.

"A son with behavioral problems," he goes on. "That was clear from the very outset, when she'd rattle off her various excuses for missing class." He slows down again, like he's expecting me to tell him to exit. "Not too late!"

"No, I don't think I want to go to Bosqueville," I say.

"Then why didn't you say so."

. . .

We're north of Madison when he finally puts on music. I thought I was going to die, going the whole way with nothing to listen to, no phone, neither of us talking about anything interesting. He plays with the dial, jazz to Bruce Springsteen to REM to classical to Taylor Swift.

"Like her?"

"Not really."

He keeps fidgeting, keeps switching, which might be even worse than bad music or no music at all. I never noticed that "Matt" was so fidgety before. Worse than me.

He returns to the jazz station. "This better?"

"Yeah. It's . . . relaxing."

He looks over at me, smug as fuck. "It irritates you."

"Not really."

"You're a bad liar, generally. An omitter, yes. That's not the same. But don't worry. It's learnable. Everything is learnable, if you're high intelligence, as we are."

Dr. Matt is still staring at me. From our sessions, I know the guy can stare a long time. But we were sitting in his office before, just listening to the tick of the clock. This is different. I'm getting nervous now, seeing how close we are getting to the big semi ahead of us with the mud flaps and a chain dragging on the highway, throwing sparks.

"It's easier to lie to my mom—omit, whatever—than to you."

He smiles and makes this sort of gee-whiz face, tucking his chin down for a second. I guess he's flattered.

"I just mean she's gullible," I say.

"She's steered by her emotions. If she wants to believe something or avoid believing something, she'll throw her whole heart into it. That makes her easy to deceive. Like most women."

It's another theme of his. Matt's divorced. He told me that a while back, but he starts getting angry when it comes up and he never makes it to the end of his story.

"But you and I were talking about music," he says. "I want you to think about something you like, something that relaxes you. Nice blue water at the bottom of the pool, a girl's breasts, whatever."

I crack up at "breasts," but I can tell he's serious.

"And stop digging the tips of your fingers into your jeans like you're trying to pry your kneecaps off," he says.

"Okay." I hadn't realized I was doing it. Relax the hands. Relax the jaw. Tits make me smile so I go for the water, instead. I'm down there, holding my breath, but it feels good. Weightless. Deep.

"Tell me you like jazz."

He called me a shitty liar, so I try the truth. "I don't like jazz."

"No, Benjamin. You're missing the point. Tell me you *like* jazz."

"Fine. I really like jazz."

"You forgot about what I was saying before. Blue water. Or breasts."

I fight the urge to crack up. Fine. Blue water. *And* breasts.

"Tell me you like jazz."

"I . . . *really* like jazz."

He laughs and turns his attention back to the dirty semi. He swerves into the left lane, directly in front of another car that was trying to pass. Cutting it close. The guy behind us lays on his horn. Who gives a fuck? The Jag accelerates effortlessly. Then we're back in the right lane, hard swerve, right in front of the big semi until he gasses it.

Matt laughs. "How's your pulse?"

"Um, high."

"Some people thrive on adrenaline. Some people actually think better in a state of high arousal." He smiles. "And some people—men—can't be aroused when there's not something at stake. A bit of risk. Resistance. The chance of being caught. The chance of something going wrong. Something . . . *extra*. What's your extra, Benjamin?"

"I don't know."

He's already given me the porn talk. That was the first week of sessions, back in Pleasant Park. I couldn't believe when he started going on about the smuttiest possible situations and explaining that he had no problem with fucking or fisting or whatever people wanted to do. The problem was that it *wasn't real*. I thought that was the point. It wasn't real, so it was okay. Actors versus—you know—versus the girl you'd actually ask to the prom.

He said it was the opposite. It wasn't real, so it was wrong. Men who watched too much porn couldn't deal with real-life sex with real-life women, Dr. C—Matt—told me. They become weak.

"Predator or prey," he says, out of the blue. "That piece-of-shit Audi didn't even belong in the left lane."

I'm just glad he's back to talking about cars. But then I sneak a look over at his face and I get that sinking feeling. He's not.

"A year from now," he keeps going, "maybe you could have done okay with Izzy Scarlatti, but you were punching above your weight. You never could have outperformed a man like Christopher Weber. Older, more suave. Not such a good driver, though..."

He pauses, chuckling, which is an improvement. Usually when he talks about Weber it's like when he talks about his ex-wife, and he gets all sulky. I guess Weber was a big disappointment to him. A good student at the institute place, and maybe okay for a while once he left, but then he got out of control. That's the part I don't like to hear about, now that I know who Weber is, or was. The shithead who gave Sid drugs and had sex with her. The pervert who was in the motel with Izzy.

"What are you thinking about, Benjamin?"

I don't want to say Weber, so I say, "Izzy."

"Still mad at her?"

"Kind of."

"Try some positive thinking. If people didn't make stupid choices, where would the rest of us be? You're one or the other. Predator..."

"Or prey," I say, giving him the answer that ends the stupid word game.

"What's your *extra*, Benjamin?" Matt asks again. We're back to that.

"I don't know," I say. Honestly.

He laughs. "Fair enough. How could you?"

He reaches across a hand and brushes my bangs, messing them up, like I'm about ten years old.

"Go for the single girls, the ones the other guys ignore,"

he says. "Not the ugly ones—I'm not saying that, though there's a good argument for it. The grateful ones. The strays."

I do my best to stare ahead and look bored. *Menomonee Falls. Germantown.*

"And here's a thing about virgins, if you happen to like younger girls, which I do. Far less trouble. They may not know how to say yes, but they also don't know how to say no. I know, you'd think they would. But chemistry is on our side. You've probably heard about the fight-or-flight response."

I nod.

"Overrated. I can tell you how many girls have ever fought me or run away." He holds up a hand, fingers splayed. "This many. Out of more than I can count. So what's the third response?"

"I don't know."

"Freeze. That's the one we want. Lower heart rate, dropping temperature, inability to respond. I don't understand wannabe necrophiliacs like Weber, personally. The truth is, a terrified girl seems dead already."

I swallow and look out the window.

He says, "You think a Jag costs a lot, but it's all about the maintenance. That's the real expense, when it comes to a car."

Thank god. A normal conversation.

"I budget two thousand a year."

"Not bad," I say. I was thinking he'd say something insane, like ten thousand.

"Oh, 'not bad.' You think you can afford two K in regular maintenance?"

"I just meant I thought it would be more."

We've taken an off-ramp onto a smaller highway now. Lots more trees and fields. Still some trucks but not as many. He gets a faraway look, picking out the next car way ahead, a nothing-special red car that looks like the sort of banged-up commuter car my mom might drive, his foot heavy on the gas as he closes the distance. Here we go again.

"When I say maintenance, I don't mean the year you can afford it. I mean every year, in and out. That's the problem with anything."

*Ninety. Ninety-five. One hundred.*

"You buy something or you start something, and you know you have to do it right or there's no point doing it at all. But you can't slip up. Once you're in, you're in. It's a commitment."

He looks over at me and rolls his eyes because he can tell. I don't get what he's talking about.

He steers hard to the right. I was so preoccupied with that red car ahead of us I didn't see the rest stop sign and the exit until he's barreling down it. He pulls into the big lot and whips into a parking space, two slots down from the next car.

He kills the engine. "Let's go see what they've got for us."

*Like, besides toilets?*

But then I see a girl who's close to my age or I guess a year younger—fourteen, fifteen—sitting on the grass with a sign that says STEVENS POINT over a childish-looking rainbow done in streaky markers. Next to her is a golden retriever puppy with a rope instead of a regular leash. Matt's staring at her.

Maybe he just means a pop machine.

"You go ahead in," he says. He didn't even ask me if I have

to pee. "Wait, here's a couple of dollars." He pulls two worn ones from his wallet, then puts them back and hands me a black credit card instead. "Just tap it. Whatever you want." He flashes white teeth. "And get her one, too."

"Really?"

"When someone offers you something, the correct response is thank you."

"Right. Thank you, Dr. . . . Matt." It's never going to sound right.

"If she asks, tell her I'm your uncle or your cousin. Don't mention the word *doctor*. Ever. It makes girls uptight."

"I don't think she'll ask."

"Yes, she will," he says, reaching for a pair of sunglasses and sliding them onto his face. "Especially when you tell her we're giving her a ride."

# 38

## ABBY

Robert wasn't answering my texts. That wasn't a real surprise, considering how pissed off I'd been with him at Ray's. Even when I texted in the morning to say I was concerned about Benjamin—that I thought I'd discovered something new and important, the reason Benjamin had been acting up—Robert still didn't reply.

Fine. I was alone with this, just as I'd been alone with the hypnosis transcript. I needed to stuff those old memories back where they belonged, and I needed to find a way to contact Benjamin, not to confront him but to reassure myself he was okay.

But first, I had to get through my day at Grove.

I made a fifth call to the number I had for Curtis, but it always went to voicemail. I'd sent him an email as well. He'd never said he was taking his own break from screens or phones. Maybe his father had a landline. I'd feel better if I knew where Benjamin was, precisely. An address, an alternate phone number. I couldn't remember Curtis's father's first name. With only a common surname, I couldn't find any contact information online.

All of this was keeping me from my teaching obligations. My students had just left for lunch and I hadn't finished adding captions to the "Mental Resiliency During the College Application Process" presentation I planned to show them at the end of the day. When I inserted a thumb drive, I was surprised by the document names that popped up. Where I expected to see slideshows and PDFs I'd developed for Summit, I instead saw a dozen unfamiliar documents.

Not *completely* unfamiliar. There was the file, WBL52024, that I'd printed for Curtis. I pulled out the thumb drive to inspect it closer. It was white and generic-looking, with nothing to distinguish it from several I owned. I'd accidentally given Curtis the wrong thumb drive back.

I opened the file and started scrolling quickly in search of the acknowledgments, where I hoped he would thank someone local with a distinctive name—a close colleague or relative I could track down as a way of finding Curtis. But I was only halfway there when my eye started to fall on certain phrases. *The war on masculinity*. Halfway down the page: *Honest talk about boys' libido*. Next paragraph: *Defending primal urges*.

I slowed down, reading more carefully, waiting for the moment Curtis would explain these were the ideas of misogynist influencers—arguments he was detailing in order to dismiss them. But the dismissal never came.

"Are you kidding me?"

The book was called *What Boys Learn*. But Curtis wasn't saying that boys learn the wrong lessons from social media or each other. He was saying they learn the wrong lessons from an "overly feminized culture, one that actively denies and suppresses the natural drives and rites of passage by which boys become men."

He was blaming the #MeToo movement. Accusing girls and women of making false rape charges. Criticizing consent culture for prioritizing women's "need to be coddled" over men's "need for sexual expression and empowerment."

I couldn't believe this was the Curtis I knew. I didn't have time to read any more. I scrolled to the end but there were no personal acknowledgments, only a dozen pages of endnotes justifying his claims. Lunch period was halfway over.

I recalled the other files I'd seen on the thumb drive. One of them was about Benjamin. I no longer gave a shit about confidentiality.

I found the Rosso2024 file and started reading. The first paragraph didn't surprise me—"below average student"—yes, a fair-enough description of Benjamin.

*Yesterday, when we met again by chance . . .*

A little odd, that he had started entering notes just after we all re-met at the pool, many days before Benjamin had his first session.

*. . . she disregarded cues that I was occupied reading and working . . .*

She?

*. . . moved a magazine I had placed on a lounge chair to maintain space intentionally between us so that I could focus on the work I'd brought, but she disregarded those and other cues.*

What the . . . ?

*He* didn't want to talk? The person who asked about

Benjamin's flip turns and talked about his divorce? The one who recounted a long story about meeting Benjamin when he was a grade schooler? The one who asked me out for a glass of wine?

*Given what I recalled from the last time I knew her—elements of antisocial personality disorder but with significant traits missing and without the positive attributes we expect from non-impulsive ASPD (high degree of success, confidence, charm), I was admittedly curious from a research standpoint, especially given the possibility of making familial and even multigenerational comparisons.*

Multigenerational comparisons.

I had to go back to the top and read again.

This wasn't a document about Benjamin. It was about me. And not just about me, but about our whole family. Curtis had seen something in me, in college, and he saw something in Benjamin. It made him curious.

But if he'd thought I had antisocial personality disorder, it hadn't stopped him from asking me out for wine. Or flirting. Or going to lunch. Or seeming on the verge of starting an affair that day in Ray's that only fizzled out at the last moment.

I stared at the screen, remembering. He'd mentioned the hypnosis manuscript, challenging me to read it. That's when things cooled off.

No, that wasn't quite right. It cooled off minutes earlier, when he asked me to release Benjamin into his charge for the rest of the summer, and I said no. My refusal to grant him full control was the pivot point when charming Curtis became severe Curtis.

I reread the last sentence on the screen.

*. . . I was admittedly curious from a research standpoint,*

*especially given the possibility of making familial and even multigenerational comparisons.*

Multigenerational.

I thought about the day I came home with Benjamin after his night in jail. The intervention by Curtis. The kindness, and the patience, and the pad thai. The question, *And your brother, was he the same way?*

But Curtis didn't know about my brother. I hadn't talked about my brother. Twenty minutes at the pool, and less than a week later, twenty minutes eating takeout. There wasn't time, never mind the fact that I didn't discuss my biggest source of familial shame with just anyone. I hadn't even told Robert why Ewan had gone to prison until we'd been dating half a year.

Curtis knew about Ewan. Maybe he'd heard about him from another psychologist, or maybe he'd met him long ago, at Menkoka, when Ewan was first held there.

I tried to picture that day at the pool. Curtis watching Benjamin with such interest.

And then I thought farther back, to that day in college when I'd brought Benjamin with me, because he'd gotten in trouble at school and I couldn't find anyone to watch him and I couldn't risk failing a psych class, either. All of which I'd explained to Curtis, feeling embarrassed that I had a disobedient young child and a chaotic life, unlike most of the other undergrads.

I pictured the look on Dr. Curtis Campbell's face, then— the tilt of his head, the softening of his features, that moment when my crush started, because it was just incredible that this professor cared, that he was interested—*really* interested. In me. In my son.

Especially in my son.

# 3 9

## BENJAMIN

"I don't know what to say to her."

"Go ask her about her dog. Say you're thinking of getting a new one. But not until the current one passes away. Say you have an old black Lab, on its last legs—"

"I'm supposed to pretend I have an old dog?"

"Yes, and you'll get a new puppy, but only after the old one dies. You just haven't decided on the breed."

I must look surprised.

"Pretend dogs are the best kind, Benjamin," he says, smiling. "A good excuse for why you have to be home, or why you can't do a favor when asked. Pretend *people*, too."

I don't ask what that means. I'm too nervous about the girl. One thing at a time.

I wander over, we chat, the dog opener works just like he said it would. At one point I look toward the car and I don't see Matt at all, but I know he's watching from somewhere. I point to the Jag. She's impressed, enough to take out her phone. I ask her what's in Stevens Point. Her sister, at college. We joke around. I'm in no hurry and neither is she. Everything's going great when suddenly Matt's at my side, harsh-whispering into my ear. "Get the fuck back to the car."

Jade—that's her name—makes a face and I make a face back. *Sorry?*

He's got my arm, literally dragging me.

"Get in."

He speeds out of the rest stop, blasting some piece of classical music, only one shade better than the jazz. I know a lecture's coming but I don't have a clue. He told me to talk to her. He even told me what to say. I don't get it.

He kills the music.

"You never, *ever* let them take a photo."

"Sorry. What?"

"She was taking a photo of my car, over your shoulder."

"I don't think you were in it."

"Doesn't matter. You tried to show off, pointing to the Jag. She pulled out her phone. One snap and she's sending it to her family or her social media, and that ends the whole game."

*What game.* I don't say it.

He bangs the side of his hand against the steering wheel. "Every person in the world would know she got in my car."

I don't think it's illegal to give someone a ride, but maybe it is? In some cases?

"Okay. I get it."

"Do you really, Benjamin? Do you *get it*?"

"They'd know you gave her a ride. You don't want people to know you gave a teenage girl a ride. Because she's too young. Maybe a runaway."

He pinches the very middle of his forehead with two fingers, like he's trying to find patience.

"She took a photo. Did you, also, take a photo?"

"No."

"You left your phone at home, is that correct?"

I nod. It was the agreement. A stupid fucking agreement, but I understand. I don't like social media, either.

"It's my fault," he says after he's calmed down and he's no longer got a death grip on the steering wheel. "I didn't give you adequate instructions. I thought you might have . . . *intuition*."

At least he's apologizing.

"Christopher Weber had intuition," he says. "Good looks. Charisma. Without that he wouldn't have appealed to two pretty girls like Sidney and Izzy. But he was undisciplined. He didn't understand his *extra*. He went after two girls in the same social circle. Girls who lived close to where he worked. He left digital trails and visited one in a public motel where people could see them, for Christ's sake, when he could have just as easily been in a car or in a park, at least until he knew what he wanted, at least until he knew what he was doing, what he needed from those girls, whether it was for them to lie still or not breathe or to be on the edge, almost not breathing, warm or cold. I don't judge. What I can't condone is a lack of self-knowledge, patience, caution. He was shitting where he planned to eat, Benjamin, do you understand what that means?"

It's the longest thing he's said all day.

"Shitting where he . . . planned to eat?"

"His work. His play. The two sides of his life. Too close. That foul motel was a mistake but it wasn't the worst part.

The worst part is where you first meet, that's where people will first look. I shouldn't have let him stay in the carriage house, even for a few nights. And the clothes and the weights he left behind—I never told him he could do that. I spent hours wiping down prints. I should have put a knife between his ribs the moment he showed up at the pool, looking for work. You're not the only one who makes mistakes, Benjamin. I made the biggest mistake: investing in a loser."

A state trooper passes on our left, slowly. No wonder all the cars in our lane have been going the speed limit.

"Wait. So *were* you trying to help Christopher Weber get better?"

That's why he's so mad. His old patient did bad things. Stuff he wasn't supposed to do.

Dr. C—I can't keep calling him *Matt*—rolls his eyes. "Yes, I was trying to help him, Benjamin. Do better. *Be better.*"

"As in—not going after girls?"

He pinches his forehead again and does a strange sort of nasal groan.

"I'm sorry!"

He glares at me. "Don't. Just, don't. I know you're smarter than you're pretending to be."

"Maybe I'm . . . not?"

He exhales through his nose. "Okay. Everything's okay. We'll take this more slowly."

# 40

## ABBY

"You're being paranoid," Robert said over the phone when I finally got him to pick up, halfway through Grove's forty-minute lunch period. "I'm almost sorry I ever bad-mouthed him, if it's just going to make you obsess."

"You said something at Ray's about his ex-wife."

"There was some talk about their various disputes. She filed a restraining order."

Curtis's story had seemed credible when he first told me, but now it seemed like a typical abuser's elaborate, self-serving lie.

"I think Curtis has been covering up a lot of things. And I think he's been interested in Benjamin since he saw him at the pool, or maybe even before that." I lowered my voice to a whisper. "I'm not saying he's a pedophile. I think he's too much of a womanizer to be interested in a boy that way. But he's fixated on Benjamin. He doesn't just want to mentor him. He wants to mold him."

*But mold him how? To what end?* I couldn't articulate my

discomfort. Robert had already called me paranoid. Maybe I was. But even paranoid thoughts are sometimes justified.

Robert said, "He might just be a psychologist who knows society isn't fair to troubled boys. And isn't that the whole point of the book he's supposedly writing?"

"The book! I started reading a chapter, and it's unhinged. And I'm not the only one who thinks so. I found a message from his editor in a long document of back and forth emails, along with an unfinished response he seemed to be cobbling together for a lawyer, in case the publisher sues him to get the advance back."

"Why would they ask for it back?"

"Because they've decided not to publish the book. Curtis is a star author no longer."

Peggy Keller was the editor's name. I'd only started skimming her email when Robert finally returned my call.

"I'll tell you what," Robert said. "I'll see if I can locate information about Curtis's father so you have an address at least. You go back to your analysis of his imploding career."

We hung up. I pulled up the Keller memo.

> Dr. Campbell,
> You've always been provocative and we appreciate both your expertise and your ardor. But the chapters on sexual development and the chapter you've titled "Reconsidering Pathologies" are problematic. Given the increasingly strident nature of your editorial exchanges with Margaret, and given also that your agent has informed us you may no longer be working together, I took

it upon myself to phone you personally, but you haven't replied to my messages.

It's one thing to suggest that adolescent experimentation is normal. It's another to suggest that girls exist to serve as vehicles or objects for the actualization of boys' or men's fetishes and fantasies, including risky ones. Surely you don't think that a guide meant for parents should encourage the acceptance of the behaviors you are describing in graphic detail. It's one thing to establish the frequency of certain kinks in the adult population, but you seem to be advocating for something that goes beyond sexual diversity, toward nonconsensual behaviors punishable by law—in a book about children, Curtis. Children.

We originally asked for a revision of chapters 9 to 11 but based on your last email and lack of communication in the weeks following, I think it's time to consider terminating our plans for this book. I've cc'd your (former?) agent and our lawyers. I hope you'll supply an agreeable time and date for a call, as I've already requested twice in the last month without receiving the courtesy of your reply.

"Hello? Professor Rosso?"

I tore myself away from the scathing publisher letter. Ayako stood in front of my desk, with Mei Ling behind her, already back from lunch. Technically, we still had five more minutes, but every last international student was already present. Over the next hour, we'd be watching the presentations they'd prepared for their parents about life at Grove.

"Can I go first, please?" Ayako asked.

"Certainly. Mei Ling, do you want to dim the lights for us? *Dim* as in make them a little lower?" I pointed across the room, to get the concept across.

A minute later, Ayako's slideshow, titled "Why I Want to Attend Grove This Fall," began to play. After several slides showing summer students doing chemistry experiments, gathered around a Virgin Mary statue, and playing field hockey, I started sneaking glances at my phone under the table.

Robert hadn't known Curtis's ex-wife's name, but after a few searches I found her, LISA CAMPBELL, posed next to Curtis in a local society column photo. On a different website she was ELISA in a photo from a Chicago charity ball, ELISABETH on a North Shore doubles tennis ranking site, and E. V. CAMPBELL, proud mom of VADA, on the home page of a real estate firm where she evidently worked in the early 2000s.

Glancing up, I directed Ayako, "There's no hurry. Try to read your slides more slowly."

A Vada seemed easier to track down than a Lisa/Elisa/Elisabeth, or so I thought. But on YouTube and TikTok I found plenty of Vadas, all the wrong age. I focused on the ex-wife again, restricting the search to the last five years, but that turned up nothing. If she'd remarried, she might be using a different surname. I'd find some way to contact her. I just needed more time.

On the screen at the front of the room, Ayako's presentation had gone full montage—a scrapbook-like page of dozens of tiny photos, the expected product of a girl who couldn't resist cramming all of her new friends onto at least one messy slide.

I looked down at my phone again. No more searches, especially now that Ayako was finished and her fellow students were clapping. I looked up in time to see Ayako's final slide—one elegant, centered photo with the words THANK YOU at the bottom.

I put my hands together to clap, but then I recognized the girl in the photo. I froze.

Mei Ling was asking me something. She wanted to give her presentation next. Her words were white noise. Ayako's slide was still on the screen. Those braces. Those bangs. There was no doubt.

"Actually, I think some of you need a bathroom break. Ayako, can you stay here a minute?"

When everyone else was out of earshot, I asked Ayako why she used that photo as her final slide. Her eyes widened, like she'd been caught cheating on a test.

"You're not in trouble," I said. "It's just that all of your other photos are of international students from the summer school."

She looked down. "We don't wear the uniform yet. She wears the uniform."

"Oh," I said, doing my best to mask my surprise with admiration. "So you just found a photo online of a girl wearing a typical Catholic school uniform."

"The Grove uniform," she corrected me. "I didn't find it online. I found the photo outside the chapel."

# 41

## BENJAMIN

It took two and a half days to mow Dr. C's dad's place and dig out a huge stand of bamboo and cut back some blackberry bushes that left scratches all over my arms. The place looks like a horror movie set, all stone and vines and with a turret on one corner. Dr. C sat on a creaky plastic lawn chair the whole time, looking at old leather-bound books while he slathered oil on his legs. I sweat. He tans.

"Getting the idea?" he says when I finished mowing the back.

"My mom always said she had to tire me out when I was a toddler so I wouldn't get into trouble."

I say it thinking he'll laugh. Adults like toddler stories. But Dr. C doesn't laugh.

"I'm not draining your energy just to make you compliant. I'm allowing you to learn discipline and practice deferred gratification. Which isn't to say you know nothing about deferred gratification, because you're better in that regard than many of my boys. But we need to balance out your sporadically nasty temper."

He smiles at that last part. Whatever. At least he hands me a can of Coke. It tastes amazing. I drink half the can without taking a breath.

"Good. Let's go inside."

There's a real estate sign out front. It says SOLD, but it's not completely sold, Dr. C told me. There's still something called a closing going on. I keep waiting to meet Dr. C's father. I picture an old bald man who looks like Professor Xavier from the X-Men in a really old-fashioned wheelchair with a blanket over his lap, sitting in some dark library next to stained glass windows. There are so many rooms in this house, it's possible. Since we got here, I haven't seen a single person, but it doesn't mean they're not here.

We eat lunch—cold turkey and American cheese sandwiches sitting on a back patio. One apple for each of us, which he chews extra loud, but I try not to show him it bothers me, because anything that bothers me becomes a lecture, which I can do without.

Then Dr. C points to the big toolbox we took out of the back of the Jag. He tells me to take it down to the basement and I go down there, a step at a time, ahead of him. It's spidery and cold, and it smells like a wet cave. The only lights are bulbs with long fuzzy strings.

"Open it up. Get out your wrench set."

I take a guess and pull out what I think are the wrenches.

"You might need a screwdriver, too."

The box has a bunch of them.

"Are we building the shed?"

"No shed."

He points to a thing that looks like a weight lifting machine in the corner.

"You're taking this apart so we can move it before the new owners show up."

There's a light string we didn't pull yet, close to the machine. I pull it.

"You ever seen anything like that?" he asks.

"Only in movies." I don't say what kind of movies. Truth is, I've seen something like this only once. There's a sort-of saddle and levers and a few parts that make it clear muscle building isn't the goal. Anyway, I know he doesn't like porn movies so I shouldn't have said anything about movies to begin with.

"You remember the conversation we had during our first week of sessions, in my office?"

I nod.

"Use words," he says—like I'm a toddler and he's my mom.

"Yes. I remember."

"We talked about . . . ?"

"Experimentation." I hope I'm picking the right word. "Life instead of fantasy."

"Yes. And we deconstructed the 'men as visual creatures' myth. Both genders respond to visual stimuli equally. No matter, it's a canard."

I try not to laugh. He uses that word a lot. *Canard*. I looked it up. It means duck.

"Visual is nothing compared to actual," he says, stroking a metal pole that connects the saddle thing to an overhead frame attached to some other parts that are hanging down, with circle things at the end. Not handcuffs. I look closer. Yes, handcuffs.

"Men are stubborn in their misunderstandings of women," he lectures in that pompous way that almost sounds British, except he's not. "If you want them to do exactly what you want, it's better to understand them. Not obey them—I never said that. Get inside their heads. Physical control is one thing, but mental control is much more powerful. Many of my patients have extremely simple desires. Domination. But there are many ways to dominate. Make it a game. Make her do what *you* want. Make her forget what *she* wants. Make her forget that she has any choice in the matter. Isolate, confuse, dismiss, refute. That, my friend, is better than any physical restraint in the world."

A few feet away is a gigantic cardboard box I'm supposed to put all the disassembled parts into. Lots of bolts and nuts. Lots of screws. The dildo thing attached to the saddle is only one part of the job.

"I'll be upstairs getting dinner ready," he says. "Mac and cheese?"

It's all pretty funny, I keep telling myself. It's a story I'm going to tell when I get back to school. The fancy car that he finally let me drive for the last twenty miles into Fond du Lac. The Addams family mansion. The superhero fuck machine in the basement.

And no, he didn't come on to me, I can already see myself saying after people start laughing. It wasn't like that.

*So what was it like?*

It was like spending a week with a supervillain who wants to tell you about all the minivillains he trained. The Christopher Webers and the John Darbys and the Benvolio

Rizzos—yeah, that guy. The one who picked up girls at bus stations and left them all in dumpsters, and yet, even though he did the same thing over and over, the cops took eight years to smoke him out.

He keeps telling me that I'm smarter than them. He keeps telling me that everything I've ever been criticized for is actually *my* superpower. I get bored easy. I don't care if a girl is upset or crying. I get mad when someone talks shit about me. I think I'm better than most people.

"You are, Benjamin. There's nothing wrong with thinking that."

We're up in the dining room now, eating mac and cheese on these fancy gold-rimmed plates at a big table under a chandelier. It's dope, but it would be a lot more dope with better food.

He starts lecturing me about all of the famous, successful people who are the way we are, and I nod and try to look interested, which is easier because I can nod while I'm eating and he doesn't get mad and say, "Use your words."

I've heard this lecture twice now.

Stock traders. Surgeons. Pilots. The best of them are like us.

CEOs. Chefs. Top salespeople. The best of them are like us.

It took me this whole road trip to realize he doesn't want me to be good. He wants me to be the right kind of bad—which isn't really bad, he keeps saying. It's just different in a way that most people won't ever understand. He compares it to how people used to think of other people with different brains. Even if they were good at things—good at math or artistic or whatever—they were still locked up or mistreated. But the world was changing.

"Someday, Ben, you'll give a TED Talk about the societal contributions of people like you and me. But not yet. For now, we hide our lights under a bushel." He looks at me and sighs. "That's from the Bible. You haven't read the Bible, have you? Just as well."

He tells me we need more time together—that things can't be rushed. I must *find my extra* and *come to appreciate my gifts*. He doesn't think I'll make as many mistakes as some people do. He has to *give me space to learn.*

He says, "Kittens must catch their own mice."

Half the time I get what he's saying and half the time I don't. I haven't seen any mice scurrying through the mansion, thank god, because mice, rats, and cockroaches all give me the creeps.

We finish dinner and he makes me do the dishes, both washing and drying. He wraps each one in bubble wrap and puts them into a cardboard box, so now the cupboard is a few plates less full. I still keep thinking his father is going to come down in an elevator at some point, maybe with a maid pushing his wheelchair.

We're getting ready for bed—I'm in a room with a twin bed that smells dusty, but I don't care—when he says, "I can't stand this place. We're leaving tomorrow."

"Your dad's not here?"

"No. My father's not here." After a minute he says, "He's in a nursing home."

I thought the whole point was fixing up the yard and clipping bushes and stuff to make his father happy, but I guess it's really only to sell it, and it's almost sold. I was supposed to be here for two weeks. But maybe we're done.

My shoulders are killing me from the yard work. There's no swimming pool and I haven't seen a lake. I'm okay with heading back, actually.

"We're going to Oshkosh, tomorrow," he says. "Have you been to Oshkosh?"

I start shaking my head and then I remember he doesn't like that. "No. I've never been."

"There's an interesting lighthouse out there, called the Asylum Light. We'll sail past it."

It's the first time he's mentioned sailing at all. I guess he must own a boat, same way he owns the Jag, which would be nice. He starts to tell me about the history of some institution for the insane, going back over 150 years, but he must notice my eyelids getting heavy because he laughs and says, "It's just history. The same story, told over and over. Just remember, it's better to be the jailer than the jailed. It's a good thing I met you when I did, Benjamin."

He's standing in the doorway and he reaches for the light switch, which makes an extra-loud thunk when he pushes it, because the house is so old.

"Tomorrow will be more fun than today was, I promise. No mistakes this time." He wags his finger at me again. "You're going to like sailing. It's a great way to meet girls."

# 42

## ABBY

I had to wait twenty minutes for the final bell to ring before I could hurry to the hallway outside the school chapel, and there it was: a large framed portrait of Harper McKibben with her birth and death dates: 2003–2017. *Always in our hearts.*

I'd seen the photo of Harper on a news site, and I knew she went to a Catholic school, but I hadn't made the connection. She wasn't just a North Shore girl. She went to school here. Right here.

Down the hall from the chapel, I rapped at the door of Sister Lucretia's secretary, a young woman who looked up with an eager-to-please smile, wiping a spot of mustard from her cheek as I entered.

"Weird question, Raquel, but you probably know I'm a candidate for the fall position, and if I get it, Sister Lucretia said there was a chance I'd get to move into the Grove faculty house that Curtis Campbell is vacating. She even said I might be able to move in early?"

Raquel was still chewing, so I pressed on nervously.

"I know he had a dog. And I have allergies, so I might need to deep clean the place first if he lived there, what—three, four years?"

Raquel set down her sandwich.

"Dr. Campbell was here way longer than that. He came here a year after I did. After his wife passed away." She closed her eyes for a moment, thinking. "So, fall of 2017."

"Fall of 2017," I repeated back. "Poor Dr. Campbell I didn't realize he'd lost his wife."

"And daughter. Drowning accident on Lake Michigan."

I must have managed to mask my shock well because Raquel calmly continued, "But I don't think you need to worry about the allergy problem. He's never had a dog. There are rules against that."

Were we even talking about the same Dr. Campbell? *No dog?* That was the least of it. Dead wife. Dead daughter. Dead student—Harper McKibben, only weeks later.

"You don't look well."

"That was the other thing I came to tell you," I said, taking a big step back. I could feel heat flashing across my cheeks, my whole body struggling to stay calm while I thought about everything Curtis had said about his ex-wife—the one he'd supposedly visited a week ago—and the daughter who was close to Benjamin's age.

"It might be flu." I fanned my face.

"Do you need to lie down? Sister Lucretia has a couch." She pointed to an open doorway. "She's in a meeting with the cafeteria staff. She won't mind."

"Maybe for a minute."

"And Professor Rosso," Raquel called after me, "you should know that the Grove house can't be cleaned just yet. Dr. Campbell still left a few things behind. But once it's completely empty, we'll let you know—*if* you get the position, I mean."

Three minutes on Sister Lucretia's hard modern couch, with my head between my knees, were all that I needed.

*Wife and daughter dead.*

*Grove student killed just after he came to teach here, only weeks after his wife and daughter died.*

*Former patient, Christopher Weber, dead following a car accident, responsible for Sidney's and Izzy's deaths.*

It could all be coincidence. It could be bad luck, or the sort of thing that only seems like luck but has logic behind it. Curtis counseled and studied psychopathic criminals. Maybe one of those criminals did something to his wife and daughter, to get back at him for an undesirable diagnosis or damning testimony in court. Maybe one of those criminals visited Curtis at his office and crossed paths with Harper, who attended school just down the road, and who recognized him later, and trusted him to give her a ride.

And Weber, who died up in Wisconsin? Maybe it wasn't a random drunk driver. Maybe it was another patient who was jealous of the attention Curtis had paid him.

None of it was Curtis's fault, possibly, but it didn't explain the endless lies.

And another thing. *Recently dropped by his publisher.* Not for an illegitimate reason, but because of disturbing things Curtis had written. Things he didn't even seem to recognize as disturbing. Girls and women as objects. Justification for nonconsensual sex. Possibly—and maybe Peggy Keller was misreading or overreacting—the normalization of violent, pathological behaviors.

Then again, it seemed like every notable pundit, even ones with PhDs, said outlandish things all the time now. Maybe Curtis felt he had to. Maybe he was one of those people who thought the best way to make people think was to say something shocking. Start a debate. It didn't mean he had ever harmed anyone intentionally.

I had bad feelings, but no evidence, and furthermore, no way to confront him directly. Not that I wanted a confrontation. What I wanted most was to simply pick up my son and drive away, leaving Curtis's provocative viewpoints for someone else to puzzle over.

I found a tissue in my jacket pocket and used it to wipe my forehead, which was covered with a sheen of nervous sweat. Glancing around Sister Lucretia's office, my eye passed over cheerful framed photos of Grove girls doing elite girl things—riding horseback, sailing on a yacht—and stopped on a key rack, just above the nun's desk. Each key had a colored plastic tag.

I stepped closer, checking over my shoulder with each step, until I was close enough to run a finger across several, turning over the tags, but they all seemed to be labeled things like *Chemistry supply closet* and *Bake sale cash box*. Another step, and I was up against the desk, reaching for a drawer handle, when a voice stopped me.

"Raquel said you felt unwell."

It was Sister Lucretia, staring at me through thick-lensed

glasses, hands pushed down into the large pockets of a shapeless gray dress made of some coarse, thick material that looked too hot for a summer day.

"I do feel odd," I said. "I had a nice rest but I should probably get home, where I have medication. It's possible I'll need a sick day tomorrow."

"If you lived here on campus, you'd be back in a jiffy." She pointed to the couch. "But you don't. Not yet. Sit down, Ms. Rosso."

"Sister, I need to—"

"Sit."

I perched on the edge of her hard couch while she stepped closer to the desk, scanning its surface.

"Were you looking for something over here?"

"No, I was just admiring the photographs over your desk."

Her mouth remained fixed in a grim line. "Yes, our students love sports. We find it's a good balance. It was something I planned to ask—if you could coach something. Tennis? Cross-country?"

"Maybe cross-country," I hedged. "Anything that doesn't involve balls or nets."

"Good. Dr. Campbell helped us with cross-country. And with swimming. And sailing. There wasn't much he couldn't do. So good with the students. What a lovely man."

Listening to the praise was like chewing on glass. I did my best not to wince.

"I never had to worry when he was around," she continued, hint of a smile forming. "If only we had ten more like him."

Her continuing stare unnerved me, so I looked away, pretending to study the photos again. The girl in full equestrian getup on a dark brown horse jumping over a green-and-white-striped pole. The sailboat, leaning into a brisk wind, the name *Paradox* on its white stern. Monied leisure.

"Ms. Rosso, if you don't mind me asking. Why did looking at photos require you to open my desk drawer?"

"I didn't. But I was just about to when you walked in. I was only looking for a Tylenol. I hope you don't mind."

Sister Lucretia's smile faded. "It's not good to take acetaminophen if you're a heavy drinker."

"I'm not."

Articulating carefully, she said, "Dr. Campbell warned me that you had some problems with alcohol, but he assured me they were all in the past. We're strong believers in rehabilitation."

"He said I was an *alcoholic*?" The diagnoses were adding up. "And you were willing to hire me?"

"He promised to help monitor your sobriety."

"Oh, did he?"

"Yes."

I tried to rein in my indignation. It was getting harder to sort through all the strange things Curtis had said about me, some true and some not true, and that was actually worse. Pure lies wouldn't be half as sticky as a mixture laced with truths that triggered my deepest anxieties. But alcohol was not one of them. That was a bad chess move.

I looked at Sister Lucretia with all the confidence I could muster. "Talking about my alcohol use would have been a violation of confidentiality."

"He assured me you weren't a regular patient. He simply said that if he had any doubts this fall, he might not be able to send a recommendation letter, and that would be the appropriate signal."

"But he already sent a recommendation letter."

"For the summer job. It was of a 'probationary' nature."

Probationary. Another small question answered. I always wondered how Curtis could think so little of me at times and still recommend me for an important job. The answer was: he didn't. He got me a temp assignment—perfect for keeping me busy, less likely to object to Benjamin's absence, which he knew from the start I'd resist—while at the same time setting up conditions that would make a permanent position unlikely.

"I'm not an alcoholic," I said. "I swear. And I could really use the fall job. Given that it comes with housing, that would mean a lot to me, and even more to my son. His name is Benjamin."

"You've mentioned him." Sister Lucretia clasped her hands at her waist, the picture of sympathy and devotion.

"I've already explained about the girl-to-boy ratio and the weekly Mass. He doesn't mind. But if I could promise him a new *home*, that would be . . ."

"Ms. Rosso. There, there."

My sob took us both by surprise. My eyes had flooded with tears I'd never felt coming. I'd only mentioned the house as a ploy, hoping she'd offer to take me to see it. Somehow I'd spot something there—an envelope, a scrap of paper, something to lead me to wherever Curtis really was.

But the house wasn't only a tactic. It was also a house.

Attached to a job. How long I'd wanted both those things more than anything; but even when I had neither, I'd still had Benjamin. And now? He was in the hands of a dangerous man.

Sister Lucretia approached the couch but didn't sit down. "He means a lot to you, your son."

"Everything." A snotty laugh covered up the hitch in my throat. "He needs a home. And he needs for me to have a stable job. We need each other."

"Of course." Sympathetic tears seemed to be forming behind her thick lenses. But then she said in a no-nonsense voice, "The house is a two-bedroom with two baths. You can certainly tell your son that, but I wouldn't promise him anything. Sort yourself out. Get your recommendations in order. Stay on the wagon. That's all I can advise."

"Thank you."

More gently she said, "We'll let you know in August. It's not even completely empty yet." She rubbed her hands in a worried gesture that annoyed me. "Poor Dr. Campbell has been so incredibly busy. We can't blame him."

"Of course we can't." I forced myself to smile. "But you said he's only left a few things behind? I'd be happy to drive them up to his father's place in Wisconsin. I just need the house key and his father's address. I'm sure he gave you a forwarding address?"

"That's a wonderful idea. I don't have the address, unfortunately. But I do have Dr. Campbell's phone number."

Sister Lucretia went to her desk, opened the top drawer, and extracted a silver key that she held in her palm, visible for one long second until she folded her fingers over it.

"Unfortunately, I can't give you access to his belongings, few as they are, before we've talked to him."

"No, of course not! Why don't you try him then? No time like the present."

I watched as Sister Lucretia dialed, waited, then left a short message.

"It went directly to voicemail," she said.

So, he wasn't just screening my calls. He was ignoring everyone's. At best, he was being irresponsible, and I was being paranoid, and years from now I'd look back on this week and laugh.

At worst? I couldn't think of "at worst."

But I did have a plan. And it didn't rely on a stupid fucking key.

# 43

## BENJAMIN

This time, he tells me, I should know what to do. No photos, and it doesn't matter if she wants a selfie with the sailboat. Sometimes it's best for cameras and phones to simply disappear. She is not, under any circumstances, to send a photo from her phone.

Like he told me before, no "Dr.," no "Curtis" or "Matt" either. I'm not "Benjamin."

At this point, I'm just wishing we could get on the boat, him and me. I don't feel like we need company, even if the girl we saw looking at the help wanted board in the marina is cute. I don't have a choice. He forces me to go up and talk to her while he busies himself filling two water jugs at a spigot forty feet away.

The girl and I are standing about a foot apart, which seems too close, but then again, we're both trying to read the same three-by-five note cards tacked above eye level, and some of them are handwritten. One person is looking for someone to clean their sailboat, one time only. Another person wants a cook and deckhand to come along for a weeklong trip.

"It's hard to read some of these," she says, taking a half step closer to me. I look down and smile, stepping back a little. "You can tell which ones are the old men. They have really messy handwriting."

I look where she's pointing and laugh. The note card is covered with shaky blue scrawl.

"On the positive side, if that person's a pervert you can probably get away from them."

"I don't know," she says. "Old guys can get around fast with those walkers."

"And anyone can beat you with a cane."

She's still smiling, a deep dimple showing. Glossy lips, pink, not that drawn-on dark red lipstick look. She might not be wearing any makeup at all. Jaw-length light brown hair, wavy and messy, with a stripe of blue that's started to fade.

She has a daypack slung over her shoulder. Full, but not huge. A patch on her army jacket says MACMURDO ANTARCTICA RESEARCH STATION.

"Don't tell me you've sailed all the way there."

She sees where I'm pointing. "No. I got this jacket from a thrift shop."

Without looking up, I can still hear the sound of water gushing into a plastic container. He's watching. Probably overfilling the container or emptying it when no one's looking, so he has an excuse to stay within eavesdropping range. He's probably surprised I'm doing this well. *I'm* surprised. Small talk is hard, and we're not even at school where I'd have obvious things to say.

"I actually think the badge is a fake," she says, still staring straight ahead at the board. "McMurdo is spelled wrong. There's no *A* in it, really. I've thought of ripping it off, but it would leave a hole."

I keep thinking she'll reshoulder her bag and walk away, but she doesn't.

"So, you're looking for a job?"

For the first time, she turns and gives me a less-than-friendly squint. Something went wrong. I asked a question. Before, we were just taking turns. Making observations, making jokes. Keeping to our own turf.

I'm about to give up and walk away when she touches my arm. She points to Dr. C.

"Your dad keeps looking at us. I think he's wondering why you're talking to a strange girl for so long."

I resist the urge to tug at the neck of my T-shirt, even though it's feeling suddenly, uncomfortably tight. "Yeah. He tells me not to talk to strangers. Especially strangers with backpacks and suspicious badges from places they've never traveled."

She laughs. "Because I'm gonna what, rip you off?"

"Maybe. You might pretend you're a boat cleaner or a dog walker or something, and then just . . . murder me. Take our boat and sail all the way from here to the Atlantic."

I got that part from Dr. C. We are way inland but I guess it's possible, lake to river to more lakes and finally salt water.

She laughs again. "So he *is* your dad."

"Uncle," I say, taking a risk. "Not my favorite one."

She pulls a face. "I hope he doesn't know that."

"Well . . ." I'm getting a rush. It's working. But I also feel like someone in a movie, playing blackjack at a Las Vegas casino, and I don't know when to ask for a new card and when to fold. "He's probably figured out I'm not that eager to sail with him today or I wouldn't be here, hanging out at the bulletin boards for this long. Obviously, he knows I don't need a job."

"So, what did you tell him when you walked over here?"

"That I was checking the lost and found notices." I point to a small corner of the board with cards about found items: White tennis visor. One sandal. A cat. "I lost my phone yesterday."

"Aw." She turns to face me and she touches my arm again. The same spot she touched before. "That's the worst!"

I feel warm inside. Hot even. But I also feel shaky.

"That must be making your day extra long," she says, nose squished and eyes half closed. A cute face I'd find annoying if we weren't alone and she wasn't making it just for me. "I mean, at least you could half ignore an uncle if you had a phone."

Why isn't she getting it? *It's easy. Just leave.*

"I bet he knows it, too," she says. Dimple still there. Cute-sorry expression still there. "I'm Lenora," she says, reaching out to shake.

I can't refuse her hand. It's soft. A little damp.

"And you are?"

"Dennen."

"Like the singer?"

"His last name. My first name."

"Your mom must have been a fan when you were born."

I'm hoping Brett Dennen had a debut album before I was

born. No idea. Dr. C told me I should say my name was Chase. I was about to say it and I couldn't. I may not look like a Dennen but I definitely don't look like a Chase.

Lenora loops her arm in mine. In a faux-fancy voice she says, "I wouldn't mind a day sail, Dennen. If your uncle would let you have some company."

When I look shocked, she pulls her arm away. Her face falls. "I'm sorry. I didn't mean to scare you."

"Of course I'm not scared," I say, so wishing I could put her arm back through mine that I have to shove my hands in my pockets just to stop myself from doing something weird. "You were being nice. But I'm sure you have something to do."

"I don't. I'm staying on my dad's sailboat, but he never leaves his slip. His plan for the next two days is to tinker with some electronics he's switching out." She lowers her voice to a flirtatious, accented stage whisper. "*Winches. Windlasses. Yes, please.*" She resumes her normal voice. "Do you even know the difference between a winch and a—"

I look up to see Dr. C standing only ten feet away from us. I didn't hear the spigot turn off. "Weather's not getting better than this! We gotta be back by two o'clock."

I risk a sideways glance at Lenora. The blue piece of hair. The shiny lips. The dimple.

*Walk away.*

But she doesn't. She steps behind and around me and then walks right over to Matt. She introduces herself. She tells him that I just invited her on the boat for a few hours of sailing. Then she looks back at me and winks.

# 44

## ABBY

"Elisa was found washed up in Indiana Dunes National Park, on the shore of Lake Michigan, southeast of Chicago," I said when Robert answered the door of his duplex around 7 P.M.

This time, I hadn't bothered to text or phone.

"Do I know this Elisa?" he asked.

"The wife."

He stepped back as I pushed my way into the hallway, six-pack of beer in one hand and file folders in the other.

"But she went back to her maiden name, Agapov. And on formal documents her first name is Elizaveta. Which is why it took me two damn hours to find the obituary and news coverage. Vada washed up dead, too, a week later. That's Curtis's daughter, or was."

He reached out to take the beer. But I didn't plan to let go of the six-pack until I knew he was listening and believing.

"You remember that cruise she went on?" I asked. "The reason she didn't show up at the hearing, supposedly? That was in July 2017. The wife and the daughter were found in August. Accidental drownings after a private watercraft overturned, officially. No wonder Elisa—or Elizaveta—didn't make that hearing."

"She was from Pleasant Park. Did they report it locally?"

I didn't know if he was buying everything I'd discovered but I handed him the beer. It was getting too heavy anyway.

"Looks like she didn't live on the North Shore long and by the time they were breaking up, she'd already gotten herself a permanent address in Chicago. It was in the city papers. Nothing local. Easy to miss, especially in a summer with so many Chicago shootings."

Robert's place was even messier than mine. Take-out napkins and an open bag of chocolate chip cookies on the coffee table. Basket of unfolded laundry on the couch.

"You can move that," he said.

I sat down and looked around for the remote, to pause the movie he'd been watching.

"Under the cushion, maybe," he said. "I assume you've got the address of where he and Benjamin were supposed to be headed?"

"Fond du Lac. At his father's. Or come to think of it, he sometimes said 'near' Fond du Lac. And doesn't the county have the same name? I haven't been able to find the address. Did you have any luck?"

"Not yet. The father's named Campbell, right?"

"Yes. I forgot the first name. Something long and biblical. But what if it doesn't even matter, Robert? What if they drove to Canada? What if they flew to Mexico?"

"Not easy to do without a passport for Benjamin."

"Florida, then. California. They could be anywhere. They could—"

Robert popped open a beer, handing it to me. "One big swallow. One big breath. Repeat."

He gestured for me to stand up, found the remote, turned off the television, gestured for me to sit again, and said, "Two more sips. Keep breathing. Good job. Not just on the beer—on the research. I thought this guy had disabled your bullshit meter permanently. Welcome back, friend."

I looked up at Robert and saw him for the first time in weeks, maybe months. He was scruffy but clean, wearing a big gray sweatshirt and even looser black sweatpants dabbed with dried white paint—I had doubts whether that kitchen project had ever been finished, but I also knew that if it had been my renovation, he would have come through, because that's how Robert was. Ready to mobilize instantly for someone else's chore or emergency. Not always so great at dealing with his own.

I took two more sips to dissolve the egg-shaped lump at the base of my throat.

I said, "You're going to lecture me for being stupid enough to trust Curtis."

"I won't."

When he sat down hard next to me, the couch shifted an inch. He'd put on a few pounds since we broke up.

"Fond du Lac is a small town," he said. "Forty thousand people. Can't be too hard to find a man with a biblical name. *If* that's where they are. And if he meant the town, not the county. But you remember him saying 'near'?"

Sour beer rose up in my throat. "I think so."

Fond du Lac, the town or the county. *Fond du Lac.* You didn't just invent Fond du Lac out of thin air. And then again, Green Bay? His wife and daughter had never lived in Green Bay, from what I could tell following two hours of online searches. And the dog? What the fuck was up with pretending to have a dog?

"His father isn't doing well," I said, still clinging to islands of fact in a sea of deception. "Curtis has been busy trying to help him."

Robert had just popped open his own beer when I shouted, "Mattathias! That's his father's name. Both of their legal names. Mattathias Campbell, and Curtis's father was a doctor, too." I allowed myself one breath of relief. "I've got to pee now."

When I came back from the bathroom, Robert's face was pink, like he'd been rubbing it, the way he'd often done when we were a couple and he was feeling uncomfortable.

"This whole thing is beyond weird. It doesn't all add up." He said it gently, watching my face. "I'm worried there's stuff you haven't told me. But don't worry. I'm gonna go first. This shit has been weighing on me, anyway." He set his can on the coffee table. "I didn't resign just because they were going to fire me for the Sidney Mayfield diary thing. I got into some other trouble over the last year."

"Oh, crap."

"And," he held up a finger, cautioning me not to interrupt, "I said some nasty things when Hernández was hired. Personal things. I was jealous he got the job I wanted. It wasn't a cool thing to do."

"Okay."

"And then I was pulled over, leaving a bar. I put my badge on my lap to give the sign. I was with another off-duty cop and he even knew the guys. But it didn't matter."

"It shouldn't matter."

"Yeah. So, we got reported. The diary thing was just one strike, but it was the third one."

"All in one year, huh?"

"It's been a tough fucking year."

"Is that it?"

"That's never *it*. If you looked into my background, Abby, you'd find lots of things. Stupid bar fights. Girls I shouldn't have dated. Even more girls who shouldn't have dated me. Things I wish I hadn't done and that I'd never tell my mother. Know what I'm saying?"

I'd met Robert's mother, Stella. She seemed like a woman you could tell anything, especially if you were one of her three handsome sons. According to her, they could do no wrong.

"Things that would get you cancelled now," he added, "if you were someone important, and I'm not. You called me a caveman once, and that's probably true." He rolled his shoulder back, neck cracking. He'd always said the long hours in the patrol car were bad for his back, as was the time he'd executed a flying tackle in order to stop a man intent on stabbing his wife. "So now you know I never could have been the right role model for Benjamin. I'm a bad influence, just like you always worried I might be."

"Maybe a little. No one's perfect." I leaned over the low table between us, to take a better look at his face. "Plus you've been drinking a lot since you stopped working. Even if you've stayed at home to do it."

"Guilty." He hesitated. "But now you know what I've been holding back. I know it means losing your respect all over again. But I'm doing it for a reason. I think you're holding out on something, too, and I want you to tell me. It's not for us. It's for Benjamin. No more secrets."

I walked over to his desktop computer, on the far side of the living room under the signed and framed Bulls poster—the man would never understand interior decorating but at least he'd taken down the *Sports Illustrated* pinups—and I signed into my email account. I pulled up the full hypnosis transcript but I didn't let him read it over my shoulder. I had to be in control of this.

I started to tell him about that night—the driving, the drinking. How good it felt to be out of the house, partying with an older crowd. The fact that my brother wanted to get a discount on a used car. The fact that he was willing to offer my virginity for that discount.

"I'll never know whether he was joking," I said.

I fast-forwarded to the arrival of the cops, walking down the trail, finally getting picked up again by Grant and Ewan, the girl I had no memory of seeing. Then the accident and the failure to report it.

"I knew Ewan was convicted for what—obstruction of justice?"

"That was one of the charges. They weren't able to prove that he withheld aid from Grant purposefully or even that he was part of the reason the accident happened in the first place. The only reason he's still in prison is because he's assaulted people in jail many times since."

"But . . . geez. The girl?"

"She never came forward. Grant predicted she wouldn't. But the next part is worse."

I told him about Grant and what happened when the driver stopped to ask if Ewan and I needed help.

Robert stared at me, perplexed. "I just can't see you as a young girl, failing to get help for someone, even if that guy was a jerk."

"I don't remember it, but I don't want that to sound like an excuse. Obviously, I repressed it."

"You were in shock from the accident. We can't predict what we'll do in those situations." He scooted closer and put a big arm around me, carefully. "I'm sorry, Abby."

I hugged him back, stiffly, then rolled my chair a foot away, needing more space, more time. Just talking about it made it all seem real in a way that made everything worse.

"So Curtis Campbell has something on you."

"And that's only half of it." I'd saved the hardest for last—telling him about Benjamin possibly giving Izzy the clonidine that had caused her fatal reaction. "Curtis has something on Benjamin, too."

Robert offered me another beer but I declined. It was nearly 11 P.M. No one would be coming and going to Curtis's vacated place at this hour. I knew what I needed to do next, and I knew I would do it alone.

## 45

## BENJAMIN

I expect Dr. C to introduce himself to Lenora as Matt. Instead he says his name is Troy and he's a podiatrist. He leads us aboard his boat and corrects me when I call it a yacht.

"Yachts are thirty-three feet and up," Lenora says. "This is a Catalina 22."

It's written on the side, I realize now. And the boat's name is written on the back. Lenora asks Dr. C—"Troy"—about the sailboat's cutesy name, as I'm sure every person must, and now I see why he called himself a podiatrist, in order not to veer so far from the truth that she'd get suspicious.

"Pair of docs, get it?" he says.

"Oh. I get it now."

"Good for you, dear. It's a double entendre."

They keep talking to each other—"bonding" my mother would call it—the whole time we're getting ready to sail. I barely exist. He talks about her name and asks her if she likes

Edgar Allan Poe and together they talk about engine sizes and jib sails. Just the stuff I thought she wanted to leave behind.

Matt-Troy-Dr. C taps his nose. "You know, I think I know your father. Maybe he came in to see me for—let me remember—bunions, was it?"

"Could be," Lenora says, glancing over like she wishes I'd rescue her from the boring conversation.

Dr. C makes a smarmy face. "Should we give him a quick call to make sure you have permission to be out for a spin?"

"I already asked him," she says too quickly. She knows, and I know, and Dr. C definitely knows that she didn't ask, just like Dr. C knows that he didn't plan to place any phone call.

That's the kind of confidence he keeps wanting me to observe and imitate. Give them a lifeline and see if they take it. Get inside their heads and find out what's working, what's missing. Take a scalpel to the interesting parts.

We're motoring away from the dock when Lenora says, "Not to worry anyone, but I'm only a so-so swimmer. I mean, I can doggy paddle, but my father always makes me wear a PFD."

I ignore her. If she and "Troy" want to be buddies, that's fine with me.

"Um, Dennen?" she tries again.

"*Now* you're talking to me," I snap.

Dr. C rolls his eyes, shakes his head, and sighs loudly. The big faker. "*Dennen.* That's rude."

But I am mad. I'm fucking mad. I didn't want him to bring her along but I didn't expect her to ignore me either.

"Temper," Dr. C says, and this time he isn't using his fake voice.

This is what I am supposed to be working on. This is one of the thousand things we talked about in his office. Self-control. Self-regulation. In addition to confidence and understanding how to be a success in a world that tells boys and men they have to be great, saddles them with responsibilities, and then shits on them for being what they were always supposed to be, the hunters, leaders, and risk-takers. Some of us can't sit still. Some of us feel less. Some of us need to vent more. Some of us need to . . . need to . . .

*The genes you and I have helped our species survive. Don't ever apologize for who you are. Hone it. Master it. Use it.*

I close my eyes. Chill out.

Dr. C is saying to Lenora, "When it comes to adolescents, a lot of bad behavior boils down to sugar levels. Once we're out of the harbor and are under sail, we'll get a snack."

"And the life jacket?"

"Certainly," he says. "Just two ticks, please."

I know shit-all about sailing. It always looks good in movies but now that we're out here on the lake, with choppy blackish water beneath us and Dr. C shouting out orders I don't understand, it's not so great. He can't trust me with the tiller. I keep getting in his way as he manages the sails, which he doesn't even call "sails" half the time. Anything he tells me to get—from the cockpit cushions to the lockers where they're supposedly kept—I can't find.

"For godsake," he snaps louder than I've ever heard him snap, "go down below if you can't help with anything. And show her the head!"

"Fine!"

Lenora comes up behind me in the crowded cabin,

whispering. "Sorry. You warned me that he wasn't your favorite uncle."

She isn't talking about Ewan, the only uncle I have. That's the problem with lies. You have to keep them straight.

"My dad sometimes keeps the cushions in the V-berth," she says, pointing. I awkwardly turn to face her, still in a half squat. "That's where people sleep. In the front."

The ceiling is so low I can't stand up straight. There's only one space with a bench to the right and a table to the left and a flat V-shaped area with bedding straight ahead and I've never felt so claustrophobic in my life.

"And the head," she says, leaning so close I can feel her breath on my cheek, and it's warm and it's sweet, "is what we landlubbers would call the bathroom."

She smells like strawberries, and her skin looks so soft I want to touch it but I also need to get far away from it. I'm starting to freak out. I can't believe she actually said "landlubbers."

"Okay, you're laughing at least," she says. "For a second, I thought you were going to puke. Have you *never* been on your uncle's sailboat before?"

I shake my head, swallowing back acid. I can't believe rich people spend money to do this.

"Or on any sailboat?"

Headshake. Hard swallow.

"Okay," she says, hands touching my hips from behind, like each knobby side of my pelvis is a handle. I flinch. "Oh my god, sorry." She pulls her hands away. "That's how my dad and I pass each other. I shouldn't have—"

"No," I huff. Now I sound like I have asthma on top of everything else. "It's okay."

The sailboat leans hard left and I fall into the table and she falls into me, but it's not sexy or cute. I don't like all these sudden movements. I've punched kids for less.

*You're a man now*, Dr. C likes to tell me. *New rights, new responsibilities.*

It takes a second to rebalance ourselves.

"And *that's* why I just grabbed on to you," she says, laughing. "For stability. To prevent what just happened." She claps once. "Okay! We need something to drink. Did your uncle mention the sugar thing because you have a problem? Just like diabetes, I mean." She looks over my shoulder, out through the low narrow doorway. "The waves are getting rougher. Maybe not the best day to be out here. It's still hot as balls but it's that sort of gray-white muggy hot, you know? Maybe that's what's making you sick."

She's so busy taking care of me that she's forgotten about herself. As girls do.

Lenora opens a cooler under the small table and pulls out what looks like a big juice container—screw-top, no label—and two red plastic cups. She sniffs. "Lemonade? This must be what we're supposed to drink."

She hands me a cup, fills it, fills her own. Sips.

"Hm. I'm gonna say there's vodka in this."

She peers out toward Matt-Troy-Dr. C, occupied at the tiller, wind whipping his smug smiling face.

"All right," she says with a cute little grin, like we're getting away with something. "I'm game."

*Sedation is your friend*, Dr. C kept saying to me on the drive. *And don't forget what I told you about phones.*

# 46

## ABBY

I started with the office. Through the closed window, my phone light swept over left-behind objects, lengthening their shadows. Stacks of books were lined up against the wall. The desk was still there, too, topped with miscellaneous items. I never thought a hole puncher would give me hope, but this one did. I needed proof that Curtis had left in a hurry, too busy to empty those desk drawers. Somewhere there could be an envelope from his father, a printout of an air itinerary. Anything with an address or a destination. Anything to stop me from heading the wrong direction.

I squatted and looked around for anything big and hard enough to break a window, but I couldn't find a single rock, only thick, luxuriant grass. I slapped a mosquito on my neck and felt the wetness on my fingers, just a squishy touch. It was enough to make me grimace. I was a wuss. No tolerance for even a little blood or violence of any kind. But was that true?

With mosquitoes feasting on my bare ankles, I felt my

body filling with hatred—like it was flowing through my veins, pumping into my muscles, preparing them for action. The sane part of me said I should breathe deeply—let it all flow back out. Find calm. But I didn't want to find calm. I wanted to find Curtis and face him. And then I wanted to bring back my boy.

I pushed on the window and it slid to one side, so effortlessly it almost made me laugh. Of course he'd leave the windows unlocked. What did he ever have to fear? This was a posh community, and he was a man.

The screen popped off easily. I jumped up and wiggled inside, scraping my leg across the sill and landing inside with an awkward grunt.

In seconds, my elation soured. One drawer and the next—empty or almost, save for some paper clips and loose change. I swept a hand through the deepest drawer and managed only to press my thumb against a tack. Swearing, I knelt down, sucking the sore spot. There, under the desk, was the dictation machine, still connected by a long cord to a spindly headset. I aimed my phone light and saw a microcassette tape, still inside. I popped it out to take a look. No label, but it had to be recent.

It wasn't what I'd come for, but I'd take anything that gave me a sense of control over my secrets, which were never meant to be in his hands. But what if Curtis had recorded sessions after mine? A small box of twenty or more tapes was farther under the desk. I couldn't fit them all in my pockets. I didn't want to leave any sure sign I'd stolen something. One missing tape could be overlooked, but a whole box?

My phone lit up with a text from Robert. I covered it

quickly with my hand, not wanting the glare to fill up the room.

*I found the address. Father is a doc who closed his practice a few years ago. Retired now. I know a cop in the area who will be on duty starting 6 a.m. Friend of a friend. I can ask him to do a drive-by.*

The relief poured through me. I typed *Thanks*. I considered adding a heart, but I pressed Send instead.

Robert followed up: *My advice we don't make a scene. You know how Benjamin will react if we came up there no reason or do anything in a panic.*

It was nearly over, then. We'd wait for the cop's report, then drive up by midmorning and pretend we were in the area, just sightseeing and checking in. Robert had found Curtis, or at least Curtis's father. Things were going to be okay.

I didn't need scraps of paper after all, but I didn't regret breaking and entering. My glance fell on the dictation machine again. I had time.

Crouched under the desk, I reinserted the tape and started listening to the words I'd already read in the transcript. From the very start, my slurred voice surprised me. I sounded drunk. Not hypnotized. Drunk, or drugged from that tea he'd encouraged me to drink, to *calm me down*, of course. Even Benjamin had noticed I came out of Curtis's office a little loopy. No wonder I'd felt so weird later that night, all the way through making dinner. The tape captured the halting quality of my words and the lengthening gaps between them, as Curtis barely acknowledged my soft and senseless rambling.

And then our voices stopped. It couldn't have been more than ten minutes into the session. I forwarded a little. Forwarded again. The only sound was a dry hiss of moving tape and Curtis's occasional throat clearing. He'd kept recording. Another fast-forward. Nothing. I flipped the thirty-minute tape over and pressed Play again. Nothing and nothing and nothing, until finally, my startled voice, as I woke at the end of the hour: *Do we need to start over?*

*No*, Curtis had told me. *Our time is up.*

I stared at the tiny white reels, coming to a sudden stop. The tape was done.

But where were all those parts where I talked about the half-naked girl I'd seen jump out of the car? Where was the accident in horrific detail? Where were my shameful, remorseless confessions?

I briefly considered whether Curtis had simply recorded over them, exchanging my problematic confession for white noise. But the throat clearing proved it wasn't so. He'd kept recording.

There was only one possibility left. I hadn't said most of the things in that transcript.

I pulled out the tape, staring at it, the magnitude paralyzing for a moment. Who would *do* that?

It's what I'd asked of myself after reading the transcript, but now the question doubled back on itself. Who would defraud a patient into thinking she'd seen and heard things that never happened?

A few details were there—things I'd told Curtis at the start of the session, other moments he could have gleaned from Ewan. But most of it was invention. He didn't bother to implant a false memory during the session itself. He didn't even bother with conventional hypnosis. He just drugged me into submission and then wrote utter falsehoods into the transcript, knowing I'd believe them.

I crawled out of the window, came around the office, and continued toward the front of the darkened main house. I tried the front door—locked. And several windows—but most of them were picture windows, and the only one that looked possible to slide open was high above my head. Every room inside looked empty, as best I could tell in the dim light. I had nearly circled the house when my eye fell on a large tarp-covered object in the back yard. Riding lawn mower? Immense pile of firewood?

When I got close enough, I saw it was a vehicle supported by several tire jacks, the wheels completely removed. That was a lot of trouble to go through in order to store a car in summertime, especially if Curtis would be coming back to retrieve it soon.

The tarp was fastened down on all sides by a web of bungee cords. I unhooked two from the rear of the SUV, spotting the removal of the back plates, and worked my way around the front, panning with my phone light until I stopped. The front of the car was buckled. Grill dented, front edge of the hood curled back like a lip, sneering.

My mind searched for the last time I'd seen the SUV. I could picture it shooting past—the car a white blur, disappearing around the house, the one and only time Curtis was late for one of Benjamin's appointments. I could see him moments later, face shiny, pushing back his dark hair.

That's when I'd driven from his place to a café, the same

place I'd gotten the call from Willa about Christopher Weber, who had died sometime before dawn, hit by a driver who was never found. The accident hadn't surprised Curtis at all. He was smug. Weber was reckless. *Maybe he pissed someone off.*

What had the police said? Something about the tires and the car color being common. Curtis's SUV was white. Tires, missing.

I stared at the crumpled bumper, making space in my mind for this new thing. Bigger than the microcassette tape, which mattered only to me. Bigger than any of the wild speculations I had half indulged, still trying to keep open the possibility that Curtis could be surrounded by death without any of it being his fault.

And if it was his fault?

You didn't crash into the car of a former patient on a backcountry road several hours away by accident. You had to hunt that person, first. You had to be arrogant enough to believe that you'd get away with it, no matter the evidence left behind. Tire tracks. Paint chips. And if you could get away with such a thing you were probably both lucky and smart, smarter than the man you wanted to kill, even if he was a killer and a psychopath.

I startled at the buzzy call of some night bird, coming from behind me, in the woods that surrounded Grove Academy. Just through those trees, the school was so close.

*Harper*, I thought, picturing her as I'd seen her in the school portrait—awkward, spotty, and so very young.

*Stupid and impulsive.*

I remembered the expression on Curtis's face when he said those words. Impulsivity was what he hated most in his failed clients. The thing he would hate the most in himself if one time—a time of strong desires only recently unbottled—he gave in and did something rash.

Harper McKibben.

Too close to home. Broad daylight. No witnesses, but still, what a risk.

Harper McKibben was picked up in Lake Forest. She was disposed of in a ravine two miles from Lake Forest.

*Too close too close too close.*

I pulled onto my residential street and parked at the curb. My car doors were locked. I was parked under a bright streetlight. Even though I was physically and mentally exhausted, the whole night had made me so jittery that I didn't even want to step out of my car. I gripped my phone, like it had the answers I still needed.

Curtis Campbell. Out of grad school for about twenty years. A therapist and researcher at a time when the most heinous crimes against women in our area seemed to be on the wane.

The timeline kept troubling me, as did the paradox of Curtis's professional identity. If he was someone trying to cure psychopaths, he would have been heartened to know something was working, there were fewer murders by strangers, fewer serial killers especially. But if he harbored his own dark appetite, how would that make him happy?

I had to keep reminding myself: None of Robert's maps and graphs really proved there were fewer serial killers from the 2010s on. There were fewer serial killers identified by the police. Fewer serial killers who were caught. And even the ones who were caught had changed their behavior. They drove farther to dump their bodies. They'd become more careful. It meant something. I could tell that it did, just as Harper's name had meant something the first time I heard it. It was the sound of the past opening up—a sinkhole—strange proof of unseen forces. Violence under the surface of everyday life.

I sent a text to Robert: *Home safe.*

It was one in the morning. He didn't answer.

I kept wondering why I wasn't bursting to tell Robert what I'd discovered from the tapes—that I hadn't known about the girl in the back of Grant's car, and I hadn't been the one to suggest leaving Grant. Why wasn't it a revelation worth celebrating? Because those two claims, upsetting as they were, didn't clear my record entirely. I was a messed-up kid. I did bad things. I wouldn't have believed Curtis's made-up stories otherwise.

Still sitting in my car, I watched as a teenage girl stepped out of an idling car three doors down from my apartment, walked up to the front door of her house, and bent down to move a geranium pot.

*Bad idea, leaving that key there*, I thought automatically. *Wouldn't be hard to get into that house.*

The voice wasn't an adult voice. It wasn't Abby the neighbor, the counselor, or the mom. It was Abby the teenager, seeing opportunities even when she wasn't searching for them. Abby, the bad seed. The hypnosis transcript was a hoax, but that didn't change what I thought of my younger self.

When I was living at my second foster home—age fourteen, fifteen—a group of us kids were sent to a church group run by Pastor Baxter, my foster dad at the time. We were supposed to talk about the bad things we did and promise to be better. The problem wasn't that we paid no attention during our little group sessions. We paid excellent attention. Others' confessions were valuable, something we all figured out quickly.

One kid pretended to be sorry about all the cars he'd hot-wired, but he also told us how he did it. Great lesson. I went next, saying how bad I felt about the makeup I'd shoplifted but I also explained how easy it was. Another lesson. A third kid explained his best tips for making and selling impressive fake IDs. It took Pastor Baxter a month to realize we were all using the group sessions not to cleanse our souls but to learn how to be more successful petty criminals.

Sitting in my car, I felt the tumblers turn.

Criminals learn from each other. Serial killers learn from each other—or they could. Even Curtis had said it. They'd used group therapy at Menkoka for a while, but it backfired. *The problem with housing and treating psychopaths together is that instead of getting better together, they get worse. They study each other. Learn from each other.*

I'd thought he was calling me out as a bad influence—and he was trying to. But he was also speaking to a larger truth.

Psychopaths learn from each other. But not only from each other. They could learn even more effectively from a leader. A teacher. A therapist. A *mentor*.

I was never going to sleep, now.

I was just about to drive to Robert's duplex four hours later when he showed up at my curb. The sky was lightening to pink in the east. I got to his car before he could come out.

"Yeah, yeah. Text first," he said, gesturing to a cup of coffee in the passenger side cup holder. "Extra cream, two sugars, right? I know you didn't sleep."

I tossed a gym bag into the back seat, then I came around front and pulled the microcassette from my pocket. "You're right. But I didn't explain why I took so long getting home."

I needed to tell him, before we pulled away from the curb, just in case he wanted to distance himself from all of this—the laws I'd already broken, never mind the ones I might be willing to break in the hours ahead. The last four hours had given me a lot of time to think about what I wanted to do to Curtis.

"You stole private property," he said. "Wonders never cease."

"It was worth it. This tape proves I didn't say what Curtis claimed I said, in his so-called transcript. All the most important stuff was made up."

Robert seemed oddly unsurprised.

"So, there it is. He's been gaslighting you. You must feel much better now."

I didn't feel better. I felt even more confused and conflicted, especially whenever I pictured Curtis the only way I ever wanted to see him again: on his knees, in pain, begging for mercy.

"And here's part two," I said. "Curtis's SUV is still at his house, and it has all the signs of hitting another car, head-on."

This time, Robert leaned back in his seat, eyes wide.

"You're kidding."

"I am not."

"That cocky little fucker." Robert frowned. "That makes

this more serious, you know. He has a lot more skin in the game." We were both buckled in, but Robert hadn't started driving. "Is Benjamin's phone in the house?"

"I assume he brought it on the trip and handed it over to Curtis."

"Makes sense, if Curtis was a good guy and he only wanted to make sure Benjamin wasn't using his phone on the sly. But if Curtis is who you say he is, and if he wanted no possibilities for tracking their location, then he would have told Benjamin to leave it behind."

We unbuckled simultaneously and hurried into my apartment. Robert took the living room and kitchen. I started in Benjamin's bedroom, feeling a sense of déjà vu as I opened drawers and dug under the mattress.

I came out five minutes later holding up the phone. "Hasn't been plugged in for days, but at least we have it. It was in his pillowcase."

Back in the car, I waited until we'd made it to the highway, giving the caffeine a few minutes to percolate through my veins, before I told Robert my idea about killers learning from each other.

"The only problem with that theory is that our area's most notorious killers—John Darby, Benvolio Rizzo, Keith Lagrange—only went to prison after they committed their crimes."

"But I bet at least some of them went to Menkoka when they were too young for prison," I said. "It's an institute for troubled adolescent boys. Ewan went there briefly. Weber went there. I'm sure we could find out whether Darby or Rizzo or Lagrange did. But I don't care if Curtis was mentoring all of our area's most notorious psychopaths or just a few. The point is, he was their mentor. They learned from *him*."

"You're thinking this is some *Dexter* situation—a crazy guy like Curtis channels his dark urges into stopping other sadistic guys?"

"The opposite. Curtis didn't want to teach his favorite protégés how to be good. He wanted to teach them how to be more disciplined. How to be less impulsive. How to not *get caught*."

"But all those guys were caught, eventually."

"And that pisses Curtis off," I said. "Don't you see?"

We were on Highway 41, heading north, when a chiming sound reminded me. We'd plugged in Benjamin's dead phone, and now it was coming to life with notifications from an app, saying that Benjamin hadn't practiced guitar for over a week. He must have downloaded it after meeting our downstairs David.

Robert's phone rang ten minutes later, around 5:20. It was his Wisconsin cop friend, calling early. He hadn't waited to get to work, but had stopped on his way, driving a civilian car that wouldn't raise any alarms.

"Thanks, Pete," Robert said, hanging up just as we passed the last exit to a town called Hartford, halfway between Milwaukee and Fond du Lac.

To me he said, "There's a sold sign. Pete knocked, but no answer, no visible vehicles and no lights."

"Sold sign," I said, incredulous. "His father doesn't live there anymore."

"The name rang a bell for Pete. Campbell Senior was a well-known doctor in the area."

"*Was*. Is he dead?"

"Not dead. Just in a nursing home. Pete will try to find out which one."

The engine revved as Robert laid a heavier foot on the gas. If the house was empty and we had no destination, it didn't help for him to drive any faster.

I said, "Our best chance is to find someone who knows Curtis and has talked to him recently." We'd already passed signs to Madison, before Milwaukee, and now we passed another side route—longer and less direct. But it would take us where we needed to go.

I'd always hated this part of Wisconsin. Now I remembered why.

## 47

### BENJAMIN

Dr. C told me that people like us don't worry. We live in the moment. One of our many evolutionary advantages.

But I've been worrying since the first minute I saw Lenora at those bulletin boards in the marina. I've been looking ahead, trying to find a different way out of this, and I've looked back from looking ahead—if that makes sense—like I can already see the day when I'll wish I'd done something different. So much for living in the moment.

Dr. C has already told me that people with antisocial personality disorder come in many types, but I don't think he wants to know I could be the wrong one. He wants me to be aware of consequences, because that reduces the chance of doing dumb-shit things, but he doesn't want me to consider the consequences of things *he* wants me to do.

Dr. C says he's teaching me to operate from a position of strength. No apologies.

"But don't look to the internet for role models. Influencers need attention. They put themselves in the public eye at every opportunity, talking about how wealthy and brilliant they are, and how many bitches they can attract, like the best a man can hope for in life is to be a pimp making videos for gullible prepubescent followers. You don't spend time watching those idiots, I hope?"

Before I could answer, he reminded me that attention is a problem. Attention limits your freedom. Attention gets you *caught*. "The worst thing that ever happened to me is all the attention I got when my first book became a bestseller. I didn't anticipate that. I shouldn't have started on the next."

So why did he? To share his immense wisdom with the world. When I get home to my phone, I've got to look up narcissism. I'm not understanding who has it and who doesn't.

I'm supposed to think about the consequences, even if it's just using cold logic, like not wanting to get caught—which is still living in the moment, I guess, but with an awareness of the future. But not a fear of it. Some emotions aren't helpful, Dr. C tells me, and we don't have to give in to the NTs—neurotypicals—who want us to think differently. Our default to cold logic is an asset.

The problem is, I *am* using logic, and not the way he wants me to. This isn't worth it. Not for sex, not for thrills.

Do I feel for Lenora? I feel something: annoyance mainly, I guess. She should have walked away. She should know better. Most men are fucking perverts. I told Izzy that; did she listen? Lenora may deserve a lesson but I'm not feeling pumped about being the one to give it to her.

Dr. C slides behind the dining table, next to me on the bench. Lenora is in "the head." He whispers in my ear, "Do you have it?"

Her phone, he means.

"Yeah."

I made up a story, or really, I added to the story I'd already made up. Hate my uncle. Lost my phone. While she's in the head could I please oh please oh please make one quick phone call without my uncle noticing?

*Sure thing.*

I went outside and leaned over, so that Dr. C couldn't watch me from inside the cabin. Then I started dialing my mom's phone. Halfway through I stopped. I couldn't remember the last four numbers. Part of it was nerves. I never dial her number. I just click on her name.

I can hear Dr. C inside the boat now, humming to himself. I try one combination and it goes to a wrong voicemail. I dial another and get an automated message from a phone company. *Fuck!*

I have only one idea left. I punch in my own phone number. That one I know, at least.

I bob as I wait for the ring, knees bending, face in the wind, picturing my mother in our apartment. It's early in the morning but she has to be home. She never goes anywhere.

It goes to my voicemail. At least I have the right number.

"Dennen!" Dr. C calls with fake cheer. "Come help make the sandwiches, if you please!" When I clamber back into the cabin, he whispers, "She's taking too long."

"Said she was changing into a bathing suit."

He wiggles his eyebrows suggestively. I hate him.

"Don't drink too much of the lemonade," he says. "That's for her. You'll want your own head on straight." He looks down, toward my crotch, as if it's not only my head he's worrying about. "Also, I told her you have diabetes. So, she's going to worry that you're overdoing the sugar."

"Why would you tell her that?"

"Why not? Little problems are great for sympathy. Nothing big. Nothing that would scare a girl."

I think about this a minute.

"My mom said you were dyslexic."

He winks. "That one has come in tremendously handy over the years. Extra office help. Deadline extensions."

"So you're not, then."

He points to all the sandwich fixings. I start making my ham and cheese. I dip the butter knife into the mustard, feeling its insufficient weight in my hand. I lick it clean and set it down. I reach past Dr. C and grab the sharper serrated knife and use it to cut my sandwich in two. Dr. C keeps humming. When he reaches under the table for something in the cooler, I lick the serrated knife clean and slip it into the back pocket of my jeans, already bulging with the pack of playing cards I swiped a few minutes ago.

When he's back, head above the table, pickle jar in hand, he whispers, "Did you get rid of it while you were out there?"

"I will. When she comes out." I swallow. "I want her to see me lose it, so she believes."

He smiles and pats my thigh. I think of the knife in my back pocket. I almost wish he would touch me again.

"Soon," he says.

# 48

## ABBY

We passed high fences strung with razor wire and pulled into the visitors' lane, passing a sign that said WEAPONS PROHIBITED with the image of a handgun and a diagonal line through it. It seemed like an obvious warning, but perhaps not. I thought back to that morning, when I'd almost stashed a knife inside my gym bag, and then settled for a tire iron instead. Why? Because I can't stand blood. But the sound of a skull crunching, possibly. I kept picturing it, asking myself if I could really do it. Trying to prepare myself for the weight of the iron, the adrenaline pumping, the expression on Curtis's face. Maybe I could.

A guard in a booth asked if I was on the approved visitor list.

"I don't know. It's been a long time."

The guard looked me up. No sign that I came here seventeen years ago.

"This is urgent," I said, leaning over to try to make direct eye contact.

"Everyone says the same thing. Your family member should have mailed you the form. Then we have to wait for processing."

Oh, Jesus.

Robert asked, "Can't she do one of those phone or video calls?"

Same answer. Visitor's list.

Down at hip level, Robert flashed an ID card that I couldn't read from a distance.

"I'm on the approved list. And I'm really hoping I can set up a video call."

"Preapproved for this particular individual? Oh yes, there you are."

The guard typed some data into his computer, then handed Robert a slick pamphlet with instructions.

"Good luck, and don't even try it from your car. No loitering."

We'd turned around, heading away from the prison, when I started thwapping Robert's arm. "You're on the fucking *list?*"

He ignored me, head ducking lower as he squinted, trying to locate the Best Western we'd seen on our way here.

"You shithead!"

"Hey," he said without any loss of composure. "I didn't realize they wouldn't let you in. I thought they made me jump through the hoops because I wasn't family."

"Jump through the hoops *when?*"

After we pulled into the motel lot, he closed the car door with a calm click, leaving me to watch him saunter into reception to pay for a room we'd only be using for an hour or two. I felt angry just imagining the front desk clerk assuming we were here for sex.

When Robert came back, he opened the door and said in a low voice, "I visited him once, about six months ago. Right after you and I broke up. I thought he might have . . . I don't know. Insights."

"About?"

"How to get you back."

"Curtis seems to be visiting him and talking about me. Benjamin wrote to him. *You* visited him. What is wrong with you people?"

I stomped up the metal steps to our second-floor room. Inside, I yanked the mustard-colored curtains shut. "That's probably why Ewan started sending even more letters this year."

Robert dug a finger into his eye, wiping away sleepy crust. "He asked me a lot of questions about Benjamin. He knew stuff about him, like he was getting information from some other source. It seemed odd at the time."

"And you didn't *tell me*?"

"You would have been pissed I'd visited him in the first place. Right?"

"Right. But then I might have figured out that Curtis was visiting him. Fuck!" I shouted and disappeared into the bathroom, slamming the thin door.

I took a shower because I was one big heat rash from top to bottom. Robert was in the next room, setting up the account for the online visit. When I was finished, I still needed several more minutes, sitting on the toilet, wrapped in a towel, trying to cool down.

When I came out, I heard a stilted recorded voice, full of sunshine and bullshit. It was an instructional video explaining all the rules and regulations for the video call to come, provided by a private company. At the top of the screen, the Stars and Stripes flapped. This wasn't Zoom. A reminder flowed across the screen, ticker-style, letting us know the call was being recorded and monitored live. Violations of the agreement would lead to a visitor ban for that individual and additional restrictions for the inmate. A final robotic voice reminder: *This call is being monitored and recorded.*

And there, finally, was Ewan's face, filling the screen. The similarities were enough to take my breath away. Eyes—same as Benjamin's. Large and dark brown. Light eyelashes, but long. The same arc of eyebrow. No wonder I preferred Benjamin in glasses. Without them, he and my brother were nearly identical, give or take years and pounds.

Unlike those movie prisoners who spend all their time getting buff, Ewan had gone the opposite route. Wide belly and rail-thin arms. Puffy cheeks. Pale skin. Acne. A thick, soft neck, with a white scar running like a necklace above his collarbone.

"You look good," Robert said to Ewan—one liar to another—while I stayed off-screen to avoid getting our call shut down.

"You too, dude. How's work?"

"Changing careers, actually."

From jobs they segued into sports, and then Ewan started talking about the appeal he planned to make, in relation to his conviction for assaulting the prison dentist, which would require a lawyer and tons of money, of course.

"You think my sister would help with that?"

"Not likely. But speaking of," Robert said, then went conspicuously quiet.

Ewan cocked his head. I could tell he'd picked up on Robert's silent message. In the corner of the screen, a timer had been running down from fifteen minutes; now only five minutes remained.

"Here's a question," Robert said, glancing my way to remind me to stay quiet and let him lead. Ewan focused, lips tighter, eyebrows lifted with anticipation. We were alleviating his boredom, at the very least.

"Your frequent visitor," Robert said. "We need to find him. Do you have any idea where he might be?"

Ewan answered quickly, like he was on a game show and determined to win. "Menkoka, near Madison, or Fond du Lac. Those are my best guesses."

"Okay. But we need an address. Not for Fond du Lac. We've got that one—"

"Not the father's house. He sold it."

I nodded, satisfied. He knew things, and he didn't seem hell-bent on pulling our legs from the start.

Robert said, "We could use help narrowing it down. Did your visitor explain what he planned to do . . . on his vacation?"

"Just more of what he usually does. Coaching. Teaching. Young men, especially. Fresh meat." Ewan moved closer to the screen, head angled down, so his forehead and eyes looked too wide. "I tried to warn you in my letters. Why didn't you listen when I said someone was asking questions about you?"

I pulled my chin into my chest, feeling suddenly vulnerable, my gut still remembering the punches he'd land if I wasn't careful.

"I wasn't supposed to tell," he said. "But if you'd come in person, if you'd cared, I could have told you that someone was asking about Benjamin. I could have told you to be more careful about the men you let into your life. What do you say about that?"

We both knew the call might get cut off if I answered him.

Remembering his role, Robert said, "So, you're saying that we've been missing some important information."

"Not my fault." Ewan grinned, lips split wide enough that I could see two molars missing, behind his right canine. Fight probably. Or maybe just rot. "About the appeal . . ."

"Yeah, maybe we can help with that. Especially if we sort out some other things. Get the family back together, first."

"I know my sister has money—"

"Dude." Robert's voice changed. He'd dropped the role-playing voice. "I'm serious. I'll pay for your lawyer myself, if we can just get through this week with no damage. I care about this kid. With your help, we can find him. Then I'll take care of the bill."

"Your 'career change' will allow that?"

"I'll sell my condo if I have to."

"Swear on . . . oh, I don't know. What should we swear on, Robert? You fail me and the Cubs never win another World Series?"

Robert answered with more patience than I could have managed. "I'm talking man-to-man, here. I'm making a pledge. We get everyone home safe, and you get a lawyer."

Ewan sat back in his chair. "Well, we have an arrangement, then!"

Robert nodded, with a grim smile that said he was calm but still meant business. "We need a location."

"I'd like an apology," Ewan said primly. "A real one."

"Your sister is very, very sorry."

"Not enough."

"She should have paid more attention to your warnings. It was a misunderstanding and a mistake."

"And?"

"And it will not happen again."

Ewan nodded. "See? I believe you, Robert. Because *you* understand the importance of family. How's your mom doing, by the way?"

"Stella's great. My brothers are great. Back to the point. Maybe there's a specific place you've forgotten about. A getaway that's been mentioned? A cabin? Maybe farther afield than what we're assuming?"

Ewan scoffed. "Our mutual friend is not a cabin kind of guy."

Three minutes left on the screen timer.

"Some northern place?" Robert guessed.

"Like a hunting cabin? I don't think he'd tolerate a cabin. Or even a motel." Ewan started laughing. "Though I heard that one of his pretty boys made the mistake of meeting a girl in one. Why do people go to motels? Use a van. Use a car. Enjoy yourself out under the starry skies. That's what I miss. The open road."

We waited silently for his daydream to end.

"I'm impressed you're doing all this for my sister," Ewan

said after a moment. "I knew you broke up. I didn't know you were back together. Any wedding bells ringing?"

"Let's stay on topic."

"*Here's* a topic," Ewan said, leaning into the screen, looking eager again. "Make sure you know the person you're marrying. Don't fall for any innocence act. Ask questions. Examine the product."

Robert said, "I already know that your friend—your visitor—has been trying to confuse Abby about what happened the night of the car accident. I'm wise to it. So don't bother."

Ewan laughed. "I'm sure she didn't like being reminded I was going to pimp her out."

Robert's eyes flashed. "So that wasn't a joke."

Ewan folded his hands across his belly, looking pleased with himself. "I couldn't afford that car without a discount! Come on, man!"

I couldn't take my eyes off that face. The one I looked up to.

"What's the big deal? It wouldn't have taken more than five minutes. And I needed a car. A person can't do anything without a car. What the fuck's a girl for, anyway?"

I could see Robert's chest moving in and out. Even though I couldn't hear him breathing, he was doing what he had to do. Big inhale. Big exhale. Don't get riled up.

"I'm going to warn you, Robert. *Know the product.* Abby isn't who you think she is."

Thirty seconds left on the screen timer.

I couldn't take it anymore. Couldn't spend even half a minute, never mind a lifetime, being too afraid to look him in the eye. I shifted over so that I was on the screen.

"Hi." I felt thirteen years old again, and I hated him for it.

"Well hello there," he said, with what sounded like tenderness. "Dogface."

The name froze me.

He leaned forward. "You're not about to cry, are you?"

I clenched my hands into fists, nails digging into my palms.

"You look surprisingly good," he said.

Robert started to speak but I shook my head. This was my brother. My job.

"Ewan, please. We need a location. It isn't about me. It's about Benjamin."

Ewan nodded. He moved even closer. Eyes right up to the camera. "Don't worry, Dogface. I'm not going to be the one to tell Robert what you did."

Ice crept into my veins.

"I'm asking if you know where Curtis is hiding."

"And I didn't tell Curtis," Ewan said. "Not the important thing."

"Focus," I said. "Please."

"I would *never* tell him," Ewan said. "Don't you owe me for that? For keeping my word? For twenty-four fucking years?"

Robert said, "Stop screwing around—"

But Ewan was done with Robert. He only cared about me, now.

Ten seconds.

"I'm glad it's stayed between us. It keeps us connected. So that when you realize we're more alike than different, when you're ready to stop pretending you're better than me . . ."

Ewan's face shrank to nothingness. Black screen.

They'd closed the connection, possibly even five seconds early. Someone had noticed I'd joined the call. Either that or they'd heard Ewan cursing.

Robert turned to me, extending an arm for a hug, but I slid away.

"I'm sorry, Abby."

I needed to leave this room.

I needed to leave this town.

Robert wasn't going to ask the question and Ewan was never going to tell. But that didn't matter. The truth was never going away, and it had nothing to do with the night of the car accident.

Ewan and I both knew what I'd done.

# 49

## BENJAMIN

We're all in the stern—Dr. C seated with his hand on the tiller, Lenora standing and pointing to a lidded bench. "Are the life jackets in there?" she asks.

He gestures for her to lift the lid and take a look—I know he's just bullshitting—and I use the diversion to sit down on the opposite bench, pull the pack of cards out of my pocket, and fling them into the water behind me.

"Oh, shit!"

Dr. C and Lenora look up in time to see a splash.

"Nooo," she says, long and low.

"I was getting ready to take your photo," I say. "It just slipped out of my hand."

Her face crumples. "No!"

She hurries over to my side of the stern, looking down into the water. Behind her, Dr. C smirks approvingly. I look away, because I can't see his face anymore without imagining how it would feel to put a finger in the smirky side of his mouth and pull hard, like he's a fish caught on a line.

Lenora spins around, hands on her cheeks. "I just *got* that phone."

"Don't worry, dear," Dr. C says. "We'll replace it." He touches her knee. My face feels hot. Time warps. His fingers on her knee, squeezing in slow motion. His blink, slower yet. Her startle reflex, his eyes opening again, his grin spreading. Slow, slow, slow. Then just as my hatred is cresting like a wave, everything returns to normal speed.

Lenora looks at me, smiling cautiously. I know what she's doing. Trying to make me feel less bad. Even though I'm the jackass who dropped her phone, supposedly.

I can't bring myself to smile back. I just keep staring, watching her expression change. Another wince, as if something is hurting her.

"Are you feeling seasick?" Dr. C asks, sliding even closer, arm around her shoulder. "You should go inside. Try resting for a bit."

The sails are down. Dr. C pulled them in when the wind died. Now we're in choppy seas, wallowing in the stifling heat, the fancy sailboat about as elegant as a hippo, the outboard motor glug-glugging along, gassy smell in the hot still air.

"No," she says, "that'll make it worse."

She cradles her forehead in her hand, face pinched. Her orange bikini top pooches forward in that position, so she has more cleavage. Her belly has three creases only because she's folded over, too sick to be self-conscious, and that makes me like her more than I've liked her since she boarded the boat, because she's not showing off and trying to pose or be pretty, she's just trying to get comfortable. "My stomach hurts. I think I need air."

Dr. C pulls hard on the long tiller and the sailboat leans into the waves, forcing Lenora to push back into her seat, bracing herself, head up, bare legs extended out in front of her to maintain stability. I feel tired, too, and queasy, but I had only a sip of the lemonade. She had two cups.

"Take her inside," Dr. C says firmly, fussing with the tiller again, slipping it into a locking gadget that keeps us moving straight even after he lets go.

"She doesn't want to."

He fake smiles, all his teeth showing. "We need her to be safe. The waves are picking up."

"You've been saying that all day."

He frowns. "If you both go inside, you can help her find the life jacket she's been looking for."

"Good idea," Lenora says, groggy.

She tries to get up but manages only a half crouch before stumbling forward. I leap up in time to grab her arm before she falls. With one free hand she reaches toward the cabin doorway, insistent now.

"I thought you wanted fresh air," I say, tugging her away from the cabin.

"I wanna . . . I need . . ." She pulls away from my grip and rushes to the side of the cockpit, vomiting over the side. "Oh." A few seconds of recovery, and she vomits again. She wipes her mouth with the back of her hand, apologizing. "I'm so sorry."

Dr. C points to a streak of vomit inches from his foot. He glares at me. "Clean that up."

"I'll get it," says Lenora, eyes half closed, struggling against another rising tide of discomfort.

Dr. C stabs the air with a finger. "I changed my mind. Stay here. I don't want you vomiting inside. Dennen will go get a rag."

She ignores him. "Sorry. I need to lie down." She stumbles toward the cabin doorway, gripping the edges with both hands.

Lenora trips as she enters, landing hard on the inner cabin floor, just barely missing the edge of the table. When she moans, I lock eyes with Dr. C, trying to understand. What is the *least* I can do to please him, so that he'll sail back to the marina?

For all his talk of "finding my extra," he's never put it into words, exactly what he wants me to do, other than not get caught. When I asked him about Christopher Weber the last time, yesterday, he ranted again about Weber's mistakes. Then he started talking about all the favors he'd already done for me, like planting the pills in Weber's car, pills like my mom's, but not exactly my mom's, after he drove Weber off the road. That way, when the toxicology from Izzy ever came back, they'd just trace the clonidine back to Weber. He's going to be holding that over my head forever.

*Half of my time is spent covering for you boys*, he said, like a martyr. But he also seemed pleased. For once, I felt like I was getting him, because he's like guys I've met before. The whiny overworked teacher. The underappreciated coach. The guy who's just trying to teach you lessons for your own good. Lessons Dr. C never got. *Look at my marriage*. If he'd known what he knows now, he wouldn't have put up with his wife as long as he did. Women cost a lot, he reminded me sternly, but they cost the most when you don't handle them right from the beginning. *Disposal is 90 percent of the problem.*

Which is why, he keeps telling me now, this sailing plan was so much better than his original plan, taking that Veronica girl from the sports bar and locking her up in a room, just because I said she was hot after seeing her photo on my mom's phone. I never should have told him that. Never should have showed him Veronica's photo. He kidnapped her for me! I never asked him to do that. I had *no idea* he was going to. But he didn't blame me for that one. He admitted it was a weak plan, since I wasn't involved from the start. *Kittens must catch their own mice.* Fucking weirdo.

"I think we should sail back," I say, now that Lenora is in the cabin and can't hear us talking over the wind and the rough water. "If I do anything, she'll tell."

"She won't. You're not going to find an opportunity like this again. No one knows where she is. No one saw us leave with her." He gestures in a circle. "And when you're done, the next step is easy."

I feel stupid. For thinking he just wanted me to have sex with her. I was so nervous about that part I couldn't see past it, and part of me thought she might even want to. It was a remote possibility, anyway. I never planned to let Dr. C watch. That's gross. And even if Lenora and I only fooled around a little, I knew I could tell him lies. He *approves* of lies.

"We can bring her back. She won't remember. She's too drunk," I say, trying to sound confident, even if I'm not feeling it. Instead, I'm feeling the way I get at school when I'm in a class and I hear people behind my desk, whispering about me. I'm feeling the way I get at night when I can't sleep, and I just need to walk. I just want to go. Leave. Before I do something I'll regret.

"No, she's not going to remember, *Dennen*. That's the point."

"But I don't *want* this."

"But you do," he says. "And if you do it on your own terms, you're going to get too excited and fuck it up. It's like losing your virginity."

I *would* be losing my virginity, but that's not what he means, because he seems to care less about the sex part than what comes after.

He shows his white teeth again. It's not even a smile. It's a pretend smile, and I know he's stressed, unless that's just how he shows his excitement. His disgusting appetite for whatever this is—being in control of her but also me. Making us do things so he can watch and play teacher.

More quietly, he whispers my real name. "*Benjamin. Get the first time out of the way. Trust me. First times are tricky. Even my first time was. You'll enjoy it more after that.*"

I grab for the small serrated knife in my pocket and I lunge forward, knee on the cockpit bench, sharp point against the hot sun-reddened skin of his neck. He leans away from me but I just press harder.

"Well, this is a surprise," he whispers.

"Don't move."

His left hand drops limply into his lap. His body untenses. Now his mouth is at my cheek, our breath mixing. I don't like being this close to him. His smell makes me sick.

Calmly he says, "And what do we do now, Benjamin? You've ruined my shirt."

I push the tip in and hear him sigh, like it doesn't even

hurt, and my hand starts to cramp from the pressure even as I feel wetness dripping down my forearm.

"You wouldn't even know how to get this sailboat back to land," he says quietly.

"I'd figure it out."

"With no one to teach you?"

Everything is a boring lesson with him. The Asylum Lighthouse and how many people were mistreated there. This boat and how it shows you can do what you want and get what's coming to you—boats and cars and girls. If he's so happy and so popular, why does he need me?

"I don't want you to teach me," I tell him.

"But you need me to. You're friendless and fatherless. Your future is bleak, and it would have been even bleaker if I hadn't covered for your stupid mistake giving Izzy those pills."

"Stop talking!" I say, pushing the tip of the blade in, just a little more.

When he swallows hard, I feel his Adam's apple move. His pulse beats against the damp side of my hand. I like it, feeling his blood and heart in my hands, the softness of his neck. One big push and he'd stop talking, finally. That would feel good.

He asks, "You know what Lenora asked me, about you, just before we got on the boat?"

I move my left forearm against his chest, finding a better position for pushing him into the hard backrest of the cockpit bench, cutting off some of his air, so he has to fight for each word.

"She asked if you were autistic. Isn't that cute? In just a few minutes she knew you were different. They'll always know, Benjamin. They won't get the right diagnosis, but they'll know there's something wrong."

"I'm not what you think I am."

"So you're the better diagnostician now. You're not like me, after all."

"I can't be. Because I don't want the things you want."

His voice sounds shaky but his smile looks real. "You're starting to get a taste."

I do want it. The thing I didn't want with Lenora, but with him—absolutely. Maybe that is my *extra*. For me, it's not about girls. It's about something else. The ultimate *fuck you* to anyone who just keeps talking and talking and talking.

I bring my left forearm higher and harder against his neck. I envision what will come soon—eyes rolling back, more blood dripping down my arm. And then I feel a bolt of queasiness, like I'm a kid again at a birthday party and I just ate too much cake. That dripping blood is something else. Maybe I'd settle for temporary silence.

If only he'd just pass out, I wouldn't have to make him bleed more. Then we could tie him up. That thought eases the queasiness. I'm up on my knees, trying to find a better position for cutting off Dr. C's oxygen when a hard kick to the back sends me sprawling. I'm on the cockpit floor, gasping. Lenora is standing over me. The knife has flown across the cockpit.

"I'm okay," Dr. C calls out in a thin, shaky voice. "Well done, Lenora."

I look up at her face, full of fear and disgust. She doesn't think I'm just some shy kid on the spectrum. She thinks I want to rape her. Kill her. Dump her. Even if I somehow got her safely to land now, she wouldn't understand. She'd tell everyone.

# 50

## ABBY

"Need to talk about it?" Robert asked when we were thirty minutes south of Fond du Lac.

It was the first thing either of us had said in an hour. I'd been thinking about what Ewan had said, thinking about why I let myself get so bothered by the fake transcript and all it alleged—and why, in comparison, my own hand in Martha's death bothered me hardly at all.

"Abby?" Robert asked.

"Can we put on music? Just for a while. I need to think."

"Okay," he said, sounding hurt.

He had no idea where my thoughts were going. How could he? But I couldn't have a normal conversation, just like I couldn't have a normal relationship.

Martha kept talking about getting Ewan out of the house, sending him away, even before the night of the accident. She kept saying it to our father, all those nights as they sat on their grubby matching recliners and I stood in the kitchen, listening.

She wouldn't stop. Ewan couldn't make her stop. She would have liked that—a threat, or an actual physical act she could report. She deserved it.

It wasn't that I did what I did, knowing it would end in death. I just pictured her falling. One big, funny slip-on-a-banana-peel whoopsie, and her coral lips pulling back into a sloppy round circle of surprise before one leg swung up and her wide rear crashed down, followed by the sound of something cracking—a shinbone, a broken arm, maybe a hip.

She'd be silenced, chastened, reminded that she drank too much at night, reminded that she slammed around the kitchen and left food out to spoil, reminded that we were part of this family, too. We weren't the leeches she made us out to be. If she was in a cast, maybe I'd have to grocery shop. Ewan could drive me. Maybe she'd decide to go to her sister's place in Florida for a month, to heal up somewhere prettier and more comfortable.

Those were the images that swam through my head as I poured the green dishwashing detergent into the pine-scented floor cleaner and then added a few glops of vegetable oil to be sure, the way I'd done at a sleepover once, when we made Brittany's kitchen floor into a super slide, so slippery that we fell again and again, laughing until Brittany wet her pants.

Brittany got in trouble for that. But I wouldn't, because I'd never tell anyone.

Robert was still fussing with the radio dial when I picked up Benjamin's phone, which I couldn't unlock. I shoved it aside in order to stare at the long line of motor homes ahead of us and tried to get my head back in the game, figuring out where Curtis might be hiding.

This was vacation country. Motorcycles, lots of them. People going camping. Maybe Curtis would tolerate an RV, one of those enormous ones.

"I always wondered if we'd end up with a weekend place up here," Robert said. "Would have been nice."

I sighed. The last thing I could think about now was our relationship.

"I'm sorry. Someday, you'll buy a nice cabin with someone else. It'll happen."

Under his breath he said, "I never understood why."

"Why'd I break up with you?"

"That's the question."

"Boundaries."

"But what does that mean?"

"You don't know what *boundaries* are?"

"Like when you don't want me to come over, unless I call or text first."

"Yes."

"But when we were going out, that made no sense. Once, I dropped by and left a note on your door and you were really happy about it. Another time, I brought you flowers—"

I groaned. "Okay, better example. When you got all up in my face about not deleting my dating apps."

"Okay. I get that. 'Put a ring on it,' right?"

"No, Robert! I never wanted you to propose to me."

His hands flew off the steering wheel. "Hey! Sorry!" A long line of Harleys continued making their way around us.

"Put your hands back. Okay, the Blue Lives Matter T-shirt you gave Benjamin."

"That was a *joke*."

"He didn't think so."

"Yes, he did! Your son has an ironic sense of humor. And he's smart, Abby. Sometimes I think you forget that."

"So you went and bought him an offensive T-shirt."

"No. I got it from a buddy. I didn't buy it, and I didn't want it. We were repainting your old apartment kitchen, remember? And I brought over a bunch of T-shirts we could use for rags and stuff. Benjamin saw the Blue Lives one. He thought it was hilarious. He asked if he could have it. I said, of course! I thought he was using it to protect his clothes from the paint. I never thought he'd wear it to school."

I took all that in. The Carrie Underwood song on the radio ended. Now there was a guy singing about how beer never broke his heart. "Why didn't you ever tell me all that?"

"Why didn't you ask?"

I turned off the radio.

"Robert, I might just be a person who can't have a long-term relationship with anyone, for a long list of reasons."

"So, boundaries are one."

"And worse than crossed boundaries were the excessive gifts."

"Gifts, *bad*. Not what my mama taught me, but okay."

"Too much, too soon. You know?"

I looked over and saw his eyes were red.

"You're a good man, Robert. Most of the time."

He forced a laugh. "And you're a good woman, Abby. Most of the time."

Exactly. But I still never planned to tell him about the times I hadn't been.

Then I thought of Benjamin, refusing to tell me about

the clonidine pills. Maybe it wasn't so hard to understand, after all. Maybe other people would call it guilt, but it wasn't that simple. You didn't want someone to die, but you weren't careful, either. You did something wrong, but not as wrong as everyone will think, and you're used to that, because no one has understood you for as long as you can remember. You did something, but you couldn't see how it would play out. You want to forget, but you know you won't.

It's a scab you'll keep picking at, forever.

The sign at the bottom of the vast, sloping yard said SOLD, just as Robert's cop friend told us it would.

"The grass is recently mowed," I pointed out, trying to sound hopeful.

We knocked on the front door and peered in the windows. I called the realtor listed on the sign and she tried to interest me in other similar properties for sale, but when I told her I was only trying to reach Curtis Campbell, and I had one phone number for him already but he wasn't answering, she had nothing to add.

At the last minute, the realtor said, "Is his trailer gone from the driveway? I asked him to move it."

"I don't see any trailer—or car."

"Good."

I hung up and relayed the conversation to Robert.

"You should have asked what kind of trailer she meant. Are we talking camper trailer, ATV trailer . . . ?"

I called back and got a voicemail. Crossing my arms, I looked up and down the road for anyone to talk to. The grand houses were spaced far apart, some newer, some older. "I just don't see Curtis Campbell going camping or off-roading. This was a waste of time. We should have started with the nursing homes, instead."

In my purse, Benjamin's phone rang once, then stopped. I just missed it.

"Someone was trying to reach him," I said, showing Robert. I googled the area code. "Someone who lives in central Wisconsin."

"Someone who doesn't realize he doesn't have his phone."

"So, not Curtis then."

"Maybe someone he met?"

It felt like good news. If someone was trying to call Benjamin in central Wisconsin, then chances were that's where he was—not Mexico or Canada, not Florida or California. But who would be calling him?

Robert and I exchanged looks, clueless. Afternoon was mellowing, low purple clouds spreading like a bruise above the lake. Robert's friend Pete hadn't been able to find us the name of Dr. Campbell Senior's nursing home.

"I see at least a dozen facilities in the area," Robert said. "Independent, assisted, downtown, hinterlands . . ."

"He has money—or he used to. Let's pick the nicest one and start there."

"What makes a nursing home nice?"

"I don't know. The view?"

"We were a pair, he and I," Mattathias Campbell Sr. said a half hour later, ladling another spoonful of creamy leek soup into his mouth.

Robert pointed at the old man's shirtfront. "You got some there."

Outside the nursing home's dining room window, past the lakeside streets of downtown Fond du Lac, Lake Winnebago shimmered in golden light. It had been a lucky guess.

When Campbell Sr. reached a shaking hand toward me, I thought he was following Robert's suggestion, asking me to pass him a cloth napkin, but he was only gesturing for a wicker basket filled with plastic-wrapped Saltine crackers. I was about to slide one packet over to him when a staff member of the nursing home came toward us. "Woah, woah. Not for him. He chokes. You doing okay, Mr. Campbell?"

Over a mouthful of lumpy soup, he said, "Dr. Campbell."

"I apologize. *Dr.* Campbell."

Meanwhile, another elderly man at the opposite end of the round tablecloth-covered table finished his soup and stared out into space. He didn't talk, but he was an excellent chewer. A dozen bits of cracker plastic littered his side of the table.

The room held about ten tables in all, each one occupied by two, three, or four elderly people. It wasn't a bad-looking place, and instead of giving us a hard time at the front desk, as I'd expected, they'd welcomed us almost too enthusiastically, explaining that Dr. Campbell Sr. received few visitors.

*Not even his son?*

*Not lately.*

When we'd introduced ourselves to Dr. Campbell himself and said we'd both been his patients, he'd beamed, eager to tell every staff member who came by. *Look how well they're doing. My patients. See that?*

"You were saying?" I jogged his memory. "About your son?"

"He doesn't come by as much, now that he's married."

No point in explaining that Curtis's wife and daughter were dead.

"But he was helping you sell the house, wasn't he?"

Dr. Campbell Sr. grimaced, like his dentures had slipped—or maybe it was nothing physical at all, only the painful interruption of a helpful delusion.

He worked his jaw a few times, squinting. "Oh, we don't have to sell the house. It's not a bother, and I'll be cutting back my hours soon. Then I'll have more time to look after things. These rotations are murder."

Robert raised his eyebrow at "rotation." He pulled out his phone in response to a chime and mouthed the word *Jaguar* to me. Then he leaned into my shoulder, whispering. "Someone saw it parked in a restaurant lot in downtown Fond du Lac. That's our best lead. Let's get out of here."

"Not yet," I said, hand up. I needed focus. Dr. Campbell Sr. needed it even more.

"You've always been busy, isn't that right?" I asked, trying to grab the thread that was slipping away.

"Jenny complains I work too many hours. I keep telling her, it'll be worth it. Wait and see. 'Learn to defer gratification,' I always told our son. Can't be a success if you're a hothead, always *now now now, gimme gimme*. That's how he was as a little boy. But he mastered himself. I give him that."

We'd been going in circles like this since we'd sat down, but at least Dr. Campbell Sr. seemed pleased rather than agitated each time either of us steered the subject back to Curtis.

"Did you ever practice together? You said you were quite the pair. I don't know if you meant you were just similar or if you worked side by side?"

"We couldn't have worked together. He's his own man. That's fine. You do things your way and I'll do them mine."

Robert and I exchanged glances, both of us looking for the lost key to the man's memories.

Robert asked, "You both like to camp, fish, anything like that?"

Dr. Campbell Sr.'s mouth split into a loose, wet grin. He pushed the mostly empty soup bowl away. "Ohhhh, yes. Fishing. Certainly. Even better when we didn't catch anything, though. That's what Jenny said. Have fun and don't catch anything!"

"Any particular spot?"

A waiter interrupted, removing the soup bowl.

Dr. Campbell Sr. set his liver-spotted hands on the table and leaned forward, fingers pressed into the tablecloth, stilling his tremor. "I can tell you just where to go. You leave the marina—"

"Which marina?" Robert interrupted.

"Well, the one with the yacht club, of course."

"Is this club on the lake near your house, on Lake Winnebago, or is it on Lake Michigan? At Sheboygan? Where are we talking about?"

"Let him answer," I cautioned Robert, grabbing my phone. I saw a public boat launch in Fond du Lac, on Lake Winnebago. Only one yacht club, close to town. Sheboygan, on Lake Michigan, was forty-five minutes away, to the east. When Dr. Campbell Sr. was younger, I reminded myself, he was a busy, busy man. Back and forth to Lake Michigan would take too long. The nearest yacht club, on Winnebago, was convenient.

"You and Curtis would go," I prompted. "When he was a boy? When he was all grown up?"

Dr. Campbell Sr. frowned. We were confusing him.

"Your son, Curtis, the doctor."

Now he showed his gums, smiling. "That's what I'm trying to tell you."

Behind us, a rattly cart pulled up with the next course. Pale, overcooked pink salmon next to a lump of mashed potatoes. Dr. Campbell Sr. clapped his hands with anticipation. We were losing him.

"The pair of us," he said, removing his hands slowly, so that the waiter could set down the plate. "Pair of docs. See? Curtis came up with that. Jenny wanted something else, but Curtis gets what he wants. Always has. Pair of docs."

"Pair of docs," I repeated, watching his shaky hand reach slowly for the fork.

He frowned. "You're saying it wrong."

Robert looked to me. Deepening his Chicago working-class accent, he tried, "Pair o' docs?"

"That's better."

I tensed with frustration. "Pair o' docs. *Pair o' docs.*"

Dr. Campbell Sr. had just started reaching for the crackers again when I jumped up from my seat, startling everyone at the table. "Robert. I've got it."

# 51

## BENJAMIN

"Lenora," Dr. C shouts, "I won't let him touch you." He lunges between us, like he's protecting her, both of them wedged into a corner of the cockpit. The knife is on the deck, between us.

"He's lying!" I shout, but I can tell, as she peeks out from behind his back, that she doesn't believe me and will *never* believe.

Eye on the knife, I pull Lenora's phone from my back pocket. "Look. I didn't lose it. Your phone, see?"

I'm only helping to convince her that I'm a liar. A manipulator.

I struggle to dial my own number with my thumb. In seconds I hear my mother's voice, faint and tinny. I shout, "Mom! Mom! We're on a boat! Can you track us? I've got a phone—"

But my distraction has cost me. Dr. C darts forward and grabs the knife, with Lenora still behind him.

To the tinny voice still squawking from the phone in my lowered hand, he shouts, "Call the police, Abby! Send help!"

My mom can't believe his side of things. She just can't. And Lenora—even if she thinks I was trying to rape her, she knows I didn't. Right?

"Tell them your name," Dr. C orders her.

"Lenora!" she shouts. "Lenora Young! Call my father, please! Brad Young. His boat's called *Siren II*. Please!"

"Mom," I say, holding the phone to my ear. "Mom!"

The sun is low on the horizon to our left. West, I mean. I can see the shoreline, only barely. A few sailboats so small they look like seagulls bobbing on the waves. A smear of green. One tall structure—maybe the same lighthouse we saw when we launched.

"Mom!"

Lenora is sobbing. Dr. C catches her, turning as she buckles, wrapping an arm around her waist.

The call has dropped. I try to redial, eye on the knife in Dr. C's right hand. He leans forward and all I see is the winking metal and I don't understand what he's doing until the boat suddenly leans hard and I stumble forward, catching myself only feet away from the blade he's holding at chest level.

I steady myself again, on the edge of hyperventilating. Phone on the cockpit deck, where I dropped it. Tiller freed from the lock that was holding our position. Boat circling, so we won't keep advancing toward shore, but we're not that far away and he knows it. If someone is looking, they'll find us.

He gives Lenora a shove toward the cabin. "You'll be safer in there. Go." But she's too scared to move.

"He'll lock you in," I warn her. "Don't do it."

She stares at me, then risks a hesitant side step away from Dr. C, with a quick glance back for encouragement. I see the confusion in her eyes. Even my mom doesn't look at me that hard. A few seconds, maybe, then she flits away. My mom tries not to let me see, but I know she's afraid.

Izzy wasn't, though. She trusted me with her secrets. She begged me for the pills. She said she had to meet one last time with the Weber guy. Face-to-face. As if she couldn't just say forget it, never mind, the game's over.

I should have gone with Izzy, to the motel. Instead I just gave her the pills, like she asked, so she'd feel less nervous. I told her they worked for my mom. They weren't strong.

So, in a way, I did kill her. By accident, but I did.

If Dr. C stabs Lenora or suffocates her inside the cabin, it will be the same. I set the trap.

"Lenora, please," I say. "Look at me. Please. Please please *look* at me."

"For fuck's sake," Dr. C says, dropping the knife, which gives me hope until I see he simply wants both hands free. He wraps his arms around Lenora's narrow waist and hauls her up, feet off the ground, pedaling. Her eyes widen with surprise. He looks proud and in control, like a dad who's lifted a crying toddler out of a sandbox and is going to show the kid what's what. He risks loosening one arm to grab a hank of her hair. She's tiny. He's strong.

"Fucking help me with this," he shouts at me, more annoyed than irate, and I know I'll be forgiven if I just follow his orders.

"She fell overboard," he says, as if it's already done. He clamps his hand over her mouth. "It happens. Especially when teens are foolish enough to drink."

He tries to heave her over the side, but she has his shirt clutched in one fist. She lands a kick to his knee. A less powerful one to his gut. No more swearing from Dr. C. No more requests. Not a word. He's furious and he's focused.

Her feet pedal—*thunk thunk thunk*—on the shiny white molded cockpit bench, tip of her sandal trying to find purchase on the edge of the boat, but it's white and rounded, slippery smooth, like the edge of a bathtub. Dr. C grunts as he tries to lift her higher. Almost. Almost.

I'm paralyzed.

He grunts and twists and then . . . he drops her and she sort of bounces off the outer side of the sailboat. I hear the splash.

*If she's really not a good swimmer, like she said. And even if she were. If she hit her head.*

I try to think. Quotes I memorized. Song lyrics. Swift comebacks. How to be strong. How to fight back. How to be a man. How to make them sorry. How to make them *see* you.

It's all noise. And Dr. C's eyes, locked on mine, are the opposite.

There's no way to think my way through what comes next so I don't. I just close my eyes and jump.

# 52

## ABBY

In the yacht club office, I ask the young attendant to look again—you're sure the Campbells let their membership lapse, and there's no *Paradox* in a slip here?—when Robert comes closer, pointing to his phone. I follow him outside, expecting him to tell me for a third time that I'm on the wrong track. He wanted to go find the orange Jaguar. Curtis would be nearby. But I didn't like it. That damn car, so obvious, so visible. It's a decoy. Why else would a man of bad intentions drive such a memorable vehicle?

Of course, Curtis was having a midlife crisis at the time, so it might have been a lapse in judgment, even for him. I look over at Robert, still busy on the phone.

A midlife crisis. And not the only thing he indulged. Is that the time he bought the sailboat, too? Not likely. His father gave the impression they had owned it a long time.

I try to remember what else Curtis said. *I could have sold it, but the car's a souvenir in a way.*

I see, unbidden, the face of Harper McKibben again. I feel her hovering behind all of this.

*Appetites long suppressed.*

*Less stable times.*

*A souvenir.*

*We all have those less stable times in our lives . . .*

But he's not going to get away with this one.

"They're already searching?" Robert says into the phone. "Okay. Thanks, Pete. Next time you're near Chicago . . ."

After hanging up he tells me, "Bad news is we can't go with them, because they left the marina a half hour ago. Good news is that they're already on it. Girl's father didn't put out an Amber Alert, because he assumed it wasn't an abduction, just bad teen judgment. She evidently texted him that she'd met a new friend at the Oshkosh docks. When he couldn't get her on the phone, he put in a call to the sheriff, asking him to keep an eye out."

"Oshkosh?" That's twenty miles north.

"Thought she'd be home by two o'clock. At least she described the boat. Twenty-two-foot Catalina."

"Trailerable size, right?" I say, remembering. "That's why they don't belong to the yacht club anymore."

The sailboat in the framed photo in Sister Lucretia's office looked elegant, but I know nothing about boat types and sizes. It was only the name that had struck me briefly. *Paradox.*

"The Coast Guard started the search from Fond du Lac, though?"

"That's where the auxiliary is. No regular CG in Oshkosh, only sheriff's boats. Anyway, Curtis's car was in town—"

"Because he wants people to think he's in Fond du Lac. Misdirection. An alibi."

"Stop worrying."

"But boats are pretty slow, right?"

"Coast Guard boats are faster. They'll be putting word out to other boats in the area, looking."

I shake my head. Lake Winnebago is an inland lake, but it's huge. And can't you go from the north side of Lake Winnebago up the Fox River into the whole Great Lakes system? Just go and go, and never come back?

Robert puts his hands on my shoulders. "She gave her dad the name of the boat. The CG got it from us, too, so they know we're onto something. They're taking this very seriously."

My relief has seeped away. Dread has taken its place. "They've got a girl, Robert."

"Curtis does, you mean."

"No. Both of them. He's talked Benjamin into something."

"But Benjamin wouldn't do anything to her—"

I think of Martha, and how I knew she would get hurt. Not die, but get hurt.

I think of the tire iron in my gym bag and how I'd like to hold it like a baseball bat and swing it, hard, right into Curtis's skull.

"He might, Robert."

"No, Abby."

"You don't understand, but I do."

No more denial. Love, and no lies. It's all gone too far. And maybe this is the first time I get it: the real cost of unconditional love. You have to truly know the condition before you can decide to accept it and keep loving, regardless. Anyone who thinks otherwise hasn't really pictured the worst that could happen. What your kid could do. What he could become. Until then, it's just empty promises.

I drive and Robert phones around until he's connected with Sheriff Bruckner, in Oshkosh. Twenty minutes later we're at the dock, hurrying toward the sheriff's boat, which still hasn't left its slip, because the sheriff isn't half as worried as we are. He's already put out a call to recreational boats in the area and no one has responded with a sighting yet, but it's no problem, now. The Coast Guard is on its way.

Bruckner keeps talking about how short-staffed they are, down two men who are on vacation and won't be back until July fourth week, their busiest time, when the *real stuff happens*, accidents and alcohol and *you'd never imagine what people get up to*.

Robert has a word with him, out of my earshot, and then he's waving me over. We're going. All of us.

"Thank you," I whisper when I reach him. "What'd you tell him?"

"I promised I'd have you out of his hair in under two hours if we could just get going, but if he stayed here at the dock, all bets would be off."

We're motoring slowly out of the harbor when Benjamin's phone starts buzzing again, but this time I grab it and answer in time.

"Mom!" Benjamin shouts. "Mom!"

I can't believe what I'm hearing—*Call the police!* And

*Help!*—but it's disrupted by other people shouting, clatter and static, a girl's voice, too.

The call drops.

Moments later, Curtis's voice breaks through the crackle of the sheriff's marine radio, asking for help.

"There you go." The sheriff nods at Robert, avoiding my glance. "Mystery solved. Everyone accounted for." He thought I was being hysterical from the start.

Curtis repeats the call. "Mayday, Mayday, this is *Paradox*. I am a twenty-two-foot white Catalina. One man aboard . . ."

I grab Robert from behind, pulling hard on his arm. "*One man?*"

The sheriff responds laconically. Curtis's radio message is fragmented. The sheriff repeats back the location to confirm it, but there's no response.

"He's saying Mayday! Why is everyone so damn calm?"

Sheriff Bruckner turns to me. "That doesn't mean he's sinking. He may just have a broken motor or something. He should have said 'Pan-pan' but a lot of boaters, they think they're the goddamn *Titanic* . . ."

Another crackle, Curtis's voice barely audible. "Two . . . I can't . . . board . . . Copy?"

"Did you hear that? *Two overboard.*"

"No ma'am. He said he only had one person on his boat."

"Yes, because two are overboard! That's my son and the girl! Benjamin and Lenora! Can't we go any faster?"

We're motoring into a stiff wind, the sky getting that green-gray tinge I associate with bad Midwestern weather, tornados, downpours, lightning. I smell it, too: that hyper-oxygenated smell before the rains splash down.

"Why people are still out in this, you gotta wonder," the sheriff says, turning back to steering, lips pressed thin. In an outrageously slow maneuver, he passes a large pair of black binoculars directly in front of my face, blocking my vision, holding them out for Robert, who is too distracted to notice until I thump him on the back.

The sheriff drawls, "*Paradox*, did you report two people overboard . . . ?"

I step back into the open-air stern, hand on my gym bag, keeping a tight grip on my impulse to do something I may or may not regret. The motor kicks up to a higher whine, waves rushing past us, bow lifting higher, fresh water speckling my face. Finally. He didn't believe me.

I point, shouting. "I can see it! That's the *Paradox*!"

Robert calls back, his voice twangier ever since he started talking to Bruckner, goddamn chameleon, though I know it works. "We know, honey!"

Robert told me to make a good impression. Be calm and cooperative. *Don't make them think you're crazy; don't say anything incriminating about Curtis or about Benjamin either. You don't know what we're walking into. You might be forced to repeat all of it on a witness stand. Watch your mouth.*

He was right. I'm watching it.

Even if Benjamin did something to the girl, I still love him. I always will.

I sit with that for a moment, expecting the feeling to fall away, like water poured into the cup of your hand. But it doesn't. It stays. I think of the day he was born, the first time I saw his face, the first time I heard him cry. Everyone was innocent at one time. Everyone needs one person, no matter what they've done or who they've become. I tell myself to remember that.

Whatever happened, they're both in danger now, in the water. There's no telling how far the *Paradox* has moved. The newspaper story about Curtis's dead wife and daughter flashes into my mind. Bodies found washed up in Indiana, weeks later.

"Benjamin!" I scream at the top of my lungs, over the water, even though I can't see anything. "Lenora!"

Dark clouds send ribbons of light and shadow over the choppy gray waters. The waves are small but irregular. Ahead and to the right, at one o'clock, I see a glint of something rising up from a patch of confused water. The sheriff's boat swerves left, and I try not to lose sight of the area as it moves from one to two o'clock and then even farther to the right, almost three o'clock. A cloud parts and a bright ray of light strikes the water and it doesn't help, it only highlights a horizontal band of water where there's nothing except for glinting chop. Diamonds sparkling across a graveyard.

I shout for Robert to come out back and I try to point out the spot as we continue veering away from it. "Keep looking! Do you see anything?"

Up at the controls, the sheriff is busy over the radio, talking to the Coast Guard, and meanwhile steering up close to the *Paradox*, which seems to be dead in the water, several hundred feet away.

"There!" I shout again. A thousand feet or more beyond the boat. A spot so far and pale it could be anything. A plastic bag, a lost buoy, a silver beer can. "Do you see?"

Robert raises the binocs. I dare not glance away from the place I'm tracking.

I urge him, "We need to tell the sheriff to aim for that spot, first."

"He won't. He's set on boarding the boat."

The *Paradox* pivots slowly, presenting its side to us, and then its stern, with Curtis at the back, waving and beckoning.

"But if they're out there?" I reach for the binoculars, but by the time I have them up, I've lost it. "Did you see anything?"

"I'm not sure."

We're so close now to the *Paradox* that I can hear Curtis's voice, and the sheriff replying. The former, distraught. The latter, still laconic, but lower pitched. The serious voice of a man talking to another man. Believing him.

Curtis is saying something about teens. Drinking. Swimming. A problem with the engine. A problem with the radio. And between every one of Curtis's phrases, the sheriff's "uh-huh," "uh-huh," "uh-huh."

From behind us to the right, five o'clock, another boat speeds into view—the Coast Guard Auxiliary. It passes behind us, pushing a deep V of white churning water in front of its bow, slowing for barely twenty seconds before it accelerates again. It keeps going, past the *Paradox*, even farther past the place I thought I might have seen a face, a hand, something. Taking directions from the sheriff. From Curtis.

"This is just another way to stall," I shout to Robert. "He knows where they went overboard. He's going to direct everyone to the wrong place."

I lift the binoculars to my eyes, scanning the horizon,

breaking it into organized strips, like mowing a lawn. Back and forth, back and forth, until I'm startled by a wave striking hard against our stern, the Coast Guard boat's wake. I lurch forward, catching myself just in time. *What did I see? What did I miss?*

A flash of white, and then a flash of neon orange, but then the orange vanishes beneath gray waves. I grip the textured rubber and push the binocs so hard into my face it hurts, while a series of lesser waves slap our stern like a series of punishing laughs.

# 53

## BENJAMIN

The hardest part when someone else is panicking is not letting their panic take you down. It's been at least fifteen minutes that I've had my arms under her armpits, trying to keep Lenora's head above water.

*You're more logical. That's why people think you're cold.*

That's what Dr. C told me during our sessions, before he got weird. And he was right. I am logical. But I'm still at a disadvantage now. All of the rescues I practiced in the pool, using the rescue tube and the rescue board—they don't help. Here, I've got no props. No easy way to signal. No team.

*You may find yourself overwhelmed,* the Red Cross manual said. But I'm not. Too much to focus on. Too much to do. A relief to have no arguments, no boring thoughts, no more stupid therapy questions. *Do you feel remorse? Do you feel shame? Do you care what others think? When things go wrong is it someone else's fault? Do you think about the future? Do you think about the past?*

I know how long I can hold my breath. *That's* what I'm thinking about right now. I know how far I can swim.

What'd he call it when you brag about yourself? *Grandiosity.* Maybe.

I know that even once my arms and legs start to feel like lead, I've still got time. Right now, I'm losing dexterity in my fingers. My toes are numb. Probably means we've been in longer than I thought. Fifteen to thirty minutes. At this water temperature? I see the multiple-choice lifeguard test in front of my eyes. I choose *D) Two to forty hours.*

It's a wide range. She has more body fat. We're both young. The air temperature is twenty degrees warmer than the water. I'm stubborn as a mule. There are so many factors, it's probably not something you could put into a calculator, like you can't look at a kid and see that he gets angry and know for sure he'll end up in prison. So why do they?

"You're doing great," I tell Lenora, even though I think she's still passed out and my lips are stiff with the cold. *Say the accident victim's name. Provide hope.* "I see two more boats out there. One's coming closer, Lenora. They're going to find us."

I never doubted the need to save her. It wasn't like one of those morality tests they give you—that even Dr. C tried to give me—about pushing the man onto the tracks to save those five people. It felt like a trick question. This rescue didn't. There were no other people, besides Lenora. I wasn't even thinking about myself. It was such a relief—the closest thing I've ever felt to bliss—to *not* think about myself. You don't know what you'll do until you get a chance to do it. Or to *not* do it. It wasn't like an impulse, either. It just happened, and when something happens without you having to think about it, that feels great, even when everything else is going to shit.

"We're all right," I say out loud. "You're going to be home soon. You're going to see your dad." I start feeling my throat tighten up but I say it anyway. "I'm going to see my mom."

I shift Lenora's body up higher on mine, hoping some of my heat is warming her from below—that our two bodies, sandwiched and floating near the top of the water, will survive longer than one.

I tuck my chin down and peer down her front, to the neon-orange bikini top she changed into, and I think, *Good choice.* I'm never wearing dark swim trunks again.

When the whine of the boat gets louder, I try to angle my head to see it, its bow riding super high, with big red letters on the side. But I can't keep looking for long. Water splashes into my mouth and I gag. I lift one arm, trying to wave, but when Lenora slumps down into the water I have to slide the arm back again, under her armpit.

"Okay," I say, leaning far back, arching my back so that I can lift her higher, staring up at the sky, not all gray like I thought, but gray and blue. Holes opening up. "You're doing great, Lenora."

A muffled voice echoes across the water from a megaphone. I repeat the arm maneuver, trying to wave, but it's not worth it. Too much water into her mouth and mine. I can't keep signaling. But that's all right.

The louder it gets, the more I know what my job is: to wait and stay calm and get through it, which I can. I know I can. I've never felt this peaceful for as long as I can remember. I've never felt this good. What the fuck that means, I'm not sure.

That I should be a Coast Guard person? Marine? Mercenary? Something sick.

The Coast Guard boat is only feet away and there's a second boat coming up behind it, motoring fast, and I know we did it right, and if my mom was talking to the Coast Guard then she might be on one of those boats, too, and it's almost over.

I feel Lenora convulse once, spitting up water. Her moan is the best thing I've heard all day, because it means she's conscious. She's going to make it.

"You're going to want your eyes open for this, Lenora."

# 54

## ABBY

The moment we pulled up close enough for me to see Benjamin, already lifted from the water by the Coast Guard patroller that got to him before we did, I broke into a grin and he grinned back, blue lips and all, a proud look on his face I hadn't seen in ages.

But once they had him transferred to the sheriff's boat, wrapped in a blanket and wedged between Robert's warm body and my own, he broke down. Sobbing and shuddering. Trying to form the words about Curtis, the drive, the car, the girls—not just Lenora, but the other one they almost picked up. Victims that narrowly escaped.

Curtis, too, might have escaped if a second Coast Guard boat hadn't arrived just as Sheriff Bruckner was departing, before the authorities finally understood this was no accident, certainly no mere instance of engine trouble, but something that would take hours of interviews to untangle.

The first thing that struck me, seeing Benjamin and Lenora, both, was not only how near death they appeared in their hypothermic states, but how young. Even though Benjamin had been in a growth spurt. Even though Lenora was a young woman, with curves. She was fifteen, we were told by the sheriff, who kept shaking his head and saying, "You'd think a girl would have more smarts than that."

He'd said it three times already when I interrupted. "Her prefrontal cortex won't be mature until she's in her mid-twenties, and boys are two years behind the girls. They're basically babies. Could you stop blaming them, just for a little while? Her, especially?"

Robert looked across Benjamin's shivering body at me, with a wistful smile. The sheriff moved to the back of the boat to rummage through a box for some winter hats and toe warmers for the kids, Lenora especially. Least he could do, instead of judging her.

"I might have an extra sweatshirt," I started to say, then stopped, remembering. I'd never had to take the tire iron out, because we weren't the ones who boarded Curtis's boat. Was I glad to have been deprived of that opportunity? Probably. Not entirely.

The hot fire of panic had smoldered down to a red-hot coal that would burn a long time. However many detectives or lawyers or journalists I had to talk to, I'd make sure he got what was coming to him.

The ride back was fast but windy, cold, and bumpy, and the whole time, my thoughts toggled back and forth. Seeing how Lenora looked at fifteen, I had to think about myself at thirteen. So much less developed. So much more naïve. Unable, truly, to think about consequences. No wonder Martha's funeral had been so strange and surreal, as had everything that followed. No wonder I had talked so little for years—not because I was good at keeping secrets, but because I was in long-term shock. I hadn't just clung to my brother, the night of the car accident and the first years after, because of a twisted morality. I'd clung to him because I had nothing and nobody else, and I was stupid besides.

No, not stupid. Just young.

Then I thought about Curtis again. About how even now, with the worst of the danger past and the resolve to pursue justice clear in my mind, I could still imagine that rough, cold tire iron in my hand. I could visualize the sensation of metal cracking skull, the vibration that would have flowed up my arm, into my shoulder—the sheer determination it would have taken. I could understand, intellectually at least, the pleasure of seeing him collapse. But would I have done any of that, really? I could have held the tire iron, but would I have swung it? And kept swinging?

Back and forth—Martha and Curtis. Martha and Curtis. And me, of course. Thirteen, thirty-seven, a girl who knew nothing, a mother who thought she knew more. I thought about how little we know, truly, about anyone. What they're thinking about. What they're feeling. What they're capable of.

After the kids were cleared by paramedics and before we gave complete police statements, it was suggested we might stay overnight, locally, just in case the police wanted to talk to us in person more than once over the next twenty-four hours. But Benjamin wanted to go home that night, and no one said we couldn't, as long as we could handle talking a couple of hours or however long it took—a sign I took as further confirmation that no one blamed my kid and he was being treated, appropriately, as a victim.

Benjamin explained everything he knew about Curtis and his connection to Weber and to Ewan. He told the police that Curtis groomed him, or tried to. The more I heard, the more I felt like someone whose car dies on a railroad crossing and manages to get it restarted just yards away from an advancing locomotive. How lucky I was, in some ways, that Benjamin was stubborn and skeptical, even while he was also vulnerable and difficult.

We weren't home yet when Robert got a call from his friend on the force in Fond Du Lac. We'd seen Curtis arrested, but in the time since, the police had also gotten a warrant and found Curtis's damaged SUV, parked in Lake Forest. Benjamin had already told the police about Curtis's braggy account of playing some role in Christopher Weber's accident. Now, they'd believe it.

Robert said, "Once the Weber accident is locked down, they'll look into the suspicious drowning of his wife and daughter. You'll see."

Maybe it was because I'd spent the last many years aware of famous, powerful men who had gotten away with galling crimes. Maybe it was because I knew, as Ewan's sister, that the sickest men are the best at manipulating people and evading punishment. I had a hard time believing Curtis would serve time.

"He will," Robert insisted. "Do you trust me? Do you think maybe I know a thing or two, now?"

"I do."

. . .

First, I just wanted Benjamin home. Then I wanted him *better*. But it isn't fair, expecting trauma to lead to instant growth.

Two weeks after the rescue, Lenora's father wanted to drive down to Pleasant Park and take Benjamin to dinner, to thank him.

"I don't want him to thank me," Benjamin said, turning away.

I held out the phone. "Please."

Reluctantly, he took it. I watched and listened as he mostly nodded, except for a few words. *Okay.* And, *No, it's all right.* And, *No, I . . . no, I, don't really want . . . I mean, thanks but . . . No.*

We tell our children they can set boundaries, and then we take it back when we ourselves want them to do something. To go along. But Benjamin wasn't going to go along with this.

When he got off, his face was red. But he didn't get angry. He didn't withdraw. He talked to me.

"Lenora's dad kept offering me things, like money. Or gift cards. Like I'm some charity case."

"No, like you're a kid who saved his daughter's life."

"I told him she can text me. That's fine. I like her. But I'm not going anywhere with him."

I wondered aloud if Benjamin was just skittish of strangers now, especially older male strangers, after what happened with Curtis.

"Oh my god," he said, frustrated. Then he tried to explain why he did what he did. How he felt when he first knew

Lenora was coming onto the boat. How angry he felt with her—the same way he was angry with Izzy, at times.

"Because you knew Izzy was putting herself in danger. So you cared for them both, in your own way. That's empathy, Benjamin."

"No! It's not! Why do we all have to use the same words—empathy, love, guilt—when we don't feel those things the same way. You can't get in my head. You can't get into anyone's head—"

"Well, a person can. That's what empathy *is*."

"So maybe I don't feel empathy! Who cares!" He closed his eyes, breathed in and out, the way he'd seen me practicing for years. "I did what was right. What *I* thought was right. And now yet another rich pushy asshole wants to fuck it up with external validation. I don't need that. Nobody needs that."

"I get it," I said. "I think."

For the rest of the summer, Benjamin read every book he could find at the library about psychopaths. Most of them were bullshit, he informed me, but not all of them.

"Don't tell me we may someday have another psychologist in the family?" I asked him one morning after he'd monologued about his latest deep dive via Google Scholar.

"Not *another* psychologist. You're only a counselor, without a PhD."

"You can be a psychologist with a PsyD."

"But you don't have that degree, either."

"Thanks for being a snob. I don't know what I think about your latest career plan," I said, reaching to pull him in for a hug. He ducked away just in time.

# EPILOGUE
## SIX MONTHS LATER

We still have a long road ahead. A new evaluation with someone who believes in the spectrum of antisocial personality disorder, who won't just put a sticker on Benjamin's head and say he's a psychopath or close to it. I'm tired of labels, frankly. For him and for myself and maybe even for Ewan. The science is new and unproven. If Benjamin ever has his own kids someday, they'll have a whole new *DSM* by then. New words, new rules, new treatments.

Shortly after Curtis's arrest, we told police about Benjamin's involvement in giving Izzy the pills that led to her death. Ralph King was at his side. The facts would emerge at Curtis's trial, anyway. Then we waited. Nothing. That doesn't mean charges won't be pressed or an investigation can't be reopened later, even years later. But for now, Izzy's family and the justice system seem much more interested in Curtis and Christopher Weber.

I once asked Benjamin if being unpunished for a publicly acknowledged crime felt like having a genetic predisposition to a disease—like some biological time bomb was ticking away, ready to go off anytime or never at all.

"No, it's more like waiting for a tax audit."

I worried he was misunderstanding the severity of his situation or forgetting his promise to at least try to feel remorse, even if it was a thought exercise more than an intuitive feeling. But he set me straight.

"No one's to blame for an inherited disease, Mom. But you *are* to blame for cheating on your taxes."

I exhaled. "Right—"

"But on top of that, you also know the IRS is pretty fucked so you'll probably get away with it."

He was right, but I had to press the point. "You don't think you deserve to get away with it."

"Of course not," he scoffed. "But do I want to go to juvie or prison? Does anyone? Not my fault the government is so hobbled it can't prosecute everything it should. I mean, we could talk about the benefits of our current administration—"

"Let's not."

Benjamin has a year and a half left at his new public high school. He's not a fan. But with every passing month he's seeing farther into the future, learning even more about himself. In addition to reading lots of psychology, he still loves sports, like swimming and cross-country. He doesn't have lots of close friends, but he has teammates. He's never been a social kid, and nothing's going to change that, except for the right partner someday, maybe. I can hope.

Robert feels an even tighter bond with Benjamin after what we all went through, and I don't get in the way. We aren't dating, but we do see each other about twice a week. When he asks me why we don't call it dating, I shrug. Maybe it *is* dating, or maybe it will be, once Benjamin is off to college or whatever he chooses to do after high school.

I didn't get the fall job at Grove. The Sisters will never forgive me for being quoted in the exposé that ran in the *Chicago Tribune* about Curtis. What with various pretrial motions to dismiss and a long discovery process, he still hasn't gone to trial for multiple pending murder charges, but we expect it to happen in the next year.

I didn't get another job at Summit, either. I got a job working, instead, for a lawyer. Ralph King, in fact. Counseling families with kids inside the juvenile detention system. We moved from Pleasant Park back to Waukegan—not my favorite place, but it's the hub for Lake County. Court system, good tacos, cheaper rent. The downtown's trying hard and those old houses on Sheridan Road are beautiful, if not quite within our reach.

When we made the move, I pulled the shoebox out from the high shelf in my closet. I took it into the bathroom and I locked the door. Then I looked at each item inside. One satiny pair of underwear. Another, older pair—and no wonder I overreacted so strongly when I saw the underwear in Benjamin's drawer, because this other memento had bothered me for so long. And the third item, the one that gave the whole box its inescapable smell—the empty dish detergent bottle.

Just one sniff and I could remember holding it, pouring it, the aroma blending with that of the pine-scented floor cleaner. Ewan would have done it differently, using some kind of motor oil or WD-40, something the cops or paramedics would have noticed as soon as they came and picked Martha's broken, cold body off the slippery floor. Ewan or me: I thought those were the only choices. I didn't realize that loving someone didn't need to mean hurting someone else.

I've tried my new thoughts about unconditional love on some of the families I work with. We talk about that stage when you realize you have to see *what is* before you can even hope for a *what will be*. Some get it. Some don't. There's always the more extreme case of a kid who has done something so clearly beyond explanation that a parent is having a hard time forgiving or even understanding. They want to stay in denial because it's safer. They don't know how far their hearts might be able to stretch, once they know everything.

With my clients, I don't fight the denial head-on. I try to be the one willing to *see* a troubled and even violent young offender. I don't shock easily. Not even when it's a kid who's been accused of taking a life, such as that of a family member who was abusive or simply unloving.

*I get why you may have done what you did*, I'll say, which often surprises a young client, especially when they're used to all the grown-ups collaborating and covering up. *But here's what I'm offering you. A fresh start. The person you are today is not the person who did that.*

They look at me as if I'm tricking them.

Sometimes I wish I could tell them a story, about a girl who loved her brother so much that she wanted to protect him from another bad person. Sometimes I wish I could tell them about the mistakes any person can make, doing the wrong thing for what seems like the right reason.

Then I remember what Benjamin has said, about how

talking is the part of therapy he likes least. I remind myself to expand my activities with juvenile clients. We don't stop talking, of course, but we mix it up. We draw and paint or go roller-skating. We visit with therapy dogs and horses. I think of Benjamin, rescuing that girl. I think of myself, rescuing Benjamin.

I tell my clients, you just need to find the thing that sets you free. The thing that assures you of your own value on this earth. It's like trying to open one door after another. You're going to keep trying, locked door after locked door, but one day you'll find the one that opens. You'll stop revisiting the worst memories from your past, the dark and slippery moments that threaten to trip you up.

You'll take the next step.

You'll walk through that door.

You'll never turn back.

# ACKNOWLEDGMENTS

Thanks to my agent, Michelle Brower, and to the amazing Soho Press team: Bronwen Hruska, Juliet Grames, Alexa Wejko, Rachel Kowal, Janine Agro, Paul Oliver, Lily DeTaeye, Emma Levy, Rudy Martinez, and Shandela Contreras. I look forward to working together on many books to come. An additional round of applause to Julie McCarroll; copy editors are heroes and I am grateful for every error corrected.

My early readers patiently slogged through many drafts and encouraged me to keep stretching my new suspense-writer muscles. Thankful hugs to Brian Lax, Tziporah Lax, Karen Ferguson, Ellen Bielawski, Deborah Williams, Allison K. Williams, Sky Burr-Drysdale, Shana Wilson, Shannon Kelley, Stephanie Dardenne, Caitlin Wahrer, and Donna Freitas. For reading my books but also for supporting me in many other ways, thanks to Honoree, Eliza, and Nikki.

I can still envision the bookshelves on which my late mother, a neuropsychologist and college psychology instructor, kept her *PDR* copy and the filing cabinets in which her various psychological tests were stored, including ones about which she held significant reservations. From the teaching podium and from across the kitchen table, my mother shaped my early understanding of psychology, inculcating me with both respect and skepticism for her chosen field.

To the many independent booksellers who have championed my novels in the past and to Barnes & Noble booksellers who helped more readers discover my first suspense novel, *The Deepest Lake*, I am profoundly grateful.

For readers interested in reading credible, evidence-backed nonfiction about psychopathology, my strongest recommendations are *The Psychopath Whisperer: The Science of Those Without Conscience* by Kent A. Kiehl, *The Psychopath Inside: A Neuroscientist's Personal Journey into the Dark Side of the Brain* by James Fallon, and for equal parts humor and science journalism, *The Psychopath Test: A Journey Through the Madness Industry* by Jon Ronson.